STORIES

ALSO BY AL SARRANTONIO

NOVELS

The Orangefield Trilogy *(Hallow Eve, Horrorween, Halloweenland)*
Masters of Mars *(Haydn of Mars, Sebastian of Mars, Queen of Mars)*
The Five Worlds Trilogy *(Exile, Journey, Return)*
Moonbane
Skeletons
October
House Haunted
West Texas
Kitt Peak
Cold Night
Summer Cool
The Boy with Penny Eyes
Totentanz
Campbell Wood

STORY COLLECTIONS
Toybox
Hornets and Others
Halloween and Other Seasons

AS EDITOR
999: New Stories of Horror and Suspense
Redshift: Extreme Visions of Speculative Fiction
Flights: Extreme Visions of Fantasy
The National Lampoon Treasury of Humor
The Fireside Treasury of New Humor
The Fireside Treasury of Great Humor

STORIES

All-New Tales

Edited by Neil Gaiman and Al Sarrantonio

wm

WILLIAM MORROW
An Imprint of HarperCollins*Publishers*

"Introduction: Just Four Words" by Neil Gaiman. Copyright © 2010 by Neil Gaiman.
"Blood" by Roddy Doyle. Copyright © 2010 by Roddy Doyle.
"Fossil-Figures" by Joyce Carol Oates. Copyright © 2010 by the *Ontario Review*.
"Wildfire in Manhattan" by Joanne Harris. Copyright © 2010 by Frogspawn, Ltd.
"The Truth Is a Cave in the Black Mountains" by Neil Gaiman. Copyright © 2010 by Neil Gaiman.
"Unbelief" by Michael Marshall Smith. Copyright © 2010 by Michael Marshall Smith.
"The Stars Are Falling" by Joe R. Lansdale. Copyright © 2010 by Joe R. Lansdale.
"Juvenal Nyx" by Walter Mosley. Copyright © 2010 by Walter Mosley.
"The Knife" by Richard Adams. Copyright © 2010 by Richard Adams.
"Weights and Measures" by Jodi Picoult. Copyright © 2010 by Jodi Picoult.
"Goblin Lake" by Michael Swanwick. Copyright © 2010 by Michael Swanwick.
"Mallon the Guru" by Peter Straub. Copyright © 2010 by Peter Straub.
"Catch and Release" by Lawrence Block. Copyright © 2010 by Lawrence Block.
"Polka Dots and Moonbeams" by Jeffrey Ford. Copyright © 2010 by Jeffrey Ford.
"Loser" by Chuck Palahniuk. Copyright © 2010 by Chuck Palahniuk.
"Samantha's Diary" by Diana Wynne Jones. Copyright © 2010 by Diana Wynne Jones.
"Land of the Lost" by Stewart O'Nan. Copyright © 2010 by Stewart O'Nan.
"Leif in the Wind" by Gene Wolfe. Copyright © 2010 by Gene Wolfe.
"Unwell" by Carolyn Parkhurst. Copyright © 2010 by Carolyn Parkhurst.
"A Life in Fictions" by Kat Howard. Copyright © 2010 by Kat Howard.
"Let the Past Begin" by Jonathan Carroll. Copyright © 2010 by Jonathan Carroll.
"The Therapist" by Jeffery Deaver. Copyright © 2010 by Jeffery Deaver.
"Parallel Lines" by Tim Powers. Copyright © 2010 by Tim Powers.
"The Cult of the Nose" by Al Sarrantonio. Copyright © 2010 by Al Sarrantonio.
"Human Intelligence" by Kurt Andersen. Copyright © 2010 by Kurt Andersen.
"Stories" by Michael Moorcock. Copyright © 2010 by Michael Moorcock.
"The Maiden Flight of McCauley's *Bellerophon*" by Elizabeth Hand. Copyright © 2010 by Elizabeth Hand.
"The Devil on the Staircase" by Joe Hill. Copyright © 2010 by Joe Hill.

STORIES. Copyright © 2010 by Neil Gaiman and Al Sarrantonio. All rights reserved. Printed in the United States of America. No part of this book may be used or reproduced in any manner whatsoever without written permission except in the case of brief quotations embodied in critical articles and reviews. For information address HarperCollins Publishers, 10 East 53rd Street, New York, NY 10022.

HarperCollins books may be purchased for educational, business, or sales promotional use. For information please write: Special Markets Department, HarperCollins Publishers, 10 East 53rd Street, New York, NY 10022.

Library of Congress Cataloging-in-Publication Data has been applied for.

ISBN 978-0-06-123092-9

10 11 12 13 14 OV/RRD 10 9 8 7 6 5 4 3 2 1

For all the storytellers and tale spinners who entertained the public and kept themselves alive, for Alexandre Dumas and Charles Dickens, for Mark Twain and Baroness Orczy and the rest, and most of all, for Scheherazade, who was the storyteller and the story told.

CONTENTS

Many loving thanks to Jennifer Brehl and Merrilee Heifetz, dual rudders on a long boat, for steering us safely to shore.

STORIES

INTRODUCTION
JUST FOUR WORDS

AL SARRANTONIO AND I WERE DISCUSSING anthologies of short stories. He had edited a huge anthology of cutting-edge horror, and another of cutting-edge fantasy, each book, in its way, definitive. And in talking, we realised that we had something in common: that all we cared about, really, were the stories. What we missed, what we wanted to read, were stories that made us care, stories that forced us to turn the page. And yes, we wanted good writing (why be satisfied with less?). But we wanted more than that. We wanted to read stories that used a lightning flash of magic as a way of showing us something we have already seen a thousand times as if we have never seen it before. Truly, we wanted it all.

And slowly, the wish becomes the deed . . .

When I was a child, I pestered my elders for stories. My family would improvise, or read me stories from books. As soon as I was old enough to read, I was one of those children who needed to have a book within reach. I would read a book a day, or more. I wanted stories, and I wanted them always, and I wanted the experience that only fiction could give me: I wanted to be inside them.

Television and cinema were all very well, but these stories happened to other people. The stories I found in books happened inside my head. I was, in some way, there.

It's the magic of fiction: you take the words and you build them into worlds.

As time passed, I became a more discriminating reader (I remember the first time I realised I did not have to finish reading a book; the first time I realised that the way a story was told was getting in the way of the story). But even as I became more discriminating as a reader I started to feel that the thing that kept me reading, the place the magic occurred, the driving force of narrative was sometimes being overlooked. I would read beautiful prose, and I would simply not care.

It came down to four words.

There are the kind of readers who read only nonfiction: who read biographies, perhaps, or travel writing. Readers who read nothing but concrete poetry. There are those who read things that will improve them and their lot, who only read books that tell them how to survive the coming financial crisis, or have confidence in themselves, or play poker, or build beehives. I myself can sometimes be found reading books about beekeeping and, because I write fiction, am always happy to read strange factual things. Whatever we read, we are part of the community of the story.

There are nonreaders, of course. I knew a man in his nineties who, when he learned that I was a writer, admitted to me that he had tried to read a book, once, long before I was born, but he had been unable to see the point of it, and had never tried again. I asked him if he remembered the name of the book, and he told me, in the manner of someone who tried to eat a snail once and did not care for it, and who does not need to remember the breed of the snail, that one was much like another, surely.

Still. Four words.

And I didn't realise it until a couple of days ago, when someone wrote in to my blog:

Dear Neil,

If you could choose a quote—either by you or another author—to be inscribed on the wall of a public library children's area, what would it be?

Thanks!
Lynn

I pondered for a bit. I'd said a lot about books and kids' reading over the years, and other people had said things pithier and wiser than I ever could. And then it hit me, and this is what I wrote:

I'm not sure I'd put a quote up, if it was me, and I had a library wall to deface. I think I'd just remind people of the power of stories, of why

they exist in the first place. I'd put up the four words that anyone telling
a story wants to hear. The ones that show that it's working, and that
pages will be turned:

" . . . and then what happened?"

The four words that children ask, when you pause, telling them a story. The four words you hear at the end of a chapter. The four words, spoken or unspoken, that show you, as a storyteller, that people care.

The joy of fiction, for some of us, is the joy of the imagination, set free from the world and able to imagine.

Talking to Al Sarrantonio I realised that I was not alone in finding myself increasingly frustrated with the boundaries of genre: the idea that categories which existed only to guide people around bookshops now seemed to be dictating the kind of stories that were being written. I love the word *fantasy*, for example, but I love it for the almost infinite room it gives an author to play: an infinite playroom, of a sort, in which the only boundaries are those of the imagination. I do not love it for the idea of commercial fantasy. Commercial fantasy, for good or for ill, tends to drag itself through already existing furrows, furrows dug by J. R. R. Tolkien or Robert E. Howard, leaving a world of stories behind it, excluding so much. There was so much fine fiction, fiction allowing free reign to the imagination of the author, beyond the shelves of genre. That was what we wanted to read.

It seemed to us that the fantastic can be, can do, so much more than its detractors assume: it can illuminate the real, it can distort it, it can mask it, it can hide it. It can show you the world you know in a way that makes you realise you've never looked at it, not *looked* at it. G. K. Chesterton compared fantastic fiction to going on holiday—that the importance of your holiday is the moment you return, and you see the place you live through fresh eyes.

And so the call went out from Mr. Sarrantonio and from me, and the stories began to come back to us. Writers rose to the challenge. We learned to expect only the unexpected.

" . . . and then what happened?"

The real magic of this little invocation is that it has inspired hundreds of millions of words, has made people who never imagined themselves as storytellers into tale-tellers who could have given Scheherazade or Dunsany's Joseph Jorkens a run for their money or their whiskey or their lives. We turn the page, and the adventure begins.

There is something waiting for you. So turn the page.

Neil Gaiman
December 2009

BLOOD

•

Roddy Doyle

HE GREW UP IN DRACULA'S CITY. He'd walked past Bram Stoker's house every day on his way to school. But it had meant nothing to him. He'd never felt a thing, not the hand of a ghost or a shiver, not a lick on his neck as he passed. In fact, he was nearly eighteen, in his last year at school, before he'd even noticed the plaque beside the door. He'd never read the book, and probably never would. He'd fallen asleep during Coppola's *Dracula*. One minute his wife was screaming, grabbing his knee; the next, she was grabbing the same knee, trying to wake him up. The cinema lights were on and she was furious.

-How can you do that?

-What?

-Sleep during a film like that.

-I always fall asleep when the film's shite.

-We're supposed to be out on a date.

-That's a different point, he said. –For that, I apologise. How did it end, anyway?

-Oh, fuck off, she said, affectionately—that was possible in Dublin.

So the whole thing, the whole Dracula business, meant absolutely nothing to him.

Nevertheless, he wanted to drink blood.

Badly.

The *badly* was recent, and dreadful. The itch, the urge, the leaking tongue—it was absolutely dreadful.

He wasn't sure when it had started. He was, though—he knew when he'd become aware.

-How d'you want your steak?

-Raw.

His wife had laughed. But he'd been telling her the truth. He wanted the slab of meat she was holding over the pan, raw and *now*—fuck the pan, it wasn't needed. He could feel muscles holding him back, and other muscles fighting for him—neck muscles, jaw muscles.

Then he woke.

But he was awake already, still standing in the kitchen, looking at the steak, and looking forward to it.

-Rare, so, he said.

She smiled at him.

-You're such a messer, she said.

He hid behind that, the fact that he acted the eejit, that it was *him,* as he bent down to the charred meat on the plate a few minutes later, and licked it. The kids copied him and they all ended up with brown gravy on their noses. He made himself forget about his aching jaws and the need to bite and growl. They all watched a DVD after dinner, and everything was grand.

And it was; it was fine. Life was normal. For a while. For quite a while. Weeks—he thought. He opened the fridge one day. There were two fillet steaks on a plate, waiting. It must have been weeks later because she—her name was Vera—she wouldn't have bought steak all that frequently. And it wasn't the case that Vera did all the shopping, or even most of it; she just went past the butcher's more often than he did. She bought the food; he bought the wine. She bought the soap and toilet paper—and he bought the wine. *You're such a messer.*

He grabbed one of the steaks and took it over to the sink. He looked behind him, to make sure he was alone, and then devoured it as he leaned over the sink. But he didn't *devour* it. He licked it first, like an ice-pop; it was cold. He heard the drops of blood hit the aluminum beneath him, and he felt the blood running down his chin, as if it—the blood—was coming from him. And he started to suck it, quickly, to drink it. It should have been warm. He knew that, and it disgusted him, the fact that he was already planting his disappointment, setting himself up to do it again—*this*—feeding a need, an addiction he suddenly had and accepted. He growled—he fuckin' growled. He looked behind him—but he didn't care. *You're such a messer.* He chewed till it stopped being meat and spat the pulp into the bin. He rubbed his chin; he washed his hands. He looked at his shirt. It was clean. He ran the hot tap and watched the black drops turn red, pink, then nothing. He took the remaining fillet from the fridge and slid it off the plate, into the bin. He tied the plastic liner and brought it out to the wheelie bin.

-Where's the dinner? Vera wanted to know, later.

-What?

-I bought fillet steaks for us. There.

She stood in front of the fridge's open door.

-They were off, he said.

-They were not.

-They were, he said. –They were minging. I threw them out.

-They were perfect, she said. –Are they in here?

She was at the bin.

-The wheelie, he said.

He hadn't expected this; he hadn't thought ahead.

-I'm bringing them back, she said, as she moved to the back door. –The fucker.

She was talking about the butcher.

-Don't, he said.

He didn't stand up, he didn't charge to block her. He stayed sitting at the table. He could feel his heart—his own meat—hopping, thumping.

-He's always been grand, he said. –If we complain, it'll—I don't know—change the relationship. The customer-client thing.

He enjoyed listening to himself. He was winning.

-We can have the mince, he said.

-It was for the kids, she said. –Burgers.

-I like burgers, he said. –You like burgers.

The back door was open. It was a hot day, after a week of hot days. He knew: she didn't want to open the wheelie and shove her face into a gang of flies.

They had small burgers. The kids didn't complain.

That was that.

Out of his system. He remembered—he saw himself—attacking the meat, hanging over the sink. He closed his eyes, snapped them shut—the idea, the thought, of being caught like that. By a child, by his wife. The end of his life.

He'd killed it—the urge. But it came back, days later. And he killed it again. The fridge again—lamb chops this time. He sent his hand in over

the chops, and grabbed a packet of chicken breasts, one of those polystyrene trays, wrapped in cling-film. He put a finger through the film, pulled
it away. He slid the breasts onto a plate—and drank the pink, the near-
white blood. He downed it, off the tray. And vomited.

Cured. Sickened—revolted. Never again. He stayed home from work
the next day. Vera felt his forehead.

-Maybe it's the swine flu.

-Chicken pox, he said. *You're such a messer.*

-You must have had the chicken pox when you were a boy, she said.
–Did you?

-I think so, he said.

She looked worried.

-It can make adult males sterile, she said.

-I had a vasectomy, he told her. –Three years ago.

-I forgot, she said.

-I didn't.

But he was cured; he'd sorted himself out. The thought, the memory—the taste of the chicken blood, the polystyrene tray—it had him
retching all day. He wouldn't let it go. He tortured himself until he knew
he was fixed.

It was iron he was after. He decided that after he'd done a bit of
Googling when he went back to work. It made sense; it was fresh air across
his face. Something about the taste, even the look, of the cow's deep red
blood—it was metal, rusty. That was what he'd craved, the iron, the metal.
He'd been looking pale; he'd been falling asleep in front of the telly, like an
old man. Anaemia. Iron was all he needed. So he bought himself a carton
of grapefruit juice—he knew the kids would never touch it—and he went
into a chemist on his way home from work, for iron tablets. He regretted
it when the woman behind the counter looked at him over her specs and
asked him if they were for his wife.

-We share them, he said.

She wasn't moving.

-I'd need to see a letter from your GP, she said.

-For iron?

-Yes.

He bought condoms and throat lozenges, and left. By the time he got
home he knew his iron theory was shite and he'd pushed the grapefruit

juice into a hedge, with the condoms. The kids were right; grapefruit juice was disgusting. There was nothing wrong with him, except he wanted to drink blood.

He had kids. That was the point. A boy and a girl. He had a family, a wife he loved, a job he tolerated. He worked in one of the banks, not high enough up to qualify for one of the mad bonuses they'd been handing out in the boom days, but high enough to have his family held hostage while he went to the bank with one of the bad guys and opened the safe—although that event had never occurred. The point was, he was normal. He was a forty-one-year-old heterosexual man who lived in Dublin and enjoyed the occasional pint with his friends—Guinness, loads of iron—played a game of indoor football once a week in a leaking school hall, had sex with his wife often enough to qualify as regularly, just about, and would like to have had sex with other women, many other women, but it was just a thought, never a real ambition or anything urgent or mad. He was normal.

He took a fillet steak into the gents' toilet at work, demolished it, and tried to flush the plastic bag down the toilet. But it stayed there like a parachute, on top of the water. He fished it out and put it in his pocket. He checked his shirt and tie in the mirror, even though he'd been careful not to let himself get carried away as he went at the meat in the cubicle. He was clean, spotless, his normal self. He checked his teeth for strings of flesh, put his face right up to the mirror. He was grand. He went back to his desk and ate his lunch with his colleagues, a sandwich he'd made himself that morning, avocado and tomato—no recession in his fridge. He felt good, he felt great.

He was controlling it, feeding it. He was his own doctor, in very good hands. He'd soon be ironed up and back to his even more normal self.

So he was quite surprised when he went over the wall, even as he went over. *What the fuck am I doing?* He knew exactly what he was doing. He was going after the next-door neighbours' recession hens. At three in the morning. He was going to bite the head off one of them. He'd seen the hens—he wasn't sure if you called them hens or chickens—from one of the upstairs windows. He saw them every night when he was closing his daughter's curtains, after he'd read to her. (See? He's normal.) There were three of them, scrabbling around in the garden. He hated them, the whole idea of them. The world economy wobbled and the middle classes immediately started growing their own spuds and carrots, buying their own chickens, and denying they had property portfolios in Eastern Europe. And they stopped talking to him because he'd become the enemy, and evil, because he worked in a bank. The shiftless bitch next door could pretend she was busy all day looking after the hens. Well, she'd have one less to look after, because he was over the wall. He'd landed neatly and quietly—he was fit; he played football—and he was homing in on the hens.

He knew what he was up to. He was hoping a light would go on, upstairs—or better, downstairs—or next door, in his own house. Frighten the shite out of him, send him scrambling back over the wall. *I was just looking to see if I could see the space shuttle. It's supposed to be coming over Ireland tonight.* He'd bluff his way out of it—*Although it won't be stopping*—while his heart thumped away at his ribs. It would sort him out for another few days, a week; it would get him over the weekend.

But no light went on.

And the chickens cluck-clucked: *We're over here.*

He grabbed one. It was easy, too easy. It was a lovely night; they were as clear there as they could have been, standing in a row, like a girl band, the Supremes. Shouldn't they have been cooped up—was that the phrase?—and let out again in the morning? The city's foxes were famous; everyone had seen one. He'd seen one himself, strolling down the street when he was walking home from the station a few months before.

He grabbed his hen, expected the protest, the pecks. But no, the hen settled into his arms like a fuckin' kitten. The little head in one hand, the hard, scrawny legs in the other, he stretched it out like a rubber band and brought it up to his mouth. And he bit—kind of. There was no burst of blood or even a clean snap. The neck was still in his mouth. He could feel a pulse on his tongue. The hen was terrified; he could feel that in the legs. But he didn't want to terrify the bird—he wasn't a cruel man. He just wanted to bite its head off and hold his mouth under its headless neck. But he knew: he didn't have it in him. He wasn't a vampire or a werewolf. And he needed a filling—he could feel that. *I was biting the head off a chicken, Doctor.* He'd put the hen down now and get back over the wall.

But a light went on—and he bit. Downstairs, right in front of him— and the head came clean off. There was no blood, not really, just—well— bone, gristle, something wet. He wouldn't vomit. They'd be staring out at him, the neighbours, him or her or him *and* her—Jim and Barbara. But he was quick, he was calm. He knew they couldn't see him because the light was on in the kitchen and it was dark out here. Although, now that he thought of it—and he *was* thinking—they might have seen him before they turned on the light.

And now the chicken, the headless, dead chicken, decided to protest. A squawk came out of something that couldn't have been its beak, because the head, detached or at least semidetached, was in one of his hands. He was holding the body by the neck and it was wriggling. *Let me down, let me down.*

He dropped the hen, heard it running away, and he charged. He ran at the wall. Not his own wall—he was *thinking*. The wall on the other side, two houses down from his own. He was up, no sweat, and he was over. He sat down for a while, to get his breath back, to work out his route home. He listened. He hadn't heard the kitchen door being opened and the hen seemed to have accepted that it was dead. The other two hadn't noticed, or they were in mourning. It was very quiet.

He was safe—he thought he was safe. He was stupid, exhilarated, appalled, ashamed, fuckin' delighted, and safe. He looked up at the sky. And he saw it, the shuttle. The brightest star, moving steadily across the night. The *Endeavour*—he remembered the name.

He was back in the bed.

She woke—half woke. His cold feet, his weight on the mattress.

-What's wrong?

-Nothing, he said. –I got up to see the shuttle.

-Great.

She was asleep already.

-It was amazing, he said, addressing her back. –Amazing.

He kissed her neck.

He actually slept. It was Friday night, Saturday morning.

The bed was empty when he woke. It was a long time since that had happened, since she'd been awake before him. He felt good—he felt great. He'd flossed and brushed before he'd got back into bed, no trace of the hen between his teeth. He'd gargled quietly till his eyes watered. No bad taste, and no guilt. He shouldn't have done what he'd done, but a more important consideration quickly smothered any guilt. It was the thought he'd fallen asleep with, clutching it like a teddy bear, just after he'd kissed his wife's neck.

Necks.

It was as simple as that.

The blood was a red herring, so to speak, sent to distract him—by his psyche or whatever, his conscience—to stop him from seeing the much healthier obvious. It was necks he'd been craving, not blood. He didn't want to drink blood and he was no more anaemic than a cow's leg. The simple, dirty truth was, he wanted to bite necks. It was one of those midlife things. And that was grand, it was fine, because he was in the middle of his life, give or take a few years.

Sex.

Simple.

He wanted to have sex with everything living. Not literally. He wanted to have sex with most things. Some things—most women. He was a normal man, slipping into middle age. His days were numbered. He knew this, but he didn't *think* it. A year was 365 days. Ten years was 3,650. Thirty years gave him 14,600. *You have 14,600 days to live. That's fine, thanks.* As he lay on the bed, he felt happy. The urge was gone, because he understood. His mind was fine, but something in him had been running amok. His biology, or something like that. Not long ago, only a few generations back, he'd have been dead already or at least drooling and toothless. Middle age and the autumn years were modern concepts. His brain understood them, but his biology—his manhood—didn't. He only had a few years of riding left—that was what biology thought. More to the point, a few years of reproducing. And maybe the vasectomy had made things worse, or more drastic, sent messages haywire—he didn't know.

The human mind was a funny thing. He'd been dying for a ride, so he bit the head off a neighbour's chicken.

He went downstairs.

-A fox got one of Barbara's hens last night, said Vera.

-Well, that was kind of inevitable, wasn't it?

-That's a bit heartless.

-It's what foxes do, he said. –When?

-What?

-Did the fox strike?

-Last night, she said. –Did you hear anything when you were looking at the shuttle?

-Not a thing, he said. –Just the astronauts chatting.

She smiled. *You're such a messer.*

-About what?

-Oh, just about how much they love Ireland. How's Barbara?

-In bits.

-Did she say she felt violated?

-She did, actually, but you're such a cynical bastard.

She was laughing. And he knew: he was home and dry.

It was later now, night again, and he kissed her neck. He bit her neck. They were a pair of kids for half an hour, and still giddy half an hour after that.

-Well, she said. —I'm ready for afters.

Her hand went exploring.

-Back in a minute, he said.

He went downstairs, went to the fridge—two mackerel on a plate. He looked in the freezer, pulled out a likely bag. A couple of pork chops. He put the bag under the hot tap, till the plastic loosened. Then he tore away the plastic and went at one of the chops. But it was too hard, too cold. He gave it thirty seconds in the microwave and hoped—and dreaded—that the ding would bring her downstairs. He stood at the kitchen window and nibbled at the edges of the chop and hoped—and dreaded—that she'd come in and see his reflection—the blind was up—before she saw him, that he'd turn and reveal himself, some kind of vampire having a snack, and she'd somehow find it sexy or at least reasonable, and forgive him, and put her hands through his hair, like she did, and maybe even join him in the chop, and he'd bring her over the wall so they could get Barbara's last two hens, one each.

He binned the rest of the chop, shook the bin so it would disappear under the other rubbish.

He'd wait for the right moment. The visuals were important; there was a huge difference between being caught devouring raw steak and licking a frozen pork chop, or inviting your life partner to do the same. There was no hurry, no mad rush. No madness at all; he was normal.

He went back upstairs.

She was waiting for him. But not in the bed, or *on* the bed. She was standing far away from the bed.

-What's this? she asked.

She turned on the light.

She was holding a head on the palm of her open hand. A small head.

-A chicken's head, he said.

-Where did you get it?

-I found it.

He was a clown, an eejit; he'd hidden it under his socks.

-It's Barbara's, she said. –Isn't it?

-Barbara's head would be a bit bigger, he said.

It didn't work; she didn't smile.

-Did the fox drop it in the garden? she asked.

She was giving him an escape route, offering him a reasonable story. But it was the wrong one. He'd found a chicken's head and hidden it? He wasn't going to admit to the lie. It was sad, perverse.

-No, he said.

-Well, she said, and looked away. –What happened?

-I bit it off, he said.

She looked at him again. For quite a while.

-What was that like?

-Great, he said. –Great.

FOSSIL-FIGURES

•

Joyce Carol Oates

1.

INSIDE THE GREAT BELLY where the *beat beat beat* of the great heart pumped life blindly. Where there should have been one, there were two: the demon brother, the larger, ravenous with hunger, and the other, the smaller brother, and in the liquidy darkness a pulse between them, a beat that quivered and shuddered, now strong, now lapsing, now strong again, as the demon brother grew even larger, took the nourishment as it pulsed into the womb, the heat, the blood, the mineral strength, kicked and shuddered with life so the mother, whose face was not known, whose existence could only be surmised, winced in pain, tried to laugh but went deathly pale, trying to smile gripping a railing *Ah! My baby. Must be a boy.* For in her ignorance the mother did not yet know that inside her belly there was not one but two. *Flesh of my flesh and blood of my blood and yet not one but two.* And yet not two equally, for the demon brother was the larger of the two, with but a single wish to suck suck suck into his being the life of the other, the smaller brother, all of the nourishment of the liquidy-dark womb, to suck into himself the smaller brother about whom he was hunched as if embracing him, belly to curving spine and the forehead of the demon brother pressed against the soft bone of the back of the head of the smaller brother. The demon brother had no speech but was purely appetite *Why there be this other here—this thing! Why this, when there is me! There is me, me, me, there is only me.* The demon brother did not yet feed by mouth, had not yet sharp teeth to tear, chew, devour and so could not swallow up the smaller brother into his gut, and so the smaller brother survived inside the swollen belly where the *beat beat beat* of the great heart pumped life blindly and in ignorance until the very hour of the birth, when the demon brother forced his way out of the womb headfirst, a diver, a plunger, eager for oxygen, thrusting, squawling, struggling to declare himself, drew his first breath in a shudder of astonishment and began to bawl loudly, hungrily, kicking his small legs, flailing his small arms, a furious purple-flushed face, half-shut glaring eyes, strands of startlingly dark and coarse hair on the flushed infant scalp *A boy! Nine-pound boy! A beautiful—perfect—boy!* Swathed in mother's oily blood, glistening like pent-up fire, a sharp scream and frenzied kicking as the umbilical cord attached to his navel was deftly severed. And what shock then—was it possible?—there was yet another baby inside the mother, but this was not a perfect baby, a runt, cloaked in oily blood, a tiny aged man with a wizened face expelled from the mother after fourteen grunting minutes in a final spasm of waning contractions *Another! There is another boy* yet so tiny, malnourished, five pounds nine ounces, most of this weight in the head, bulbous blue-veined head, purple-flushed skin, the skull forceps dented at the left temple, eyelids stuck together with bloody pus, tiny fists weakly flailing, tiny legs weakly kicking, tiny lungs weakly drawing breath inside the tiny rib cage *Oh but the poor thing won't live—will he?* Tiny caved-in chest, something twisted about the tiny spine, and only faintly, as if at a distance, came the choked bleating cries. In contempt the demon brother laughed. From his place at the mother's breast suck suck sucking the mother's rich milk yet the demon brother laughed in contempt and anger for *Why there be this other here, why this, why "brother," why "twin," when there is me. Only be one of me.*

Yet not one: two.

AT A FEVER PITCH childhood passed for the demon brother who was first in all things. At a glacial pace childhood passed for the smaller brother who trailed behind his twin in all things. The demon brother was joyous to behold, pure infant fire, radiant thrumming energy, every molecule of his being quivering with life, appetite, *me me me.* The smaller brother was often sick, lungs filled with fluids, a tiny valve in his heart fluttered, soft bones of his curving spine, soft bones of his bowed legs, anemia, weak appetite, and the skull subtly misshapen from the forceps delivery, his cries were breathy, bleating, nearly inaudible *me? me?* For the demon brother was first in all things. In the twins' crib the first to roll onto his stomach, and the first to roll onto his back. The first to crawl. The first to rise on shaky baby legs. The first to toddle about wide eyed in triumph at being vertical. The first to speak: Mama. The first to drink in, to swallow up, to suck nourishment from all that he encountered, eyes widened in wonder, in greed, his first word Mama not an appeal or a plea but a command: Mama! Belatedly the smaller brother followed the demon brother, uncertain in his movements, poorly coordinated in his legs, his arms, the very tilt of his head questionable, and his head quivering on frail shoulders, the eyes rapidly blinking, watery, seemingly weak as the facial features were less defined than those of the demon brother of whom it was claimed proudly *He's all boy!* while of the smaller brother it was murmured *Poor thing! But he is growing.* Or it was murmured *Poor thing! But what a sweet sad smile.* In these early years the smaller brother was often sickly and several times had to be hospitalized (anemia, asthma, lung congestion, heart-valve flutter, sprained bones) and in these interims the demon brother did not seem to miss the smaller brother but basked in the full attention of their parents and grew yet taller and stronger and soon it could scarcely be claimed that the brothers were twins—even "fraternal" twins—for observers would react with baffled smiles *Twins? How can that be possible?* For by the age of four, the demon brother was several inches taller than the smaller brother whose spine curved, and whose chest caved in upon itself, and whose eyes blinked, teary and vaguely focused, and it came to seem that the brothers were not twins but, simply, brothers: the one older than the other by two or three years, and much healthier. *We love the boys equally. Of course.* At bedtime the demon brother sank into sleep with the abruptness of a rock sinking into dark water, come to rest in the soft dark mud below. At bedtime the smaller brother lay with opened eyes and stem-thin limbs twitching, for he feared sleep as one might fear sinking into infinity *Even as a young child I understood that infinity is a vast fathomless chasm inside the brain into which we fall and fall through out lives, fall and fall unnamed, faceless and unknown where even, in time, the love of our parents is lost. Even the love of our mothers is lost. And all memory* waking from a thin tormented sleep like frothy water spilled across his face and he's struggling to breathe, choking and coughing, for the demon brother has sucked up most of the oxygen in the room, how can the demon brother help it, his lungs are so strong, his breath so deep and his metabolism so heated, naturally the demon brother will suck up the oxygen in the brothers' room where each night at bedtime their parents tuck the boys in, in twin beds, kissing each, declaring their love for each, and in the night the smaller brother is wakened from a nightmare of suffocation, his weak lungs unable to breathe, panicked and whimpering, in a plea for help managing to crawl from his bed and out of the room and into the hall, collapsed partway between the brothers' room and their parents' room where in the early morning the parents will discover him.

Such meager life, yet such life struggles to save itself!—so the demon brother would recall, in contempt.

OF COURSE WE LOVE Edgar and Edward equally. They are both our sons.

This declaration the demon brother knew to be a lie. Yet was angered by the thought that, when the parents uttered the lie, as they did frequently, those who heard it might believe. And the smaller brother, the sickly brother, with his caved-in chest, crooked spine, wheezy asthmatic breath, yearning teary eyes and sweet smile wished to believe. To rebuke him, the demon brother had a way of turning on him when they were alone, for no (evident) reason pushing him, shoving him, wrestling him to the floor, as the smaller brother drew breath to protest straddling him with his knees, gripping the breakable rib cage like a vise, thump-thump-thumping the little freak's head against the floor, the moist hard palm of a hand clamped over the little freak's mouth to prevent him from crying for help *Mama mama mama* faint as a dying lamb's bleating and so unheard by the mother in another part of the house downstairs in her bliss of ignorance not hearing the thump-thump-thump of the smaller brother's head against the carpeted floor of the boys' room until at last the smaller brother goes limp, ceases to struggle, ceases to struggle for breath, his pinched little face has turned blue, and the demon brother relents, releases him panting and triumphant.

Could've killed you, freak. And I will, if you tell.

For why were there two and not one? As in the womb, the demon brother felt the injustice, and the illogic.

School! So many years. Here the demon brother, who was called Eddie, was first in all things. As the smaller brother, who was called Edward, lagged behind. Immediately in elementary school the brothers were not perceived to be twins but only just brothers, or relatives sharing a last name.

Eddie Waldman. Edward Waldman. But you never saw them together.

At school, Eddie was one of the popular boys. Adored by girls, emu-
lated and admired by boys. He was a big boy. A husky boy. He was a natural
leader, an athlete. Waved his hand, and the teachers called upon him. His
grades were never less than a B. His smile was a dimpled smile, sly-sincere.
He had a way of looking you frankly in the eye. By the age of ten Eddie
had learned to shake hands with adults and to introduce himself *Hi! I'm
Eddie* provoking smiles of admiration *What a bright precocious child!* and, to
demon brother's parents *How proud you must be of your son* as if in fact there
was but one son, and not two. In sixth grade, Eddie ran for president of his
class and was elected by a wide margin.

I am your brother, remember me!

You are nothing of mine. Go away!

But I am in you. Where can I go?

Already in elementary school the smaller brother Edward had dropped
behind his twin. The problem wasn't his schoolwork—for Edward was a
bright, intelligent, inquisitive boy—his grades were often As, when he was
able to complete his work—but his health. So frequently absent from his
fifth-grade classes, he'd had to repeat the year. His lungs were weak, he
caught respiratory infections easily. His heart was weak, in eighth grade
he was hospitalized for weeks following surgery to repair the faulty heart
valve. In tenth grade he suffered a "freak accident"—observed only by his
brother Eddie, in their home—falling down a flight of stairs, breaking
his right leg and kneecap and his right arm and several ribs and injuring his
spine and thereafter he had to hobble about stricken with shyness, wincing
in pain, on crutches. His teachers were aware of him, the younger Waldman boy. His teachers regarded him with sympathy, pity. In high school,
his grades became ever more erratic: sometimes As but more often Cs, Ds,
Incompletes. The smaller brother seemed to have difficulty concentrating
in his classes, he fidgeted with pain, or stared open eyed in a haze of painkillers, scarcely aware of his surroundings. When he was fully awake, he
had a habit of hunching over his notebooks, which were unusually large,
spiral notebooks with unlined pages, like sketchbooks, and in these notebooks he appeared to be constantly drawing, or writing; he frowned and
bit his lower lip, lost in concentration, ignoring the teacher and the rest of
the class *Slipping into infinity, a pleat in time and a twist of the pen and there's
freedom!* The pen had to be a black felt-tip with a fine point. The notebooks
had to have marbled black-and-white covers. The teacher had to call upon
"Edward" several times to get the boy's full attention and in his eyes then,

a quick flaring up, like a match lighted, shyness supplanted by something like resentment, fury. *Leave me alone why can't you, I am not one of you.*

By the time the brothers were eighteen, Eddie was a senior bound for college, president of his class and captain of the football team and in the school yearbook "most likely to succeed" and Edward was trailing behind by a year, with poor grades. He'd begun to arrive at school with a wheelchair, brought by his mother, now in the throes of spinal pain from a slipped disk, and in this wheelchair he was positioned at the front, right-hand corner of his classes, near the teacher's desk, a broken, freaky figure with a small pinched boy's face, waxy skin and slack lips, drowsy from painkillers, or absorbed in his spiral notebooks in which he only pretended to take notes while in fact drawing bizarre figures—geometrical, humanoid—that seemed to spring from the end of his black felt-tip pen.

In the spring of his junior year, stricken with bronchitis, Edward didn't complete his courses and never returned to school: his formal education had ended. In that year, Eddie Waldman was recruited by a dozen universities offering sports scholarships and, shrewdly, he chose the most academically prestigious of the universities, for his goal beyond the university was law school.

Resembling each other as a shadow can be said to resemble its object. Edward was the shadow.

By this time the brothers no longer shared a room. The brothers never longer shared—even!—the old, cruel childish custom of the demon brother's wish to harm his smaller twin; the demon brother's wish to suck all the oxygen out of the air, to swallow up his smaller twin entirely. *Why be this other here—this thing! Why this, when there is me!*

Here was the strange thing: the smaller brother was the one to miss the bond between them. For he had no other so deeply imprinted in his soul as his brother, no bond so fierce and intimate. *I am in you, I am your brother, you must love me.*

But Eddie laughed, backing away. Shook hands with his sickly brother for whom he felt only a mild repugnance, the mildest pang of guilt, and he said good-bye to his parents, allowed himself to be embraced and kissed and went away, smiling in anticipation of his life he went away with no plan to return to his hometown and to his boyhood house except for expediency's sake as a temporary visitor who would be, within hours of his return, restless, bored, eager to escape again to his "real" life elsewhere.

2.

NOW IN THEIR TWENTIES the brothers rarely saw each other. Never spoke on the phone.

Eddie Waldman graduated from law school. Edward Waldman continued to live at home.

Eddie excelled, recruited by a prominent New York City law firm. Edward suffered a succession of "health crises."

The father divorced the mother, abruptly and mysteriously it seemed for the father, too, had a "real" life elsewhere.

Eddie entered politics, under the tutelage of a prominent conservative politician. Edward, suffering spinal pain, spent most days in a wheelchair. Inside his head calculating numbers, imagining equations in which the numerical, the symbolic, and the organic were combined, inventing music, rapidly filling large sheets of construction paper with bizarre yet meticulously detailed geometrical and humanoid figures in settings resembling those of the surrealist painter de Chirico and the visionary artist M. C. Escher. *Our lives are Möbius strips, misery and wonder simultaneously. Our destinies are infinite, and infinitely recurring.*

In the affluent suburb of the great American city, on a residential street of large, expensive houses, the Waldman house, a clapboard colonial on a two-acre lot, began by degrees to fall into disrepair, decline. The front lawn was unmowed and spiky, moss grew on the rotting shingle boards of the roof and newspapers and flyers accumulated on the front walk. The mother, once a sociable woman, began to be embittered, suspicious of neighbors. The mother began to complain of ill health. Mysterious "hexes." The mother understood that the father had divorced her as a way of divorcing himself from the misshapen broke-backed son with the teary yearning eyes who would never grow up, would never marry, would spend the rest of his life in the fevered execution of eccentric and worthless "art."

Frequently the mother called the other son, the son of whom she was so proud, whom she adored. But Eddie seemed always to be traveling, and rarely returned his mother's messages.

In time, within a decade, the mother would die. In the now derelict house (visited, infrequently, by a few concerned relatives) Edward would live as a recluse in two or three downstairs rooms, one of which he'd converted into a makeshift studio. The embittered mother had left him enough money to enable him to continue to live alone and to devote himself to his work; he hired help to come to the house from time to time to clean it, or to attempt to clean it; to shop for him, and to prepare meals. *Freedom! Misery and wonder!* On large canvases Edward transcribed his bizarre dream-images, among galaxies of hieroglyphic shapes in a sequence titled *Fossil-Figures*. For it was Edward's belief, which had come to him in a paroxysm of spinal pain, that misery and wonder are interchangeable and that one must not predominate. In this way time passed in a fever heat for the afflicted brother, who was not afflicted but blessed. Time was a Möbius strip that looped back upon itself, weeks, months and years passed and yet the artist grew no older in his art. (In his physical being, perhaps. But Edward had turned all mirrors to the wall and had not the slightest curiosity about what Edward now "looked like.")

The father, too, died. Or disappeared, which is the same thing.

Relatives ceased to visit, and may have died.

Into infinity, which is oblivion. But it is out of that infinity we have spring: why?

It began to be, as if overnight, the era of the Internet. No man need be a recluse now. However alone and cast off by the world.

Via the Internet *E.W.* communicated with companions—soul mates—scattered in cyberspace, of whom, at any given time, there were invariably a few—but E.W.'s needs were so minimal, his ambition for his art so modest, he required only a few—fascinated by the *Fossil-Figures* he displayed on the Web, who negotiated to buy them. (Sometimes, bidding against one another, for unexpectedly high sums.) And there were galleries interested in exhibiting the works of *E.W.*—as the artist called himself—and small presses interested in publishing them. In this way, in the waning years of the twentieth century, *E.W.* became something of an underground cult figure, rumored to be impoverished, or very wealthy; a crippled recluse living alone in a deteriorating old house, in a deteriorating body, or, perversely, a renowned public figure who guarded his privacy as an artist.

Alone yet never lonely. For is a twin lonely?

Not so long as his twin-self continues to exist.

The brothers were never in contact now, yet, on TV, by chance as sometimes Edward flicked through channels like one propelling himself through the chill of intergalactic space, he came upon images of his lost brother: giving impassioned speeches ("sanctity of life"—"pro-life"—"family values"—"patriotic Americans") to adoring crowds, being interviewed, smiling into the camera with the fiery confidence of one ordained by God. There was the demon brother elected to the U.S. Congress from a district in a neighboring state the smaller brother hadn't known he was living in; there, the demon brother beside an attractive young woman, gripping the young woman's hand, a wife, a Mrs. Edgar Waldman, the smaller brother hadn't known he had married. The demon brother had been taken up by rich, influential elders. In a political party, such elders look to youth to further their political heritage, their "tradition." In this political party the "tradition" was identical with economic interests. This was the triumphant politics of the era. This was the era of the self. *Me, me, me! There is me, me, me there is only me.* Cameras panned rapturous audiences, fervently applauding audiences. For in *me*, there is the blind wish to perceive *we*. As in the most primitive, wrathful, and soulless of gods, humankind will perceive *we*. In the most distant galaxies, infinities of mere emptiness, the ancient yearning *we*.

So Edward, the left-behind brother, hunched in his wheelchair, regarded the demon brother glimpsed on TV with no bitterness nor even a sense of estrangement as one might feel for a being of another species but with the old, perverse yearning *I am your brother, I am in you. Where else can there be, that I am?*

HERE WAS THE INESCAPABLE fact: the brothers shared a single birthday. Even beyond their deaths, that fact would never change.

January 26. The dead of winter. Each year on that day the brothers thought of each other with such vividness, each might have imagined that the other was close beside him, or behind him, a breath on his cheek, a phantom embrace. *He is alive, I can feel him* Edward thought with a shiver of anticipation. *He is alive, I can feel him* Edgar thought with a shiver of revulsion.

3.

THERE CAME A JANUARY 26 that marked the brothers' fortieth birthday. And a few days later there came to an exhibit of E.W.'s new exhibit *Fossil-*

Figures in a storefront gallery in the warehouse district near the Hudson
River at West and Canal streets, New York City, U.S. Congressman Edgar Waldman, who'd given a political speech that afternoon in midtown,
alone now, a limousine with U.S. federal plates waiting at the curb. Noting with satisfaction that the exhibit rooms were nearly deserted. Noting
with disgust how the old, cracked linoleum stuck against the bottom of
his expensive shoes. The handsome congressman wore very dark glasses,
he looked at no one, in dread of being recognized in this sordid place. Especially he was in dread of seeing the crippled brother—"E.W"—whom
he had not seen in nearly twenty years but believed that he would recognize immediately though by this time the twins—"fraternal twins"—
looked nothing alike. Edgar anticipated the stunted broken figure in a
wheelchair, yearning teary eyes and wistful smile that maddened, made
you want to strike with your fists, that offer of forgiveness where forgiveness was not wanted. *I am your brother, I am in you. Love me!* But there was
no one.

Only E.W.'s work, pretentiously called by the gallery "collage paintings." These *Fossil-Figures* lacked all beauty, even the canvases upon which
they were painted looked soiled and battered and the walls upon which
they were (unevenly) hung were streaked as if the hammered-tin ceiling leaked rust. What were these artworks covered in dream/nightmare
shapes, geometrical, yet humanoid, shifting into and out of one another
like translucent guts, deeply offensive to the congressman who sensed
"subterfuge"—"perversion"—"subversion" in such obscure art, and what
was obscure was certain to be "soulless"—even "traitorous." Most upsetting, the *Fossil-Figures* seemed to be taunting the viewer, anyway this
viewer, like riddles, and he had no time for God-damned riddles, the rich
man's daughter he'd married to advance his career was awaiting him at the
St. Regis, this visit to West and Canal streets was an (unmarked) stop in
Congressman Waldman's itinerary for the day. Wiping his eyes to better
see an artwork depicting the night sky, distant galaxies, and constellations,
almost there was beauty here, suns like bursting egg yolks swallowing
up smaller suns, comets shaped like—was it male sperm?—blazing male
sperm?—colliding with luminous bluish-watery planets; and, protruding
from the rough surface of the canvas, a thing so unexpected, so ugly, the
congressman stepped back in astonishment: was it a nestlike growth of
some kind? a tumor? composed of plasticine flesh and dark crinkly hairs

and—could it be baby teeth? arranged in a smile?—and a scattering of baby bones?

A fossil, it was. A thing removed from the human body. Something very ugly discovered a cavity of a surviving twin's body. The fossil-soul of the other, which had never breathed life.

Stunned, quivering with disgust, the congressman turned away.

Walked on, in a haze of denunciations, denials. Seeing that some of the canvases were beautiful—were they?—or were they all ugly, obscene, if you knew how to decode them?—he was made to think that he was endangered, something was going to happen to him, there was a blunt statistical fact that in the last election he'd been reelected to his seat in Congress by a smaller majority than in any of the preceding elections, in such victory there is the presentiment of defeat. Through the maze of rooms circling back to the start of the exhibit and at a glass-topped counter there was a bored-looking girl with dead-white skin and a face glittering with piercings who seemed to be working for the gallery and he asked of her in a voice that quavered with indignation if these ridiculous "fossil-figures" were considered "art" and she told him politely yes of course, everything the gallery exhibited was art and he asked if the exhibit was supported by public funds and seemed but partly mollified to learn that it was not. He asked who the "so-called artist" E.W. was and the girl spoke vaguely saying nobody knew E.W. personally, only the proprietor of the gallery had ever seen him, he lived by himself outside the city and never came into the city, not even to oversee the exhibit, didn't seem to care if his artworks sold, or what prices they were sold for.

"He's got some 'wasting-away' disease, like muscular dystrophy, or Parkinson's, but last we knew, E.W. is alive. He's alive."

AND I WON'T GO away. You will come to me instead.

EACH YEAR: JANUARY 26. One year, one insomniac night, Edward is flicking restlessly though TV channels and is surprised to see a sudden close-up of—is it Edgar? The demon brother Edgar? TV news footage from earlier in the day, rerun now in the early hours of the morning, suddenly this magnification of a man's head, thick-jawed face, an aging face obscured by dark glasses, skin gleaming with oily sweat, an arm lifted to shield the disgraced congressman from a pack of pursuing reporters, photographers and TV camera crews, there's Congressman Edgar Waldman being briskly walked into a building by plainclothes police officers. *Indicted on multiple charges of bribe-taking, violations of federal campaign laws, perjury before a federal grand jury.* Already the rich man's daughter has filed for divorce, there's a quick smile, a suggestion of bared teeth. In the brothers' childhood house in which Edward lives in a few downstairs rooms Edward stares at the TV screen from which his lost brother has faded, uncertain if the thumping sensation in his head is a profound shock, a pang of hurt that must beat within the brother, or his own excitement, eagerness. *He will come to me now. He will not deny me, now.*

Epilogue

IT WAS SO. THE demon brother would return home, to his twin who awaited him.

For he knew himself now *Not one but two.* In the larger world he'd gambled his life and lost his life and would retreat now, to the other. In retreat a man sets aside pride, disgraced, divorced, bankrupt and a glisten of madness in the washed-out blue eyes. His heavy jaws were silvery-dark with stubble, a tremor in his right hand that had been lifted in a federal court to swear that Edgar Waldman would tell the truth the whole truth and nothing but the truth *Yes I swear* and in that heartbeat it was all over for him, a taste like bile rising at the back of his mouth.

Still the wonder. Disbelief. The corroded ruin of a face like clay that has been worn down by rivulets of water, wind. And that glisten of madness in the eyes: *Me?*

In retreat now returning to his childhood home he had shunned for years. The left-behind, broke-backed younger brother who'd been living alone since their mother's death, now many years ago. As a young man he'd never considered time as anything other than a current to bear him aloft, propel him into his future, now he understood that time is a rising tide, implacable inexorable unstoppable rising tide, now at the ankles, now the knees, rising to the thighs, to the groin and the torso and to the chin, ever rising, a dark water of utter mystery propelling us forward not into the future but into infinity, which is oblivion.

Returning to the suburban town of his birth and to the house he's shunned for decades, seeing now with a pang of loss how the residential neighborhood had changed, many of the large houses converted to apartment buildings and commercial sites, and most of the plane trees lining the street severely trimmed or removed altogether. And there was the old Waldman home that had once been their mother's pride, once so splendidly white, now a weatherworn gray with sagging shutters and a rotting roof and a lush junglelike front lawn awash in litter as if no one had lived there for a long time. Edgar had been unable to contact Edward by phone, there was no directory listing for a phone under the name Edward Waldman, now his heart pounded in his chest, he felt a wave of dread *He has died, it is too late.* Hesitantly knocking at the front door and listening for a response from within and knocking again, more loudly, hurting his knuckles, and at last there came from within a faint bleating sound, a voice asking who it was and he called out *It's me.*

Slowly as if with effort the door opened. And there, in his wheelchair, as Edgar had imagined him, but not so ravaged as Edgar has imagined him, was his brother Edward whom he hadn't seen in more than two decades: a shrunken individual of no obvious age with a narrow, pale, pinched yet unlined face, a boy's face, and his hair threaded with gray like Edgar's, and one bony shoulder higher than the other. Pale blue eyes filling with moisture he swiped at with the edges of both hands and in a scratchy voice that sounded as if it hadn't been used in some time he said *Eddie. Come in.*

. . . WHEN IT HAPPENED COULD never be determined precisely since the bodies were frozen and preserved from decay found together on a leather sofa made up as a bed pulled up to within a foot of a fireplace heaped with ashes in a downstairs room of the old clapboard colonial crowded with furniture and what appeared to be the accumulated debris of decades but which may have been materials for artworks or the very artworks themselves of the eccentric artist known as E.W., the elderly Waldman brothers in layers of bulky clothing must have fallen asleep in front of a fire in the otherwise unheated house, the fire must have burnt out in the night and the brothers died in their sleep in a protracted January cold

spell: the brother to be identified as Edgar Waldman, eighty-seven, embracing his brother Edward Waldman, also eighty-seven, from behind, protectively fitting his body to his brother's crippled body, forehead tenderly pressed to the back of the other's head, the two figures coiled together like a gnarled organic material that has petrified to stone.

WILDFIRE IN MANHATTAN

•

Joanne Harris

IT'S NOT MY NAME—WELL, NOT *QUITE*—but you can call me Lucky. I live right here in Manhattan, in the penthouse suite of a hotel just off Central Park. I'm a model citizen in every way, punctual, polite and orderly. I wear sharp suits. I wax my chest hair. You'd never think I was a god.

It's a truth often overlooked that old gods—like old dogs—have to die sometime. It just takes longer, that's all; and in the meantime citadels may fall, empires collapse, worlds end and folk like us end up on the pile, redundant and largely forgotten.

In many ways, I've been fortunate. My element is fire, which never quite goes out of style. There are Aspects of me that still wield power—there's too much of the primitive left in you Folk for it to be otherwise, and although I don't get as many sacrifices as I used to, I can still get obeisance if I want it (who doesn't?)—after dark, when the campfires are lit. And the dry lightning strikes across the plains—yes, they're mine—and the forest fires; and the funeral pyres and the random sparks and the human torches—all mine.

But here, in New York, I'm Lukas Wilde, lead singer in the rock band Wildfire. Well, I say *band*. Our only album, *Burn It Up*, went platinum when the drummer was tragically killed on stage by a freakish blast of lightning.

Well, maybe not so freakish. Our only U.S. tour was stalked by lightning from beginning to end; of fifty venues, thirty-one suffered a direct hit; in just nine weeks we lost three more drummers, six roadies and a truckload of gear. Even I was beginning to feel I'd taken it just a *little* too far.

Still, it was a great show.

Nowadays, I'm semiretired. I can afford to be; as one of only two surviving band members I have a nice little income, and when I'm feeling bored I play piano in a fetish bar called the Red Room. I'm not into rubber myself (too sweaty), but you can't deny it makes a terrific insulator.

By now you may have gathered—I'm a night person. Daylight rather cramps my style; and besides, fire needs a night sky to show to best advantage. An evening in the Red Room, playing piano and eyeing the girls, then downtown for rest and recreation. *Not* a scene that my brother frequents; and so it was with some surprise that I ran smack into him that night, as I was checking out the nicely flammable back streets of the Upper East Side, humming "Light My Fire" and contemplating a spot of arson.

I didn't say? Yes, in this present Aspect, I have a brother. Brendan. A twin. We're not close; Wildfire and Hearth Fire have little in common, and he rather disapproves of my flamboyant lifestyle, preferring the more domestic joys of baking and grilling. Imagine that. A firegod running a restaurant—it makes me burn with shame. Still, it's his funeral. Each of us goes to hell in his own way, and besides, his flame-grilled steaks are the best in the business.

It was past midnight, I was a little light-headed from the booze—but not so drunk that you'd have noticed—and the streets were as still as they get in a city that only ever shuts one eye. A huddle of washouts sleeping in cardboard boxes under a fire escape; a cat raiding a Dumpster. It was November; steam plumed from the sewer grates and the sidewalks were shiny with cold sweat.

I was just crossing the intersection of Eighty-First and Fifth, in front of the Hungarian meat market when I saw him, a familiar figure with hair the colour of embers tucked into the collar of a long grey coat. Tall, slim and ballet quick; you might almost have been forgiven for thinking it was me. Close scrutiny, however, reveals the truth. *My* eyes are red and green; his, on the other hand, are green and red. Anyway, I wouldn't be seen dead wearing those shoes.

I greeted him cheerily. "Do I smell burning?"

He turned to me with a hunted expression. "Shh! Listen!"

I was curious. I know there's never been much love between us, but he usually greets me, at least, before he starts with the recriminations. He called me by my true name. Put a finger to his lips, then dragged me into a side alley that stank of piss.

"Hey, Bren. What gives?" I whispered, correcting my lapels.

His only reply was a curt nod in the direction of the near-deserted alley. In the shadows, two men, boxy in their long overcoats, hats pulled down over narrow, identical faces. They stopped for a second on the kerb, checked left, checked right and crossed over with swift, effortless choreography before vanishing, wolfish, into the night.

"I see." And I did. I'd seen them before. I could feel it in my blood. In another place, in another Aspect, I knew them, and they knew me. And believe me, they were men in form alone. Beneath those cartoon-detective overcoats they were all teeth. "What d'you think they're doing here?"

He shrugged. "Hunting."

"Hunting who?"

He shrugged again. He's never been a man of words, even when he wasn't a man. Me, I'm on the wordy side. I find it helps.

"So you've seen them here before?"

"I was following them when you came along. I doubled back—I didn't want to lead them home."

Well, I could understand that. "What are they?" I said. "Aspects of what? I haven't seen anything like this since Ragnarók, but as I recall—"

"Shh—"

I was getting kinda sick of being shoved and shushed. He's the elder twin, you know, and sometimes he takes liberties. I was about to give him a heated reply when I heard a sound coming from nearby, and something swam into rapid view. It took me a while to figure it out; derelicts are hard to see in this city, and he'd been hiding in a cardboard box under a fire escape, but now he shifted quick enough, his old overcoat flapping like wings around his bony ankles.

I knew him, in passing. Old man Moony, here as an Aspect of Mani, the Moon, but mad as a coot, poor old sod (it often happens when they've been at the juice, and the mead of poetry is a heady brew). Still, he could run, and was running now, but as Bren and I stepped out of his way, the two guys in their long overcoats came to intercept him at the mouth of the alley.

Closer this time—I could smell them. A rank and feral smell, half rotted. Well, you know what they say. You can't teach a carnivore oral hygiene.

At my side I could feel my brother trembling. Or was it me? I wasn't sure. I was scared, I knew that—though there was still enough alcohol carousing in my veins to make me feel slightly removed from it all. In any case I stayed put, tucked into the shadows, not quite daring to move. The two guys stood there at the mouth of the alley, and Moony stopped, wavering now between fight and flight. And—

Fight it was. Okay, I thought. Even a rat will turn when cornered. That didn't mean *I* had to get involved. I could smell him too, the underpinning stench of him, like booze and dirt and that stinky sickly poet smell. He was scared, I knew that. But he was also a god—albeit a beat-up Aspect of one—and that meant he'd *fight* like a god, and even an old alky god like Moony has his tricks.

Those two guys might yet have a shock coming.

For a moment they held their position, two overcoats and a mad poet in a dark triangle under the single streetlight. Then they moved—the guys with that slick, fluid motion I'd seen before, Moony with a lurch and a yell and a flash from his fingertips. He'd cast Týr—a powerful rune—and I saw it flicker through the dark air like a shard of steel, hurtling towards the two not-quite-men. They dodged—no pas de deux could have had more grace—parting, then coming together again as the missile passed, moving in a tight axe-head formation towards the old god.

But throwing Týr had thrown Moony. It takes strength to cast the runes of the Elder Script, and most of his glam was already gone. He opened his mouth—to speak a cantrip, I thought—but before he could, the overcoats moved in with that spooky superhuman speed and I could smell their rankness once more, but so much stronger, like the inside of a badger's sett. They closed in, unbuttoning their coats as they ran—but *were* they running? Instead they seemed to *glide,* like boats, unfurling their long coats like sails to hide and envelop the beleaguered moongod.

He began to chant—the mead of poetry, you know—and for a second the drunken voice cracked and changed, becoming that of Mani in his full Aspect. A sudden radiance shone forth—the predators gave a single growl, baring their teeth—and for a moment I heard the chariot chant of the mad moongod, in a language you could never learn, but of which a single word could drive a mortal crazy with rapture, bring down the stars, strike a man dead—or raise him back to life again.

He chanted, and for a beat the hunters paused—and was that a single trace of a tear gleaming in the shadow of a black fedora?—and Mani sang a glamour of love and death, and of the beauty that is desolation and of the brief firefly that lights up the darkness—for a wing's beat, for a breath—before it gutters, burns and dies.

But the chant did not halt them for more than a second. Tears or not, these guys were *hungry*. They glided forward, hands outstretched, and now I could see *inside* their unbuttoned coats, and for a moment I was sure there was no body beneath their clothes, no fur or scale, no flesh or bone. There was just *the shadow;* the blackness of Chaos; a blackness beyond colour or even its absence; a hole in the world, all-devouring, all-hungry.

Brendan took a single step, and I caught him by the arm and held him back. It was too late anyway; old Moony was already done for. He went down—not with a crash, but with an eerie sigh, as if he'd been punctured—and the creatures that now no longer even *looked* like men were on him like hyenas, fangs gleaming, static hissing in the folds of their garments.

There was nothing human in the way they moved. Nothing superfluous. They Hoovered him up from blood to brain—every glamour, every spark, every piece of kith and kindling—and what they left looked less like a man than a cardboard cutout of a man left lying in the dirt of the alleyway.

Then they were gone, buttoning up their overcoats over the terrible absence beneath.

A silence. Brendan was crying. He always was the sensitive one. I wiped something (sweat, I think) from my face and waited for my breathing to return to normal.

"That was nasty," I said at last. "Haven't seen anything quite like that since the End of the World."

"Did you hear him?" said Brendan.

"I heard. Who would have thought the old man had so much glam in him?"

My brother said nothing, but hid his eyes.

I suddenly realized I was hungry, and thought for a moment of suggesting a pizza, but decided against it. Bren was so touchy nowadays, he might have taken offence.

"Well, I'll see you later, I guess," and sloped off rather unsteadily, wondering why brothers are always so damned hard, and wishing I'd been able to ask him home.

I wasn't to know, but I wish I had—I'd never see that Aspect of him again.

———

I SLEPT TILL LATE the next day. Awoke with a headache and a familiar post-cocktail nauseous feeling, then remembered—the way you remember doing something to your back when you were in the gym, but didn't realize how bad it was going to be until you'd slept on it—and sat bolt upright.

The guys, I thought. *Those two guys.*

I must have been drunker than I'd thought last night, because this morning the memory of them froze me to the core. Delayed shock; I know it well, and to combat its effects I called room service and ordered the works. Over coffee, bacon, pancakes and rivers of maple syrup, I worked on my recovery, and though I did pretty well, given the circumstances, I found I couldn't quite get the death of old Moony out of my mind, or the slick way the two overcoats had crawled over him, gobbling up his glam before buttoning up and back to business. Poetry in motion.

I pondered my lucky escape—well, I guessed that if they hadn't sniffed out Moony first, then it would have been Yours Truly and Brother Bren for a double serving of Dish of the Day—but my heart was far from light as it occurred to me that if these guys were really after our kind, this was at best a reprieve, not a pardon, and that sooner or later those overcoats would be sharpening their teeth at my door.

So I finished breakfast and called Bren. But all I got was his answering machine, so I looked up the number of his restaurant and dialled it. The line was dead.

I would have tried his mobile, but, like I said, we're not close. I didn't know it, or the name of his girl, or even the number of his house. Too late now, right? Just goes to show. Carpe diem, and all that. And so I showered and dressed and went off in haste under gathering clouds to the Flying Pizza, Bren's place of work (but what a dumb name!), in the hope of getting some sense out of my twin.

It was there that I realized something was amiss. Ten blocks away I knew it already, and the sirens and the engines and the shouting and the smoke were just confirmation. There was something ominous about those gathering thunderclouds, and the way they sat like a Russian hat all spiky with needles of lightning above the scene of devastation. My heart sank lower the closer I got. Something was amiss, all right.

Looking around to ensure that I was unobserved, I cast the visionary rune Bjarkán with my left hand, and squinted through its spyglass shape.

Smoke I saw; and lightning from the ground; my brother's face looking pale and strained; then fire; darkness; then, as I'd feared, the Shadow—and its minions, the wolves, the shadow hunters, boxed into their heavy overcoats.

Those guys, I thought, and cursed. *Again.*

And now I knew where I'd known them before—and they were pretty bad in that Aspect, too, though I had more on my plate at that time than I do nowadays, and I'll admit I didn't give them my full attention. I did now, though, casting runes of concealment about me as I skirted the funnel of black smoke, the funeral pyre of my brother's restaurant—and for all I knew, of Brendan himself, who had looked pretty wasted in my vision.

I got there at last, keeping an eye out for overcoats, to find fire engines and cop cars everywhere. A line had been cordoned off at the end of the road, and there were men trying to spray water over the great fizzing spume of fire that had already dug its roots deep into the Flying Pizza.

I could have told them they were wasting their time. You can't put out the work of a firegod—even a god of hearth fire—like it was just a squib. The flames sheeted up, thirty, forty, fifty feet high, clean and yellow and shot through with glamours that would probably have looked like dancing sparks to your kind, but which, if they'd touched you, would have stripped you, flesh to bone, in one.

And Brendan? I thought. *Could he still be alive somewhere?*

Well, if he was, he must have run. There was no way anyone could have survived that blaze. And it wasn't like Bren to flee the scene. He had turned and fought; I'd seen as much in my vision, and my brother was so dead set against the use of glamours among the Folk that he wouldn't have used them if he'd had any kind of choice.

I used Ós—the rune of mystery—to scry my brother's fate. I saw their faces, thin and wolfish; saw his smile, teeth bared, so that for a second in my vision he could have been me, wild and furious and filled with killing rage. He could be okay, my brother, you know; it just took more time to fire him up. I saw him draw his mindsword—flaming, it was, with an edge that shivered translucent light. A sword that could have cut through granite or silk with the same easy slice; a sword I hadn't seen since the last time the world ended, a flickering flame of a firegod's sword that just *touched* the shadow inside an unbuttoned overcoat and went out like a puff of smoke.

Then, in the dark, they were on him. Question answered. Well, at least my brother went out in style.

I wiped my face and pondered the points. Point one: I was now an only twin. Point two: unless he'd taken his assailants with him (which I doubted), by now the two coats would be on my tail. Point three—

I was just embarking on point three when a heavy hand fell onto my shoulder, another grasped my arm just above the elbow and then both applied a painful pressure, which soon became excruciating as the joint locked and a low, familiar voice rasped in my ear.

"Lucky. I should have known you were in this somehow. This shambles has got your mark all over it."

I yelped and tried to free my arm. But the other bastard was holding me too tight.

"Move, and I'll break it," snarled the voice. "Hell, perhaps I ought to break it anyway. Just for old times' sake."

I indicated to him that I'd rather he didn't. He locked my arm a little further—I felt it begin to go and screamed—then he shoved me hard towards the alley wall. I hit it, bounced, spun round with mindsword ready, half drawn, and found myself staring into a pair of eyes as grim and colourless as a rainy day. Just my luck—a friend with a grievance, which is the only kind I tend to have nowadays.

Well, I say *friend*. He's one of our kind, but you know how it is. Fire and rainstorm—we don't get along. Besides, in his present Aspect he stood taller, weighed heavier, hit harder than me. His face was a thundercloud, and any thought I had of fighting the guy evaporated like cheap perfume. I sheathed the sword and took the better part of valour.

"Hey," I said. "It's Our Thor."

He sniffed. "Try anything, and I'll douse you cold," he said. "I've got an army of stormclouds ready to roll. You'll be out like a light before you can blink. Want to try it?"

"Did I ever? Nice greeting, friend. It's been a long time."

He grunted. "Arthur's the name in this present Aspect. Arthur Pluviôse—and *you're* dead." He made it sound like some weird kind of naming ceremony.

"Wrong," I said. "*Brendan's* dead. And if you think I'd be a party to the murder of my own brother—"

"Wouldn't put it past you," Arthur said, though I could tell the news had shaken him. "Brendan's *dead*?" he repeated.

"'Fraid so." I was touched—I'd always thought he hated us both.

"Then this wasn't you?"

"My, you're fast."

He glowered. "Then how?"

"How else?" I shrugged. "The Shadow, of course. Chaos. Black Surt. Choose your own damn metaphor."

Arthur gave a long, soft sigh. As if it had preyed on his mind for such a long time that any news—even bad news—even *terrible* news—could come as a relief. "So it's true," he said. "I was beginning to think—"

"Finally—"

He ignored the gibe and turned on me once more, his rainy-day eyes gleaming. "It's the wolves, Lucky. The wolves are on the trail again."

I nodded. Wolves, demons, no word exists in any tongue of the Folk to describe exactly what they were. I call them *ephemera*, though I had to admit there was nothing ephemeral about their present Aspect.

"Skól and Haiti, the Sky-Hunters, servants of the Shadow, Devourers of the Sun and Moon. And of anything else that happens to be in their way, for that matter. Brendan must have tried to tackle them. He never did have any sense."

But I could tell he was no longer listening. "The Sun and—"

"Moon." I gave him the abridged version on the events of last night. He listened, but I could tell he was distracted.

"So, after the Moon, the Sun. Right?"

"I guess." I shrugged. "That is, assuming there's an Aspect of Sól in Manhattan, which, if there is—"

"There is," said Arthur grimly. "Her name's Sunny." And there was something about his eyes as he said it, something even more ominous than the rain-swelled clouds above us, or his hand on my shoulder, horribly pally and heavy as lead, that made me think I was in for an even lousier day than I'd had so far.

"Sunny," I said. "Then she'll be next."

"Over my dead body," said Arthur. "And yours," he added, almost as an afterthought, keeping his hand hard on my shoulder and smiling that dangerous, stormy smile.

"Sure. Why not?" I humoured him. I could afford to—I'm used to running, and I knew that at a pinch, Lukas Wilde could disappear within an hour, leaving no trace.

He knew it too. His eyes narrowed, and above us the clouds began to move softly, gathering momentum like wool on a spindle. A dimple appeared at its nadir—soon, I knew, to become a funnel of air, stitched and barbed with deadly glamours.

"Remember what they say," said Arthur, addressing me by my true name. "Everywhere you go, you always take the weather with you."

"You wrong me." I smiled, though I'd never felt less like it. "I'll be only too happy to help your friend."

"Good," said Arthur. He kept that hand on my shoulder, though, and his smile was all teeth. "We'll keep to the shadows. No need to involve the Folk any more than we have to. Right?"

It was a dark and stormy afternoon. I had an idea that it was going to be the first of many.

SUNNY LIVED IN BROOKLYN Heights, in a loft apartment on a quiet street. Not a place I visit often, which accounts for my not having spotted her sooner. Most of our kind take the discreet approach; gods have enemies too, you know, and we find it pays to keep our glam to ourselves.

But Sunny was different. For a start, according to Arthur (what a dumb name!), she didn't know what she was anymore. It happens sometimes; you just forget. You get all wrapped up in your present Aspect; you start to think you're like everyone else. Perhaps that's what kept her safe for so long; they say gods look after drunks and half-wits and little children, and Sunny certainly qualified. Transpires that my old pal Arthur had been looking after her for nearly a year without her knowing it, making sure that she got the sunshine she needed to be happy, keeping sniffers and prowlers away from her door.

Because even the Folk start getting suspicious when someone like Sunny lives nearby. It wasn't just the fact that it hadn't rained in months; that sometimes all of New York City could be under a cloud but for the two or three streets surrounding her block; or the funny northern lights that sometimes shone in the sky above her apartment. It was *her*, just *her*, with her face and her smile, turning heads wherever she went. A man—a *god*—could fall in love.

Arthur had dropped his raingod Aspect, and was now looking more or less like a regular citizen, but I could tell he was making a hell of an effort. As soon as we crossed the Brooklyn Bridge I could see him beginning to hold it in, the way a fat man holds in his gut when a pretty girl comes into the room. Then I saw her colours—from afar, like lights in the sky, and the look on his face—that look of truculent yearning—intensified a little.

He gave me the critical once-over. "Tone it down a bit, will you?" he said.

Well, *that* was offensive. I'd looked a lot flashier as Lukas Wilde, but looking at Arthur right then I thought it a bad time to say so. I turned down the volume on my red coat, but kept my hair as it was, hiding my mismatched eyes behind a pair of snappy shades.

"Better?"

"You'll do."

We were standing outside the place now. A standard apartment at the back of a lot of others; black fire escape, small windows, little roof garden throwing down wisps of greenery into the guttering. But at the window there was a light, something rather like sunlight, I guess, occasionally strobing here and there—following her movements as she wandered about her flat.

Some people have no idea of how to go unnoticed. In fact, it was astonishing that the wolves hadn't seized on her before. She'd not even tried to hide her colours, which was frankly beyond unwise, I thought—hell, she hadn't even pulled the drapes.

Arthur gave me one of his looks. "We're going to protect her, Lucky," he said. "And *you're* going to be nice. Okay?"

I made a face. "I'm always nice. How could you possibly doubt me?"

SHE INVITED US IN straightaway. No checking of credentials; no suspicious glance from behind the open drapes. I'd had her down as pretty, but dumb; now I saw she was a genuine innocent, a little-girl-lost in the big city. Not my type, naturally, but I could see what Arthur saw in her.

She offered us a cup of ginseng tea. "Any friend of Arthur's," she said, and I saw his painful grimace as he tried to fit his big fingers around the little china cup, all the while trying to hold himself in so that Sunny could have her sunshine . . .

Finally, it was too much for him. He let it out with a gasp of release, and the rain started to come down in snakes, hissing into the gutters.

Sunny looked dismayed. "Damn *rain!*"

Arthur looked like someone had punched him hard, right in the place where thunder gods keep their ego. He gave that feeble smile again. "It doesn't make you feel safe?" he said. "You don't think there's a kind of poetry in the sound, like little hammers beating down onto the roof-tops?"

Sunny shook her head. "Yuck."

I lit the fire with a discreet cantrip and a fingering of the rune Kaen. Little flames shot out of the grate and danced winsomely across the hearth. It was a good trick, though I say it myself—especially as it was an electric fire.

"Neat," said Sunny, smiling again.

Arthur gave a low growl.

"So—have you seen anything strange around here lately?" Stupid damn question, I told myself. Move a sun goddess onto the third floor of a Manhattan brownstone, and you're apt to see more than the occasional pyrotechnics. "No guys in suits?" I went on. "Dark overcoats and fedora hats, like someone from a bad fifties comic strip?"

"Oh, *those* guys." She poured more tea. "Yeah, I saw them yesterday. They were sniffing around in the alleyway." Sunny's blue eyes darkened a little. "They didn't look friendly. What do they want?"

I was going to tell her about Bren, and what had happened to Old Man Moony, but Arthur stopped me with a glance. Sunny has that effect, you know; makes guys want to do stupid things. Stupid, noble, self-sacrificing things—and I was beginning to understand that I was going to be a part of it, whether or not I wanted to be.

"Nothing *you* need to worry about," Arthur said with a big smile, clamping a hand on my upper arm and marching me onto the balcony. "They're just some guys we're looking for. We'll camp out here tonight and keep an eye out for them for you. Any trouble, we'll be here. No need for you to worry. Okay?"

"Okay," said Sunny.

"Okay," I said between gritted teeth (my arm felt like it had been pounded several times with a hammer). I waited until we were alone, and Sunny had drawn the curtains, then I turned on him. "What's the deal?" I said. "We can't hold back the Shadow-wolves. You must know that by now, right? You saw what they did to Moony and Bren. Our only chance is to outrun them, to take your lady friend with you and to run like the blazes to another city, to another continent if we can, where the Shadow has less influence—"

Arthur looked stubborn. "I won't run."

"Fine. Well, it's been a blast— *Ow!* My *arm!*"

"And neither will you," said Our Thor.

"Well, if you put it *that* way—"

I may be a trifle impetuous, but I know when to surrender to force majeure. Arthur had his mind set on both of us being heroes. My only remaining choice was whether to set *my* mind to helping him, thereby possibly saving both our hides, or to make a run for it as soon as the bastard's guard was down—

Well, I might have gone down either path, but just then I caught sight of our boys in the alleyway, sniffing and snarling like wolves in suits, and I was down to no choice at all. I drew my mindsword, he drew his. Glamours and runes distressed the night air. Not that *they* would help us, I thought; they hadn't helped my brother Bren, or the mad old moongod. And Shadow—or Chaos, if you prefer—had plenty of glamours of its own with which to strike down three renegade gods, fugitives left over from the End of the World—

"Hey! Up here!" yelled Our Thor.

Two pairs of eyes turned up towards us. A hiss like static as the ephemera tuned into our whereabouts. A glint of teeth as they grinned—and then they were crawling up the fire escape, all pretence of humanity gone, slick beneath those boxy black coats, nothing much in there but tooth and claw, like poetry with an appetite.

Oh, great, I thought. Way to keep a low profile, Our Thor. Was it an act of self-sacrifice, a ploy to attract their attention, or could he possibly have a plan? If he did, then it would be a first. Mindless self-sacrifice was about his level. I wouldn't have minded *that* much, but it was clear that in his boundless generosity he also meant to sacrifice *me*.

"Lucky!" It was raining again. Great ropes and coils of thunderous rain that thrashed down onto our bowed heads, all gleaming in the neon lights in shades of black and orange—from the static-ridden sky, great flakes of snow lumbered down. Well, that's what happens around a raingod under stress; but that didn't stop me getting soaked, and wishing I'd brought my umbrella. It didn't stop the ephemera though. Even the bolts of lightning that crashed like stray missiles into the alleyway (I have skills too, and

I was using them like the blazes by then) had no effect on the wolves of Chaos, whose immensely slick and somehow snakelike forms were now poised on the fire escape beneath us, ten feet away and ready to pounce.

One did—a mindbolt flew. I recognized the rune Hagall. One of my colleague's most powerful, and yet it passed right through the ephemera with a squeal of awesome feedback, then the creature was on us again, unbuttoning its overcoat, and now I was sure there were *stars* in there, stars and the mindless static of space—

"Look," I said. "What do you want? Girls, money, power, fame—I can get all those things for you, no problem. I've got influence in this world. Two handsome, single guys like yourselves—hey, you could make a killing in showbiz."

Perhaps not the wisest choice of words.

The first wolf leered. *"Killing,"* it said. By then I could smell it again, and I knew that words couldn't save me. First, the thing was ravenous. Second, *nothing* with that level of halitosis could possibly hope to make it in the music business. Some guys, I knew, had come pretty close. My daughter Hel, for instance, has, in spite of her—shall we say *alternative*—looks, a serious fan base in certain circles. But not these guys. I mean, *Ew.*

I flung a handful of mindrunes then: Týr; Kaen; Hagall; Ýr—but none of them even slowed it down. The other wolf was onto us now, and Arthur was wrestling with it, caught in the flaps of its black coat. The balcony was pulling away from the wall; sparks and shards of runelight hissed into the torrential rain.

Damn it, I thought. *I'm going to die wet.* And I flung up a shield using the rune Sól, and with the last, desperate surge of my glam I cast *all* the firerunes of the First Aettir at the two creatures that once had been wolves but were now grim incarnations of revenge, because nothing escapes from Chaos, not Thunder, not Wildfire, not even the Sun—

"Are you guys okay out there?" It was Sunny, peering through a gap in the curtains. "Do you want some more ginseng tea?"

"Ah—no thanks," said Arthur, now with a demon wolf in each hand and that stupid grin on his face again. "Look, ah, Sunny, go inside. I'm kinda busy right now—"

The thing that Our Thor had been holding at bay finally escaped his grasp. It didn't go far, though; it sprang at me and knocked me backwards against the rail. The balcony gave way with a screech, and we all fell together, three floors down. I hit the deck—damned hard—with the ephemera on top of me, and all the fight knocked out of me and I knew that I was finished.

Sunny peered down from her window. "Do you need help?" she called to me.

I could see right *into* the creature now, and it was grim—like those fairy tales where the sisters get their toes chopped off and the bad guys get pecked to death by crows and even the little mermaid has to walk on razor blades for the rest of her life for daring to fall in love . . . Except that I knew Sunny had got the Disney version instead, with all the happy endings in it, and the chipmunks and rabbits and the goddamned squirrels (I hate squirrels!) singing in harmony, where even the wolves are good guys and no one ever *really* gets hurt—

I gave her a sarcastic smile. "Yeah, wouldya?" I said.

"Okay," said Sunny, and pulled the drapes and stepped out onto the balcony.

And then something very weird happened.

I WAS WATCHING HER from the alleyway, my arms pinned to my sides now and the ephemera straddling me with its overcoat spread like a vulture about to spear an eyeball. The cold was so intense that I couldn't feel my hands at all, and the stench of the thing made my head swim, and the rain was pounding into my face and my glam was bleeding out so fast that I knew I had seconds, no more—

So the first thing she did was put her umbrella up.

Ignored Arthur's desperate commands—besides, he was still wrestling with the second ephemera. His colours were flaring garishly; runelight whirled around them both, warring with the driving rain.

And then she smiled.

It was as if the sun had come out. Except that it was night, and the light was, like, sixty times more powerful than the brightest light you've ever known, and the alley lit up a luminous white, and I screwed my eyes shut to prevent them from being burnt there and then out of their sockets, and all these things happened at once.

First of all, the rain stopped. The pressure on my chest disappeared, and I could move my arms again. The light, which had been too intense

even to see when it first shone out, diffused itself to a greenish-pink glow.
Birds on the rooftops began to sing. A scent of something floral filled the
air—strangest of all in that alleyway, where the smell of piss was predomi-
nant—and someone put a hand on my face and said:

"It's okay, sweetie. They've gone now."

Well, that was it. I opened my eyes. I figured that either I'd taken more
concussion than I'd thought, or there was something Our Thor hadn't told
me. He was standing over me, looking self-conscious and bashful. Sunny
was kneeling at my side, heedless of the alleyway dirt, and her blue dress
was shining like the summer sky, and her bare feet were like little white
birds, and her sugar blond hair fell over my face and I was glad she really
wasn't my type, because that lady was nothing but trouble. And she gave
me a smile like a summer's day, and Arthur's face went dangerously red,
and Sunny said:

"Lucky? Are you okay?"

I rubbed my eyes. "I think so. What happened to Skól and Haiti?"

"Those guys?" she said. "Oh, they had to go. I sent them back into
Shadow."

Now Arthur was looking incredulous. "How do you know about
Shadow?" he said.

"Oh, Arthur, you're so *sweet*." Sunny pirouetted to her feet and planted
a kiss on Our Thor's nose. "As if I could have lived here this long and not
have known I was different—" She looked at the illuminated sky. "Northern lights," she said happily. "We ought to have them more often here. But
I really do appreciate it," she went on. "You guys looking out for me, and
everything. If things had been different, if we hadn't been made from such
different elements, then maybe you and I could have—you know—"

Arthur's face went, if possible, even redder.

"So, what are you going to do now?" she said. "I guess we're safe—for
a while, at least. But Chaos knows about us now. And the Shadow never
really gives up . . ."

I thought about it for a while. And then an idea came to me. I said:
"Have you ever thought of a career in entertainment? I could find a job for
you with the band . . ." I wondered if she could sing. Most celestial spheres
can, of course, and anyway, she'd light up the place just by stepping onto
the stage—we'd save a fortune on pyrotechnics . . .

She gave that megawatt smile of hers. "Is Arthur in the band, too?"

I looked at him. "He could be, I guess. There's always room for a drummer."

Come to think of it, there's a lot to be said for going on the road right now. New people, new lineup, new places to go—

"That would be nice." Her face was wistful. His was like that of a sick puppy, and it made me even more relieved that I'd never been the romantic type. I tried to imagine the outcome: sun goddess and thunder god on stage together, every night—

I could see it now, I thought. Wildfire, on tour again. I mean, we're talking rains of fish, equatorial northern lights; hurricanes, eclipses, solar flares, flash floods—and lightning. Lots of lightning. Might be a little risky, of course.

But all the same—a hell of a show.

THE TRUTH IS A CAVE
IN THE BLACK MOUNTAINS

•

Neil Gaiman

YOU ASK ME IF I CAN FORGIVE MYSELF? I can forgive myself for many things. For where I left him. For what I did. But I will not forgive myself for the year that I hated my daughter, when I believed her to have run away, perhaps to the city. During that year I forbade her name to be mentioned, and if her name entered my prayers when I prayed, it was to ask that she would one day learn the meaning of what she had done, of the dishonour that she had brought to my family, of the red that ringed her mother's eyes.

I hate myself for that, and nothing will ease that, not even what happened that night, on the side of the mountain.

I had searched for nearly ten years, although the trail was cold. I would say that I found him by accident, but I do not believe in accidents. If you walk the path, eventually you must arrive at the cave.

But that was later. First, there was the valley on the mainland, the whitewashed house in the gentle meadow with the burn splashing through it, a house that sat like a square of white sky against the green of the grass and the heather just beginning to purple.

And there was a boy outside the house, picking wool from off a thorn-bush. He did not see me approaching, and he did not look up until I said, "I used to do that. Gather the wool from the thorn-bushes and twigs. My mother would wash it, then she would make me things with it. A ball, and a doll."

He turned. He looked shocked, as if I had appeared out of nowhere. And I had not. I had walked many a mile, and had many more miles to go. I said, "I walk quietly. Is this the house of Calum MacInnes?"

The boy nodded, drew himself up to his full height, which was perhaps two fingers bigger than mine, and he said, "I am Calum MacInnes."

"Is there another of that name? For the Calum MacInnes that I seek is a grown man."

The boy said nothing, just unknotted a thick clump of sheep's wool from the clutching fingers of the thorn-bush. I said, "Your father, perhaps? Would he be Calum MacInnes as well?"

The boy was peering at me. "What are you?" he asked.

"I am a small man," I told him. "But I am a man, nonetheless, and I am here to see Calum MacInnes."

"Why?" The boy hesitated. Then, "And why are you so small?"

I said, "Because I have something to ask your father. Man's business." And I saw a smile start at the tips of his lips. "It's not a bad thing to be small, young Calum. There was a night when the Campbells came knocking on my door, a whole troop of them, twelve men with knives and sticks, and they demanded of my wife, Morag, that she produce me, as they were there to kill me, in revenge for some imagined slight. And she said, 'Young Johnnie, run down to the far meadow, and tell your father to come back to the house, that I sent for him.' And the Campbells watched as the boy ran out the door. They knew that I was a most dangerous person. But nobody had told them that I was a wee man, or if that had been told them, it had not been believed."

"Did the boy call you?" said the lad.

"It was no boy," I told him, "but me myself, it was. And they'd had me, and still I walked out the door and through their fingers."

The boy laughed. Then he said, "Why were the Campbells after you?"

"It was a disagreement about the ownership of cattle. They thought the cows were theirs. I maintained the Campbells' ownership of them had ended the first night the cows had come with me over the hills."

"Wait here," said young Calum MacInnes.

I sat by the burn and looked up at the house. It was a good-sized house: I would have taken it for the house of a doctor or a man of law, not of a border reaver. There were pebbles on the ground and I made a pile of them, and I tossed the pebbles, one by one, into the burn. I have a good eye, and I enjoyed rattling the pebbles over the meadow and into the water. I had thrown a hundred stones when the boy returned, accompanied by a tall, loping man. His hair was streaked with grey, his face was long and wolfish. There are no wolves in those hills, not any longer, and the bears have gone too.

"Good day to you," I said.

He said nothing in return, only stared; I am used to stares. I said, "I am seeking Calum MacInnes. If you are he, say so, I will greet you. If you are not he, tell me now, and I will be on my way."

"What business would you have with Calum MacInnes?"

"I wish to hire him, as a guide."

"And where is it you would wish to be taken?"

I stared at him. "That is hard to say," I told him. "For there are some who say it does not exist. There is a certain cave on the Misty Isle."

He said nothing. Then he said, "Calum, go back to the house."

"But da—"

"Tell your mother I said she was to give you some tablet. You like that. Go on."

Expressions crossed the boy's face—puzzlement, hunger, happiness—and then he turned and ran back to the white house.

Calum MacInnes said, "Who sent you here?"

I pointed to the burn as it splashed its way between us on its journey down the hill. "What's that?" I asked.

"Water," he replied.

"And they say there is a king across it," I told him.

I did not know him then at all, and never knew him well, but his eyes became guarded, and his head cocked to one side. "How do I know you are who you say you are?"

"I have claimed nothing," I said. "Just that there are those who have heard that there is a cave on the Misty Isle, and that you might know the way."

He said, "I will not tell you where the cave is."

"I am not here asking for directions. I seek a guide. And two travel more safely than one."

He looked me up and down, and I waited for the joke about my size, but he did not make it, and for that I was grateful. He just said, "When we reach the cave, I will not go inside. You must bring out the gold yourself."

I said, "It is all one to me."

He said, "You can take only what you carry. I will not touch it. But yes, I will take you."

I said, "You will be paid well for your trouble." I reached into my jerkin, handed him the pouch I had in there. "This for taking me. Another, twice the size, when we return."

He poured the coins from the pouch into his huge hand, and he nodded. "Silver," he said. "Good." Then, "I will say good-bye to my wife and
son."

"Is there nothing you need to bring?"

He said, "I was a reaver in my youth, and reavers travel light. I'll bring
a rope, for the mountains." He patted his dirk, which hung from his belt,
and went back into the whitewashed house. I never saw his wife, not then,
nor at any other time. I do not know what colour her hair was.

I threw another fifty stones into the burn as I waited, until he returned,
with a coil of rope thrown over one shoulder, and then we walked together
away from a house too grand for any reaver, and we headed west.

THE MOUNTAINS BETWEEN THE rest of the world and the coast are grad-
ual hills, visible from a distance as gentle, purple, hazy things, like clouds.
They seem inviting. They are slow mountains, the kind you can walk up
easily, like walking up a hill, but they are hills that take a full day and more
to climb. We walked up the hill, and by the end of the first day we were
cold.

I saw snow on the peaks above us, although it was high summer.

We said nothing to each other that first day. There was nothing to be
said. We knew where we were going.

We made a fire, from dried sheep dung and a dead thorn-bush: we
boiled water and made our porridge, each of us throwing a handful of oats
and a fingerpinch of salt into the little pan I carried. His handful was huge,
and my handful was small, like my hands, which made him smile and say,
"I hope you will not be eating half of the porridge."

I said I would not and indeed, I did not, for my appetite is smaller than
that of a full-grown man. But this is a good thing, I believe, for I can keep
going in the wild on nuts and berries that would not keep a bigger person
from starving.

A path of sorts ran across the high hills, and we followed it and encountered almost nobody: a tinker and his donkey, piled high with old pots, and
a girl leading the donkey, who smiled at me when she thought me to be a
child, and then scowled when she perceived me to be what I am, and would
have thrown a stone at me had the tinker not slapped her hand with the
switch he had been using to encourage the donkey; and, later, we overtook

an old woman and a man she said was her grandson, on their way back across the hills. We ate with her, and she told us that she had attended the birth of her first great-grandchild, that it was a good birth. She said she would tell our fortunes from the lines in our palms, if we had coins to cross her palm. I gave the old biddy a clipped lowland groat, and she looked at my palm.

She said, "I see death in your past and death in your future."

"Death waits in all our futures," I said.

She paused, there in the highest of the high lands, where the summer winds have winter on their breath, where they howl and whip and slash the air like knives. She said, "There was a woman in a tree. There will be a man in a tree."

I said, "Will this mean anything to me?"

"One day. Perhaps." She said, "Beware of gold. Silver is your friend." And then she was done with me.

To Calum MacInnes she said, "Your palm has been burned." He said that was true. She said, "Give me your other hand, your left hand." He did so. She gazed at it, intently. Then, "You return to where you began. You will be higher than most other men. And there is no grave waiting for you, where you are going."

He said, "You tell me that I will not die?"

"It is a left-handed fortune. I know what I have told you, and no more."

She knew more. I saw it in her face.

That was the only thing of any importance that occurred to us on the second day.

We slept in the open that night. The night was clear and cold, and the sky was hung with stars that seemed so bright and close I felt as if I could have reached out my arm and gathered them, like berries.

We lay side by side beneath the stars, and Calum MacInnes said, "Death awaits you, she said. But death does not wait for me. I think mine was the better fortune."

"Perhaps."

"Ah," he said. "It is all nonsense. Old-woman talk. It is not truth."

I woke in the dawn mist to see a stag, watching us curiously.

The third day we crested those mountains, and we began to walk downhill.

My companion said, "When I was a boy, my father's dirk fell into the cooking fire. I pulled it out, but the metal hilt was as hot as the flames. I did not expect this, but I would not let the dirk go. I carried it away from the fire, and plunged the sword into the water. It made steam. I remember that. My palm was burned, and my hand curled, as if it was meant to carry a sword until the end of time."

I said, "You, with your hand. Me, only a little man. It's fine heroes we are, who seek our fortunes on the Misty Isle."

He barked a laugh, short and without humour. "Fine heroes," was all he said.

The rain began to fall then, and did not stop falling. That night we passed a small croft house. There was a trickle of smoke from its chimney, and we called out for the owner, but there was no response.

I pushed open the door and called again. The place was dark, but I could smell tallow, as if a candle had been burning and had recently been snuffed.

"No one at home," said Calum, but I shook my head and walked forward, then leaned my head down into the darkness beneath the bed.

"Would you care to come out?" I asked. "For we are travellers, seeking warmth and shelter and hospitality. We would share with you our oats and our salt and our whisky. And we will not harm you."

At first the woman, hidden beneath the bed, said nothing, and then she said, "My husband is away in the hills. He told me to hide myself away if the strangers come, for fear of what they might do to me."

I said, "I am but a little man, good lady, no bigger than a child, you could send me flying with a blow. My companion is a full-sized man, but I do swear that we shall do nothing to you, save partake of your hospitality, and dry ourselves. Please do come out."

All covered with dust and spiderwebs she was when she emerged, but even with her face all begrimed, she was beautiful, and even with her hair all webbed and greyed with dust it was still long and thick, and golden red. For a heartbeat she put me in the mind of my daughter, but that my daughter would look a man in the eye, while this one glanced only at the ground fearfully, like something expecting to be beaten.

I gave her some of our oats, and Calum produced strips of dried meat from his pocket, and she went out to the field and returned with a pair of scrawny turnips, and she prepared food for the three of us.

I ate my fill. She had no appetite. I believe that Calum was still hungry when his meal was done. He poured whisky for the three of us: she took but a little, and that with water. The rain rattled on the roof of the house, and dripped in the corner, and, unwelcoming though it was, I was glad that I was inside.

It was then that a man came through the door. He said nothing, only stared at us, untrusting, angry. He pulled off his cape of oiled sacking, and his hat, and he dropped them on the earth floor. They dripped and puddled. The silence was oppressive.

Calum MacInnes said, "Your wife gave us hospitality, when we found her. Hard enough she was in the finding."

"We asked for hospitality," I said. "As we ask it of you."

The man said nothing, only grunted.

In the high lands, people spend words as if they were golden coins. But the custom is strong there: strangers who ask for hospitality must be granted it, though you have a blood feud against them and their clan or kind.

The woman—little more than a girl she was, while her husband's beard was grey and white, so I wondered if she was his daughter for a moment, but no: there was but one bed, scarcely big enough for two—the woman went outside, into the sheep pen that adjoined the house, and returned with oatcakes and a dried ham she must have hidden there, which she sliced thin, and placed on a wooden trencher before the man.

Calum poured the man whisky, and said, "We seek the Misty Isle. Do you know if it is there?"

The man looked at us. The winds are bitter in the high lands, and they would whip the words from a man's lips. He pursed his mouth, then he said, "Aye. I saw it from the peak this morning. It's there. I cannot say if it will be there tomorrow."

We slept on the hard-earth floor of that cottage. The fire went out, and there was no warmth from the hearth. The man and his woman slept in their bed, behind the curtain. He had his way with her, beneath the sheep-skin that covered that bed, and before he did that, he beat her for feeding us and for letting us in. I heard them, and could not stop hearing them, and sleep was hard in the finding that night.

I have slept in the homes of the poor, and I have slept in palaces, and I have slept beneath the stars, and would have told you before that night that all places were one to me. But I woke before first light, convinced we had to be gone from that place, but not knowing why, and I woke Calum by putting a finger to his lips, and silently we left that croft on the mountainside without saying our farewells, and I have never been more pleased to be gone from anywhere.

We were a mile from the place when I said, "The island. You asked if it would be there. Surely, an island is there, or it is not there."

Calum hesitated. He seemed to be weighing his words, and then he said, "The Misty Isle is not as other places. And the mist that surrounds it is not like other mists."

We walked down a path worn by hundreds of years of sheep and deer and few enough men.

He said, "They also call it the Winged Isle. Some say it is because the island, if seen from above, would look like butterfly wings. And I do not know the truth of it." Then, "'And what is truth?' said jesting Pilate."

It is harder coming down than it is going up.

I thought about it. "Sometimes I think that truth is a place. In my mind, it is like a city: there can be a hundred roads, a thousand paths, that will all take you, eventually, to the same place. It does not matter where you come from. If you walk toward the truth, you will reach it, whatever path you take."

Calum MacInnes looked down at me and said nothing. Then, "You are wrong. The truth is a cave in the black mountains. There is one way there, and one only, and that way is treacherous and hard, and if you choose the wrong path you will die alone, on the mountainside."

We crested the ridge, and we looked down to the coast. I could see villages below, beside the water. And I could see high black mountains before me, on the other side of the sea, coming out of the mist.

Calum said, "There's your cave. In those mountains."

The bones of the earth I thought, seeing them. And then I became uncomfortable, thinking of bones, and to distract myself, I said, "And how many times is it you have been there?"

"Only once." He hesitated. "I searched for it all my sixteenth year, for I had heard the legends, and I believed if I sought I should find. I was seventeen when I reached it, and came back with all the gold coins I could carry."

"And were you not frightened of the curse?"

"When I was young, I was afraid of nothing."

"What did you do with your gold?"

"A portion I buried and I alone know where. The rest I used as bride-price for the woman I loved, and I built a fine house with it."

He stopped as if he had already said too much.

There was no ferryman at the jetty. Only a small boat, hardly big enough for three full-sized men, tied to a tree trunk on the shore, twisted and half dead, and a bell beside it.

I sounded the bell, and soon enough a fat man came down the shore.

He said to Calum, "It will cost you a shilling for the ferry, and your boy, three pennies."

I stood tall. I am not as big as other men are, but I have as much pride as any of them. "I am also a man," I said. "I'll pay your shilling."

The ferryman looked me up and down, then he scratched his beard. "I beg your pardon. My eyes are not what they once were. I shall take you to the island."

I handed him a shilling. He weighed it in his hand, "That's ninepence you did not cheat me out of. Nine pennies are a lot of money in this dark age." The water was the colour of slate, although the sky was blue, and whitecaps chased one another across the water's surface. He untied the boat and hauled it, rattling, down the shingle to the water. We waded out into the cold water, and clambered inside.

The splash of oars on seawater, and the boat propelled forward in easy movements. I sat closest to the ferryman. I said, "Ninepence. It is good wages. But I have heard of a cave in the mountains on the Misty Isle, filled with gold coins, the treasure of the ancients."

He shook his head dismissively.

Calum was staring at me, lips pressed together so hard they were white. I ignored him and asked the man again, "A cave filled with golden coins, a gift from the Norsemen or the Southerners or from those who they say were here long before any of us: those who fled into the West as the people came."

"Heard of it," said the ferryman. "Heard also of the curse of it. I reckon that the one can take care of the other." He spat into the sea. Then he said, "You're an honest man, dwarf. I see it in your face. Do not seek this cave. No good can come of it."

"I am sure you are right," I told him, without guile.

"I am certain I am," he said. "For not every day is it that I take a reaver and a little dwarfy man to the Misty Isle." Then he said, "In this part of the

world, it is not considered lucky to talk about those who went to the West."
We rode the rest of the boat journey in silence, though the sea became
choppier, and the waves splashed into the side of the boat, such that I held
on with both hands for fear of being swept away.

And after what seemed like half a lifetime the boat was tied to a long
jetty of black stones. We walked the jetty as the waves crashed around us,
the salt spray kissing our faces. There was a humpbacked man at the landing selling oatcakes and plums dried until they were almost stones. I gave
him a penny and filled my jerkin pockets with them.

We walked on into the Misty Isle.

I am old now, or at least, I am no longer young, and everything I see
reminds me of something else I've seen, such that I see nothing for the first
time. A bonny girl, her hair fiery red, reminds me only of another hundred
such lasses, and their mothers, and what they were as they grew, and what
they looked like when they died. It is the curse of age, that all things are
reflections of other things.

I say that, but my time on the Misty Isle, that is also called, by the wise,
the Winged Isle, reminds me of nothing but itself.

It is a day from that jetty until you reach the black mountains.

Calum MacInnes looked at me, half his size or less, and he set off at a
loping stride, as if challenging me to keep up. His legs propelled him across
the ground, which was wet, and all ferns and heather.

Above us, low clouds were scudding, grey and white and black, hiding
each other and revealing and hiding again.

I let him get ahead of me, let him press on into the rain, until he was
swallowed by the wet, grey haze. Then, and only then, I ran.

This is one of the secret things of me, the things I have not revealed
to any person, save to Morag, my wife, and Johnnie and James, my sons,
and Flora, my daughter (may the Shadows rest her poor soul): I can run,
and I can run well, and, if I need to I can run faster and longer and more
sure-footedly than any full-sized man; and it was like this that I ran then,
through the mist and the rain, taking to the high ground and the black-
rock ridges, yet keeping below the skyline.

He was ahead of me, but I spied him soon, and I ran on and I ran past
him, on the high ground with the brow of the hill between us. Below us
was a stream. I can run for days without stopping. That is the first of my
three secrets, and one secret I have revealed to no man.

We had discussed already where we would camp that first night on the Misty Isle, and Calum had told me that we would spend the night beneath the rock that is called Man and Dog, for it is said that it looks like an old man with his dog by his side, and I reached it late in the afternoon. There was a shelter beneath the rock, which was protected and dry, and some of those who had been before us had left firewood behind, sticks and twigs and branches. I made a fire and dried myself in front of it and took the chill from my bones. The woodsmoke blew out across the heather.

It was dark when Calum loped into the shelter and looked at me as if he had not expected to see me that side of midnight. I said, "What took you so long, Calum MacInnes?"

He said nothing, only stared at me. I said, "There is trout, boiled in mountain water, and a fire to warm your bones."

He nodded. We ate the trout, drank whisky to warm ourselves. There was a mound of heather and of ferns, dried and brown, piled high in the rear of the shelter, and we slept upon that, wrapped tight in our damp cloaks.

I woke in the night. There was cold steel against my throat—the flat of the blade, not the edge. I said, "And why would you ever kill me in the night, Calum MacInnes? For our way is long, and our journey is not yet over."

He said, "I do not trust you, dwarf."

"It is not me you must trust," I told him, "but those that I serve. And if you left with me but return without me, there are those who will know the name of Calum MacInnes, and cause it to be spoken in the shadows."

The cold blade remained at my throat. He said, "How did you get ahead of me?"

"And here was I, repaying ill with good, for I made you food and a fire. I am a hard man to lose, Calum MacInnes, and it ill becomes a guide to do as you did today. Now, take your dirk from my throat and let me sleep."

He said nothing, but after a few moments, the blade was removed. I forced myself neither to sigh nor to breathe, hoping he could not hear my heart pounding in my chest; and I slept no more that night.

For breakfast, I made porridge, and threw in some dried plums to soften them.

The mountains were black and grey against the white of the sky. We saw eagles, huge and ragged of wing, circling above us. Calum set a sober pace and I walked beside him, taking two steps for every one of his.

"How long?" I asked him.

"A day. Perhaps two. It depends upon the weather. If the clouds come down then two days, or even three . . ."

The clouds came down at noon and the world was blanketed by a mist that was worse than rain: droplets of water hung in the air, soaked our clothes and our skin; the rocks we walked upon became treacherous and Calum and I slowed in our ascent, stepped carefully. We were walking up the mountain, not climbing, up goat paths and craggy sharp ways. The rocks were black and slippery: we walked, and climbed and clambered and clung, we slipped and slid and stumbled and staggered, and even in the mist, Calum knew where he was going, and I followed him.

He paused at a waterfall that splashed across our path, thick as the trunk of an oak. He took the thin rope from his shoulders, wrapped it about a rock.

"This was not here before," he told me. "I'll go first." He tied one end of the rope about his waist and edged out along the path, into the falling water, pressing his body against the wet rock face, edging slowly, intently through the sheet of water.

I was scared for him, scared for both of us: holding my breath as he passed, only breathing when he was on the other side of the waterfall. He tested the rope, pulled on it, motioned me to follow him, when a rock gave way beneath his foot, and he slipped on the wet rock, and fell into the abyss.

The rope held, and the rock beside me held. Calum MacInnes dangled from the end of the rope. He looked up at me, and I sighed, anchored myself by a slab of crag, and I wound and pulled him up and up. I hauled him back onto the path, dripping and cursing.

He said, "You're stronger than you look," and I cursed myself for a fool. He must have seen it on my face for, after he shook himself (like a dog, sending droplets flying), he said, "My boy Calum told me the tale you told him about the Campbells coming for you, and you being sent into the fields by your wife, with them thinking she was your ma, and you a boy."

"It was just a tale," I said. "Something to pass the time."

"Indeed?" he said. "For I heard tell of a raiding party of Campbells sent out a few years ago, seeking revenge on someone who had taken their cattle. They went, and they never came back. If a small fellow like you can kill a dozen Campbells . . . well, you must be strong, and you must be fast."

I must be *stupid*, I thought ruefully, telling that child that tale.

I had picked them off one by one, like rabbits, as they came out to piss or to see what had happened to their friends: I had killed seven of them before my wife killed her first. We buried them in the glen, built a small cairn of stacking stones above them, to weigh them down so their ghosts would not walk, and we were sad: that Campbells had come so far to kill me, that we had been forced to kill them in return.

I take no joy in killing: no man should, and no woman. Sometimes death is necessary, but it is always an evil thing. That is something I am in no doubt of, even after the events I speak of here.

I took the rope from Calum MacInnes, and I clambered up and up, over the rocks, to where the waterfall came out of the side of the hill, and it was narrow enough for me to cross. It was slippery there, but I made it over without incident, tied the rope in place, came down it, threw the end of it to my companion, walked him across.

He did not thank me, neither for rescuing him, nor for getting us across; and I did not expect thanks. I also did not expect what he actually said, though, which was: "You are not a whole man, and you are ugly. Your wife: is she also small and ugly, like yourself?"

I decided to take no offence, whether offence had been intended or no. I simply said, "She is not. She is a tall woman, almost as tall as you, and when she was young—when we were both younger—she was reckoned by some to be the most beautiful girl in the lowlands. The bards wrote songs praising her green eyes and her long red-golden hair."

I thought I saw him flinch at this, but it is possible that I imagined it, or more likely, wished to imagine I had seen it.

"How did you win her, then?"

I spoke the truth: "I wanted her, and I get what I want. I did not give up. She said I was wise and I was kind, and I would always provide for her. And I have."

The clouds began to lower, once more, and the world blurred at the edges, became softer.

"She said I would be a good father. And I have done my best to raise my children. Who are also, if you are wondering, normal-sized."

"I beat sense into young Calum," said older Calum. "He is not a bad child."

"You can only do that as long as they are there with you," I said. And then I stopped talking, and I remembered that long year, and also I remembered Flora when she was small, sitting on the floor with jam on her face, looking up at me as if I were the wisest man in the world.

"Ran away, eh? I ran away when I was a lad. I was twelve. I went as far as the court of the King over the Water. The father of the current king."

"That's not something you hear spoken aloud."

"I am not afraid," he said. "Not here. Who's to hear us? Eagles? I saw him. He was a fat man, who spoke the language of the foreigners well, and our own tongue only with difficulty. But he was still our king." He paused. "And if he is to come to us again, he will need gold, for vessels and weapons and to feed the troops that he raises."

I said, "So I believe. That is why we go in search of the cave."

He said, "This is bad gold. It does not come free. It has its cost."

"Everything has its cost."

I was remembering every landmark—climb at the sheep skull, cross the first three streams, then walk along the fourth until the five heaped stones and find where the rock looks like a seagull and walk on between two sharply jutting walls of black rock, and let the slope bring you with it . . .

I could remember it, I knew. Well enough to find my way down again. But the mists confused me, and I could not be certain.

We reached a small loch, high in the mountains, and drank fresh water, caught huge white creatures that were not shrimps or lobsters or crayfish, and ate them raw like sausages, for we could not find any dry wood to make our fire, that high.

We slept on a wide ledge beside the icy water and woke into clouds before sunrise, when the world was grey and blue.

"You were sobbing in your sleep," said Calum.

"I had a dream," I told him.

"I do not have bad dreams," Calum said.

"It was a good dream," I said. It was true. I had dreamed that Flora still lived. She was grumbling about the village boys, and telling me of her time in the hills with the cattle, and of things of no consequence, smiling her great smile and tossing her hair the while, red-golden like her mother's, although her mother's hair is now streaked with white.

"Good dreams should not make a man cry out like that," said Calum. A pause, then, "I have no dreams, not good, not bad."

"No?"

"Not since I was a young man."

We rose. A thought struck me: "Did you stop dreaming after you came to the cave?"

He said nothing. We walked along the mountainside, into the mist, as the sun came up.

The mist seemed to thicken and fill with light, in the sunshine, but did not fade away and I realized that it must be a cloud. The world glowed. And then it seemed to me that I was staring at a man of my size, a small, humpty man, his shadow, standing in the air in front of me, like a ghost or an angel, and it moved as I moved. It was haloed by the light, and shimmered, and I could not have told you how near it was or how far away. I have seen miracles and I have seen evil things, but never have I seen anything like that.

"Is it magic?" I asked, although I smelled no magic on the air.

Calum said, "It is nothing. A property of the light. A shadow. A reflection. No more. I see a man beside me, as well. He moves as I move." I glanced back, but I saw nobody beside him.

And then the little glowing man in the air faded, and the cloud, and it was day, and we were alone.

We climbed all that morning, ascending. Calum's ankle had twisted the day before, when he had slipped at the waterfall. Now it swelled in front of me, swelled and went red, but his pace did not ever slow, and if he was in discomfort or in pain, it did not show upon his face.

I said, "How long?" as the dusk began to blur the edges of the world.

"An hour, less, perhaps. We will reach the cave, and then we will sleep for the night. In the morning you will go inside. You can bring out as much gold as you can carry, and we will make our way back off the island."

I looked at him, then: grey-streaked hair, grey eyes, so huge and wolfish a man, and I said, "You would sleep outside the cave?"

"I would. There are no monsters in the cave. Nothing that will come out and take you in the night. Nothing that will eat us. But you should not go in until daylight."

And then we rounded a rockfall, all black rocks and grey half-blocking our path, and we saw the cave mouth. I said, "Is that all?"

"You expected marble pillars? Or a giant's cave from a gossip's fireside tales?"

"Perhaps. It looks like nothing. A hole in the rock face. A shadow. And there are no guards?"

"No guards. Only the place, and what it is."

"A cave filled with treasure. And you are the only one who can find it?"

Calum laughed then, like a fox's bark. "The islanders know how to find it. But they are too wise to come here, to take its gold. They say that the cave makes you evil: that each time you visit it, each time you enter to take gold, it eats the good in your soul, so they do not enter."

"And is that true? Does it make you evil?"

" . . . No. The cave feeds on something else. Not good and evil. Not really. You can take your gold, but afterwards, things are," he paused, "things are *flat*. There is less beauty in a rainbow, less meaning in a sermon, less joy in a kiss . . ." He looked at the cave mouth and I thought I saw fear in his eyes. "Less."

I said, "There are many for whom the lure of gold outweighs the beauty of a rainbow."

"Me, when young, for one. You, now, for another."

"So we go in at dawn."

"You will go in. I will wait for you out here. Do not be afraid. No monster guards the cave. No spells to make the gold vanish, if you do not know some cantrip or rhyme."

We made our camp, then; or rather we sat in the darkness, against the cold rock wall. There would be no sleep there.

I said, "You took the gold from here, as I will do tomorrow. You bought a house with it, a bride, a good name."

His voice came from the darkness. "Aye. And they meant nothing to me, once I had them, or less than nothing. And if your gold pays for the King over the Water to come back to us and rule us and bring about a land of joy and prosperity and warmth, it will still mean nothing to you. It will be as something you heard of that happened to a man in a tale."

"I have lived my life to bring the king back," I told him.

He said, "You take the gold back to him. Your king will want more gold, because kings want more. It is what they do. Each time you come back, it will mean less. The rainbow means nothing. Killing a man means nothing."

Silence then, in the darkness. I heard no birds: only the wind that called and gusted about the peaks like a mother seeking her babe.

I said, "We have both killed men. Have you ever killed a woman, Calum MacInnes?"

"I have not. I have killed no woman, no girls."

I ran my hands over my dirk in the darkness, seeking the wood and center of the hilt, the steel of the blade. It was there in my hands. I had not intended to ever tell him, only to strike when we were out of the mountains, strike once, strike deep, but now I felt the words being pulled from me, would I or never-so. "They say there was a girl," I told him. "And a thorn-bush."

Silence. The whistling of the wind. "Who told you?" he asked. Then, "Never mind. I would not kill a woman. No man of honour would kill a woman . . ."

If I said a word, I knew, he would be silent on the subject, and never talk about it again. So I said nothing. Only waited.

Calum MacInnes began to speak, choosing his words with care, talking as if he was remembering a tale he had heard as a child and had almost forgotten. "They told me the kine of the lowlands were fat and bonny, and that a man could gain honour and glory by adventuring off to the southlands and returning with the fine red cattle. So I went south, and never a cow was good enough, until on a hillside in the lowlands I saw the finest, reddest, fattest cows that ever a man has seen. So I began to lead them away, back the way I had come.

"She came after me with a stick. The cattle were her father's, she said, and I was a rogue and a knave and all manner of rough things. But she was beautiful, even when angry, and had I not already a young wife, I might have dealt more kindly to her. Instead I pulled a knife, and touched it to her throat, and bade her to stop speaking. And she did stop.

"I would not kill her—I would not kill a woman, and that is the truth—so I tied her, by her hair, to a thorn tree, and I took her knife from her waistband, to slow her as she tried to free herself, and pushed the blade of it deep into the sod. I tied her to the thorn tree by her long hair, and I thought no more of her as I made off with her cattle.

"It was another year before I was back that way. I was not after cows that day, but I walked up the side of that bank—it was a lonely spot, and if you had not been looking, you might not have seen it. Perhaps nobody searched for her."

"I heard they searched," I told him. "Although some believed her taken by reavers, and others believed her run away with a tinker, or gone to the city. But still, they searched."

"Aye. I saw what I did see—perhaps you'd have to have stood where

I was standing, to see what I did see. It was an evil thing I did, perhaps."

"Perhaps?"

He said, "I have taken gold from the cave of the mists. I cannot tell any longer if there is good or there is evil. I sent a message, by a child, at an inn, telling them where she was, and where they could find her."

I closed my eyes but the world became no darker.

"There is evil," I told him.

I saw it in my mind's eye: her skeleton picked clean of clothes, picked clean of flesh, as naked and white as anyone would ever be, hanging like a child's puppet against the thorn-bush, tied to a branch above it by its red-golden hair.

"At dawn," said Calum MacInnes, as if we had been talking of provisions or the weather, "you will leave your dirk behind, for such is the custom, and you will enter the cave, and bring out as much gold as you can carry. And you will bring it back with you, to the mainland. There's not a soul in these parts, knowing what you carry or where it's from, would take it from you. Then send it to the King over the Water, and he will pay his men with it, and feed them, and buy their weapons. One day, he will return. Tell me on that day that there is evil, little man."

WHEN THE SUN WAS up, I entered the cave. It was damp in there. I could hear water running down one wall, and I felt a wind on my face, which was strange, because there was no wind inside the mountain.

In my mind, the cave would be filled with gold. Bars of gold would be stacked like firewood, and bags of golden coins would sit between them. There would be golden chains and golden rings, and golden plates, heaped high like the china plates in a rich man's house.

I had imagined riches, but there was nothing like that here. Only shadows. Only rock.

Something was here, though. Something that waited.

I have secrets, but there is a secret that lies beneath all my other secrets, and not even my children know it, although I believe my wife suspects, and it is this: my mother was a mortal woman, the daughter of a miller, but my father came to her from out of the West, and to the West he returned when he had had his sport with her. I cannot be sentimental about my parentage: I am sure he does not think of her, and doubt that he ever knew of me. But he left me a body that is small, and fast, and strong; and perhaps I take after him in other ways—I do not know. I am ugly, and my father was beautiful, or so my mother told me once, but I think that she might have been deceived.

I wondered what I would have seen in that cave if my father had been an innkeeper from the lowlands.

You would be seeing gold, said a whisper that was not a whisper, from deep in the heart of the mountain. It was a lonely voice, and distracted, and bored.

"I would see gold," I said aloud. "Would it be real, or would it be an illusion?"

The whisper was amused. *You are thinking like a mortal man, making things always to be one thing or another. It is gold they would see, and touch. Gold they would carry back with them, feeling the weight of it the while, gold they would trade with other mortals for what they needed. What does it matter if it is there or no if they can see it, touch it, steal it, murder for it? Gold they need and gold I give them.*

"And what do you take, for the gold you give them?"

Little enough, for my needs are few, and I am old; too old to follow my sisters into the West. I taste their pleasure and their joy. I feed, a little, feed on what they do not need and do not value. A taste of heart, a lick and a nibble of their fine consciences, a sliver of soul. And in return a fragment of me leaves this cave with them and gazes out at the world through their eyes, sees what they see until their lives are done and I take back what is mine.

"Will you show yourself to me?"

I could see, in the darkness, better than any man born of man and woman could see. I saw something move in the shadows, and then the shadows congealed and shifted, revealing formless things at the edge of my perception, where it meets imagination. Troubled, I said the thing it is proper to say at times such as this: "Appear before me in a form that neither harms nor is offensive to me."

Is that what you wish?

The drip of distant water. "Yes," I said.

From out of the shadows it came, and it stared down at me with empty sockets, smiled at me with wind-weathered ivory teeth. It was all bone, save its hair, and its hair was red and gold, and wrapped about the branch of a thorn-bush.

"That offends my eyes."

I took it from your mind, said a whisper that surrounded the skeleton. Its jawbone did not move. *I chose something you loved. This was your daughter, Flora, as she was the last time you saw her.*

I closed my eyes, but the figure remained.

It said, *The reaver waits for you at the mouth of the cave. He waits for you to come out, weaponless and weighed down with gold. He will kill you, and take the gold from your dead hands.*

"But I'll not be coming out with gold, will I?"

I thought of Calum MacInnes, the wolf-grey in his hair, the grey of his eyes, the line of his dirk. He was bigger than I am, but all men are bigger than I am. Perhaps I was stronger, and faster, but he was also fast, and he was strong.

He killed my daughter, I thought, then wondered if the thought was mine or if it had crept out of the shadows and into my head. Aloud, I said, "Is there another way out of this cave?"

You leave the way you entered, through the mouth of my home.

I stood there and did not move, but in my mind I was like an animal in a trap, questing and darting from idea to idea, finding no purchase and no solace and no solution.

I said, "I am weaponless. He told me that I could not enter this place with a weapon. That it was not the custom."

It is the custom now, to bring no weapon into my place. It was not always the custom. Follow me, said the skeleton of my daughter.

I followed her, for I could see her, even when it was so dark that I could see nothing else.

In the shadows it said, *It is beneath your hand.*

I crouched and felt it. The haft felt like bone—perhaps an antler. I touched the blade cautiously in the darkness, discovered that I was holding something that felt more like an awl than a knife. It was thin, sharp at the tip. It would be better than nothing.

"Is there a price?"

There is always a price.

"Then I will pay it. And I ask one other thing. You say that you can see the world through his eyes."

There were no eyes in that hollow skull, but it nodded.

"Then tell me when he sleeps."

It said nothing. It melded into the darkness, and I felt alone in that place.

Time passed. I followed the sound of the dripping water, found a rock pool, and drank. I soaked the last of the oats and I ate them, chewing them until they dissolved in my mouth. I slept and woke and slept again, and dreamed of my wife, Morag, waiting for me as the seasons changed, waiting for me just as we had waited for our daughter, waiting for me forever.

Something, a finger I thought, touched my hand: it was not bony and hard. It was soft, and humanlike, but too cold. *He sleeps.*

I left the cave in the blue light, before dawn. He slept across the cave-mouth, catlike, I knew, such that the slightest touch would have woken him. I held my weapon in front of me, a bone handle and a needlelike blade of blackened silver, and I reached out and took what I was after, without waking him.

Then I stepped closer, and his hand grasped for my ankle and his eyes opened.

"Where is the gold?" asked Calum MacInnes.

"I have none." The wind blew cold on the mountainside. I had danced back, out of his reach, when he had grabbed at me. He stayed on the ground, pushed himself up onto one elbow.

Then he said, "Where is my dirk?"

"I took it," I told him. "While you slept."

He looked at me, sleepily. "And why ever would you do that? If I was going to kill you I would have done it on the way here. I could have killed you a dozen times."

"But I did not have gold then, did I?"

He said nothing.

I said, "If you think you could have got me to bring the gold from the cave, and that not bringing it out would have saved your miserable soul, then you are a fool."

He no longer looked sleepy. "A fool, am I?"

He was ready to fight. It is good to make people who are ready to fight angry.

I said, "Not a fool. No. For I have met fools and idiots, and they are happy in their idiocy, even with straw in their hair. You are too wise for foolishness. You seek only misery and you bring misery with you and you call down misery on all you touch."

He rose then, holding a rock in his hand like an axe, and he came at me. I am small, and he could not strike me as he would have struck a man of his own size. He leaned over to strike. It was a mistake.

I held the bone haft tightly, and stabbed upward, striking fast with the point of the awl, like a snake. I knew the place I was aiming for, and I knew what it would do.

He dropped his rock, clutched at his right shoulder. "My arm," he said. "I cannot feel my arm."

He swore then, fouling the air with curses and threats. The dawn light on the mountaintop made everything so beautiful and blue. In that light, even the blood that had begun to soak his garments was purple. He took a step back, so he was between me and the cave. I felt exposed, the rising sun at my back.

"Why do you not have gold?" he asked me. His arm hung limply at his side.

"There was no gold there for such as I," I said.

He threw himself forward, then, ran at me and kicked at me. My awl blade went flying from my hand. I threw my arms around his leg, and I held on to him as together we tumbled off the mountainside.

His head was above me, and I saw triumph in it, and then I saw sky, and then the valley floor was above me and I was rising to meet it and then it was below me and I was falling to my death.

A jar and a bump, and now we were turning over and over on the side of the mountain, the world a dizzying whirligig of rock and pain and sky, and I knew I was a dead man, but still I clung to the leg of Calum MacInnes.

I saw a golden eagle in flight, but below me or above me I could no longer say. It was there, in the dawn sky, in the shattered fragments of time and perception, there in the pain. I was not afraid: there was no time and no space to be afraid in, no space in my mind and no space in my heart. I was falling through the sky, holding tightly to the leg of a man who was trying to kill me; we were crashing into rocks, scraping and bruising and then . . .

. . . we stopped. Stopped with force enough that I felt myself jarred, and was almost thrown off Calum MacInnes and to my death beneath. The side of the mountain had crumbled, there, long ago, sheared off, leaving a sheet of blank rock, as smooth and as featureless as glass. But that was below us. Where we were, there was a ledge, and on the ledge there was a miracle: stunted and twisted, high above the treeline, where no trees have any right to grow, was a twisted hawthorn tree, not much larger than a bush, although it was old. Its roots grew into the side of the mountain, and it was this hawthorn that had caught us in its grey arms.

I let go of the leg, clambered off Calum MacInnes's body, and onto the side of the mountain. I stood on the narrow ledge and looked down at the sheer drop. There was no way down from here. No way down at all.

I looked up. It might be possible, I thought, climbing slowly, with fortune on my side, to make it up that mountain. If it did not rain. If the wind was not too hungry. And what choice did I have? The only alternative was death.

A voice: "So. Will you leave me here to die, dwarf?"

I said nothing. I had nothing to say.

His eyes were open. He said, "I cannot move my right arm, since you stabbed it. I think I broke a leg in the fall. I cannot climb with you."

I said, "I may succeed, or I may fail."

"You'll make it. I've seen you climb. After you rescued me, crossing that waterfall. You went up those rocks like a squirrel going up a tree."

I did not have his confidence in my climbing abilities.

He said, "Swear to me by all you hold holy. Swear by your king, who waits over the sea as he has since we drove his subjects from this land. Swear by the things you creatures hold dear—swear by shadows and eagle feathers and by silence. Swear that you will come back for me."

"You know what I am?" I said.

"I know nothing," he said. "Only that I want to live."

I thought. "I swear by these things," I told him. "By shadows and by eagle feathers and by silence. I swear by green hills and standing stones. I will come back."

"I would have killed you," said the man in the hawthorn bush, and he said it with humour, as if it was the biggest joke that ever one man had told another. "I had planned to kill you, and take the gold back as my own."

"I know."

His hair framed his face like a wolf-grey halo. There was red blood on his cheek where he had scraped it in the fall. "You could come back with ropes," he said. "My rope is still up there, by the cave mouth. But you'd need more than that."

"Yes," I said. "I will come back with ropes." I looked up at the rock above us, examined it as best I could. Sometimes good eyes mean the difference between life and death, if you are a climber. I saw where I would need to be as I went, the shape of my journey up the face of the mountain. I thought I could see the ledge outside the cave, from which we had fallen as we fought. I would head for there. Yes.

I blew on my hands, to dry the sweat before I began to climb. "I will come back for you," I said. "With ropes. I have sworn."

"When?" he asked, and he closed his eyes.

"In a year," I told him. "I will come here in a year."

I began to climb. The man's cries followed me as I stepped and crawled and squeezed and hauled myself up the side of that mountain, mingling with the cries of the great raptors; and they followed me back from the Misty Isle, with nothing to show for my pains and my time, and I will hear him screaming, at the edge of my mind, as I fall asleep or in the moments before I wake, until I die.

It did not rain, and the wind gusted and plucked at me but did not throw me down. I climbed, and I climbed in safety.

When I reached the ledge, the cave entrance seemed like a darker shadow in the noonday sun. I turned from it, turned my back on the mountain, and from the shadows that were already gathering in the cracks and the crevices and deep inside my skull, and I began my slow journey away from the Misty Isle. There were a hundred roads and a thousand paths that would take me back to my home in the lowlands, where my wife would be waiting.

UNBELIEF

•

Michael Marshall Smith

IT HAPPENED IN BRYANT PARK, a little after six o'clock in the evening. He was sitting by himself in lamp shadow amongst the trees, at one of the rickety green metal tables along the north side, close to where the Barnes & Noble library area is during the day. He was warmly dressed in nondescript, casual clothing and sipping from a Starbucks in a seasonally red cup, acquired from the outlet on the corner of Sixth, right opposite one of the entrances to the park. He queued, just like any normal person: watching through the window you'd have no idea of who he was, or the power he wielded over this and other neighbourhoods.

He had done exactly the same on the preceding two evenings. I'd followed him down from Times Square both times, watched him buy the same drink from the same place and then spend half an hour sitting in the same chair, or near enough, watching the world go by. Evidently, as I had been assured, it was what this man always did at this time of day and this time of year. Habit and ritual are some of our greatest comforts, but they're a gift to people like me.

He might as well have tied himself up with a bow.

ON THE PREVIOUS OCCASIONS I had merely observed, logged his actions, and walked on by. The thing had been booked for a specific date, for reasons I neither knew nor cared about.

That day had come, and so I entered the park by the next entrance along, by the restrooms, strolling in casually and without evident intent.

I paused for a moment on the steps. He didn't appear to be there with protection. There were other people sparsely spread over the park, perched at tables or walking in the very last of the twilight, but there was no indication they were anything more than standard-issue New Yorkers, taking a little time before battling the subway or bridges and tunnels or airports, heading home to their families or friends or real partners for the holidays. Grabbing a last few seconds' blessed solitude, an unwitnessed cigarette, or an illicit kiss and a promise not to forget, before entering a day or two of enforced incarceration with the people who populated their real lives.

Their presence in the park did not concern me. They were either absorbed in their companions or in something within themselves, and none would notice me until it was too late. I have done harder jobs under more difficult conditions. I could have just taken the shot from twenty feet away, kept on walking, but I found I didn't want it to happen like that. Not with this guy. He deserved less.

I watched him covertly as I approached his position. He appeared relaxed, at ease, as if savoring his own few private moments of peace before tackling some great enterprise. I knew what he thought that was going to be. I also knew it wasn't going to happen.

There was an empty chair on the other side of his table. I sat down on it.

He ignored me for a couple minutes, peering in a vaguely benign way at the skeletal branches of the tall trees that stand all around the park's central grassy area: at them, or perhaps at all the buildings around the square revealed by the season's dearth of leaves. Being able to see these monoliths makes the park seem both bigger and yet more intimate, stripped.

Defenseless.

"Hello, Kane," he said, finally.

I'd never actually seen him before—not in the flesh at least, only in pictures—so I have no idea how he'd managed to make me straightaway. I guess it's his job to know things about people.

"You don't seem surprised," I said.

He glanced at me finally, then away again, seemingly to watch a young couple perched at a table twenty yards up the path. They were bundled up in thick coats and scarves and necking with cautious optimism. After a few minutes they separated, tentatively smiling, still with their arms around each other's shoulders, and turned to look at the lights strung in the trees, to listen to the sound of cars honking, to savour being where they were. A recent liaison, the legacy of an office party, perhaps, destined to be a source of embarrassed silences in the office by Valentine's Day. Either that, or pregnancy and marriage and all the silences after that.

"I knew it could happen," the man said, taking the lid off his coffee and peering inside, as if gauging how long he had left. "I'm not surprised it's you sitting there."

"Why's that?"

"Accepting a job for this evening? That's cold. Takes a certain kind of person. Who else they going to call?"

"That supposed to be a compliment? You think if you butter me up then I won't do it?"

The man looked calmly at me through the steam of what smelt like a gingerbread latte.

"Oh, you'll do it. I have no doubt of that."

I didn't like his tone, and I felt the thing start to uncurl inside me. If you've ever tried to give up smoking, you'll have felt something like it—the sudden, lurid desire to lay waste to the world and everything in it, starting right here, right now, and with the person physically closest to you.

I don't know what this thing is. It doesn't have a name. I just know it's there, and I feel it when it wakes. It has always been a very light sleeper.

"No, really," I said. "Just because I live in a big house these days, and I got a wife and a child, you think I can't do what I do?"

"You've still got it. You'll always have it."

"Fucking right I will."

"And that's something to be proud of?" He shook his head. "Shame of it is, you were a good kid."

"Isn't everyone?"

"No. Some people come out of the womb broken. You can nurture all you want, sooner or later they're going to pass the damage on. With you, it could have been different. That makes it worse, somehow."

"I am who I chose to be."

"Really? Everyone in the neighbourhood knows the kind of person your father was."

My hands twitched, involuntarily.

"He had no faith in anything," the man said. "He was a hater. And a hurter. I remember watching him when he was young, knowing how he'd grow up. Either dead inside, or affectionate in inappropriate ways. Maybe both. Am I right?"

"If you'd like this to play out in a civilised fashion," I said, my voice tight, "you want to drop this line of discussion."

"Forgive me. But you've come here to kill me, Kane. That's pretty personal too, wouldn't you say?"

I knew I should get on with it. But I was also aware that this was the biggest job of my career, and when it was done, it would be over.

I was also simply curious. "What the fuck makes you think you're better than me?" I said. "What you do isn't so different."

"You really think so?"

"You put yourself in a position of power, made it so you get to choose who gets what. Who prospers, who gets nothing. And then you point the finger and lives get fucked up forever. Same as me."

"I don't see it that way." He looked into his cup again. The habit was beginning to get on my nerves.

"Yeah, drink up," I said. "Time's running out."

"One question."

"How'd I find you?"

He nodded.

"People talk."

"My people?"

I shook my head, irritably. The truth was, his own soldiers had held the line. I'd tracked down a couple of them (one slurping pho in a noodle bar under a bridge in Queens, the other sleeping in a tree deep in Central Park) and leaned on them hard—to the point where one of them would not be working for him, or anyone else, ever again. Both had merely looked up at me with their cold, strange eyes and waited for whatever I was going to do. It was not they who'd told me to go and stand in Times Square at the end of any December afternoon, and wait there until this man appeared, arriving there from directions unknown.

"So, who, then?"

"It's too late for you to be taking names," I said, with some satisfaction. "That's all over now."

He smiled again, but more coldly, and I saw something in his face that had not been there before—not on the surface, at least. The steady calm of a man who was used to making judgment calls, decisions upon which the lives of others had hung. A man who had measured, assayed, and who was now about to pay the price, at the behest of people who had fallen on the wrong side of the line he had believed it was his God-given right to draw.

"You think you're this big, bountiful guy," I said. "Everybody's old man. But some understand the real truth. They realise it's all bullshit."

"Have I not made my rules clear? Have I not looked out for the people who deserved it?"

"Only to make them do what you want."

"And what do *you* want? Why are you really here tonight, Kane?"

"Someone paid me to be. More than one, in fact. A syndicate. People saying that enough is enough. Getting back for what you did to them."

"I know about that," he interrupted, as if bored. "I can even guess who these people are. But I asked why *you're* here."

"For the money."

"No. Otherwise you'd have done it from ten yards away and be on your way home by now."

"So you tell me why, if you're so fucking wise."

"It's personal," he said. "And that's a mistake. You've made a good living out of what you do, and have something of a life. On your terms. That's because you've merely been for hire. But you want this one for yourself. Admit it. You hate me on your own account."

This man was smart enough to know a lie when he heard it, so I said nothing.

"Why, Kane? Did something happen, some night, when there was snow on the ground outside and everything should have been carols and fairy lights? Did your presents come with conditions, or costs? Payments that came due in the middle of the night, when Mom was asleep?"

"That's enough."

"How many people have you killed, Kane? Can you even remember?"

"I remember," I said, though I could not.

"When you let it get personal, the cost becomes personal too. You're opening your own heart here. You sure you want to do that?"

"I'd do it for free. For the bullshit you are, and have always been."

"Disbelief is easy, Kane. It's faith that takes courage, and character."

"You're out of time," I said.

He sighed. Then he tipped the cup, drained the last of his coffee, and set it down on the table between us.

"I'm done," he said.

In the fifteen minutes we'd been talking, nearly half the people had left the park. The necking couple had been amongst them, departing hand in hand. The nearest person was now about sixty yards away. I stood up, reached in my jacket.

"Anything you want to say?" I asked, looking down at his mild, rosy face. "People do, sometimes."

"Not to you," he said.

I pulled out the gun and placed the silenced end in the middle of his forehead. He didn't try to move. I took hold of his right shoulder with my other hand, and pulled the trigger once.

With all the traffic around the square, I barely even heard the sound. His head jerked back.

I let go of his shoulder and he sagged slowly around the waist, until the weight of his big, barrel chest pulled his body down off the chair to slump heavily onto the path, nearly face-first.

A portion of the back of his head was gone, but his eyes were still open. His beard scratched against the pavement as he tried to say something. After a couple of times I realised it was not words he was forcing out, but a series of sounds. I put the barrel to his temple and pulled the trigger again. A portion of the opposite temple splatted out onto the stones.

Yet still he was trying to push out those three short syllables, each the same.

I pulled the trigger a final time, and he was quiet. I bent down close to make sure, and to whisper in the remains of his ear.

"Check it twice, right, asshole?"

Then I walked out of the park. A few blocks away I found a cab, and started the long, slow journey home to New Jersey.

I WOKE EARLY THE next morning, like most fathers, to the sound of my son hurrying past our bedroom and down the stairs. On his way to the fireplace, no doubt.

Good luck with that, I thought, though I knew his stocking would be full nonetheless.

A few minutes later Lauren levered herself into a sitting position. She pulled on her robe and went to the window, yanking aside the drapes.

She smiled at something she saw out there, then turned and quickly left the room.

By the time I'd got my own robe on and gone down to the kitchen to make coffee, I knew what she'd seen through the window. It had snowed overnight, covering the yard and hanging off the trees. The whole nine yards of Winter Wonderland set dressing. Probably I would have to help build a snowman later, whether I felt like it or not.

In the living room my wife and child were sitting together Indian style in the middle of the floor, cooing over the stockings they'd already taken down from the fireplace. Candy, little gifts, pieces of junk that were supposed to mean something just because they'd been found in a sock. I noticed that the cookie left on the table near the hearth had a large bite taken out of it. Lauren has always been good with detail.

"Happy Christmas, guys," I said, but neither of them seemed to hear.

I stepped around them and went to the fireplace. I took down the remaining stocking. I knew something was different before it was even in my hand.

It was empty.

"Lauren?"

She looked up at me. "Ho ho ho," she said. There was nothing in her face.

Then she smiled, briefly, before going back to chattering with our son, watching for the third or fifth time as he excitedly repacked and then unpacked his stocking. Her smile went straight through me. But then they always have.

I left the stocking on the arm of one of the chairs and walked out into the kitchen.

I opened the back door, and went to stand outside in the snow.

It was very quiet, and it was nothing but cold.

THE STARS ARE FALLING

•

Joe R. Lansdale

BEFORE DEEL ARROWSMITH CAME BACK from the dead, he was crossing a field by late moonlight in search of his home. His surroundings were familiar, but at the same time different. It was as if he had left as a child and returned as an adult to examine old property only to find the tree swing gone, the apple tree cut down, the grass grown high, and an outhouse erected over the mound where his best dog was buried.

As he crossed, the dropping moon turned thin, like cheap candy licked too long, and the sun bled through the trees. There were spots of frost on the drooping green grass and on the taller weeds, yellow as ripe corn. In his mind's eye he saw not the East Texas field before him or the dark rows of oaks and pines beyond it, or even the clay path that twisted across the field toward the trees like a ribbon of blood.

He saw a field in France where there was a long, deep trench, and in the trench were bloodied bodies, some of them missing limbs and with bits of brains scattered about like spilled oatmeal. The air filled with the stinging stench of rotting meat and wafting gun smoke, the residue of poison gas, and the buzz of flies. The back of his throat tasted of burning copper. His stomach was a knot. The trees were like the shadowy shades of soldiers charging toward him, and for a moment, he thought to meet their charge, even though he no longer carried a gun.

He closed his eyes, breathed deeply, shook his head. When he opened them the stench had passed and his nostrils filled with the nip of early morning. The last of the moon faded like a melting snowflake. Puffy white clouds sailed along the heavens and light tripped across the tops of the trees, fell between them, made shadows run low along the trunks and across the ground. The sky turned light blue and the frost dried off the drooping grass and it sprang to attention. Birds began to sing. Grasshoppers began to jump.

He continued down the path that crossed the field and split the trees. As he went, he tried to remember exactly where his house was and how it looked and how it smelled, and most important, how he felt when he was inside it. He tried to remember his wife and how she looked and how he felt when he was inside her, and all he could find in the back of his mind was a cipher of a woman younger than he was in a long, colorless dress in a house with three rooms. He couldn't even remember her nakedness, the shape of her breasts and the length of her legs. It was as if they had met only once, and in passing.

When he came through the trees and out on the other side, the field was there as it should be, and it was full of bright blue and yellow flowers. Once it had been filled with tall corn and green bursts of beans and peas. It hadn't been plowed now in years, most likely since he left. He followed the trail and trudged toward his house. It stood where he had left it. It had not improved with age. The chimney was black at the top and the unpainted lumber was stripping like shedding snakeskin. He had cut the trees and split them and made the lumber for the house, and like everything else he had seen since he had returned, it was smaller than he remembered. Behind it was the smokehouse he had made of logs, and far out to the left was the outhouse he had built. He had read many a magazine there while having his morning constitutional.

Out front, near the well, which had been built up with stones and now had a roof over it supported on four stout poles, was a young boy. He knew immediately it was his son. The boy was probably eight. He had been four years old when Deel had left to fight in the Great War, sailed across the vast dark ocean. The boy had a bucket in his hand, held by the handle. He set it down and raced toward the house, yelling something Deel couldn't define.

A moment later she came out of the house and his memory filled up. He kept walking, and the closer he came to her, standing framed in the doorway, the tighter his heart felt. She was blond and tall and lean and dressed in a light-colored dress on which were printed flowers much duller than those in the field. But her face was brighter than the sun, and he knew now how she looked naked and in bed, and all that had been lost came back to him, and he knew he was home again.

When he was ten feet away the boy, frightened, grabbed his mother and held her, and she said, "Deel, is that you?"

He stopped and stood, and said nothing. He just looked at her, drinking her in like a cool beer. Finally he said, "Worn and tired, but me."

"I thought . . ."

"I didn't write cause I can't."

"I know . . . but . . ."

"I'm back, Mary Lou."

THEY SAT STIFFLY AT the kitchen table. Deel had a plate in front of him and he had eaten the beans that had been on it. The front door was open and they could see out and past the well and into the flower-covered field. The window across the way was open too, and there was a light breeze ruffling the edges of the pulled-back curtains framing it. Deel had the sensation he'd had before when crossing the field and passing through the trees, and when he had first seen the outside of the house. And now, inside, the roof felt too low and the room was too small and the walls were too close. It was all too small.

But there was Mary Lou. She sat across the table from him. Her face was clean of lines and her shoulders were as narrow as the boy's. Her eyes were bright, like the blue flowers in the field.

The boy, Winston, was to his left, but he had pulled his chair close to his mother. The boy studied him carefully, and in turn, Deel studied the boy. Deel could see Mary Lou in him, and nothing of himself.

"Have I changed that much?" Deel said, in response to the way they were looking at him. Both of them had their hands in their laps, as if he might leap across the table at any moment and bite them.

"You're very thin," Mary Lou said.

"I was too heavy when I left. I'm too skinny now. Soon I hope to be just right." He tried to smile, but the smile dripped off. He took a deep breath. "So, how you been?"

"Been?"

"Yeah. You know. How you been?"

"Oh. Fine," she said. "Good. I been good."

"The boy?"

"He's fine."

"Does he talk?"

"Sure he talks. Say hello to your daddy, Winston."

The boy didn't speak.

"Say hello," his mother said.

The boy didn't respond.

"That's all right," Deel said. "It's been a while. He doesn't remember me. It's only natural."

"You joined up through Canada?"

"Like I said I would."

"I couldn't be sure," she said.

"I know. I got in with the Americans, a year or so back. It didn't matter who I was with. It was bad."

"I see," she said, but Deel could tell she didn't see at all. And he didn't blame her. He had been caught up in the enthusiasm of war and adventure, gone up to Canada and got in on it, left his family in the lurch, thinking life was passing him by and he was missing out. Life had been right here and he hadn't even recognized it.

Mary Lou stood up and shuffled around the table and heaped fresh beans onto his plate and went to the oven and brought back cornbread and put it next to the beans. He watched her every move. Her hair was a little sweaty on her forehead and it clung there, like wet hay.

"How old are you now?" he asked her.

"How old?" she said, returning to her spot at the table. "Deel, you know how old I am. I'm twenty-eight, older than when you left."

"I'm ashamed to say it, but I've forgotten your birthday. I've forgotten his. I don't hardly know how old I am."

She told him the dates of their births.

"I'll be," he said. "I don't remember any of that."

"I . . . I thought you were dead."

She had said it several times since he had come home. He said, "I'm still not dead, Mary Lou. I'm in the flesh."

"You are. You certainly are."

She didn't eat what was on her plate. She just sat there looking at it, as if it might transform.

Deel said, "Who fixed the well, built the roof over it?"

"Tom Smites," she said.

"Tom? He's a kid."

"Not anymore," she said. "He was eighteen when you left. He wasn't any kid then, not really."

"I reckon not," Deel said.

———

AFTER DINNER, SHE GAVE him his pipe the way she used to, and he found a cane rocker that he didn't remember being there before, took it outside and sat and looked toward the trees and smoked his pipe and rocked.

He was thinking of then and he was thinking of now and he was thinking of later, when it would be nighttime and he would go to bed, and he wasn't certain how to approach the matter. She was his wife, but he hadn't been with her for years, and now he was home, and he wanted it to be like before, but he didn't really remember how it was before. He knew how to do what he wanted to do, but he didn't know how to make it love. He feared she would feel that he was like a mangy cat that had come in through the window to lie there and expected petting.

He sat and smoked and thought and rocked.

The boy came out of the house and stood to the side and watched him.

The boy had the gold hair of his mother and he was built sturdy for a boy so young. He had a bit of a birthmark in front of his right ear, on the jawline, like a little strawberry. Deel didn't remember that. The boy had been a baby, of course, but he didn't remember that at all. Then again, he couldn't remember a lot of things, except for the things he didn't want to remember. Those things he remembered. And Mary Lou's skin. That he remembered. How soft it was to the touch, like butter.

"Do you remember me, boy?" Deel asked.

"No."

"Not at all?"

"No."

"'Course not. You were very young. Has your mother told you about me?"

"Not really."

"Nothing."

"She said you got killed in the war."

"I see . . . Well, I didn't."

Deel turned and looked back through the open door. He could see Mary Lou at the washbasin pouring water into the wash pan, water she had heated on the stove. It steamed as she poured. He thought then he should have brought wood for her to make the fire. He should have helped make the fire and heat the water. But being close to her made him nervous. The boy made him nervous.

"You going to school?" he asked the boy.

"School burned down. Tom teaches me some readin' and writin' and cipherin'. He went eight years to school."

"You ever go fishin'?"

"Just with Tom. He takes me fishin' and huntin' now and then."

"He ever show you how to make a bow and arrow?"

"No."

"No, sir," Deel said. "You say, no, sir."

"What's that?"

"Say yes, sir or no, sir. Not yes and no. It's rude."

The boy dipped his head and moved a foot along the ground, piling up dirt.

"I ain't gettin' on you none," Deel said. "I'm just tellin' you that's how it's done. That's how I do if it's someone older than me. I say no, sir and yes, sir. Understand, son?"

The boy nodded.

"And what do you say?"

"Yes, sir."

"Good. Manners are important. You got to have manners. A boy can't go through life without manners. You can read and write some, and you got to cipher to protect your money. But you got to have manners too."

"Yes, sir."

"There you go . . . About that bow and arrow. He never taught you that, huh?"

"No, sir."

"Well, that will be our plan. I'll show you how to do it. An old Cherokee taught me how. It ain't as easy as it might sound, not to make a good one. And then to be good enough to hit somethin' with it, that's a whole nuther story."

"Why would you do all that when you got a gun?"

"I guess you wouldn't need to. It's just fun, and huntin' with one is real sportin', compared to a gun. And right now, I ain't all that fond of guns."

"I like guns."

"Nothin' wrong with that. But a gun don't like you, and it don't love you back. Never give too much attention or affection to somethin' that can't return it."

"Yes, sir."

The boy, of course, had no idea what he was talking about. Deel was uncertain he knew himself what he was talking about. He turned and looked back through the door. Mary Lou was at the pan, washing the dishes; when she scrubbed, her ass shook a little, and in that moment, Deel felt, for the first time, like a man alive.

THAT NIGHT THE BED seemed small. He lay on his back with his hands crossed across his lower stomach, wearing his faded red union suit, which had been ragged when he left, and had in his absence been attacked by moths. It was ready to come apart. The window next to the bed was open and the breeze that came through was cool. Mary Lou lay beside him. She wore a long white nightgown that had been patched with a variety of colored cloth patches. Her hair was undone and it was long. It had been long when he left. He wondered how often she had cut it, and how much time it had taken each time to grow back.

"I reckon it's been a while," he said.

"That's all right," she said.

"I'm not sayin' I can't, or I won't, just sayin' I don't know I'm ready."

"It's okay."

"You been lonely?"

"I have Winston."

"He's grown a lot. He must be company."

"He is."

"He looks some like you."

"Some."

Deel stretched out his hand without looking at her and laid it across her stomach. "You're still like a girl," he said. "Had a child, and you're still like a girl . . . You know why I asked how old you was?"

"'Cause you didn't remember."

"Well, yeah, there was that. But on account of you don't look none different at all."

"I got a mirror. It ain't much of one, but it don't make me look younger."

"You look just the same."

"Right now, any woman might look good to you." After she said it, she caught herself. "I didn't mean it that way. I just meant you been gone a long time . . . In Europe, they got pretty women, I hear."

"Some are, some ain't. Ain't none of them pretty as you."

"You ever . . . you know?"

"What?"

"You know . . . While you was over there."

"Oh . . . Reckon I did. Couple of times. I didn't know for sure I was comin' home. There wasn't nothin' to it. I didn't mean nothin' by it. It was like filling a hungry belly, nothin' more."

She was quiet for a long time. Then she said, "It's okay."

He thought to ask her a similar question, but couldn't. He eased over to her. She remained still. She was as stiff as a corpse. He knew. He had been forced at times to lie down among them. Once, moving through a town in France with his fellow soldiers, he had come upon a woman lying dead between two trees. There wasn't a wound on her. She was young. Dark haired. She looked as if she had lain down for a nap. He reached down and touched her. She was still warm.

One of his comrades, a soldier, had suggested they all take turns mounting her before she got cold. It was a joke, but Deel had pointed his rifle at him and run him off. Later, in the trenches he had been side by side with the same man, a fellow from Wisconsin, who like him had joined the Great War by means of Canada. They had made their peace, and the Wisconsin fellow told him it was a poor joke he'd made, and not to hold it against him, and Deel said it was all right, and then they took positions next to each other and talked a bit about home and waited for the war to come. During the battle, wearing gas masks and firing rifles, the fellow from Wisconsin had caught a round and it had knocked him down. A moment later the battle had ceased, at least for the moment.

Deel bent over him, lifted his mask, and then the man's head. The man said, "My mama won't never see me again."

"You're gonna be okay," Deel said, but saw that half the man's head was missing. How in hell was he talking? Why wasn't he dead? His brain was leaking out.

"I got a letter inside my shirt. Tell Mama I love her . . . Oh, my god, look there. The stars are falling."

Deel, responding to the distant gaze of his downed companion, turned and looked up. The stars were bright and stuck in place. There was an explosion of cannon fire and the ground shook and the sky lit up bright red; the redness clung to the air like a veil. When Deel looked back at the fellow, the man's eyes were still open, but he was gone.

Deel reached inside the man's jacket and found the letter. He realized then that the man had also taken a round in the chest, because the letter was dark with blood. Deel tried to unfold it, but it was so damp with gore it fell apart. There was nothing to deliver to anyone. Deel couldn't even remember the man's name. It had gone in one ear and out the other. And now he was gone, his last words being, "The stars are falling."

While he was holding the boy's head, an officer came walking down the trench holding a pistol. His face was darkened with gunpowder and his eyes were bright in the night and he looked at Deel, said, "There's got to be some purpose to all of it, son. Some purpose," and then he walked on down the line.

Deel thought of that night and that death, and then he thought of the dead woman again. He wondered what had happened to her body. They had had to leave her there, between the two trees. Had someone buried her? Had she rotted there? Had the ants and the elements taken her away? He had dreams of lying down beside her, there in the field. Just lying there, drifting away with her into the void.

Deel felt now as if he were lying beside that dead woman, blond instead of dark haired, but no more alive than the woman between the trees.

"Maybe we ought to just sleep tonight," Mary Lou said, startling him. "We can let things take their course. It ain't nothin' to make nothin' out of."

He moved his hand away from her. He said, "That'll be all right. Of course."

She rolled on her side, away from him. He lay on top of the covers with his hands against his lower belly and looked at the log rafters.

A COUPLE OF DAYS and nights went by without her warming to him, but he found sleeping with her to be the best part of his life. He liked her sweet smell and he liked to listen to her breathe. When she was deep asleep, he would turn slightly, and carefully, and rise up on one elbow and look at her shape in the dark. His homecoming had not been what he had hoped for or expected, but in those moments when he looked at her in the dark, he was certain it was better than what had gone before for nearly four horrible years.

The next few days led to him taking the boy into the woods and finding the right wood for a bow. He chopped down a bois d'arc tree and showed the boy how to trim it with an axe, how to cut the wood out of it for a bow, how to cure it with a fire that was mostly smoke. They spent a long time at it, but if the boy enjoyed what he was learning, he never let on. He kept his feelings close to the heart and talked less than his mother. The boy always seemed some yards away, even when standing right next to him.

Deel built the bow for the boy and strung it with strong cord and showed him how to find the right wood for arrows and how to collect feathers from a bird's nest and how to feather the shafts. It took almost a week to make the bow, and another week to dry it and to make the arrows. The rest of the time Deel looked out at what had once been a plowed field and was now twenty-five acres of flowers with a few little trees beginning to grow, twisting up among the flowers. He tried to imagine the field covered in corn.

Deel used an axe to clear the new trees, and that afternoon, at the dinner table, he asked Mary Lou what had happened to the mule.

"Died," Mary Lou said. "She was old when you left, and she just got older. We ate it when it died."

"Waste not, want not," Deel said.

"Way we saw it," she said.

"You ain't been farmin', how'd you make it?"

"Tom brought us some goods now and then, fish he caught, vegetables from his place. A squirrel or two. We raised a hog and smoked the meat, had our own garden."

"How are Tom's parents?"

"His father drank himself to death and his mother just up and died."

Deel nodded. "She was always sickly, and her husband was a lot older than her . . . I'm older than you. But not by that much. He was what? Fifteen years? I'm . . . Well, let me see. I'm ten."

She didn't respond. He had hoped for some kind of confirmation that his ten-year gap was nothing, that it was okay. But she said nothing.

"I'm glad Tom was around," Deel said.

"He was a help," she said.

After a while, Deel said, "Things are gonna change. You ain't got to take no one's charity no more. Tomorrow, I'm gonna go into town, see I can buy some seed, and find a mule. I got some muster-out pay. It ain't much, but it's enough to get us started. Winston here goes in with me, we might see we can get him some candy of some sort."

"I like peppermint," the boy said.

"There you go," Deel said.

"You ought not do that so soon back," Mary Lou said. "There's still time before the fall plantin'. You should hunt like you used to, or fish for a few days . . . You could take Winston here with you. You deserve time off."

"Guess another couple of days ain't gonna hurt nothin'. We could all use some time gettin' reacquainted."

NEXT AFTERNOON WHEN DEEL came back from the creek with Winston, they had a couple of fish on a wet cord, and Winston carried them slung over his back so that they dangled down like ornaments and made his shirt damp. They were small but good perch and the boy had caught them, and in the process, shown the first real excitement Deel had seen from him. The sunlight played over their scales as they bounced against Winston's back. Deel, walking slightly behind Winston, watched the fish carefully. He watched them slowly dying, out of the water, gasping for air. He couldn't help but want to take them back to the creek and let them go. He had seen injured men gasp like that, on the field, in the trenches. They had seemed like fish that only needed to be put in water.

As they neared the house, Deel saw a rider coming their way, and he saw Mary Lou walking out from the house to meet him.

Mary Lou went up to the man and the man leaned out of the saddle, and they spoke, and then Mary Lou took hold of the saddle with one hand and walked with the horse toward the house. When she saw Deel and Winston coming, she let go of the saddle and walked beside the horse. The man on the horse was tall and lean with black hair that hung down to his shoulders. It was like a waterfall of ink tumbling out from under his slouched, gray hat.

As they came closer together, the man on the horse raised his hand in greeting. At that moment the boy yelled out, "Tom!" and darted across the field toward the horse, the fish flapping.

THEY SAT AT THE kitchen table. Deel and Mary Lou and Winston and Tom Smites. Tom's mother had been half Chickasaw, and he seemed to have gathered up all her coloring, along with his Swedish father's great height and broad build. He looked like some kind of forest god. His hair hung over the sides of his face, and his skin was walnut colored and smooth and he had balanced features and big hands and feet. He had his hat on his knee.

The boy sat very close to Tom. Mary Lou sat at the table, her hands out in front of her, resting on the planks. She had her head turned toward Tom.

Deel said, "I got to thank you for helpin' my family out."

"Ain't nothin' to thank. You used to take me huntin' and fishin' all the time. My daddy didn't do that sort of thing. He was a farmer and a hog raiser and a drunk. You done good by me."

"Thanks again for helpin'."

"I wanted to help out. Didn't have no trouble doin' it."

"You got a family of your own now, I reckon."

"Not yet. I break horses and run me a few cows and hogs and chickens, grow me a pretty good-size garden, but I ain't growin' a family. Not yet. I hear from Mary Lou you need a plow mule and some seed."

Deel looked at her. She had told him all that in the short time she had walked beside his horse. He wasn't sure how he felt about that. He wasn't sure he wanted anyone to know what he needed or didn't need.

"Yeah. I want to buy a mule and some seed."

"Well, now. I got a horse that's broke to plow. He ain't as good as a mule, but I could let him go cheap, real cheap. And I got more seed than I know what to do with. It would save you a trip into town."

"I sort of thought I might like to go to town," Deel said.

"Yeah, well, sure. But I can get those things for you."

"I wanted to take Winston here to the store and get him some candy."

Tom grinned. "Now, that is a good idea, but so happens, I was in town this mornin', and—"

Tom produced a brown paper from his shirt pocket and laid it out on the table and carefully pulled the paper loose, revealing two short pieces of peppermint.

Winston looked at Tom. "Is that for me?"

"It is."

"You just take one now, Winston, and have it after dinner," Mary Lou said. "You save that other piece for tomorrow. It'll give you somethin' to look forward to."

"That was mighty nice of you, Tom," Deel said.

"You should stay for lunch," Mary Lou said. "Deel and Winston caught a couple of fish, and I got some potatoes. I can fry them up."

"Why that's a nice offer," Tom said. "And on account of it, I'll clean the fish."

THE NEXT FEW DAYS passed with Tom coming out to bring the horse and the seed, and coming back the next day with some plow parts Deel needed. Deel began to think he would never get to town, and now he wasn't so sure he wanted to go. Tom was far more comfortable with his family than he was and he was jealous of that and wanted to stay with them and find his place. Tom and Mary Lou talked about all manner of things, and quite comfortably, and the boy had lost all interest in the bow. In fact, Deel had found it and the arrows out under a tree near where the woods firmed up. He took it and put it in the smokehouse. The air was dry in there and it would cure better, though he was uncertain the boy would ever have any-thing to do with it.

Deel plowed a half-dozen acres of the flowers under, and the next day Tom came out with a wagonload of cured chicken shit, and helped him shovel it across the broken ground. Deel plowed it under and Tom helped Deel plant peas and beans for the fall crop, some hills of yellow crookneck squash, and a few mounds of watermelon and cantaloupe seed.

That evening they were sitting out in front of the house, Deel in the cane rocker and Tom in a kitchen chair. The boy sat on the ground near Tom and twisted a stick in the dirt. The only light came from the open door of the house, from the lamp inside. When Deel looked over his shoulder, he saw Mary Lou at the washbasin again, doing the dishes, wiggling her ass. Tom looked in that direction once, then looked at Deel, then looked away at the sky, as if memorizing the positions of the stars.

Tom said, "You and me ain't been huntin' since well before you left."

"You came around a lot then, didn't you?" Deel said.

Tom nodded. "I always felt better here than at home. Mama and Daddy fought all the time."

"I'm sorry about your parents."

"Well," Tom said, "everyone's got a time to die, you know. It can be in all kinds of ways, but sometimes it's just time and you just got to embrace it."

"I reckon that's true."

"What say you and me go huntin'?" Tom said, "I ain't had any possum meat in ages."

"I never did like possum," Deel said. "Too greasy."

"You ain't fixed 'em right. That's one thing I can do, fix up a possum good. 'Course, best way is catch one and pen it and feed it corn for a week or so, then kill it. Meat's better that way, firmer. But I'd settle for shootin' one, showin' you how to get rid of that gamey taste with some vinegar and such, cook it up with some sweet potatoes. I got more sweet potatoes than I know what to do with."

"Deel likes sweet potatoes," Mary Lou said.

Deel turned. She stood in the doorway drying her hands on a dish towel. She said, "That ought to be a good idea, Deel. Goin' huntin'. I wouldn't mind learnin' how to cook up a possum right. You and Tom ought to go, like the old days."

"I ain't had no sweet potatoes in years," Deel said.

"All the more reason," Tom said.

The boy said, "I want to go."

"That'd be all right," Tom said, "but you know, I think this time I'd like for just me and Deel to go. When I was a kid, he taught me about them woods, and I'd like to go with him, for old time's sake. That all right with you, Winston?"

Winston didn't act like it was all right, but he said, "I guess."

THAT NIGHT DEEL LAY beside Mary Lou and said, "I like Tom, but I was thinkin' maybe we could somehow get it so he don't come around so much."

"Oh?"

"I know Winston looks up to him, and I don't mind that, but I need to get to know Winston again . . . Hell, I didn't ever know him. And I need to get to know you . . . I owe you some time, Mary Lou. The right kind of time."

"I don't know what you're talkin' about, Deel. The right kind of time?"

Deel thought for a while, tried to find the right phrasing. He knew what he felt, but saying it was a different matter. "I know you ended up with me because I seemed better than some was askin'. Turned out I wasn't quite the catch you thought. But we got to find what we need, Mary Lou."

"What we need?"

"Love. We ain't never found love."

She lay silent.

"I just think," Deel said, "we ought to have our own time together before we start havin' Tom around so much. You understand what I'm sayin', right?"

"I guess so."

"I don't even feel like I'm proper home yet. I ain't been to town or told nobody I'm back."

"Who you missin'?"

Deel thought about that for a long time. "Ain't nobody but you and Winston that I missed, but I need to get some things back to normal . . . I need to make connections so I can set up some credit at the store, maybe some farm trade for things we need next year. But mostly, I just want to be here with you so we can talk. You and Tom talk a lot. I wish we could talk like that. We need to learn how to talk."

"Tom's easy to talk to. He's a talker. He can talk about anything and make it seem like somethin', but when he's through, he ain't said nothin' . . . You never was a talker before, Deel, so why now?"

"I want to hear what you got to say, and I want you to hear what I got to say, even if we ain't talkin' about nothin' but seed catalogs or pass the beans, or I need some more firewood or stop snoring. Most anything that's got normal about it. So, thing is, I don't want Tom around so much. I want us to have some time with just you and me and Winston, that's all I'm sayin'."

Deel felt the bed move. He turned to look, and in the dark he saw that Mary Lou was pulling her gown up above her breasts. Her pubic hair looked thick in the dark and her breasts were full and round and inviting.

She said, "Maybe tonight we could get started on knowing each other better."

His mouth was dry. All he could say was, "All right."

His hands trembled as he unbuttoned his union suit at the crotch and she spread her legs and he climbed on top of her. It only took a moment before he exploded.

"Oh, God," he said, and collapsed on her, trying to support his weight on his elbows.

"How was that?" she said. "I feel all right?"

"Fine, but I got done too quick. Oh, girl, it's been so long. I'm sorry."

"That's all right. It don't mean nothin'." She patted him stiffly on the back and then twisted a little so that he'd know she wanted him off her.

"I could do better," he said.

"Tomorrow night."

"Me and Tom, we're huntin' tomorrow night. He's bringin' a dog, and we're gettin' a possum."

"That's right . . . Night after."

"All right, then," Deel said. "All right, then."

He lay back on the bed and buttoned himself up and tried to decide if he felt better or worse. There had been relief, but no fire. She might as well have been a hole in the mattress.

TOM BROUGHT A BITCH dog with him and a .22 rifle and a croaker sack. Deel gathered up his double barrel from out of the closet and took it out of its leather sheath coated in oil and found it to be in very good condition. He brought it and a sling bag of shells outside. The shells were old, but he had no cause to doubt their ability. They had been stored along with the gun, dry and contained.

The sky was clear and the stars were out and the moon looked like a carved chunk of fresh lye soap, but it was bright, so bright you could see the ground clearly. The boy was in bed, and Deel and Tom and Mary Lou stood out in front of the house and looked at the night.

Mary Lou said to Tom, "You watch after him, Tom."

"I will," Tom said.

"Make sure he's taken care of," she said.

"I'll take care of him."

Deel and Tom had just started walking toward the woods when they were distracted by a shadow. An owl came diving down toward the field. They saw the bird scoop up a fat mouse and fly away with it. The dog chased the owl's shadow as it cruised along the ground.

As they watched the owl climb into the bright sky and fly toward the woods, Tom said, "Ain't nothin' certain in life, is it?"

"Especially if you're a mouse," Deel said.

"Life can be cruel," Tom said.

"Wasn't no cruelty in that," Deel said. "That was survival. The owl was hungry. Men ain't like that. They ain't like other things, 'cept maybe ants."

"Ants?"

"Ants and man make war 'cause they can. Man makes all kinds of proclamations and speeches and gives reasons and such, but at the bottom of it, we just do it 'cause we want to and can."

"That's a hard way to talk," Tom said.

"Man ain't happy till he kills everything in his path and cuts down everything that grows. He sees something wild and beautiful and wants to hold it down and stab it, punish it 'cause it's wild. Beauty draws him to it, and then he kills it."

"Deel, you got some strange thinkin'," Tom said.

"Reckon I do."

"We're gonna kill so as to have somethin' to eat, but unlike the owl, we ain't eatin' no mouse. We're having us a big, fat possum and we're gonna cook it with sweet potatoes."

They watched as the dog ran on ahead of them, into the dark line of the trees.

WHEN THEY GOT TO the edge of the woods the shadows of the trees fell over them, and then they were inside the woods, and it was dark in places with gaps of light where the limbs were thin. They moved toward the gaps and found a trail and walked down it. As they went, the light faded, and Deel looked up. A dark cloud had blown in.

Tom said, "Hell, looks like it's gonna rain. That came out of nowhere."

"It's a runnin' rain," Deel said. "It'll blow in and spit water and blow out before you can find a place to get dry."

"Think so?"

"Yeah. I seen rain aplenty, and one comes up like this, it's traveling through. That cloud will cry its eyes out and move on, promise you. It ain't even got no lightnin' with it."

As if in response to Deel's words it began to rain. No lightning and no thunder, but the wind picked up and the rain was thick and cold.

"I know a good place ahead," Tom said. "We can get under a tree there, and there's a log to sit on. I even killed a couple possums there."

They found the log under the tree, sat down and waited. The tree was an oak and it was old and big and had broad limbs and thick leaves that spread out like a canvas. The leaves kept Deel and Tom almost dry.

"That dog's done gone off deep in the woods," Deel said, and laid the shotgun against the log and put his hands on his knees.

"He gets a possum, you'll hear him. He sounds like a trumpet."

Tom shifted the .22 across his lap and looked at Deel, who was lost in thought. "Sometimes," Deel said, "when we was over there, it would rain, and we'd be in trenches, waiting for somethin' to happen, and the trenches would flood with water, and there was big ole rats that would swim in it, and we was so hungry from time to time, we killed them and ate them."

"Rats?"

"They're same as squirrels. They don't taste as good, though. But a squirrel ain't nothin' but a tree rat."

"Yeah? You sure?"

"I am."

Tom shifted on the log, and when he did Deel turned toward him. Tom still had the .22 lying across his lap, but when Deel looked, the barrel was raised in his direction. Deel started to say somethin', like, "Hey, watch what you're doin'," but in that instant he knew what he should have known all along. Tom was going to kill him. He had always planned to kill him. From the day Mary Lou had met him in the field on horseback, they were anticipating the rattle of his dead bones. It's why they had kept him from town. He was already thought dead, and if no one thought different, there was no crime to consider.

"I knew and I didn't know," Deel said.

"I got to, Deel. It ain't nothin' personal. I like you fine. You been good to me. But I got to do it. She's worth me doin' somethin' like this . . . Ain't no use reaching for that shotgun, I got you sighted; twenty-two ain't much, but it's enough."

"Winston," Deel said, "he ain't my boy, is he?"

"No."

"He's got a birthmark on his face, and I remember now when you was younger, I seen that same birthmark. I forgot but now I remember. It's under your hair, ain't it?"

Tom didn't say anything. He had scooted back on the log. This put him out from under the edge of the oak canopy, and the rain was washing over his hat and plastering his long hair to the sides of his face.

"You was with my wife back then, when you was eighteen, and I didn't even suspect it," Deel said, and smiled as if he thought there was humor in it. "I figured you for a big kid and nothin' more."

"You're too old for her," Tom said, sighting down the rifle. "And you didn't never give her no real attention. I been with her mostly since you left. I just happened to be gone when you come home. Hell, Deel, I got clothes in the trunk there, and you didn't even see 'em. You might know the weather, but you damn sure don't know women, and you don't know men."

"I don't want to know them, so sometimes I don't know what I know. And men and women, they ain't all that different . . . You ever killed a man, Tom?"

"You'll be my first."

Deel looked at Tom, who was looking at him along the length of the .22.

"It ain't no easy thing to live with, even if you don't know the man," Deel said. "Me, I killed plenty. They come to see me when I close my eyes. Them I actually seen die, and them I imagined died."

"Don't give me no booger stories. I don't reckon you're gonna come see me when you're dead. I don't reckon that at all."

It had grown dark because of the rain, and Tom's shape was just a shape. Deel couldn't see his features.

"Tom—"

The .22 barked. The bullet struck Deel in the head. He tumbled over the log and fell where there was rain in his face. He thought just before he dropped down into darkness: It's so cool and clean.

DEEL LOOKED OVER THE edge of the trench where there was a slab of metal with a slot to look through. All he could see was darkness except when the lightning ripped a strip in the sky and the countryside lit up. Thunder banged so loudly he couldn't tell the difference between it and cannon fire, which was also banging away, dropping great explosions near the breast works and into the zigzagging trench, throwing men left and right like dolls.

Then he saw shapes. They moved across the field like a column of ghosts. In one great run they came, closer and closer. He poked his rifle through the slot and took half-ass aim and then the command came and he fired. Machine guns began to burp. The field lit up with their constant red pops. The shapes began to fall. The faces of those in front of the rushing line brightened when the machine guns snapped, making their features devil red. When the lightning flashed they seemed to vibrate across the field. The cannons roared and thunder rumbled and the machine guns coughed and the rifles cracked and men screamed.

Then the remainder of the Germans were across the field and over the trench ramifications and down into the trenches themselves. Hand-to-hand fighting began. Deel fought with his bayonet. He jabbed at a German soldier so small his shoulders failed to fill out his uniform. As the German hung on the thrust of Deel's blade, clutched at the rifle barrel, flares blazed along the length of the trench, and in that moment Deel saw the soldier's chin had bits of blond fuzz on it. The expression the kid wore was that of someone who had just realized this was not a glorious game after all.

And then Deel coughed.

He coughed and began to choke. He tried to lift up, but couldn't, at first. Then he sat up and the mud dripped off him and the rain pounded him. He spat dirt from his mouth and gasped at the air. The rain washed his face clean and pushed his hair down over his forehead. He was uncertain how long he sat there in the rain, but in time, the rain stopped. His head hurt. He lifted his hand to it and came away with his fingers covered in blood. He felt again, pushing his hair aside. There was a groove across his forehead. The shot hadn't hit him solid; it had cut a path across the front of his head. He had bled a lot, but now the bleeding had stopped. The mud in the grave had filled the wound and plugged it. The shallow grave had most likely been dug earlier in the day. It had all been planned out, but the rain was unexpected. The rain made the dirt damp, and in the dark Tom had not covered him well enough. Not deep enough. Not firm enough. And his nose was free. He could breathe. The ground was soft and it couldn't hold him. He had merely sat up and the dirt had fallen aside.

Deel tried to pull himself out of the grave, but was too weak, so he twisted in the loose dirt and lay with his face against the ground. When he was strong enough to lift his head, the rain had passed, the clouds had sailed away, and the moon was bright.

Deel worked himself out of the grave and crawled across the ground toward the log where he and Tom had sat. His shotgun was lying behind the log where it had fallen. Tom had either forgotten the gun or didn't care. Deel was too weak to pick it up.

Deel managed himself onto the log and sat there, his head held down, watching the ground. As he did, a snake crawled over his boots and twisted its way into the darkness of the woods. Deel reached down and picked up the shotgun. It was damp and cold. He opened it and the shells popped out. He didn't try to find them in the dark. He lifted the barrel, poked it toward the moonlight, and looked through it. Clear. No dirt in the barrels. He didn't try to find the two shells that had popped free. He loaded two fresh ones from his ammo bag. He took a deep breath. He picked up some damp leaves and pressed them against the wound and they stuck. He stood up. He staggered toward his house, the blood-stuck leaves decorating his forehead as if he were some kind of forest god.

IT WAS NOT LONG before the stagger became a walk. Deel broke free of the woods and onto the path that crossed the field. With the rain gone it was bright again and a light wind had begun to blow. The earth smelled rich, the way it had that night in France when it rained and the lightning flashed and the soldiers came and the damp smell of the earth blended with the biting smell of gunpowder and the odor of death.

He walked until he could see the house, dark like blight in the center of the field. The house appeared extremely small then, smaller than before; it was as if all that had ever mattered to him continued to shrink. The bitch dog came out to meet him but he ignored her. She slunk off and trotted toward the trees he had left behind.

He came to the door, and then his foot was kicking against it. The door cracked and creaked and slammed loudly backward. Then Deel was inside, walking fast. He came to the bedroom door, and it was open. He went through. The window was up and the room was full of moonlight, so brilliant he could see clearly, and what he saw was Tom and Mary Lou lying together in mid-act, and in that moment he thought of his brief time with her and how she had let him have her so as not to talk about Tom anymore. He thought about how she had given herself to protect what she had with Tom. Something moved inside Deel and he recognized it as the core of what man was. He stared at them and they saw him and froze in action. Mary Lou said, "No," and Tom leaped up from between her legs, all the way to his feet. Naked as nature, he stood for a moment in the middle of the bed, and then plunged through the open window like a fox down a hole. Deel raised the shotgun and fired and took out part of the window-sill, but Tom was out and away. Mary Lou screamed. She threw her legs to the side of the bed and made as if to stand, but couldn't. Her legs were too weak. She sat back down and started yelling his name. Something called from deep inside Deel, a long call, deep and dark and certain. A bloody leaf dripped off his forehead. He raised the shotgun and fired. The shot tore into her breast and knocked her sliding across the bed, pushing the back of her head against the wall beneath the window.

Deel stood looking at her. Her eyes were open, her mouth slightly parted. He watched her hair and the sheets turn dark.

He broke open the shotgun and reloaded the double barrel from his ammo sack and went to the door across the way, the door to the small room that was the boy's. He kicked it open. When he came in, the boy, wearing his nightshirt, was crawling through the window. He shot at him, but the best he might have done was riddle the bottom of his feet with pellets. Like his father, Winston was quick through a hole.

Deel stepped briskly to the open window and looked out. The boy was crossing the moonlit field like a jackrabbit, running toward a dark stretch of woods in the direction of town. Deel climbed through the window and began to stride after the boy. And then he saw Tom. Tom was off to the right, running toward where there used to be a deep ravine and a black-berry growth. Deel went after him. He began to trot. He could imagine himself with the other soldiers crossing a field, waiting for a bullet to end it all.

Deel began to close in. Being barefoot was working against Tom. He was limping. Deel thought that Tom's feet were most likely full of grass burrs and were wounded by stones. Tom's moon shadow stumbled and rose, as if it were his soul trying to separate itself from its host.

The ravine and the blackberry bushes were still there. Tom came to the ravine, found a break in the vines, and went over the side of it and down. Deel came shortly after, dropped into the ravine. It was damp there and smelled fresh from the recent rain. Deel saw Tom scrambling up the other side of the ravine, into the dark rise of blackberry bushes on the far side. He strode after him, and when he came to the spot where Tom had gone, he saw Tom was hung in the berry vines. The vines had twisted around his arms and head and they held him as surely as if he were nailed there. The more Tom struggled, the harder the thorns bit and the better the vines held him. Tom twisted and rolled and soon he was facing in the direction of Deel, hanging just above him on the bank of the ravine, supported by the blackberry vines, one arm outstretched, the other pinned against his abdomen, wrapped up like a Christmas present from nature, a gift to what man and the ants liked to do best. He was breathing heavily.

Deel turned his head slightly, like a dog trying to distinguish what it sees. "You're a bad shot."

"Ain't no cause to do this, Deel."

"It's not a matter of cause. It's the way of man," Deel said.

"What in hell you talkin' about, Deel? I'm askin' you, I'm beggin' you, don't kill me. She was the one talked me into it. She thought you were dead, long dead. She wanted it like it was when it was just me and her."

Deel took a deep breath and tried to taste the air. It had tasted so clean a moment ago, but now it was bitter.

"The boy got away," Deel said.

"Go after him, you want, but don't kill me."

A smile moved across Deel's face. "Even the little ones grow up to be men."

"You ain't makin' no sense, Deel. You ain't right."

"Ain't none of us right," Deel said.

Deel raised the shotgun and fired. Tom's head went away and the body drooped in the clutch of the vines and hung over the edge of the ravine.

THE BOY WAS QUICK, much faster than his father. Deel had covered a lot of ground in search of him, and he could read the boy's sign in the moonlight, see where the grass was pushed down, see bare footprints in the damp dirt, but the boy had long reached the woods, and maybe the town beyond. He knew that. It didn't matter anymore.

He moved away from the woods and back to the field until he came to Pancake Rocks. They were flat, round chunks of sandstone piled on top of one another and they looked like a huge stack of pancakes. He had forgotten all about them. He went to them and stopped and looked at the top edge of the pancake stones. It was twenty feet from ground to top.

He remembered that from when he was a boy. His daddy told him, "That there is twenty feet from top to bottom. A Spartan boy could climb that and reach the top in three minutes. I can climb it and reach the top in three minutes. Let's see what you can do."

He had never reached the top in three minutes, though he had tried time after time. It had been important to his father for some reason, some human reason, and he had forgotten all about it until now.

Deel leaned the shotgun against the stones and slipped off his boots and took off his clothes. He tore his shirt and made a strap for the gun, and slung it over his bare shoulder and took up the ammo bag and tossed it over his other shoulder, and began to climb. He made it to the top. He didn't know how long it had taken him, but he guessed it had been only about three minutes. He stood on top of Pancake Rocks and looked out at the night. He could see his house from there. He sat cross-legged on the rocks and stretched the shotgun over his thighs. He looked up at the sky. The stars were bright and the space between them was as deep as forever. If man could, he would tear the stars down, thought Deel.

Deel sat and wondered how late it was. The moon had moved, but not so much as to pull up the sun. Deel felt as if he had been sitting there for days. He nodded off now and then, and in the dream he was an ant, one of many ants, and he was moving toward a hole in the ground from which came smoke and sparks of fire. He marched with the ants toward the hole, and then into the hole they went, one at a time. Just before it was his turn, he saw the ants in front of him turn to black crisps in the fire, and he marched after them, hurrying for his turn, then he awoke and looked across the moonlit field.

He saw, coming from the direction of his house, a rider. The horse looked like a large dog because the rider was so big. He hadn't seen the man in years, but he knew who he was immediately. Lobo Collins. He had been sheriff of the county when he had left for war. He watched as Lobo rode toward him. He had no thoughts about it. He just watched.

Well out of range of Deel's shotgun, Lobo stopped and got off his horse and pulled a rifle out of the saddle boot.

"Deel," Lobo called. "It's Sheriff Lobo Collins."

Lobo's voice moved across the field loud and clear. It was as if they were sitting beside each other. The light was so good he could see Lobo's mustache clearly, drooping over the corners of his mouth.

"Your boy come told me what happened."

"He ain't my boy, Lobo."

"Everybody knowed that but you, but wasn't no cause to do what you did. I been up to the house, and I found Tom in the ravine."

"They're still dead, I assume."

"You ought not done it, but she was your wife, and he was messin' with her, so you got some cause, and a jury might see it that way. That's something to think about, Deel. It could work out for you."

"He shot me," Deel said.

"Well now, that makes it even more different. Why don't you put down that gun, and you and me go back to town and see how we can work things out."

"I was dead before he shot me."

"What?" Lobo said. Lobo had dropped down on one knee. He had the Winchester across that knee and with his other hand he held the bridle of his horse.

Deel raised the shotgun and set the stock firmly against the stone, the barrel pointing skyward.

"You're way out of range up there," Lobo said. "That shotgun ain't gonna reach me, but I can reach you, and I can put one in a fly's asshole from here to the moon."

Deel stood up. "I can't reach you, then I reckon I got to get me a wee bit closer."

Lobo stood up and dropped the horse's reins. The horse didn't move. "Now don't be a damn fool, Deel."

Deel slung the shotgun's makeshift strap over his shoulder and started climbing down the back of the stones, where Lobo couldn't see him. He came down quicker than he had gone up, and he didn't even feel where the stones had torn his naked knees and feet.

When Deel came around the side of the stone, Lobo had moved only slightly, away from his horse, and he was standing with the Winchester held down by his side. He was watching as Deel advanced, naked and committed. Lobo said, "Ain't no sense in this, Deel. I ain't seen you in years, and now I'm gonna get my best look at you down the length of a Winchester. Ain't no sense in it."

"There ain't no sense to nothin'," Deel said, and walked faster, pulling the strapped shotgun off his shoulder.

Lobo backed up a little, then raised the Winchester to his shoulder, said, "Last warnin', Deel."

Deel didn't stop. He pulled the shotgun stock to his hip and let it rip. The shot went wide and fell across the grass like hail, some twenty feet in front of Lobo. And then Lobo fired.

Deel thought someone had shoved him. It felt that way. That someone had walked up unseen beside him and had shoved him on the shoulder. Next thing he knew he was lying on the ground looking up at the stars. He felt pain, but not like the pain he had felt when he realized what he was.

A moment later the shotgun was pulled from his hand, and then Lobo was kneeling down next to him with the Winchester in one hand and the shotgun in the other.

"I done killed you, Deel."

"No," Deel said, spitting up blood. "I ain't alive to kill."

"I think I clipped a lung," Lobo said, as if proud of his marksmanship. "You ought not done what you done. It's good that boy got away. He ain't no cause of nothin'."

"He just ain't had his turn."

Deel's chest was filling up with blood. It was as if someone had put a funnel in his mouth and poured it into him. He tried to say something more, but it wouldn't come out. There was only a cough and some blood; it splattered warm on his chest. Lobo put the weapons down and picked up Deel's head and laid it across one of his thighs so he wasn't choking so much.

"You got a last words, Deel?"

"Look there," Deel said.

Deel's eyes had lifted to the heavens, and Lobo looked. What he saw was the night and the moon and the stars. "Look there. You see it?" Deel said. "The stars are fallin'."

Lobo said, "Ain't nothin' fallin', Deel," but when he looked back down, Deel was gone.

JUVENAL NYX

•

Walter Mosley

1.

SHE NAMED ME JUVENAL NYX and made me a child of the night.

I was attending a Saturday-night meeting at Splinter—the Radical Faction Bookstore, presenting the Amalgamation of Black Student Unions' stand on when and how we would agree to work with white radical organizations. For too long, we believed, had our systems, movements, and ultimate liberation been co-opted by white groups pretending, maybe even believing, that they were our friends and allies. But in the end we were saddled with goals outside our communities, diverted into pathways that abandoned our people's needs and ends.

The speech went very well, and the people there, both black and white, seemed to take my words seriously. I felt that the articulation of our goals was in itself a victory, a line drawn in the quick-drying cement that had been poured into the frame of the coming revolution.

I was very young.

She approached me after the series of speakers had made their comments, pleas, pledges, and calls for solidarity. She was short and white, pale actually, wearing loose-fitting jeans and a faded blue T-shirt. She wasn't pretty and didn't do much in the way of makeup. Only her eyes were arresting. They were very dark, maybe even black, with a patina of silver glowing underneath now and then.

"I like what you had to say," she told me. "Any man must stand on his own before relying on the help of others."

Her use of the word *man* made me curious. I assumed, from the way she dressed, that she'd be a feminist.

"That's right," I said. "The black man doesn't need Mr. Charlie to pave the way. It's the white man who wants our power."

"Everyone wants your strength," she said.

With that she looked into my eyes and touched my left wrist. Her fingers were cold.

"Will you have coffee with me?" she asked.

No, was in my throat but "Yes" came out of my mouth. "Only for just a bit," I added awkwardly. "I have to get back to my people and report."

"I AM FROM RUMANIA," she told me at the café across the street from the bookstore. "My parents have died and I am alone in the world. I work sometimes doing freelance copyediting and I go to meetings at night."

"Political meetings?" I asked, wondering at the moonlight that emanated from behind her eyes.

"No kind in particular," she said, dismissing all content with the shrug of a shoulder. "I go to readings and lectures, art openings and the like. I just want to be around people, to belong for a while."

"You live alone?"

"Yes. I prefer it that way. Relationships seem to lose their meaning, and after a few weeks I crave solitude again."

"How old are you?" I asked, wondering at the odd way in which she spoke.

"I am young," she said, smiling as if there was a joke hidden among her words. "Come home with me for the night."

"I don't chase after white girls, Julia," I said, because that was the name she'd given me.

"Come home with me," she said again.

"I'll walk you to your door," I said, reluctantly, "but after that I have to get back to Central House."

"What is Central House?"

"The officers and senior members of the BSUs around the city have rented a brownstone in Harlem. We live together and prepare for whatever's coming."

She smiled at my words and stood.

———

"JULIA," A MAN SAID when we were halfway down the block from the café. "Wait up."

He was tall and brawny, white and blond. He might have been a football player at some university, maybe the one I was attending.

"Martin," she said by way of a tepid greeting.

"Where you going?" He had a thick gauze wad taped to his left forearm. When she didn't answer he gave me an evil look.

"This is my, my girlfriend, dude," he said.

I didn't reply. Instead I was preparing for a fight I didn't think I could win. He was very big and I am, at best, a middleweight.

"Just walk away and you won't get hurt," the footballer added.

His tone had a pleading quality to it. This made him seem all the more dangerous.

"Hey, man," I said. "I just met the lady, but you aren't gonna make me go anywhere."

He reached for me and I got ready to throw the hardest punch I could. I wasn't about to let that white boy make me turn tail and run.

"Martin, stop," Julia said. Each syllable was the sound of a hammer driving a nail.

Martin's fingers splayed out like a fan and he drew the hand back as if it had been burned.

"Go away," she said, "and don't bother me again."

Martin was well over six feet tall and weighed maybe two-forty, most of which was muscle. He shook like a man resisting a strong wind. The muscles of his neck bunched up and corded and he grimaced, exposing his teeth in a skull-like grin. After a minute or so of this strain, Martin turned his back to us and staggered from the sidewalk into the street and away. Cowering as he stumbled off, he gave the impression of a man reeling from a beating.

"You were ready to fight him," Julia said.

I didn't answer.

"He would have hurt you," she stated.

With that she took my arm and walked me across downtown Manhattan to the pedestrian entrance of the Brooklyn Bridge. I didn't question our walk. There was a buildup of energy in my blood and muscles from the fight I'd almost had, from fear of the pounding I would have surely received.

On the way she told me about her life in Rumania, her escape from the

Communists to Munich where she lived with Gypsies for a time. It was a cool October evening and I listened, feeling no need to respond. For her part, she held on to my arm happily prattling about a life that seemed like a story out of a book.

When we got to the other side, she walked me to where there were many warehouses and few residences. We came to a stairwell leading down to a doorway below the surface of the street. She pushed the door open without using a key.

We went down a long hallway until coming to stairs that took us down at least three more levels. There we came to another hall and then to a door that she produced a key for.

IT WAS A SMALL, dimly lit room with a maple table in one corner and a single mattress on the floor. There were no windows, of course, and the room smelled dry and stale, like a tomb that had been sealed for centuries.

The door closed behind me and I turned to look Julia in the eye. The moons there were luminescent and her smile took my breath away. She shucked the blue T-shirt, stepped out of the loose pants, and she was naked. I realized as I lunged for her that this uncontrolled sexuality had been coming on ever since Martin had threatened me. I pulled down my pants and Julia started laughing. I dragged her to the small bed and we were together. My pants were around my ankles. My shoes were still on my feet but I couldn't take the time to remove them. I had to be in her. I had to fuck her and to keep on fucking. Nothing could stop me. Even my orgasm only slowed down the gyrating urgency for a moment or two.

All the while Julia was laughing and talking to me in some foreign tongue. Now and again she'd pull my hair back and examine my eyes with those eerie lights in hers.

I writhed on top of her while she entwined me with her cold legs and arms. I could not stop. I could not pull away. For the first time in my life, I felt, I knew what freedom was. I understood that this passion was the only thing that touched the core of my being.

———

I AWOKE NOT REMEMBERING having lost consciousness, yet I must have passed out, because I was now in another room in a bed with a frame. My wrists and ankles were chained to the four corners of the bed and I was naked.

This room was also windowless and stale. It felt as if I was far underground, but I yelled anyway. I screamed and hollered until my throat was raw, but no one came. No one heard me.

As hours went past I thrashed and called out, but the chains were strong and the walls thick. There was a columnlike yellow candle burning for the little light Julia had left me, and I wondered if I was meant to die in that underground tomb.

At times I worried that this was some white supremacist plot against the BSU of New York. Had they captured me to make a statement? Were they going to lynch me or burn me? Would I be a martyr for the cause?

It was many hours later when the door came open and Julia walked in. I yelled for all I was worth before she could close the door, but she wasn't bothered. She smiled and came to sit next to me on the bed.

She was wearing a red velvet robe that flowed all the way down to her bare feet. There was a hood, but it hung down behind her head.

"This is a room within a room that is itself within a larger room," she said. "We are far underground and no one can hear you."

"Why you got me chained down like this?" I asked, trying to keep the fear out of my voice.

In answer, she stood up, letting the sumptuous robe fall to the floor. She was as naked as I. The breath left my lungs, but I don't know if it was her nakedness or those eyes that left me stunned.

She smiled again and knelt down at my side. She moved her head quickly and bit into my left forearm.

I have spent many days over the next few paragraphs of description.

How can I explain a feeling completely foreign, a feeling that pushed every emotion I could possibly experience past the threshold of my ability to bear it? The pain was a song that I cried out to in cracked harmony. The flow of blood was not only my life but the lives of all who came before me. Her quivering joy was a wild animal in my chest clawing and ripping to escape my silly so-called civilized existence.

My back arched upward and I cried out for release—and for the pain to continue. I wanted to bleed into Julia more than I had craved sex. I was an infant again—so excited by the new sensations of life that I needed the chains to contain my ecstasy.

When I slumped back to the mattress, I no longer existed. I was the husk of the cocoon of a moth that had transformed itself from worm to flight. I was filled with nothing, surrounded by nothing. I was not dead because I had never truly lived. The flailing larvae and the fluttering bug had used my inert being merely for the transition, leaving me nothing but emptiness, like the transient aftermath of a weak smile.

"Juvenal Nyx," a voice whispered.

"What?" I rasped.

"That is your name."

I drifted for many hours that seemed like weeks or months. I was not unconscious or asleep but neither was I aware of the world around me. In this limbolike ether I was approached by various entities representing sentients that claimed no race, sex, or species.

"You are in danger of knowledge," one such being, who seemed to be a yellow nimbus with no origin, said.

"Of being found out?" I asked in some fashion other than speech.

"Of knowing," the empty halo of light replied.

"I don't understand."

"Then there is still hope."

"JUVENAL," A HUMAN VOICE SAID.

I opened my eyes and saw Julia, again in jeans and T-shirt, sitting at the foot of the bed. She was staring at me in a way that I can only describe as hungry.

"Julia."

The smile did not leaven her rapacious eyes.

"You are a sweet man." Though she whispered these words I heard them as a shout down a long, echoing hallway. "I scented your sweetness before I entered the bookstore. I came there for you."

"You let Martin go after biting his arm," I said, "didn't you?"

"I let them all go after the first bite," she said. "Hundreds of them . . . thousands."

I, the old me, sighed in relief.

"And I want to let you go too," she said, "but your blood sings to me."

She touched my inner right thigh halfway between knee and groin. Her cold fingers rubbed that spot. Just the touch caused an echo of dark delight.

She bent over me and hovered an inch away from the place she'd touched, her lunar eyes gazing into mine.

"Bite it," I said in spite of the panic in my chest.

OVER THE NEXT FOUR days she drank from my other arm and leg, and finally from my abdomen just above the naval. I was in constant ecstasy and dread. I didn't eat, sleep, or feel the need to relieve myself. My body was in a state of total repose except when she fed on my blood.

"We never drink much," she told me one evening after having feasted. She was lying back with her head against my thigh, savoring her perversion. "It doesn't take much to keep us alive. We aren't like your people who need to kill and squander to keep themselves going. Just a cupful of fresh blood and we can live for many days."

"Then why do you bite me every day?" I asked. There was no fear in my question. Just after the bite I felt drugged, yielding. I simply wanted to understand what she was saying.

She sat up. Her once-black eyes were now white with that strange light.

"We cannot multiply like you," she said. "We must create our progeny. Our bite contains a drug that would quickly become a poison to most people. To some, however, those that are sweet, we can pass on the trait that makes us unique. These we call our lovers."

"You love me?"

"I love your taste."

"You mean like I love a good steak?"

A wave of disgust passed over her face.

"No, not death, but the life that lives in you and in me simultaneously. The feeling of being that I carry in me that is you. This, this taste is the most exquisite experience that any living creature can know."

"What about Martin?" I asked when I got the feeling she might leave. I hated it when she left after biting me. It was as if I needed her there with me to keep the darkness away.

"Our bite, like I said, is a drug. It makes those we feed on want us. Usually they forget or remember us as a dream, but sometimes they stalk us. This is one possible consequence of the symbiosis between us. I made the mistake of taking you to the place where Martin had met me. His hunger is strong, but if I were to bite him again he would certainly die."

"How long ago did you bite him?"

"Two years."

"And the wound still needed a bandage?"

"Probably not. Sometimes they wear the dressing as a reminder."

"Do you . . . ," I began, but she put her cold hand on my forehead and I passed out.

WHEN I AWOKE, THE morning after the last bite, the chains had been removed. On a single straight-backed chair I found my clothes—neatly folded. Lying across the soft pile was a cream-colored envelope with the name JUVENAL NYX printed on it. The room was quiet and I knew somehow that Julia was gone for good.

My bites throbbed but didn't hurt.

I rushed out of the door that led into a hallway that completely encompassed my cell. There was a door from that hall into another corridor that surrounded the first hallway. There was no furniture or even a carpet in the two buffering halls. The only other room I found was a small toilet. Seeing this I realized that my body was coming back to me and I had to go.

Dear Juvenal,

You are mine from now until the far-off day when either you or I cease to exist. That may not be for many years, even centuries. You will discover many things about yourself over the next weeks and months. Do not fear them. Do not despair. You are mine as if you came from my own womb and I am yours, though we cannot see each other for a long time. Trust in your instincts and your urges. Give in to your hungers and passions. One day we will be together again—when it is safe for both of us. These rooms are now yours. Use them as I have.

I love you,

Julia

The letter was written with a fountain pen and each word was wrought for me.

I went back into the cell and looked around. The floors were bare, unfinished pine. The bed was simple. There was only the one chair. That room could have been a poem about Julia's life and now mine.

I sat down hearing far-off music, like cellos, in the distance. After a while I realized that this music was the singing in my blood.

After a long time of sitting there, wondering what drug she put in her mouth before biting me, I stood up and walked away from her subterranean chamber, never intending to return.

THE DAY WAS BRIGHT, glaring. Everything sounded crisp and loud. I had been in darkness for so long that my eyes hurt and the sun burned against my skin.

But there was also a crystalline quality to the air and vistas. I crossed the bridge feeling light, weightless. The people around me seemed burly and somewhat bumbling. I felt friendly toward them. I was halfway across the Brooklyn Bridge before I realized that I hadn't thought about race once that day. White, black, and brown, they all seemed the same to me.

I chided myself to snap out of it and see the political and racial landscape as I knew it was. I tried to tell myself that my imprisonment had damaged my sense of reality, that Julia had robbed me of my ability to see clearly.

But try as I might I couldn't find fault with the men and women going on their way. And Julia . . . her moony eyes and slight accent brought no anger or fear, recrimination or desire for revenge.

I walked on feeling lighter and happier with each step. The world seemed to be singing some joyous hymn to its own life and destiny. The birds and bugs and even the chemical scents in the air made me feel nostalgic for something that had passed away but lived on in sense memory.

I laughed and did a little jig as I went.

I decided to walk all the way up to Harlem and Central House.

I felt like some kind of prince walking up crowded Fifth Avenue. The people were my unwitting subjects and I was beneficent royalty. In amongst them, now and again, I saw bright-colored coronas reminding me of the yellow halo that had warned me about knowledge.

When I got to Central Park, the song in the sky turned strident. It was howling, but I didn't mind it. The trees whispered of their age and gravity. They had gone one way while I had taken the opposite direction. There was a thrumming in my blood and I was so light-headed that I had to take a seat on a park bench.

I was grinning at the people going past. Some glanced at me with worried looks on their faces. Long ago, last week, I would have said that it was because I was a black man, filled with the purpose of my race, but then I thought that they couldn't possibly understand the experience that flowed in my veins.

The sun was screaming at me and I decided to stand. It was only then that I realized how weak I was. I fell face forward to the pavement. It didn't hurt because I was unconscious before I hit the ground.

SOMEWHERE THE SUN WAS setting. Its final shout over the horizon was followed by a silence so profound that I was yanked out of sleep, as if someone had dumped a hundred pounds of ice on my bare skin. I leaped up from the hospital bed and gazed out of the window into the burgeoning darkness of twilight.

"What's wrong with you, guy?" a man said.

I turned to see him. He was one of six other men in beds around the room, a white man with a gray beard and a darker, though still somewhat gray, mustache.

"How did I get here?" I asked.

"They just dragged you in. We thought you was dead."

I was still dressed. The excitement of the day was replaced by the certainty of night. The thrill that filled me was dark and dangerous.

I was in the street before I realized that I had no shoes on my feet. But I wasn't bothered by the touch of my skin on the concrete and asphalt.

I headed back to the park. Once there I searched out my prey.

SHE WAS A YOUNG brown-skinned woman walking down a quiet lane. There was no fear emanating from her. I headed in her direction and, while passing, I put an arm around her waist, pulled her to me, and bit, with a lower tooth I'd never had before, into her neck. It was a pinprick, a small wound that would heal quickly. She fought me for all of eight seconds and then I felt her hand caress the back of my neck.

"Who are you?" she whispered. "What are you doing to me?"

Her blood flowed slowly into my mouth. It was the richest, most sumptuous meal I'd ever had. It was steak and butter and thick red wine that gods ate on the high holidays of their divinity.

"Please," she whispered in a wavering voice. "What's happening to me? I feel it everywhere," and she rubbed her body against mine.

I drank more and more.

She told me things in that park while people wandered past thinking that we were lovers who couldn't wait for closed doors.

As I tasted her rich bounty, she whispered the secrets of her life. Her desires and disappointments, loves and mistakes flowed as her blood. I realized somewhere in the back of my mind that I was somehow feeding on her soul as well as the serum of her life.

This delightful experience lasted for a quarter hour and then suddenly the tooth retracted painfully into my lower gum. I pulled back from her and she reached out for me.

"Who are you?" she asked.

"Juvenal Nyx," I said.

"What did you do to me?" She brought the fingers of her right hand to her neck.

"It's a drug."

"I," she hesitated, "I want more."

"Meet me here tomorrow at the same time and I will bring it to you."

She was about to say something else, but I put a finger to her lips.

"Go," I said and she obeyed immediately.

I WAS RUNNING THROUGH the park with all the fleet lightness of a young deer or the quick-footed predator on its trail. I was laughing and uncontainable. My first prey would forget me. If she didn't, if she came back, I would not return to that spot for many weeks. I knew, somehow, that the drug of my bite would turn toxic in her veins if I ever bit her again.

I sped all the way to Harlem, but when I got to the street where Central House stood I balked. For the first time I understood, in my intellect, that things had changed. I had been going on my senses up until that block.

But then I realized that I couldn't just walk into the political commune in bare feet, with blood on my breath.

I went into the alley of the building across the street and scaled the wall with little difficulty. When I reached the rooftop I hunkered down, black skin in gathering darkness, to spy on my friends.

CECIL BONTEMPS AND MINERVA Jenkins walked out of the front door of the house late in the evening. I concentrated on them with all of my senses. They talked about the meeting they'd just quit. It was a summit about me, my disappearance. They mentioned a white girl I was seen leaving with.

"Jimmy was always a flake," Cecil said. "Prob'ly shacked up and high as a kite with that chick."

An animal growled and I started, looking around the empty roof. It was only then that I realized the bestial noise had come from the anger in me.

"Jimmy don't get high," Minnie said. "You know that. Something's happened to him. We should do like Troy says and go to the police."

"We cain't have the police rummagin' around Central," he said. "What if they found our weapons?"

We had been stockpiling rifles and ammunition for the coming revolution. We kept them in a trunk in the basement, ready for the day that martial law was declared on the Black Man.

"We got to do something, Cecil."

"Okay. Yeah. All right. Let's go down to that bookstore again."

I STAYED ON THAT roof for three days eavesdropping on my onetime comrades. In the day, the sun would rise, bellowing across the sky, and I'd fall into a coma after a while. At night I roused and watched my friends as if they were prey.

On the fourth evening I chased a young man down an alley three blocks north of Central House. I yoked him in a doorway and bit into his shoulder. He whimpered and cried as I drank of the serum of his life. It felt uncomfortably sexual. I realized that unless it was necessary, I'd prefer the blood of women.

"What did you do to me?" His speech was slurred, but he was still afraid.

"Go," I said in a deep voice that was alien to me.

He ran.

I'd forgotten about Central House by that time. For the rest of the night I prowled the streets, looking but not wanting, a danger but not a threat.

At dawn I returned to the Brooklyn warehouse where Julia had taken me. Two floors below the room she'd first taken me to was the tomblike chamber that would be home from then on. She'd left the key to the door in my pocket.

In the darkness, far below the street, I could hear the faraway singing of the sun. I felt safe in my vault—dangerous too.

2.

THAT WAS THIRTY-THREE YEARS ago, October 1976. Since then I've inhabited the underground chamber that Julia somehow owned. The title had been signed over to me, and I lived there, sleeping in that bed or sitting on the straight-backed chair, going out now and again for a cupful of blood from some unwary pedestrian. Sometimes I'd bite them just enough to introduce the drug into their system, then use their money to let a hotel room where slowly, over the course of the evening, I would lick their necks and growl like a great wolf.

I have killed no one and discovered many things about my mutation.

One very important detail is that I heal very quickly.

I found this out one evening when a gang of young men decided to attack me and the woman I was feeding on in Prospect Park. There were eight of them, but I was at full strength and so fought them off after some effort. I realized later that I had been stabbed three times in the chest. Certainly my lung was pierced and possibly I'd sustained damage to my heart.

I considered going to the hospital, but something kept me from human company when I was wounded and so I went home to die.

For many days I lay on the floor of my chamber feeling the pain in my chest. But after a week or so I revived enough so that I could go out and feed. Now all that's left of my fatal wounds are three whitish scars on my chest.

I don't read books or go to movies, watch television or follow the news. The only human contact I've had up until quite recently has been primarily limited to the whispering euphoria of my victims. I've fed every few days or so and have lived on the sustenance of human blood and the soul seepage when they are under my sway. I can sit for days in my underground chamber savoring the soft murmurings of my victims. Their words about secret desires and unfulfilled dreams imbue me with the possibilities of a life that has been denied me. Sometimes I drift for hours in the secrets told me from swooning lips. I can see the images that they remember and feel the emotions they have hidden from everyone else.

For the first few years I only went after women because of the intimate nature of my bite. But as time has gone by I have also preyed upon some men. My taste for blood has been refined and I seek out certain flavors and scents. Some nights I go out and there is no one for me. And though I prefer young women, there are others who demand notice.

I have discovered other things about my nature. I am, for instance, allergic to the full moon. Those nights, if I am exposed to lunar regency, I develop a fever and a headache so powerful that I am blinded by its potency. If I go out in the full moon, I remain incapacitated for over a week.

This is how I found out another quirk in my physical characteristics. When the fever is upon me I am weak, so much so that most normal people can fend off my attack. And because the malady lasts for so long I am further weakened by the subsequent lack of sustenance. In this diminished state I am forced to seek out quarry that is likewise incapacitated.

After the first time I was weakened by the lunar allergy, I came upon an old woman confined to a wheelchair who had been left for a while by an unprofessional attendant. The attendant had gone down to the water not far from my crypt and was talking at a phone booth. While she was there I snuck up behind the old woman and bit.

Her dreams were fragmented and her blood thin, but it was all I could do. I hoped that she would not die from my attack. I find that since my transformation I have an instinctual reverence for life in all its myriad forms. Spiders and roaches, rats and human beings all have a right to life in my eyes. I drank half a dram of the old woman's tasteless blood and hurried away to revive.

Four weeks later I saw the woman walking with a new nurse. She was healthy for a woman her age and chattering happily with the new helper. I realized then that my bite has certain curative properties. I remember smiling at my elderly prey as I walked past. She looked as if she recognized something about me, though that should have been impossible seeing that I'd attacked her from behind.

ANOTHER PART OF MY life has been the coronas, empty circles of light that are seemingly invisible to the human eye. They come in every color and have a variety of natures. Some are predatory, attacking and destroying others of their kind. Some are able to communicate with me. Not many approve of my being. I don't know if it is that they don't want to be seen or if they are repulsed by my urges and needs. Regardless—we exist on different planes and cannot touch or affect each other in any physical way.

The only corona I recognize is the yellow being that approached me while Julia was making me into Juvenal Nyx. It appears to me at times, imparting cryptic messages about knowledge and perception.

"You are on the path to knowing what should be secret," it has said more than once—not in words but the meaning has crossed the void between us and settled on my mind.

I paid little attention to these messages until nine months ago.

I was down on Water Street watching the old woman who had been wheelchair bound before I bit her. By now she no longer had a nurse and was herself looking after what might have been a toddler grandchild.

I felt paternal toward the old woman and ancient in my bones. It was a summer evening and the sun was far enough behind the horizon that I didn't have to worry about light-headedness.

"Come," a voice in my head said.

I turned and saw the jagged yellow corona floating in the air behind me.

I stood to follow, but the strange piping voice then said, "Later."

"Come later?" I asked the empty air.

The corona disappeared and I went back to my subterranean home to wait for it to reappear. I had eaten quite recently and so had no need to hunt.

Late that night the yellow light appeared in my chamber. It did not speak but led the way up and out of my home. It brought me to the pedestrian entrance of the Brooklyn Bridge and faded from sight.

I walked out on the pathway. It was late in the evening and unseasonably cool, so I was one of the few people out strolling. When I had just passed the first pylon of the bridge, I caught sight of a woman who had climbed out on a girder and was now about to jump.

My condition makes me quite agile and strong. I ran straight out across the girder and caught the woman by her wrist just as she was falling over the side. I pulled her up and held her around the waist in case she wanted to try again.

"This is not a good idea," I said. My voice was dry and cracked, as I rarely spoke out loud.

"What's wrong with your eyes?" she replied.

For some reason this made me smile.

"You were going to kill yourself," I said.

"That's not going to happen now," she said, "obviously." She looked back over the side a little wistfully. "You want to buy me some coffee?"

HER NAME WAS IRIDIA Lamone. She'd been born and raised in northern California and had come to New York to study painting.

"I married my high school boyfriend, but we don't really get along anymore," she told me at the Telltale Bean in Brooklyn Heights.

There was no hint in her demeanor that she'd just tried to kill herself.

My senses were in such a heightened state from the corona and saving a life that it took me a while to identify the potency of her scent. There was a bouquet to her blood that I had never experienced before. It drew me on a primal level. I found myself having to hold back from biting her right there in the coffee shop.

"Is that why you tried to kill yourself?" I asked.

"Tarver is always depressed," she said. "He mopes around the house when he's not working and he's jealous of my painting. Whenever I'm working he finds some way to interfere. Either he needs my attention or finds something wrong with the house. He comes in with plumbing problems and unpaid bills—anything to distract me, anything so he doesn't have to feel bad about me living my life."

"That's not really an answer," I said.

"I don't owe you an answer, Juvenal. What kind of name is that anyway?"

"I was very sick once," I said. "A woman saved my life and after that she suggested that I go by the name Juvenal Nyx."

"Why?"

"It means 'child of the night.'"

"It's like you were named after a poem."

"The disease left me with certain allergies to natural light. If I go out in the sun, I get weak. If I stay out long enough, I lose consciousness."

"And do you get a rash?" she asked. She was smiling, less than an hour out from her attempted suicide.

"No, but I get a kind of allergy to bright moonlight too."

"Wow. And you call this better?"

"It is best. I know the parameters of my existence and experience ecstasy every night."

This was true though I had never spoken it. I wasn't cursed or debilitated. I didn't miss my family or friends. The life I had known decades before seemed to me like a rat trapped in a researcher's maze. My sex, my race, my repetitious existence—these were the chains of mortality, the bonds that I had shrugged.

"Ecstasy?" she uttered.

The look in her eyes told me that I loved her. The scent on her breath was the odor of procreation.

"Why did you try to jump?" I asked.

"It just all came together," she said in a matter-of-fact tone. "I didn't want to go home to Tarver and I was sure that I'd never paint again."

"Why not just leave him?"

"Because that would kill him and then I'd have his death on my head."

"And so you'll do it again?"

"I don't think so," she mused.

Iridia had dark bronze skin and large almond-shaped eyes. Her gold-brown hair was long and thick, tied back into a braid that was reminiscent of a broad rope.

"Why not?" I asked.

"Because I believe in fate and you saved me at the last possible moment, when I had given up."

"Because I saved you, you won't try to kill yourself again?"

"Not just because you saved me," she said. She reached across the table and took my cold hand in hers. "I had already jumped. I could feel the gravity give way beneath me. I had given myself up to death and then you caught me and held me."

We gazed into each other's eyes and I was lost.

"Would you ever give up the sun?" I asked.

"Never," she said. "I'm a watercolorist and I need it to feed my heart."

"But you were willing to die," I argued.

"Not anymore."

It was at that moment I came into control of my life. All that had gone before was immediately obvious and clear. I had existed as human being for twenty-two years following the pathways that were prescribed. I had a race and gender, nationality and language. I was what the world made me. And then, when Julia came, I was what she made me. So tenuous was my existence that the transformation she wrought tore apart the paper-thin fabric of my identity. I hadn't even been able to maintain my name. I had, for fifty-five years, never made a choice on my own. I was always led, always formed by others' hands. Even my school politics came from a knee-jerk desire to belong.

Iridia had found her identity with a simple gesture, had changed her direction when she saw a new light.

"Will you come home with me tonight?" I asked.

"But I have to go back to Tarver in the morning."

"All right."

I WANTED MORE THAN anything to bite Iridia, to change her from human being to predator child. The fang in my lower jaw throbbed as we kissed, as we made love, but I would not bring it out.

I knew, instinctively, that if I turned her, we would have to separate. That is why Julia left me before I awakened to my powers. The scent of love for us is fatal. Once we make our children, we are compelled to devour them.

This hunger yawned in me like the chasm under Iridia when she leaped from the Brooklyn Bridge; it is why I had never come across a being like myself. We are very rare. Our love is truly a hunger, and we, like our human forebears, are our own best prey.

"WHAT'S YOUR REAL NAME, Juvenal Nyx?" she asked in the early hours of the morning after we'd made love for hours.

I had to think for a few moments before saying, haltingly, "James Tremont of Baltimore."

"You don't sound sure," she said before kissing my naval.

"It's been so long."

"You're not that old."

"I'm older than I look."

Her nostrils flared and the gland under my jaw swelled with venom. I pressed against it and kissed her left nipple.

"Bite it," she whispered.

"A little later," I said.

"I want it now."

"How will I ever get you to come back if I don't make you wait?"

She sat up in the bed, in the empty underground room.

"I've never met a man like you," she said.

"Then we're even," I replied, thinking that I hadn't talked so much in decades.

"You really don't need music or books or even paintings on the wall?"

"For a long time I thought that the only things I needed were food and sleep."

"And now?"

"So much more that I can't even begin to articulate it."

"I'll have to tell Tarver about tonight," she said softly.

"Yeah."

"I won't leave him."

I wanted to tell her that the love wrenching my chest could never live with her—my hunger for her soul was too great.

"Will we see each other again?" I asked.

"I won't leave you either," she said with certainty.

"Why not? You hardly know me."

"I know you better than I've known any man," she said. "You saved my life. And I think that's what you were made for—saving lives."

3.

I TOOK AN OFFICE on the top floor of the Antwerp Building and put up a sign that read: JUVENAL NYX: PROBLEM SOLVER.

I fastened little business cards to phone booths and bulletin boards around the city, had Iridia's brother, Montrose, make me a small Web site, and took out an ad in two free papers. I *borrowed* the money for these investments from some of my wealthier victims. I plan to pay them back and so have chosen to overlook the undue influence I had over them.

I decided on the path of self-employment because this is against the nature of my being. Creatures like me are supposed to be hidden in the night, secreted away from the world in general. We're supposed to live off humanity, not aid people with their real and imagined plights.

It was time for me to go against the tide of my fate.

My business hours are from sunset to dawn, and I will listen to any problem, any problem at all—from severe acne to the threat of death or imprisonment. I accept and reject jobs, collect fees based on the client's ability to pay, and spend every weekend with Iridia.

I find missing persons, cure a variety of minor illnesses, and even save a life now and then.

Tarver Lamone hates me, but I don't worry about him. I can usually sense danger when it's near and it's pretty hard to do me harm. I worry about Iridia sometimes, but she is so certain about right and wrong, and her own indecipherable path, that I have not figured out how to say no to her.

And I am addicted to her nearness. Once, when she had to go home to California for three weeks, I fell into a state of near catatonia that lasted for almost a month. It took Iridia and Montrose breaking into my subterranean condo and her sitting with me for hours to bring me back to consciousness.

IT DOESN'T SOUND LIKE the good life, I know, but it has its bright sides. Every day I get calls from people who need someone like me. I've helped children with their homework and ladies shake their stalkers. I cured one man of acrophobia and permanently paralyzed a serial killer who wanted to stop his trade.

Everything was going fine until one early morning, at six minutes past twelve, when a woman walked into my office.

I'm six feet and one half inch in height. She was quite a bit taller than I, with skin whiter than maggots' flesh. Her hair was luxurious, long and black. She might have been beautiful if it hadn't been for the intensity of her laser green eyes. The gown she wore was either black or green, maybe both, and her high-heeled shoes seemed to be made from red glass.

"Mr. Nyx?" she asked.

"Yes," I said, feeling an unfamiliar wave of fear.

"You're young."

"I'm older than I look."

She glanced around my office. The décor was much like my underground home. There were three straight-backed oak chairs and a small round oak table under the window that looked out on Brooklyn. The only decoration that hung on the wall was a watercolor of a patch of weeds in the bright sun.

"May I sit?" she asked. Her voice was neither masculine nor feminine, hardly was it human, it sounded so rich and deep.

"Certainly," I said.

She lowered herself into the closest chair and I sat across from her. She looked into my eyes and I concentrated on not looking away. This made her smile. It was a predatory smile—on this subject I consider myself an expert.

She was beautiful in the way that fire is, dangerous and untouchable.

Her nostrils flared and then, after a minute had passed, she handed me a card that read MAHEY X. DEMOLA in red lettering at the lower left-hand corner.

That was all, no job title, profession, address, or phone. There was no e-mail or emblem. If you didn't know what that name meant, then you didn't know anything.

"How can I help you, Ms. Demola?"

She smiled and stared for another spate of seconds.

"The painting surprises me," she said at last.

"Why?"

"Your hours, your profession. You don't seem like a sun worshipper."

"My girlfriend's a painter. She gave me that for an office-warming present."

"Serious?" she said.

"Come again?"

"Is it serious between you?"

"Why are you here, Ms. Demola?"

"I've lost my pet." Her smile would seduce emperors and frighten children.

"Dog?"

"A rare breed, large and quite vicious."

"I don't know . . ."

"I worry that Reynard may be dangerous."

The light in her eyes shifted, and either I was made to pay attention or the words themselves moved me.

"Dangerous how?"

"He's a carnivore and he's large," she said in way of explanation.

"If a dog's attacking people in the city, I'm sure animal control will be out after it."

"Reynard is a sewer rat in spite of his size. I believe that he's found his way into the abandoned subway tunnels under the city. There are, I believe, people living down there, people who might not be on the radar of your animal control."

I'd spent some time in the various abandoned catacombs beneath the city. I've hunted there and spent some relaxing days deep under the ground, away from the sounds of the city.

"How big are we talking?"

"Big."

Mahey carried a large white bag that looked to be made of some kind of naked flesh. From the sack she took a blue velvet roll, maybe a foot and a half in length. This she handed to me.

I unfurled the cloth, revealing a simple black knife, somewhat less than a foot long. The handle was part and parcel of the metal blade.

"Carry this with you," she said.

"I didn't say I was taking the job."

"Don't let's be coy, Mr. Nyx."

I wanted to argue further, but instead I rolled the dark metal blade back up and stood.

"I guess I better be getting to work then."

"You can see me to my car downstairs," she said, a little less formal than she had been.

When we got into the close quarters of the elevator, I was assailed by the odor of deep woods. It wasn't a sweet smell, but there was lightness and dark, decay and new growth. It was almost overpowering.

On the street there was a cherry red Lincoln Town Car parked at the front door. A short, porcine man in a bright green suit stood at the ready, waiting for Ms. Demola.

As we approached him, someone shouted, "Hey, Nyx!"

He was jogging across the street, coming right at me. It was Tarver Lamone wearing white exercise pants and a gray sweatshirt. He was moving pretty quickly when he pulled a pistol out of the pouch of the sweatshirt. I was so surprised that I didn't move immediately. The chauffeur was taken off guard also, but Mahey was anything but slow. She reached out and put four fingers on the forearm of Tarver's gun hand. The whole arm turned to spaghetti and hung down, lifeless.

"He is not yours to kill," she said in an almost matter-of-fact tone. "Not tonight."

Tarver dropped the pistol and screamed. He turned and ran away. His gait was odd because the right arm was still hanging loosely at his side.

I turned away from him to stare at my Amazonian client.

"What was that?" I asked.

"You were not made for love, Mr. Nyx," she said. "Its spikes and spines will stake you as certainly as Reynard's great teeth."

With those words she moved toward the car door, now held open by the piggish driver.

I watched them drive away and wondered, for the first time, if this rebellion against my nature was a good thing.

GRAND CENTRAL STATION WAS pretty much empty at one in the morning. I moved to the entrance of the IRT and made it to the downtown platform, populated with a few midnight commuters: young lovers and drunks, street punks and the homeless. A local train came and almost everyone got on.

I went to the far end of the platform and jumped down to the track. I was moving pretty fast, and so even if anyone saw anything, they wouldn't have been able to stop me.

Half a mile north there was a metal ladder that led down to a network of sub-subterranean tunnels and corridors. One of these led to a crawl space that took me even farther down, to another set of passageways and access tunnels. Some of these paths led to offices and utility stockrooms used by subway workers for storage and relaxation. There were forgotten conduits also, some of which brought underground travelers to places that made up a city below the city.

I had been walking down a completely darkened tunnel for half an hour when a sudden stench almost brought me to my knees. I lit a match. Usually I can move in the dark with no light at all. It's one of the abilities I developed after meeting Julia. But though I can move without bumping into things, I can't really see.

The match revealed a rotting, decimated corpse. It had been human, but I couldn't tell if it was man or woman. The groin, belly, and chest had been ripped out and the face was chewed off completely. Much of the flesh was gone. Only the hands were somewhat intact, but they were gnarled and filthy.

Whoever it was, they hadn't been dead for long, but down under the subway there was lots of life that sought out dead flesh. Roaches, rats, and flies swarmed around the corpse. I staggered away wondering about Mahey X. Demola's pet.

Along the path I discovered six more corpses. The odor was cloying. The scuttling sounds in the darkness were upsetting, even for me.

I was headed for the underground commune called the City of Light, named for the electric hookup a man named Nathan Charles had connected years before. There were lamps, fans, video players, and even computers in the cavern down under East Seventy-Third Street. I had been down here before during my nocturnal wanderings, had gotten to know some of the people who inhabited this strange place.

As I made my way toward the underground cooperative, I feared that there would be more bodies—many more.

"Who's there?" a man asked and a bright light shone in my night eyes.

All my senses were temporarily blinded by the glare, but I'd recognized the voice.

"It's me, Lester, Juvenal."

"Juvy?" The light moved away. "What you doin' down here, son?"

"I heard that there was some kinda dog down here attacking your people. I thought I'd come down and help."

"Help yourself an' get your ass outta here," one of my few friends told me. "Whatever it is down here attackin' us, it ain't no dog. It's a fuckin' monster, man. Shit. It ripped off Lonnie Bingham's arm wit' just one swipe. He died screamin'."

With the light out of my face, I could see my friend Lester. He was my age (and therefore looked much older), tall like me, black, and bald. I'd met him on one of my sojourns in the underground caverns. I liked him because he hadn't been to the surface in thirty years. He ran the City of Light, a beneficent mayor of the out crowd.

"How many people have died?" I asked.

"There's a dozen missin'. We made us a bunker in the north quarter. Everybody's there right now. The thing cain't get in, but we ain't been able to get out to bring down food and supplies. We need a big gun too."

There came a howl through the vast network of tunnels, caves, and caverns. The sound entered all of my senses: a sour taste and acrid smells assailed me, my skin ached, and visions of violent screams danced before me. My entire body tingled, then suddenly my attention was drawn to a spot up ahead.

"That's it," Lester said. "That's the beast."

"It's up ahead," I said. "You go on, L. Go get your supplies and weapons. I'm gonna take care of this here dog."

"You crazy, Juvy? You just a kid, man. You cain't hurt that thing. I shot it point-blank wit' my twenty-two pistol an' he hardly even slowed down."

Lester grabbed my arm and I pushed him away. I'm much stronger than normal men. Lester hit the ground and rolled a few feet. I turned my back on him and kept going.

The thing wailed again. This cry brought on hallucinations. I could see people running from beasts of all sorts. I smelled death and the stars themselves began to cry. I saw men and women being raped then slaughtered—then eaten. Their attackers were vicious beings who looked like children but who were older than the oldest trees in the forest.

When the vision ended I found myself on my knees with a pain like a spike through my brain.

I got up and moved quickly toward the City of Light.

IT WAS LESS THAN even a shantytown in a hollowed-out grotto of stone. There were tents and lean-tos, fire cans and furniture under the electric light that had christened the town of eighty or so. At the far end from the entrance was a huge metal door. No one knew what the vault was for. Now it held the remainder of Lester's people.

Above it on a natural stone ledge crouched Mahey X. Demola's *pet*. He was covered with golden fur except for the snout, which was a striped black and blood red. His paws were nearly hands, and though he squatted down on all fours I believed that he could stand upright and tall.

A growl sounded in my throat. All rational thought fled my mind. A rage, deep and frightening, sang through my muscles, and the beast above me howled.

I saw an eye in the darkness above Mahey's *dog*. It stared at me and wondered while the creature leaped from its ledge.

I saw the golden blur coming. I wanted to dive and roll, then grab and rend and bite and tear. But instead I was dazzled by that eye, wondering what it could mean . . .

Reynard slammed into me and I went flying. He was hard as stone, and I was, for the first time in decades, merely human. Reynard swiped at me, raking his claws first across my face and then on my chest.

I hit him with both fists and had no effect whatever. He bit into my arm then butted me with his high crown. I fell to the ground, senseless but still hating. Reynard hovered above me, his mouth a stench-filled yawn of hunger, hatred, and vicious anticipation.

There came seven small pops. I thought for an instant that it was the sound of Reynard ripping off one of my limbs, but then I heard a gurgling cry. It was my name being spoken.

Juvenal.

The thoughts cascading at that moment didn't have a linear progression. Lester's face was there and his .22 pistol—that had made the pops. He used his weapon to try to save me, dooming us both in the process. The small-caliber gun was his only weapon.

The black iron knife, shoved in my belt, was mine.

I didn't try to unroll the blue velvet. While Reynard looked up to see what was stinging his face, I plunged the blue roll into his chest.

His howl was what I can only call a cacophony of exploding stars. I was falling, careening through an emptiness that was unending. I was impossible and so was the idea of me. I was bleeding and hating, killing . . .

"Juvy, stop!" Lester yelled. He was trying to pull me off the beast's corpse. I was plunging the knife into its inert body again and again. I was outraged by the visions he'd shown me. I wanted him to take them back.

"He's dead, man!" Lester cried and he managed to pull me back.

I was weakened by the wounds and loss of blood, but the rage still filled me.

The knife pulsed in my grip and I turned away.

"Juvenal," Lester called.

"Not now, man," I said. "Not now."

I STAGGERED AWAY DOWN tunnel after tunnel, having no idea where I was going. The iron knife thrummed in my hand. It felt good. It felt diseased. It felt alive and angry, like a bumblebee clenched in your fist.

I came across an abandoned campsite in a recess in a wall. There I pulled out a soiled trench coat. I put it on to hide my bloody wounds and held the blade up in the sleeve of the coat.

I climbed up into the subway and made it to the Twenty-Eighth Street stop. I climbed out and staggered into the gathering dawn.

"Mr. Nyx," a gruff voice, which maybe shouldn't have spoken in words at all, called.

It was Mahey's piggish chauffeur standing next to the cherry red limo.

He held the back door open and I didn't have the strength to refuse.

"Hello, Mr. Nyx," Mahey said when I fell into the seat beside her.

I didn't respond.

"Did you find Reynard?"

"Yeah. You didn't say what you wanted me to do, so I killed him."

"Just so. Do you have the knife?"

It was throbbing against my forearm. I didn't want to give it up. But those green lights would not be denied. I pulled out the blade and handed it to her. She took a plastic sheet from her skin purse and took the thing without actually touching it.

She placed the knife in the bag and gave me a smile that was supposed to be friendly. Then she produced a wad of cash and handed it to me.

"Where can I drop you, Mr. Nyx?"

———

I SLEPT ON MY office floor for more than sixty hours.

My small suite of offices has a bathroom with a change of clothes hanging in the closet. After two and a half days of comatose sleep, I washed off at the sink and dressed. Then I went to sit in a chair at the window and thanked the night that I was still alive.

My physical wounds were almost healed, but the memories still pained me. Reynard and I had something in common. He was a creature like me. His howls carried knowledge and his stench spoke of an alternate history to the evolutionary blunderings of known life.

And Mahey also was part of my hidden lineage. I was sure of this. And what was that black blade that she wouldn't touch? And that eye which I imagined but am also sure of its existence?

There came a knock on the door.

I wondered for a moment if it was Tarver with his gun or maybe Mahey, or one of her henchmen, with a pulsating black knife.

A creature like Reynard would not knock.

"Who is it?"

"Eerie," she said.

I opened the door and the woman I loved all the way down to the molecular level stood there before me dressed in yellow and white.

She looked me in the eye and I looked back.

"We have to talk," she said.

I ushered her in.

Perched in chairs across from each other, it was the first time in months that we'd come together without a kiss.

"Yes?" I said.

"Tarver's in a mental ward, out of his head and with his right arm completely paralyzed."

"Uh-huh?"

"He goes in and out, but at one point he said that you did this to him."

"Oh. Well, you see—"

"What's going on?" Iridia asked.

"Tarver came here with a pistol," I said.

"What?"

"He came up to me and pulled it out, but before he could shoot, the woman I was with, a client, blocked his arm. He screamed and ran away, but as far as I could see she didn't cut him or anything."

"But then how did he get paralyzed and crazy?"

I hesitated. Up until that moment, my identity, my abilities were secret. Secrets are like the night: they hide from sight that which we suspect and fear. But I no longer wanted to live in darkness. Iridia, the love of my being, was not someone I wanted to hide from. And even if the truth made me lose her, at least she would know me, if only for a while.

"I want to tell a story about a woman named Julia," I said. "She named me Juvenal Nyx and made me a child of the night."

THE KNIFE

•

Richard Adams

ALL THAT IS NARRATED IN THIS STORY took place in 1938.

It was not until Philip actually saw the knife lying in the bushes that his life changed its nature, as it were, from a fantasy to a frightening possibility. He stopped, turned his head for a glance and then took a couple of steps back, stared and remained staring, as though he needed to make sure that the knife was real.

Yes, it was real all right. It was the only thing for some time that had been able to break through the palisade of his dismal, all-absorbing dread.

Before that, his thoughts had been dominated by his horrible apprehension, the prospect of severe physical pain, inescapable and coming soon. It was as though his mind had been running a tape again and again. For its starting point it had Stafford's final words to him yesterday. "So I shall see you in the library after prayers tomorrow night, and you've got no one to thank but yourself." Next came Stafford's turning away and his own imprisonment, as it were, within those words, surrounding him like the bars of a cage. And then the intervening time; and so back to Stafford's words.

Ever since the beginning of this term and Stafford's appointment as head prefect of the house, he had become—not only in his own eyes, but in everyone else's—Stafford's principal victim. "Stafford doesn't like you, does he?" Jones had said. "And *can* you blame him?" added Brown, at which both of them had roared with laughter.

All through the term his offences had accumulated, earning themselves on the way a whole series of petty punishments, which had climaxed last week in his being beaten by Stafford in the house library. The pain had been severe—the worst he had ever undergone—and now it was apparently going to be repeated.

Last night he had hardly slept. He couldn't eat breakfast and could hardly eat lunch. Jones and Brown were the only people he had told.

And now here he was, trudging though the wet woods alone on a half-holiday afternoon. And now, here was the knife. It burst in upon his thoughts, which surrendered and came to a stop.

It was very like the knives he had seen on television, the knives which scores of people had handed in to the police as the result of a public appeal.

He stooped and picked it up. It was a good foot long in its fancy sheath and it had a very sharp point. And now, straight on cue, came the fantasy.

The knife had been sent to him by a mysterious Power, and he was under orders to use it. He was always entertaining fantasies. There was no end to them: revenge fantasies, sexual fantasies, supreme-power fantasies. To a considerable extent, he lived in solitude with his fantasies.

Under orders to use it. When and where? "My lord, I shall use it in the middle of the night, and no one will be able to tell"—He broke off. Deliberately changed his thoughts. However, the first thoughts returned. But of course he wasn't really going to use it, was he?

If he did, what would happen then? For once he couldn't imagine. However, one thing was clear. There would be a tremendous row; the most tremendous row ever. But suppose no one could tell it was him?

He wouldn't be beaten again, would he? The beating would be swallowed up in the awful row. Everything would change. Yes, that was the real point. Everything would change, including his life.

No one knew he had a knife. And no one would want to claim it after he'd used it as he meant to. Before house prayers that evening he had thought out exactly what he was going to do.

Going upstairs to bed he was so much preoccupied that he stumbled into someone without noticing who. "Oh, damn you, Jevons, why can't you look where you're going?" "Sorry, er—sorry, er—"

Most of the senior boys had single rooms. He had had one now for two terms. That night after lights out he lay silently in the dark, willing himself to keep awake.

But he fell asleep. When he woke it was two in the morning by his watch. Last chance to say no. But yes, he was still determined to do it. What had he to lose?

Got the knife? Got the torch? Got someone else's bath towel he'd pinched from the changing room? He opened the door of his room, stepped into the passage and stood listening. Not a sound anywhere. It wasn't far to the door of Stafford's room (mind, no fingerprints).

And now he was standing beside Stafford's bed, listening to his steady breathing as he lay on his back. He turned on the torch, shone it on Stafford's throat and all in one movement plunged in the knife. The point was so sharp that he hardly felt it pierce. He let go of the hilt and all in one movement spread the towel over throat, knife and all, ran back to his room, shut the torch in a drawer and got back into bed.

All this he remembered clearly. And the aftermath? Well, the tremendous row. The shock throughout the school. The shock throughout the country. The newspapers, the headmaster, the police, the fingerprinting. (To what purpose? He had readily given his own.)

Apparently, no one had told the police that he was a boy on the wrong side of Stafford. So many boys were.

His parents had not been hard to persuade when he had asked them if he could leave at the end of the term.

I'M HIS GODFATHER, AND I've always kept up a friendly interest in him. We've been close friends for many years.

One night last week, after he'd come to dinner with me, he told me everything and said that he'd often had a mind to give himself up. I've told him to dismiss that notion altogether and assured him that his secret is entirely safe with me. I wouldn't let on to a living soul.

Well, would you?

WEIGHTS AND MEASURES

•

Jodi Picoult

THE LOUDEST SOUND IN THE WORLD is the absence of a child. Sarah
found herself waiting for it, the moment she opened her eyes in the morning: that satin ribbon of a giggle, or the thump of a jump off the bed—but
instead all she heard was the hiss of the coffeemaker that Abe must have
preset in the kitchen last night, spitting angrily as it finished its brewing.
She glanced at the clock over the landscape of Abe's sleeping body. For a
moment, she thought about touching that golden shoulder or running her
hand through his dark curls, but like most moments, it was gone before she
remembered to act on it. "We have to get up," she said.

Abe didn't move, did not turn toward her. "Right," he said, and from
the pitch of his voice she knew that he hadn't been asleep either.

She rolled onto her back. *"Abe."*

"Right," he repeated. He pushed off the bed in one motion and clos-
eted himself in the bathroom, where he ran the shower long before he
stepped inside, incorrectly assuming the background noise would keep
anyone outside from hearing him cry.

THE WORST DAY OF Abe's life had not been the one you'd imagine, but the
one after that, when he went to choose his daughter's coffin. Sarah begged
him to go; said she could not sit and talk about what to do with their daughter as if she were a box of outgrown clothing that had to be stored somewhere safe and dry. The funeral director was a man with a bad comb-over
and kind, gray eyes, and his first question to Abe was whether he'd seen his
daughter . . . afterward. Abe had—once the doctors and nurses had given
up and the tubes had been removed and the crash carts pulled away, he
and Sarah were given a moment to say good-bye. Sarah had run out of the

hospital room, screaming. Abe had sat down on the edge of the bed with the plastic mattress that crinkled beneath his weight, and had threaded his fingers with his daughter's. For a brief, heart-stopping moment, he thought he'd felt her move, but it turned out to be his own sobbing, jarring the bed. He'd sat like that for a while, and then somehow managed to pull her onto his lap and crawl onto the cot himself, as if he were the patient.

What he remembered was not how still she was, or how her skin grew ashen under his touch, but how she had weighed just the tiniest bit less than she had that morning, when he'd carried her through the double doors of the emergency room. It wasn't remarkable to think that he—a man who lived by weights and measures—would be sensitive to this even at a moment as overwhelming as that one. Abe recalled hearing medical examiners say a person who died lost twenty-one grams of weight—the measure of a human soul. He realized, though, holding his daughter in his arms, that the scale was all wrong. Loss should have been measured in leagues: the linear time line he would not spend with her as she lost her first tooth, lost her heart over a boy, lost the graduation cap she tossed into a silvered sky. Loss should have been measured circularly, like angles: the minutes between the two of them, the degrees of separation.

We suggest that you dress your daughter the way she would have wanted, the funeral director had said. *Did she have a favorite party dress, or a pair of overalls she always wore to climb trees? A soccer uniform? A T-shirt from a favorite vacation?*

There were other questions, and decisions to be made, and finally, the funeral director took Abe into another room to choose a coffin. The samples were stacked against the wall, jet and mahogany sarcophagi gleaming at such a high polish he could see his own ravaged features in their reflections. The funeral director led Abe to the far end of the room, where three stunted coffins were propped like brave soldiers. They ranged from some that came up as high as his hip to one that was barely bigger than a bread box.

Abe picked one painted a glossy white, with gold piping, because it reminded him of his daughter's bedroom furniture. He kept staring at it. Although the funeral director assured him that it was the right size, it did not seem large enough to Abe to hold a girl as full of life as his daughter. It was certainly not large enough, he knew, to pack inside the turtle shell of grief that he'd armored himself in this past day. Which meant, of course, that even after his daughter was gone, the sorrow would remain behind.

THE FUNERAL WAS HELD at a church neither Abe nor Sarah attended, a service arranged by Sarah's mother, who in spite of this still managed to believe in God. At first, Sarah had fought it—how many idealistic discussions had she and Abe had about religion being akin to brainwashing; about letting their child choose her own rainbow of beliefs?—but Sarah's mother put her foot down, and Sarah—still reeling—was weak enough to be toppled. *What kind of parent*, Felicity had said tearfully, *doesn't want a man of God to say a few words over her daughter?* Now, Sarah sat in the front pew as this pastor spoke, words that flowed over the crowd like an anesthetic breeze. In her hand was a small teal green Beanie Baby, a dog that had gone everywhere with her child, to the point where it was hairless and frayed and barely even recognizable in its animalhood. Sarah squeezed it in her fist so tight that she could feel its seeded stuffing start to push at the seams.

Try to remember, as we celebrate her short and glorious life, that sadness comes out of love. Sadness is a kind of terrible privilege.

Sarah wondered why the pastor hadn't mentioned the truly important things: like the fact that her daughter could take a toilet paper roll and turn it into a pretend video camera that occupied her imagination for hours. Or that the only songs that made her stop crying when she had colic as an infant were tracks from *Sgt. Pepper's Lonely Hearts Club Band*. She wondered why he hadn't told the people who'd come here that her daughter had only just learned how to do a round off in gymnastics and that she could pick the Big Dipper out of any night sky?

Oh, Lord, receive this child of Yours into the arms of Your mercy, into the blessed rest of everlasting peace, and into the company of angels.

At that, Sarah lifted her head. *Not Your child*, she thought. *Mine.*

Ten minutes later, it was over. She remained stone still while everyone else left to get into their cars and drive to the cemetery. But she had worked out something special with Abe; the one request, really, she'd had for this funeral. She felt Abe's hand come onto her shoulder and his lips move against her ear. "Do you still—"

"Yes," she interrupted, and then he was gone too.

She walked up to the coffin, surrounded by an embarrassment of flowers. Fall flowers, like the ones she'd had in her wedding bouquet. She forced herself to glance down at her daughter—who looked, well, perfectly normal, which was the great irony here.

"Hey, baby," Sarah said softly, and she tucked the small green dog underneath her daughter's arm. Then she opened up the large purse she'd brought with her to the funeral service.

It had been critical for her to be the last one to see her daughter before that casket was closed. She wanted to be the last one to lay eyes on her girl, the same way—seven years ago—she had been the first.

The book she pulled out of her purse was so dog-eared and worn that its spine had cracked and some of its pages were only filed in between others, instead of glued into place. "'In a great green room,'" she began to read, "'there was a fireplace, and a red balloon, and a picture of . . .'"

She hesitated. This was the part where her daughter would have chimed in: *the cow jumping over the moon.* But now, Sarah had to say the words for her. She read through to the end, going by heart when the tears came so furiously that she could not see the words on the page. "'Goodnight stars,'" she whispered. "'Goodnight air. Goodnight noises everywhere.'" Then she drew in a ragged breath and touched her finger to her daughter's lips. "Sleep tight," Sarah said.

IN THE GATHERING HALL at the church, Abe thought there were obscene amounts of food, as if pastries and deviled eggs and casseroles could make up for the fact that nobody really knew what to say to him. He stood holding a plate piled high that someone had brought him, although he hadn't taken a single bite. From time to time, a friend or a relative would come up to him and say something stupid: *How are you doing? Are you holding up okay? It won't hurt as much, in time.* Things like that only made him want to put down his plate and punch the speaker until his hand bled, because that kind of pain he could understand better than the empty ache in his chest that wouldn't go away. No one said what they all were truly thinking, when they furtively glanced over at Abe with his bad-fitting black suit and his Styrofoam plate: *I'm so glad it happened to you, and not me.*

"Excuse me."

Abe turned around to find a woman he'd never met before—middle-aged, with wrinkles around her eyes that made him think she had smiled, often, in her youth. Maybe one of Felicity's church ladies, he thought. She was holding a box of daffodil bulbs. "I'm so sorry for your loss," she said, and she held out the box.

He set down the plate on a chair beside him so that he could take the bulbs. "Plant these now," she said, "and when they come up in the spring, think of her."

She touched his arm and walked off, leaving Abe holding on to this hope.

SARAH HAD MET ABE when she was new to Los Angeles, and some friends had taken her to a cigar club that was so exclusive you had to enter through a corporate office building and give the doorman the password to be let into the correct elevator bank. The club was on the roof of the building, and Sarah's friends had tried to cure her East Coast homesickness by showing off Mel Gibson's humidor. It was a dark place, one where actors who fancied themselves to be musicians were likely to pick up a guitar and jam with the band; one that only made Sarah even more aware of how much she hated this city, this new job, this departure from where she really wanted to be.

They sat at the bar, pulling up stools beside a good-looking guy with hair as dark as ink and a smile that made Sarah feel like she was caught in a whirlpool. Sarah's friends ordered cosmos and tried to outflirt each other—getting him to reveal that he was the drummer in the band, and that his name was Abe. When one of the girls came back from the bathroom and exclaimed, *Have you seen all the stars?* Abe leaned over and asked Sarah to dance. They moved like smoke over the empty dance floor, to a canned jazz track. "Why me?" Sarah asked simply.

His hand, resting on the small of her back, pulled her just that much closer. "Because," Abe said, "when your friend started talking about stars, you were the only one in this whole fucking place who looked up at the sky."

Three months later, they moved to Massachusetts together. Six months later, they got married, amid many toasts and jokes about Abraham and Sarah and their destiny to create a tribe. But like their biblical counterparts, it took years for them to have a child—eight, to be exact. Just long enough for Sarah to believe it was time to give up trying. Just short enough for her to be overwhelmed with the news of her pregnancy; to never give a second thought to the fact that this might not be the end of the struggle, but instead, the beginning.

ON THE WAY HOME from the church, Sarah turned to Abe and told him to stop at the grocery store. "There's nothing in the house," she said, as if this wasn't obvious on so many levels. They were too numb to think about how they looked, at one in the afternoon, moving through the frozen foods aisle in coat and tie and pearls and heels. They wandered through the store, picking out the items that seemed to scream normal: eggs and bread and cheese and milk; things any family could use. In the cereal aisle, Abe started to automatically reach for the berry Kix, her favorite, until he realized that they didn't need it anymore; and he covered gracefully by taking instead the cereal box beside it, some god-awful bran thing that looked like straw and that he knew he'd never eat.

They went to the line with their favorite checkout girl, the one who didn't mind when their daughter helped scan the bar codes on the soup cans and the frozen peas. She smiled when she saw them. "Wow, look at you two!" she said, glancing at their clothes and winking. "Don't tell me food shopping is what passes for a date without the kids nowadays . . ."

Abe and Sarah froze. This woman wouldn't know—how *could* she? She thought, as would any other stranger, that their daughter was home with a babysitter, watching *The Princess Diaries* for the six hundredth time or pretending the Tupperware was a drum set. As Abe signed the credit card receipt, the checkout clerk reached beneath her cash register and pulled out a lollipop. "She likes blue, right? Tell her I missed her."

"Yes," Abe said, grasping it so tightly that the stick curved. "Yes, I will."

He followed Sarah as she pushed the cart outside, where the sun was so bright it brought tears to his eyes. Sarah turned to him, speechless and staring. "What?" Abe said, his voice raw. "What did I do wrong?"

THREE DAYS LATER, SARAH woke up and pulled on her favorite sweater only to realize that her arms now stretched a good three inches past the ends of the sleeves. Annoyed—did Abe shrink it in the wash?—she pulled out another only to realize that she'd outgrown that one, too. She stared at herself in the mirror for a moment and then pushed the sleeves up to her elbows, where she could not see anything wrong.

She tried to pretend that she didn't notice when she unloaded the dishwasher and could, for the first time in her life, reach the top shelf of the cabinets without having to stand on a stool or ask Abe for his help.

ON HIS LAST DAY of paid bereavement leave, Abe remembered sitting in the hospital with his daughter. There were starfish painted on the window glass, and while they waited for the doctor and Sarah read a waiting-room magazine from the turn of the century, his daughter had wanted to play I spy. It had gotten to the point, in the past seven years, where Abe could almost do this semiconscious—since his daughter had a habit of changing midstream what her target object was, anyway, the game didn't make any linear sense. He guessed the exit sign over the door, the bathroom knob, the starfish on the far right, getting more and more impatient, and wishing the doctor would just come in already so that he didn't have to play one more damn round.

It had only been a sore throat. Her fever wasn't more than 101. That was the criteria—you weren't supposed to worry about a fever until it spiked past 102, something Sarah had learned the hard way when she'd call the pediatrician early on, freaking out over everything from hangnails to cradle cap. But over the course of their daughter's life, they'd weaned themselves into health care confidence. They didn't rush her into the office at the sign of the first cough; they made her sleep overnight on an earache to make sure it was present the next morning before they went to get it checked. And this time, Sarah had kept her home from school waiting to see if it was a virus, or strep throat. They'd done what they were supposed to do as parents; they'd listened to the doctors; they'd played by the rules—and by dinnertime, the rules didn't apply. Children weren't supposed to die of strep throat, but then again, you did not have to look far for the *shouldn'ts*. All over this world there were tsunamis sweeping entire countries out to sea; there were Eskimo women with breast milk full of mercury; there were wars being fought that had been started for the wrong reasons. All over this world impossible things were happening that never should have.

Abe realized he would play I spy for a thousand years, if he could.

THE NEXT DAY, WHEN Abe left for work, Sarah cleaned. Not just a cursory vacuum and floor mop, mind you, but toilets scrubbed by hand and radiator registers being dusted and the washing of the walls. She went into her drawers and bagged all the sweaters that did not fit, and the new pile of pants that ended above her ankles. She got rid of the travel coffee mugs and gravy boats and cherry pitters she never used, weeding through the kitchen drawers. She organized Abe's clothes by color grouping; she threw out all the medicine bottles past their expiration date. She wiped down the shelves of the refrigerator and tossed the capers and the mustard and the horseradish that hadn't been used except for that one recipe months ago.

She began to organize the closets in the house—the front one, with the winter coats still in hibernation and the boots tossed like gauntlets into a Rubbermaid bin on the floor—and then the hall closet with its piles of snowy towels and heady potpourri. It was in that one that she found herself reaching to the rear of the top shelf—the hiding spot she'd never been able to reach herself without a struggle, before, and that therefore became her cache of Christmas gifts bought and saved all year for her daughter. One by one, Sarah pulled out a remote-control robot, an art set to make flower fairies, a dress-up kit—treasures she'd found in January or March or May and had known, in that instant, that her daughter would love. She stood immobile for a long moment, holding this bounty in her elongated arms, paralyzed by the most concrete evidence she'd found yet that her daughter was Not. Coming. Home.

Sarah sat down in the middle of the hall. She opened up the plastic shrink-wrapped robot, installed its batteries, and sent him careening into the bathroom. She opened the dress-up kit and wrapped a pink boa around her own neck; peered into the tiny heart-shaped mirror to apply the fuchsia lipstick and glittery blue eye shadow, a whore's version of happiness.

When the phone rang, she ran into the bedroom to pick up an extension. "How are you doing?" Abe asked.

"Fine," Sarah said. In the bedroom mirror, she could still see the clown-red cheeks, the garish mouth. "I'm fine."

She hung up the phone and went into the kitchen for a large black trash bag, big enough to hold a yard's worth of leaves, or a closet full of the future. She scooped all the unused toys for her daughter into the trash bag and carried it over her shoulder out to the garage. Because it was not trash day, Sarah drove all the way to the municipal dump, where she let the attendant punch her ticket once for the privilege of hauling the sack over the ravine's edge. She waited, until this bag full of what she'd lost nestled itself between other bags stuffed with the things people actually chose to give away.

PHARMACISTS LIVE IN MINUTIAE, which is why Abe had learned a whole system of measurement in college that most educated folks don't even know exists. Ask anyone who has ever filled the innards of a tiny gelatin capsule with a drug, and they will know that twenty grains equals one scruple. Three scruples equal one dram apothecaries. Eight drams apothecaries equal one ounce apothecaries, which equals four hundred eighty grains, or twenty-four scruples.

Abe was trying to count the twenty-four scruples, but they had nothing to do with the pills he had spilled before him on the little rubber mat from Pfizer, a freebie he'd gotten at some conference in Santa Fe. It was funny—a scruple, by itself, was a misgiving; make it plural and it suddenly was a set of principles, of ethics. It *was* that simple, he understood now. You only had to survive one of your regrets, and it was enough to make you realize you'd been living your life all wrong.

He regretted telling his daughter to clean up her room the day before she died. He regretted the fact that he hadn't hugged her in front of her friends after her fall concert at school, because he thought her embarrassment was more important than his pride. He regretted not taking his family to Australia, when they were still a family. He regretted not having been given the chance to meet a grandchild. He regretted having seven years, instead of seventy-seven.

Abe pushed aside these thoughts and began to recount the pills. But he had to keep hiking up his pants—they were riding that low on his hips. Finally, ducking behind a wall of meds, he unbuttoned his white coat and notched his belt tighter. It would make sense that he was losing weight— he hadn't been eating, really—but the belt suddenly didn't fit at all. There simply wasn't a notch where he needed it to be; he'd grown that thin, that fast.

Frustrated, he unwound some twine in the back room used for shipments and took off his belt, looping the rope in its place. He thought of going back inside and finishing the order, but instead he walked out through the back receiving door of the pharmacy and kept walking—around the block, and then down three more, and through the traffic light, until he came to a bar he passed every day when he drove home. Olaf's, it was called, and it was open, even though it was only eleven A.M.

He was aware, as he walked through the door, that he looked like a poor man's Charlie Chaplin, with a rope holding up his pants. He was aware that he hadn't been to a bar during the day since he'd been a drummer a lifetime ago. There were five people at the bar, even this morning, and they weren't the sort of folks you found in bars at night. These were the hard-luck cases, the ones who needed whiskey (a dram!) to get through another few hours of an ordinary workday; or the call girls who needed to forget before they went home to sleep off last night's memories; or the old men who only wanted to find their youth in the bottom of a bottle of gin.

Abe climbed onto a stool—and climbed was the word; he must have been more exhausted than he thought, for all the effort that it took to get onto it. "Have you got Jameson?" he asked the bartender, and the guy looked at him with a smile as crooked as lightning.

"Nice try, kid," he said.

"Excuse me?"

The bartender shook his head. "You got any ID?"

Abe was forty-two years old, and he could not remember the last time he'd been carded. He had gray hair at the temples, for God's sake. But he reached for his wallet, only to realize that it was back at work, in his locker, like usual. "I don't," he said.

"Well, then," the bartender said. "I ain't got Jameson. Come on back when you turn twenty-one."

Abe stared at him, confounded. He jumped off the stool, landing hard. The whole way back to work, he searched for his reflection in the shiny hoods of Buicks, in plate-glass windows of bakeries, in puddles. When you lost a child, did you lose the years you'd spent with her, too?

———

A WEEK AFTER THEIR daughter's death, Sarah could not stop thinking about her. She would taste the skin of the little girl, a kiss, the moment before the chicory of the coffee kicked in, or the sweetness of the muffin blossomed on her tongue. She would pick up a newspaper and feel instead the rubbery band of small socks between her fingers as she folded them over after doing the wash. She'd be in one room and hear the music of her daughter's voice, the way grammar leaped through her sentences like a frog.

Abe, on the other hand, was starting to lose her. He would close his eyes and try to conjure up his daughter's face, and he still could, but it was unraveled at the edges a little more each day. He found himself spending hours in her bedroom, inhaling the smell of her strawberry-mango shampoo still trapped in the fibers of the pillowcase, or poring through the books on her shelves and trying to see them through her eyes. He went so far as to open her finger paints, stand stripped to the waist in front of her tiny mirror, draw her heart on his chest.

ALTHOUGH SARAH'S MO WAS usually to do the opposite of whatever her mother told her to do, this time, she took her advice. She showed up at the church, shuddering as she remembered the hymns that had been played at her daughter's funeral, steeling herself for the absence of the coffin at the altar. She knocked on the pastor's office door, and he ushered her inside and gave her a cup of tea. "So," the pastor said, "your mother's worried about you."

Sarah opened up her mouth to say something snippy and typically awful, but she caught herself in time. Of *course* her mother was worried. That was the job description, wasn't it? That was why she had come.

"Can I ask you something?" Sarah said. "Why *her*?"

"I don't understand . . ."

"I get the whole God thing. I get the kingdom of heaven. But there are millions of seven-year-olds out there. Why did God take *mine*?"

The pastor hesitated. "God didn't take your daughter, Sarah," he said. "Illness did."

Sarah snorted. "Sure. Pass the buck when it's convenient." She could feel herself dangerously at the edge of breaking down, and wondered why on earth she'd thought it was a good idea to come here.

The pastor reached for her hand. His were warm and papery, familiar.

"Heaven's an amazing place," he said softly. "She's up there, and she's looking down on us, right now, you know."

Sarah felt her throat tighten. "My daughter," she said, "can't ride a ski lift without hyperventilating. She panics in elevators. She doesn't even like bunk beds. She's terrified of heights."

"Not anymore."

"How do you know that?" Sarah exploded. "How do you know that there's anything afterward? How do you know it doesn't just . . . end?"

"I don't know," the pastor said. "But I can hope. And I truly believe that your daughter is in heaven, and even if she does still get scared, Jesus will be there to keep her safe."

She turned away as a tear streaked down her cheek. "She doesn't know Jesus," Sarah said. "She knows me."

ABE FOUND HIMSELF DEFYING gravity. He'd be standing in the kitchen, getting a glass of water, and he'd find himself rising to the balls of his feet. He could not walk fast down the street without starting to float between strides. He started to put stones in the pockets of his pants, which were all too long for him now.

He was sitting on his daughter's bed one Saturday, remembering a conversation they'd had. *Can I still live here when I get married?* she'd asked, and he'd grinned and said that would be perfectly fine.

But what about your husband? he'd asked.

His daughter had considered this carefully. *Well, we could set up the cot, like when I have a sleepover.*

The doorbell rang, and when Abe went downstairs, he found the little girl his daughter had considered her best friend—the last one who'd used that cot, actually—standing red eyed beside her mother. "Hi, Abe," the woman said. "I hope this isn't too much of an imposition."

"No!" he said, too brightly. "No! Not at all!"

"It's just that Emily's having some trouble, with, well, *you know.* She drew a picture, and wanted to bring it here. She thought maybe you could hang it up." The little girl thrust out a piece of paper toward Abe: a crayon drawing of two little girls—one dark-haired, like his daughter, one fair, like Emily. They were holding hands. There was a melting sun overhead, and grass beneath their feet.

Abe realized he was nearly at a level with Emily; he barely had to crouch down to look her in the eye. "This is beautiful, honey," he said. "I'm going to put it up right over her bed." He reached out as if to touch the crown of her head, but realized that this might hurt him more than it would offer comfort, and at the last minute pulled his arm back to his side.

"Are you all right?" Emily's mother whispered. "You look . . ." Her voice trailed off as she tried to find the right word, and then she just gave up and shook her head. "Well. Of *course* you're not all right. I'm so sorry, Abe. I truly am." With one last look, she took Emily's hand and started to walk down the driveway.

Abe held the crayon picture in his hand so tightly that it crumpled. He watched Emily kick the unraked leaves along the sidewalk, setting up small tornadoes as her mother looked straight ahead, not even aware that she was missing this one small, wonderful thing.

SARAH AND ABE DID not really speak to each other, not until Abe walked into their daughter's room and found Sarah taking the books off the shelves and putting them into boxes. "What are you doing?" he asked, stricken.

"I can't move past this," Sarah said, "knowing it's all right down the hall."

"No," Abe answered.

Sarah hesitated. "What do you mean, *no?*"

Abe reached into one of the boxes and took out a fistful of picture books, jammed them back onto the shelf. "Just because you're ready to give her up," he said, "doesn't mean *I* am."

Sarah's face bloomed with color. "Give her up?" she whispered. "Is that what you think I'm doing? For God's sake, Abe, all I want to do is *function* like a normal human being again."

"But you're not normal. *We're* not normal." His eyes filled with tears. "She *died,* Sarah."

Sarah winced, as if she had taken a blow. Then she turned on her heel and walked out of the room.

Abe sank onto the floor, his fingers speared through his hair. After a half hour, he stood up and walked down the hall to their bedroom. He found Sarah lying on her side, staring at the sun as it shamefully scuttled off the horizon. Abe lay down on the bed, curling his body around hers. "I lost her," he whispered. "Please don't tell me I've lost you."

Sarah turned to him, and rested her palm on his cheek. She kissed him, all the words she could not say. They began to comfort each other—a touch here, a brush of lips there, a kindness. But when their clothes had dissolved into pools on the floor, when Abe braced himself over his wife and took hold of her body and tried to settle her curves against his canyons, they did not come together seamlessly, the way they used to. They were off, just enough to make it uncomfortable; just enough for her to say, *Let me try this* and for him to say, *Maybe this way.*

Afterward, when Sarah had fallen asleep, Abe sat up and stared down at the end of the bed, at his wife's feet hanging long and white over its edge.

THE NEXT MORNING, ABE and Sarah lay in the dark. "Maybe I need to be alone for a while," Sarah said, although it wasn't what she'd hoped to say.

"Maybe you do," Abe replied, although it was the opposite of what he meant. It was as if, in this new world, where the impossible had actually happened, nothing fit anymore: not language, not reason, not even the two of them.

When Sarah got out of bed, she took the sheet with her—a modesty she hadn't needed for fifteen years of marriage. It prevented Abe from seeing what he would have noticed, in an instant: that the growth Sarah had experienced was exactly the same amount Abe himself had diminished; and that, if you could measure anything as insubstantial as that, it would have been exactly the same size and scope as the daughter they'd lost.

SARAH REACHED THE SUITCASE, even though it was stored in the top rafters of the attic. Abe watched her pack. At the door, they made promises they both knew they would not keep. "I'll call," Sarah said, and Abe nodded. "Be well," he answered.

She was going to stay with her mother—something that, in all the years of their marriage, Abe never would have imagined coming to pass; and yet he considered this a positive sign. If Sarah was choosing Felicity, in spite of their rocky relationship, maybe there was hope for all children to return to their parents, regardless of how impossible the journey seemed to be.

He had to pull a chair to the window, because he was no longer tall enough to see over its sill. He stood on the cushion and watched her put her suitcase into the car. She looked enormous to him, a giantess—and he considered that this is what motherhood does to a woman: make her larger than life. He waited until he could not see her car anymore, and then he climbed down from the chair.

He could not work anymore; he was too short to reach the counter. He could not drive anywhere, the pedals were too far from his feet. There was nothing for Abe to do, so he wandered through the house, even emptier than it had been. He found himself, of course, in his daughter's room. Here, he spent hours: drawing with her art kit; playing with her pretend food and cash register; sifting through the drawers of her clothing and playing a game with himself: can you remember the last time she wore this? He put on a Radio Disney CD and forced himself to listen to the whole of it. He lined up her stuffed animals, like witnesses.

Then he crawled into her dollhouse, one he'd built for her last Christmas. He closed the door behind himself. He glanced around at the carefully pasted wallpaper, the rich red velvet love seat, the kitchen sink. He climbed the stairs to the bedroom, where he could stare out the window to his heart's content. The view, it was perfect.

GOBLIN LAKE

•

Michael Swanwick

IN 1646, SHORTLY BEFORE THE END of the Thirty Years' War, a patrol of Hessian cavalrymen, fleeing the aftermath of a disastrous battle to the north wherein a botched flanking maneuver had in an hour turned certain victory to abject rout, made camp at the foot of what a local peasant they had captured and forced to serve as a guide assured them was one of the highest mountains in the Spessart region of Germany. Among their number was a young officer named Johann von Grimmelshausen, a firebrand and habitual liar who was known to his comrades as Jurgen, which in English translates as Jack.

As the front lines were distant and the countryside unwary, the patrol had picked up a great deal of food and several casks of Rhine wine on their way. So that night they ate and drank well. When the food was done, they called upon their guide to tell them of the countryside in which they found themselves. He, having slowly come to the opinion that they did not intend to kill him when they were done with his services (and, possibly, having plans of lulling them with his servility and then slipping away under cover of darkness when they were all asleep), was only too happy to oblige them.

"Directly below us, not a quarter of a mile's distance away, is the Mummelsee"—in the local dialect the name meant Goblin Lake—"which is bottomless, and which has the peculiar property that it changes whatever is thrown into it into something else. So that, for example, if any man were to tie up a number of pebbles in a kerchief and let it down into the water on a string, when he pulled it up the pebbles would have turned into peas or rubies or the eggs of vipers. Furthermore, if there were an odd number of pebbles, the number of whatever they became should invariably be even, but if they were even they would come out odd."

"That would be a very pretty way of making a living," Jack observed. "Sitting by the banks of a lake, turning pebbles into rubies."

"What they become is not predictable," the peasant cautioned. "You could not rely on them turning to gemstones."

"Even if they did so only one time in a hundred . . . Well, I have spent many a day fishing with less to show for it."

By now, several of the cavalry men were leaning forward, listening intently. Even those who stared loftily way into the distance, as if they did not care, refrained from speaking lest they miss something profitable. So, seeing too late that he had excited their avarice, the peasant quickly said, "But it is a very dangerous place! This was the very lake which Luther said was cursed and that if you threw a stone into it a terrible storm immediately blows up, with hail and lightning and great winds, for there are devils chained up in its depths."

"No, that was in Poltersberg," Jack said negligently.

"Poltersberg!" the peasant spat. "What does Poltersberg know of terrors? There was a farmer hereabout who had to kill his best plow horse when it broke a leg. Being of an inquiring turn of mind, he hauled its carcass to the lake and threw it in. Down it sank, and up it rose again, alive—but transformed horribly, so that it had teeth like knives, two legs rather than four, and wings like those of an enormous bat. It screamed in agony and flew away into the night, no man knows where.

"Worse, when the carcass hit the water, some of it was splashed over the farmer's face, erasing his eyes completely, so that from that instant onward, he was blind."

"How did he know the horse was transformed, then?" Jack asked with a sardonic little smile.

The peasant's mouth opened and then closed again. After a bit, he said, "It is also said that there were two cutthroats who brought the body of a woman they had—"

Jack cut him off. "Why listen to your stories when we can find out for ourselves?"

There was a general murmur of agreement and, after a little prodding with a knife, the peasant led them all downward.

The way down to the Mummelsee was steep and roadless, and the disposition of the soldiers was considerably soured by the time they reached it. Their grumblings, moreover, were directed as much toward Jack as toward the rascally peasant guide, for on reflection it was clear to them all that he had insisted on this journey not from any real belief that he would end up rich—for what experienced military man believes *that?*—but from his innate love of mischief.

Oblivious to their mood, Jack sauntered to the end of a crumbling stone pier. He had brought along a double handful of fresh cherries, which he carried in his cap, and was eating them one by one and spitting their stones into the water. "What is that out there?" he asked, gesturing negligently toward what appeared to be a large, submerged rock, roughly rectangular in shape and canted downward to one side. It was easily visible, for the moon was full and unobscured and its light seemed to render the nighttime bright as day.

"In my grandfather's time," the peasant said eagerly, as if anxious to restore his good reputation, "the Duke of Württemberg caused a raft to be made and put out onto the lake to sound its depths. But after the measure had been led down nine thread cables with a sinking lead and yet had found no bottom—why, then the raft, contrary to the nature of wood, began to sink. So that all made haste for the land, fearing greatly. Nor did any escape without a soaking, and terrible diseases were said to have afflicted them in their old age."

"So that's the raft, you say?"

"If you look closely, you can see where the arms of Württemberg were carved into the wood. Worn, perhaps, but clear to see." The peasant pointed earnestly at some faint markings that a credulous man might convince himself were as described.

Jack rounded on him savagely. "You scoundrel! I have been watching the cherry stones as they sank in the water, and nothing happened to them. One did not become two, two were not transformed into seventeen, and none of them—not a one!—showed the least tendency to become rubies or emeralds or vipers or oxen or even fish."

Protesting wildly, the peasant tried to scuttle around Jack and so off the pier. Jack, for his part, was equally determined not to allow him to do so. Thus it was that a game of rat-and-mastiff took place, with the peasant playing the part of the rat and the cavalrymen the mastiffs. And though the numbers were all on one side, all the desperation and cunning were on the other.

At the last, Jack made a lunge for the peasant and, just as the man escaped his enclosing arms, found himself seized by two of his laughing comrades, hoisted up into the air, and thrown into the Mummelsee.

DOWN, DOWN, DOWN, JACK sank, choking. The water was as clear as crystal, and yet far down in the distance as black as coal, for the monstrousness of its depth. So filled with anger at his comrades was he that at first he did not notice when he stopped choking. Then, before he could properly marvel at this strange turn of circumstance, he was suddenly distracted by movements in the depths of the lake. At a distance, the creatures looked like so many frogs, flitting to and fro, but as they grew closer they seemed very much like human beings, save that their skin was green and their clothes, though fine and flowing, were clearly woven of seaweeds and other underwater plants.

More and more of these water spirits rose up like diving birds and quickly surrounded Jack. So great was their number that he had no choice but to go with them when, by gestures and frowns, the sylphs indicated he was to descend to the very bottom of the Mummelsee. Like a flock of birds circling as they descend from the sky, they guided him down.

When finally Jack lightly touched one foot to the floor of the lake, pushing up a gentle puff of silt, and then with the other creating a second puff, he found there waiting for him a sylph or nix (for the taxonomy of lake spirits was not a subject he was conversant in) clad in raiment of gold and silver, by which token he took this being to be the king of the Mummelsee.

"A good day to you, Jack," said the king. "I trust you are well?"

"God save us from hurt and harm, friend!" Jack cried. "But however could you possibly know my name?"

"As for that, my dear fellow, I have been reading about your adventures, most recently with those scoundrelly false comrades who threw you into this lake." The king's Vandyke and mustachios waved lightly in the water and this made Jack clutch his throat in sudden apprehension that he was breathing a medium for which mortal men were unsuited. But then the king laughed and his laugh was so natural and warmhearted that Jack could not help but join it. So, realizing that a man who could still laugh was neither dead nor in any sense lacking breath, he put aside his fears.

"What place is this," Jack asked, "and what manner of people live here?"

"Why, as the saying goes, 'As above, so below.' We have our farms and cities and churches, though the god we worship in it may not have the same name as yours. Salt hay is harvested to thatch our roofs. Sea horses pull plows in our fields, and sea cows are milked in our barns. Catfish chase mice fish, and water gnomes drive shafts through the muck in search of mussels and precious stones. The maidens here may have scales, but they are no less beautiful nor any more slippery than those in your above-water world."

So talking, the king of the Mummelsee led Jack along a pleasant road to what destination he did not yet reveal, and all the nixies who had guided Jack down formed themselves into a casual procession behind them, laughing and talking among themselves, and flashing from side to side as they went, so that they resembled nothing so much as a great school of minnows. Above a winding road they swam and then through a forest of giant kelp, which abruptly opened up upon a shining white city.

Great were the wonders of that submarine metropolis. The walls of its buildings were so white they glowed, for they were plastered (so explained the king) with powdered pearls. While the streets were not paved with gemstones, many a fresco set into the exterior walls was made of nothing else, and the scenes they depicted were not of warfare but of children at play and lovers chastely courting. The architecture was a happy blend of Moorish and Asian influences, with minarets and pagodas existing in easy harmony, and entrances on all the upper floors as well as the bottommost. Nor did it escape Jack's attention that there were neither locks on the doors nor guards at the entrances to the palace—and this was far from the least of the wonders that he saw.

But the greatest wonder of all, so far as Jack was concerned, was the sylph maiden Poseidonia, the king's daughter, who came out to greet her father on his return to the city. The instant he clapped eyes on her slim and perfect form, Jack was determined to win her. Nor was that a difficult task, as he was a well-made man with a soldier's straight bearing, and his frank admiration drew from her a happy blush and no protests whatsoever. Further, the mer-people being a Heathen folk and not bound by Christian standards of propriety, their mutual infatuation quickly found physical expression.

Time went by. It may have been days or it may have been months.

Late one afternoon, lying in the princess's bed, with the sheets and pillows all in sensuous disarray and a greenish-blue noontide light flowing through her bedroom windows, Jack cleared his throat and hesitantly said, "Tell me something, oh my best and belovedest."

"Anything!" replied that passionate young sylph.

"One thing continues to bother me—a small thing, perhaps, but it nitters and natters at the back of my mind, and I cannot rid myself of it, however I try. When first I arrived in this rich and splendid land, your father told me he had been reading of my adventures. By what magic? In what unimaginable book?"

"Why, in this one, dearest of scoundrels." (It was the sylph's single most endearing quality that she loved Jack for exactly what he was and not one whit through any misapprehension of his character.) "What other book could it possibly be?"

Jack looked from one end of the room to the other, and replied, "I see no book."

"Well, of course not, silly. If it were *here*, how could you be in it?"

"I cannot say, oh delight of my eyes, for your answer makes absolutely no sense to me."

"Trust me, he read of you in this book, nor have you ever left it."

Now Jack began to feel the stirrings of anger. "*This* one you say—*which* one? The devil take me if I can make heads or tales of your answers!"

Then the laughter died in Poseidonia's throat, and she exclaimed, "You poor thing! You truly do not understand, do you?"

"If I understood, would I be at this very instant begging you like a fool for a simple and straightforward answer?"

She regarded him with a sad little smile. "I think it is time you talked with my father," she said at last.

"IS MY LISSOME YOUNG daughter not energetic enough to please you?" asked the king of the Mummelsee.

"That and more," said Jack, who had long grown used to the sylphs' shockingly direct manner of speaking.

"Then be content with her and this carefree existence you lead, and do not seek to go questing out beyond the confines of these ever-so-pleasant pages."

"Again you speak in riddles! Majesty, this business is driving me mad.

I beg of you, for this once, speak to me plain and simply, even as if I were but a child."

The king sighed. "You know what books are?"

"Yes, of course."

"When was the last time you read one?"

"Why, I—"

"Exactly. Or that anybody you know read one?"

"I have been in the company of rough-and-tumble soldiers, whose response to coming upon a library might typically be to use its contents to start their campfires, so this is not terribly surprising."

"You must have read books in your youth. Can you tell me the plot of any of them?"

Jack fell silent.

"You see? Characters in books do not read books. Oh, they snap them shut when somebody enters the room, or fling them aside in disgust at what they fancy is said within, or hide their faces in one which they pretend to peruse while somebody else lectures them on matters they'd rather not confront. But they do not *read* them. Twould be recursive, rendering each book effectively infinite, so that no single one might be finished without reading them all. This is the infallible method of discovering on which side of the page you lie—have you read a book this year?" The king arched an eyebrow and waited.

After a very long silence, Jack said, "No. I have not."

"Then there you are."

"But . . . how can this be? How can we possibly . . . ?"

"It is the simplest thing imaginable," replied the king. "I, for example, dwell within chapters eleven through seventeen of book five of something called *Simplicissimus*. It is, I assure you, a good life. So what if the walls of my palace are as thin as paper, the windows simply drawn on by pen, and my actions circumscribed by the whimsy of the artist? I neither age nor die, and when you, taking a brief rest from your romantic gymnastics with my daughter, care to visit me, I always find our little conversations diverting."

Glumly, Jack stared out through a window paned with nacre polished so smooth as to be transparent. "It is a hard thing," he said, "to realize that one is not actually real." Then, after a long moment's thought, "But this makes no sense. Granted that my current surroundings and condition are hardly to be improved upon. Yet I have seen things in the war that . . . Well, it doesn't bears thinking upon. Who on earth would create such a world as ours? Who could possibly find amusement in such cruelties as, I grant you, I have sometimes been a part of?"

"Sir," said the king, "I am not the artist, and he, I suspect, is nobody of any great esteem in his unimaginably larger world. He might pass you on the street unnoticed. In conversation, it is entirely possible, he would not impress you favorably. Why, then, should you expect more from him than he—or, as it may be, she—might reasonably expect from his or her vastly more potent creator?"

"Are you saying that our author's world is no better than our own?"

"It is possible it is worse. From his work we can infer certain things about the world in which he lives. Our architecture is ornate and romantic. His therefore is plain and dull—sheets of gray concrete, perhaps, with each window the exact twin of all the others—or he would not have bothered to imagine ours in such delightful detail."

"Then, since our world is so crude and violent, it stands to reason that his must be a paragon of peace and gentility?"

"Say rather that ours has an earthy vigor while his is mired down in easy hypocrisy."

Shaking his head slowly, Jack said, "How is it that you know so much about the world we live in, and yet I know so little?"

"There are two types of characters, my son. Yours is forever sailing out of windows with his trousers in his hand, impersonating foreign dignitaries with an eye to defrauding uncharitable bishops, being ambushed in lightless alleys by knife-wielding ruffians, and coming home early to discover his newlywed bride in bed with his mistress's husband."

"It is as if you had been reading my diary," Jack said wonderingly. "Had I a diary to read."

"That is because you are the active sort of character, whose chief purpose is to move the plot along. I am, however, more the reflective sort of character, whose purpose it is to expound upon and thus reveal the inner meaning of the narrative. But I see you are confused—let us step briefly out of my story."

And, as simply as one might turn a page, Jack found himself standing in a pleasant garden, awash in the golden light of a late-afternoon sun. The king of the Mummelsee was seated in a chair which, though plain and simple, suggested a throne—indeed, such a throne as a philosopher-king might inhabit.

"That is very well observed of you," the king said in response to Jack's unspoken observation. "It is possible that, with encouragement, you could be converted to a reflective character yet."

"Where are we?"

"This is my dear friend Dr. Vandermast's garden in Zayana, where it is eternally afternoon. Here, he and I have had many a long discussion of entelechy and epistemology and other such unimportant and ephemeral nothings. The good doctor has discreetly made himself absent that we may talk in private. He himself resides in a book called—but what matters that? This is one of those magical places where we may with equanimity discuss the nature of the world. Indeed, its aspect is such that we could scarce do otherwise if we tried."

A hummingbird abruptly appeared before Jack, hanging in the air like a frantic feathered jewel. He extended a finger and the bird hovered just above it, so that he could feel the delicate push of air from its madly pumping wings upon his skin. "What marvel is this?" he asked.

"It is just my daughter. Though she does not appear in this scene, still she desires to make her wishes known—and so she expresses herself in imagery. Thank you, dear, you may leave now." The king clapped his hands and the hummingbird vanished. "She will be heartbroken if you depart from our fictive realm. But doubtless another hero will come along and, being fictional, Poseidonia neither learns from her experiences nor lets them embitter her against their perpetrator's gender. She will greet him as openly and enthusiastically as she did you."

Jack felt a perfectly understandable twinge of jealousy. But he set it aside. Hewing to the gist of the discussion, he said, "Is this an academic argument, sir? Or is there a practical side to it?"

"Dr. Vandermast's garden is not like other places. If you were to wish to leave our world entirely, then I have no doubt it could be easily arranged."

"Could I then come back?"

"Alas, no," the king said regretfully. "One miracle is enough for any life. And more than either of us, strictly speaking, deserves, I might add."

Jack picked up a stick and strode back and forth along the flower beds, lashing at the heads of the taller blossoms. "Must I then decide based on no information at all? Leap blindly into the abyss or remain doubtful at its lip forever? This is, as you say, a delightful existence. But can I be content with this life, knowing there is another and yet being ignorant of what it might entail?"

"Calm yourself. If that is all it takes, then let us see what the alternative might be." The king of the Mummelsee reached down into his lap and turned the page of a leather-bound folio that Jack had not noticed before.

"ARE YOU GOING TO be sitting there forever, woolgathering, when there are chores to be done? I swear, you must be the single laziest man in the world."

Jack's fat wife came out of the kitchen, absently scratching her behind. Gretchen's face was round where once it had been slender, and there was a slight hitch in her gait, where formerly her every movement had been a dance to music only she could hear. Yet Jack's heart softened within him at the sight of her, as it always did.

He put down his goose quill and sprinkled sand over what he had written so far. "You are doubtless right, my dear," he said mildly. "You always are."

As he was stumping outdoors to chop wood, draw water, and feed the hog they were fattening for Fastnacht, he caught a glimpse of himself in the mirror that hung by the back door. An old and haggard man with a beard so thin it looked moth eaten glared back at him in horror. "Eh, sir," he murmured to himself, "you are not the fine young soldier who tumbled Gretchen in the hayloft only minutes after meeting her, so many years ago."

A cold wind blew flecks of ice in his face when he stepped outside, and the sticks in the woodpile were frozen together so that he had to bang them with the blunt end of the axe to separate them so that they might be split. When he went to the well, the ice was so thick that breaking it raised a sweat. Then, after he'd removed the rock from the lid covering the bucket of kitchen slops and started down toward the sty, he slipped on a patch of ice and upended the slops over the front of his clothing. Which meant not only that he would have to wash those clothes weeks ahead of schedule—which in wintertime was an ugly chore—but that he had to gather up the slops from the ground with his bare hands and ladle them back into the bucket, for come what may the pig still needed to be fed.

So, muttering and complaining to himself, old Jack clomped back into the house, where he washed his hands and changed into clean clothing and sat back down to his writing again. After a few minutes, his wife entered the room and exclaimed, "It is so cold in here!" She busied herself building up the fire, though it was so much work carrying wood up to his office that Jack would rather have endured the cold to save himself the extra labor later on. Then she came up behind him and placed her hands on his shoulders. "Are you writing a letter to Wilhelm again?"

"Who else?" Jack growled. "We work our fingers to the bone to send him money, and he never writes! And when he does, his letters are so brief! He spends all his time drinking and running up debts with tailors and chasing after—" He caught himself in time, and coughed. "Chasing after inappropriate young women."

"Well, after all, when you were his age—"

"When I was his age, I never did any such thing," Jack said indignantly.

"No, of course not," he wife said. He could feel the smile he did not turn around to see. "You poor foolish dear."

She kissed the top of his head.

THE SUN EMERGED FROM behind a cloud as Jack reappeared, and the garden blazed with a hundred bright colors—more of Poseidonia's influence, Jack supposed. Its flowers turned their heads toward him flirtatiously and opened their blossoms to his gaze.

"Well?" said the king of the Mummelsee. "How was it?"

"I'd lost most of my teeth," Jack said glumly, "and there was an ache in my side that never went away. My children were grown and moved away, and there was nothing left in my life to look forward to but death."

"That is not a judgment," the king said, "but only a catalog of complaints."

"There was, I must concede, a certain authenticity to life on the other side of the gate. A validity and complexity which ours may be said to lack."

"Well, there you are, then."

The shifting light darkened and a wind passed through the trees, making them sigh. "On the other hand, there is a purposefulness to this life which the other does not have."

"That too is true."

"Yet if there is a purpose to our existence—and I feel quite certain that there is—I'll be damned if I know what it is."

"Why, that is easily enough answered!" the king said. "We exist to amuse the reader."

"And this reader—who exactly is he?"

"The less said about the reader," said the king of the Mummelsee fervently, "the better." He stood. "We have talked enough," he said. "There are two gates from this garden. One leads back whence we came. The second leads to . . . the other place. That which you glimpsed just now."

"Has it a name, this 'other place'?"

"Some call it Reality, though the aptness of that title is, of course, in dispute."

Jack tugged at his mustache and chewed at the inside of his cheek. "This is, I swear, no easy choice."

"Yet we cannot stay in this garden forever, Jack. Sooner or later, you must choose."

"Indeed, sir, you are right," Jack said. "I must be resolute." All about him, the garden waited in hushed stillness. Not a bullfrog disturbed the glassy surface of the lily pond. Not a blade of grass stirred in the meadow. The very air seemed tense with anticipation.

He chose.

So it was that Johann von Grimmelshausen, sometimes known as Jurgen, escaped the narrow and constricting confines of literature, and of the Mummelsee as well, by becoming truly human and thus subject to the whims of history. Which means that he, of course, died centuries ago. Had he remained a fiction, he would still be with us today, though without the richness of experience which you and I endure every day of our lives.

Was he right to make the choice he did? Only God can tell. And if there is no God, why, then we will never know.

MALLON THE GURU

•

Peter Straub

NEAR THE END OF WHAT HE later called his "developmental period," the
American guru Spencer Mallon spent four months traveling through India
with his spiritual leader, Urdang, a fearsome German with a deceptively
mild manner. In the third of these months, they were granted an audience
with a yogi, a great holy man who lived in the village of Sankwal. However, an odd, unsettling thing happened as soon as Mallon and Urdang
reached the outskirts of the village. A carrion crow plummeted out of the
sky and landed, with an audible thump and a skirl of feathers, dead on
the dusty ground immediately in front of them. Instantly, villagers began
streaming toward them, whether because of the crow or because he and
Urdang were fair-skinned strangers, Mallon did not know. He fought the
uncomfortable feeling of being surrounded by strangers gibbering away in
a language he would never understand, and in the midst of this great difficulty tried to find the peace and balance he sometimes experienced during
his almost daily, generally two-hour meditations.

An unclean foot with tuberous three-inch nails flipped aside the dead
bird. The villagers drew closer, close enough to touch, and leaning in and
jabbering with great intensity, urged them forward by tugging at their
shirts and waistbands. They, or perhaps just he, Spencer Mallon, was being
urged, importuned, begged to execute some unimaginable service. They
wished him to perform some kind of *task,* but the task remained mysterious. The mystery became clearer only after a rickety hut seemed almost to
materialize, miragelike, from the barren scrap of land where it squatted.
One of the men urging Mallon along yanked his sleeve more forcefully
and implored him, with flapping, birdlike gestures, to go into the hut, evidently his, to enter it and *see* something—the man indicated the necessity
for vision by jabbing a black fingernail at his protuberant right eye.

I have been chosen, Mallon thought. *I, not Urdang, have been elected by these ignorant and suffering people.*

Within the dim, hot enclosure, he was invited to gaze at a small child with huge, impassive eyes and limbs like twigs. The child appeared to be dying. Dark yellow crusts ringed its nostrils and its mouth.

Staring at Mallon, the trembling villager raised one of his own hands and brushed his fingertips gently against the boy's enormous forehead. Then he waved Mallon closer to the child's pallet.

"Don't you get it?" Urdang said. "You're supposed to touch the boy."

Reluctantly, unsure of what he was actually being asked to do and fearful of contracting some hideous disease, Mallon extended one hand and lowered his extended fingers toward the boy's skeletal head as if he were about to dip them for the briefest possible moment into a pail of reeking fluid drawn from the communal cesspit.

Kid, he thought, *for the sake of my reputation, I hope we're going to see a miracle cure.*

At the moment of contact, he felt as though a tiny particle of energy, a radiant erg as quick and flowing as mercury, passed directly from his hand through the fragile wall of the boy's skull.

In the midst of this extremely interesting and in fact amazing phenomenon, the father collapsed to his knees and began to croon in gratitude.

"How do these people know about me?" he asked.

"The real question is, what do they think you did?" Urdang said. "And how do they think they know it? Once we have had our audience, I suggest we put on our skates."

Urdang, Mallon realized, had no idea of what had just happened. It was the restoration of a cosmic balance: a bird died, and a child was saved. He had been the fulcrum between death and the restoration. A perfect Indian experience had been given to him. The great yogi would embrace him as he would a son, he would open his house and his ashram and welcome him as a student of unprecedented capabilities.

Proceeding down a narrow lane in the village proper, Mallon carelessly extended two fingers and ran them along a foot or two of the mud-plastered wall at his side. He had no plan, no purpose beyond just seeing what was going to happen, for he knew that in some fashion his touch would alter the universe. The results of his test were deeply gratifying: on the wall, the two lines traced by his fingers glowed a brilliant neon blue that brightened and intensified until it threatened to sear the eyes. The villagers spun around and waved their arms, releasing an ecstatic babble threaded with high-pitched cries of joy. Along with everybody else, Mallon had stopped moving to look at the marvelous, miraculous wall. An electrical buzz and hum filled all the spaces within his body; he felt as though he could shoot sparks from his fingers.

I should touch that kid all over again, he thought. *He'd zoom right up off the bed.*

In seconds, the vibrant blue lines cooled, shrank, and faded back into the dull khaki of the wall. The villagers thrust forward, rubbed the wall, flattened themselves against it, spoke to it in whispers. Those who kissed the wall came away with mouths and noses painted white with dust. Only Mallon, and perhaps Urdang, had been chagrined to see the evidence of his magic vanish so quickly from the world.

The babbling crowd, not at all disappointed, clustered again around him and pushed him forward. Their filthy, black-nailed hands gave him many a fond pat and awed, stroking caress. Eventually they came to a high yellow wall and an iron gate. Urdang pushed himself through the crowd and opened the gate upon a long, lush flower garden. At the distant end of the garden stood a graceful terra-cotta building with a row of windows on both sides of its elaborately tiled front door. The dark heads of young women appeared in the windows. Giggling, the women retreated backward.

The villagers thrust Mallon and Urdang forward. The gates clanged behind them. Far away, an oxcart creaked. Cattle lowed from behind the creamy-looking terra-cotta building.

I am in love with all of India! Mallon thought.

"Come nearer," said a dry, penetrating voice.

A small man in a dhoti of dazzling white sat in the lotus position just in front of a fountain placed in the middle of the garden. A moment before, Mallon had noticed neither the man nor the fountain.

"I believe that you, sir, are Urdang," the man said. "But who is your most peculiar follower?"

"His name is Spencer Mallon," Urdang said. "But, Master, with all due respect, he is not peculiar."

"This man is a peculiarity entire unto himself," said the little man. "Please sit down."

They sat before him, adjusting themselves into the lotus position as well as they could, Urdang easily and perfectly, Mallon less so. He considered it extremely likely that in some deeply positive way he actually was peculiar. Peculiarity of his kind amounted to a great distinction, as the Master understood and poor Urdang did not.

Before them, the great holy man contemplated them in a silence mysteriously shaped by the harsh angles and shining curves of his shaven head and hard, nutlike face. Mallon gathered from the quality of the silence that the yogi was after all not unreservedly pleased by the homage of their visit. Of course the difficult element had to be Urdang—the presence of Urdang in this sacred place. After something like nine or ten minutes, the yogi turned his head to one side and, speaking either to the flowers or the splashing fountain, ordered sweet tea and honey cakes. These delights were delivered by two of the dark-haired girls, who wore beautiful, highly colored saris and sandals with little bells on the straps.

"Is it true that when you came into our village, a carrion crow came toppling dead from the sky?" asked the holy man.

Urdang and Mallon nodded.

"That is a sign, Urdang. We must consider the meaning of this sign."

"Let us do so, then," Urdang said. "I believe the sign to be auspicious. That which eats death is itself devoured by it."

"Yet death comes tumbling into our village."

"Immediately afterward, this young man touched the forehead of a dying child and restored him to good health."

"No one of this young man's age and position can do this," said the yogi. "Such a feat requires great holiness, but even great holiness is not sufficient. One must have spent decades in study and meditation."

"And yet it happened. Death was banished."

"Death is never banished, it merely travels elsewhere. Your student greatly distresses me."

"Dear Master, as the villagers led us toward your house, this man I have brought to you extended one arm and—"

The yogi silenced him with a wave of the hand. "I am not concerned with such displays. Fireworks do not impress me. Yes, they indicate the presence of a gift, but of what use is this gift, to what purposes will it be turned?"

Mallon had touched a dying child, the Master said, yet had he restored it to health? Even if he had, was the healing truly his work? Mere belief could heal as successfully as other forces, temporarily. Was Mallon well schooled in the sutras? How great was his knowledge of Buddhist teachings?

Urdang replied that Mallon was not a Buddhist.

"Then why have you come?"

Mallon spoke from his heart. "I come for your blessing, dear Master."

"You cannot have my blessing. I ask for yours instead." The holy man spoke as if to an ancient enemy.

"My blessing?" Mallon asked.

"Render it unto me as you did to the child."

Confused and irritated, Mallon scooted forward and extended a hand. Almost, he wished to withhold his blessing, as had the yogi, but he could not behave so childishly in front of Urdang. The holy man leaned forward and permitted his brow to be brushed. If any molten particle of energy flew from his hand into the yogi's brain pan, Mallon did not feel its passage.

The Master's face contracted, no mean trick, and for a moment he closed his eyes.

"Well?" Mallon said. Urdang gasped at his rudeness.

"It is very much as I thought," said the Master, opening his eyes. "I cannot be responsible for your Spencer Mallon, and you must not request any more of me. I see it all very clearly. Already, this most peculiar, this most dangerously peculiar man has awakened disorder within our village. He must leave Sankwal immediately, and you who brought him here, Urdang, you must leave with him."

"If that is your wish, Master," Urdang said. "But perhaps—"

"No. No more. You would be wise to separate yourself from this student as soon as you can do so honorably. And as for you, young man . . ."

He turned his sorrowful eyes upon Mallon, and Mallon could feel his spirit hovering near, irate and fearful.

"I advise you to take great, great care in everything you do. But it would be wisest if you did nothing at all."

"Master, why are you afraid of me?" Mallon asked. "I want only to love you." In truth, he had wished to love the Master before he met him. Now, he wanted only to leave the village and its frightened, envious yogi far behind him. And, he realized, if Urdang wanted to leave him, that would be fine, too.

"I am grateful you do not," the Master said. "You will go from my village now, both of you."

When Urdang opened the gates, the lanes were empty. The villagers had fled back to their homes. The air darkened, and rain began to fall. Before they reached open ground, the earth had been churned to mud. A loud cry came from the hut of the poor man with the sick child, whether of joy or pain they could not say.

CATCH AND RELEASE

•

Lawrence Block

WHEN YOU SPENT ENOUGH TIME FISHING, you got so you knew the waters. You had certain spots that had worked for you over the years, and you went to them at certain times of the day in certain seasons of the year. You chose the tackle appropriate to the circumstances, picked the right bait or lure, and tried your luck.

If they weren't biting, you moved on. Picked another spot.

HE WAS CRUISING THE interstate, staying in the right-hand lane, keeping the big SUV a steady five miles an hour below the speed limit. As he passed each exit, he let up on the gas pedal while he kept an eye out for hitch-hikers. There was a string of four exits where they were apt to queue up, college students looking to thumb their way home, or to another campus, or wherever they felt a need to go. There were so many of them, and they were always going someplace, and it hardly mattered where or why.

He drove north, passed four exits, took the fifth, crossed over and got on the southbound entrance ramp. Four more exits, then off again and on again and he was once more heading north.

Taking his time.

There were hitchhikers at each exit, but his foot never touched the brake pedal. It would hover there, but he always saw something that made him drive on. There were plenty of girls out there today, some of them especially alluring in tight jeans and braless T-shirts, but they all seemed to have boys or other girls as companions. The only solitary hitchhikers he saw were male. And he was not interested in boys. He wanted a girl, a girl all by herself.

———

LUKE 5:5. LORD, WE *fished all night and caught nothing.*

Sometimes you could drive all day, and the only reason you'd have to stop was to fill the gas tank. But the true fisherman could fish all night and catch nothing and not regard the time as ill spent. A true fisherman was patient, and while he waited he gave his mind over to the recollection of other days at the water's edge. He'd let himself remember in detail how a particular quarry had risen to the bait and taken the hook. And put up a game fight.

And sizzled in the pan.

WHEN HE STOPPED FOR her, she picked up her backpack and trotted up to the car. He rolled down the window and asked her where she was headed, and she hesitated long enough to have a look at him and decide he was okay. She named a town fifty or sixty miles up the road.

"No problem," he said. "I can just about take you to your front door."

She tossed her pack in the back, then got in front beside him. Closed the door, fastened her seat belt.

She said something about how grateful she was, and he said something appropriate, and he joined the stream of cars heading north. What, he wondered, had she seen in that quick appraising glance? What was it that had assured her he was all right?

His face was an unmemorable one. The features were regular and average and, well, ordinary. Nothing stuck out.

Once, years ago, he'd grown a mustache. He had thought it might give his face some character, but all it did was look out of place. What was it doing there on his lip? He kept it there, waiting to get used to it, and one day he realized that wasn't going to happen, and shaved it off.

And went back to his forgettable face. Unremarkable, unthreatening. Safe.

"A FISHERMAN," SHE SAID. "My dad likes to go fishing. Once, twice a year he'll go away for the weekend with a couple of his buddies and come back with an ice chest full of fish. And my mom gets stuck with cleaning them, and for a week the house totally smells of fish."

"Well, that's a problem I'm spared," he told her. "I'm what they call a catch-and-release fisherman."

"You don't come home with a full ice chest?"

"I don't even have an ice chest. Oh, I used to. But what I found over time was that it was the sport I enjoyed, and it was a lot simpler and easier if the game ended with the fish removed from the hook and slipped gently back into the water."

She was silent for a moment. Then she asked if he thought they enjoyed it.

"The fish? Now that's an interesting question. It's hard to know what a fish does or doesn't enjoy, or even if the word *enjoy* can be applied to a fish. You could make the case that a fish fighting for its life gets to be intensely alive in a way it otherwise doesn't, but is that good or bad from the fish's point of view?" He smiled. "When they swim away," he said, "I get the sense that they're glad to be alive. But I may just be trying to put myself in their position. I can't really know what it's like for them."

"I guess not."

"One thing I can't help but wonder," he said, "is if they learn anything from the experience. Are they warier the next time around? Or will they take the hook just as readily for the next fisherman who comes along?"

She thought about it. "I guess they're just fish," she said.

"Well now," he said. "I guess they are."

SHE WAS A PRETTY THING. A business major, she told him, taking most of her elective courses in English because she'd always like to read. Her hair was brown with auburn highlights, and she had a good figure, with large breasts and wide hips. Built for childbearing, he thought, and she'd bear three or four of them, and she'd gain weight with each pregnancy and never quite manage to lose all of it. And her face, already a little chubby, would broaden and turn bovine, and the sparkle would fade out of her eyes.

There was a time when he'd have been inclined to spare her all that.

"REALLY," SHE SAID, "YOU could have just dropped me at the exit. I mean, this is taking you way out of your way."

"Less so than you'd think. Is that your street coming up?"

"Uh-huh. If you want to drop me at the corner—"

But he drove her to the door of her suburban house. He waited while she retrieved her backpack, then let her get halfway up the path to her door before he called her back.

"You know," he said, "I was going to ask you something earlier, but I didn't want to upset you."

"Oh?"

"Aren't you nervous hitching rides with strangers? Don't you think it's dangerous?"

"Oh," she said. "Well, you know, everybody does it."

"I see."

"And I've always been okay so far."

"A young woman alone—"

"Well, I usually team up with somebody. A boy, or at least another girl. But this time, well . . ."

"You figured you'd take a chance."

She flashed a smile. "It worked out okay, didn't it?"

He was silent for a moment, but held her with his eyes. Then he said, "Remember the fish we were talking about?"

"The fish?"

"How it feels when it slips back into the water. And whether it learns anything from the experience."

"I don't understand."

"Not everyone is a catch-and-release fisherman," he said. "That's probably something you ought to keep in mind."

She was still standing there, looking puzzled, while he put the SUV in gear and pulled away.

HE DROVE HOME, FEELING fulfilled. He had never moved from the house he was born in, and it had been his alone ever since his mother's death ten years ago.

He checked the mail, which yielded half a dozen envelopes with checks in them. He had a mail-order business, selling fishing lures, and he spent the better part of an hour preparing the checks for deposit and packing the orders for shipment. He'd make more money if he put his business online and let people pay with credit cards, but he didn't need much money, and he found it easier to let things remain as they were. He ran the same ads every month in the same magazines, and his old customers reordered, and enough new customers turned up to keep him going.

He cooked some pasta, heated some meat sauce, chopped some lettuce for a salad, drizzled a little olive oil over it. He ate at the kitchen table, washed the dishes, watched the TV news. When it ended he left the picture on but muted the sound, and thought about the girl.

Now, though, he gave himself over to the fantasy she inspired. A lonely road. A piece of tape across her mouth. A struggle ending with her arms broken.

Stripping her. Piercing each of her openings in turn. Giving her physical pain to keep her terror company.

And finishing her with a knife. No, with his hands, strangling her. No, better yet, with his forearm across her throat, and his weight pressing down, throttling her.

Ah, the joy of it, the thrill of it, the sweet release of it. And now it was almost as real to him as if it had happened.

But it hadn't happened. He'd left her at her door, untouched, with only a hint of what might have been. And, because it hadn't happened, there was no ice chest full of fish to clean——no body to dispose of, no evidence to get rid of, not even that feeling of regret that had undercut his pleasure on so many otherwise perfect occasions.

Catch and release. That was the ticket, catch and release.

THE ROADHOUSE HAD A name, Toddle Inn, but nobody ever called it anything but Roy's, after the man who'd owned it for close to fifty years until his liver quit on him.

That was something he would probably never have to worry about, as he'd never been much of a drinker. Tonight, three days after he'd dropped the young hitchhiker at her door, he'd had the impulse to go barhopping, and Roy's was his fourth stop. He'd ordered a beer at the first place and drank two sips of it, left the second bar without ordering anything, and drank most of the Coke he ordered at bar number three.

Roy's had beer on draft, and he stood at the bar and ordered a glass of it. There was an English song he'd heard once, of which he recalled only one verse:

The man who buys a pint of beer
Gets half a pint of water;
The only thing the landlord's got
That's any good's his daughter.

The beer was watery, to be sure, but it didn't matter because he didn't care about beer, good or bad. But the bar held something to interest him, the very thing he'd come out for.

She was two stools away from him, and she was drinking something in a stemmed glass, with an orange slice in it. At first glance she looked like the hitchhiker, or like her older sister, the one who'd gone wrong. Her blouse was a size too small, and she'd tried to cope by unbuttoning an extra button. The lipstick was smeared on her full-lipped mouth, and her nail polish was chipped.

She picked up her drink and was surprised to find that she'd finished it. She shook her head, as if wondering how to contend with this unantici-pated development, and while she was working it out he lifted a hand to catch the barman's eye, then pointed at the girl's empty glass.

She waited until the fresh drink was in front of her, then picked it up and turned toward her benefactor. "Thank you," she said, "you're a gentle-man."

He closed the distance between them. "And a fisherman," he said.

SOMETIMES IT DIDN'T MATTER what you had on your hook. Sometimes it wasn't even necessary to wet a line. Sometimes all you had to do was sit there and they'd jump right into the boat.

She'd had several drinks before the one he'd bought her, and she didn't really need the two others he bought her after that. But she thought she did, and he didn't mind spending the money or sitting there while she drank them.

Her name, she told him repeatedly, was Marni. He was in no danger of forgetting that fact, nor did she seem to be in any danger of remembering his name, which she kept asking him over and over. He'd said it was Jack— it wasn't—and she kept apologizing for her inability to retain that informa-tion. "I'm Marni," she'd say on each occasion. "With an *i*," she added, more often than not.

He found himself remembering a woman he'd picked up years ago in a bar with much the same ambience. She'd been a very different sort of drunk, although she'd been punishing the Harvey Wallbangers as industriously as Marni was knocking back the gandy dancers. She'd grown quieter and quieter, and her eyes went glassy, and by the time he'd driven them to the place he'd selected in advance, she was out cold. He'd had some very interesting plans for her, and here she was, the next thing to comatose, and wholly incapable of knowing what was being done to her.

So he'd let himself imagine that she was dead, and took her that way, and kept waiting for her to wake up, but she didn't. And it was exciting, more exciting than he'd have guessed, but at the end he held himself back.

And paused for a moment to consider the situation, and then very deliberately broke her neck. And then took her again, imagining that she was only sleeping.

And that was good, too.

"AT LEAST I GOT the house," she was saying. "My ex took the kids away from me, can you imagine that? Got some lawyer saying I was an unfit mother. Can you imagine that?"

The house her ex-husband had let her keep certainly looked like a drunk lived in it. It wasn't filthy, just remarkably untidy. She grabbed him by the hand and led him up a flight of stairs and into her bedroom, which was no neater than the rest of the place, then turned and threw herself into his arms.

He disengaged, and she seemed puzzled. He asked if there was anything in the house to drink, and she said there was beer in the fridge, and there might be some vodka in the freezer. He said he'd be right back.

He gave her five minutes, and when he returned with a can of Rolling Rock and a half-pint of vodka, she was sprawled naked on her back, snoring. He set the beer can and the vodka bottle on the bedside table, and drew the blanket to cover her.

"Catch and release," he said, and left her there.

FISHING WAS NOT JUST a metaphor. A couple of days later he walked out his front door into a cool autumn morning. The sky was overcast, the humidity lower than it had been. The breeze was out of the west.

It was just the day for it. He got his gear together, made his choices, and drove to the bank of a creek that was always good on this kind of day. He fished the spot for an hour, and by the time he left he had hooked and landed three trout. Each had put up a good fight, and as he released them he might have observed that they'd earned their freedom, that each deserved another chance at life.

But what did that mean, really? Could a fish be said to earn or deserve anything? Could anyone? And did a desperate effort to remain alive somehow entitle one to live?

Consider the humble flounder. He was a saltwater fish, a bottom fish, and when you hooked him he rarely did much more than flop around a little while you reeled him in. Did this make him the trout's moral inferior? Did he have less right to live because of his genetically prescribed behavior?

He stopped on the way home, had a hamburger and a side of well-done fries. Drank a cup of coffee. Read the paper.

Back home, he cleaned and sorted his tackle and put everything away where it belonged.

THAT NIGHT IT RAINED, and did so off and on for the next three days. He stayed close to home, watched a little television.

Nights, he'd lean back in his recliner and close his eyes, letting himself remember. Once, a few months back, he'd tried to count. He'd been doing this for years, long before his mother died, and in the early years his appetite had been ravenous. It was, he sometimes thought, a miracle he hadn't been caught. Back then he'd left DNA all over the place, along with God knew what else in the way of trace evidence.

Somehow he'd gotten away with it. If they'd ever picked him up, if he'd ever attracted the slightest bit of official attention, he was sure he'd have caved immediately. He'd have told them everything, confessed to everything. They wouldn't have needed trace evidence, let alone DNA. All they'd have needed was a cell to lock him into and a key to throw away.

So there had been many, but he'd ranged far and wide and little of what he did ran to pattern. He'd read about other men who had very specific tastes, in essence always hunting the same woman and killing her in the same fashion. If anything, he'd deliberately sought variety, not for precautionary reasons but because it was indeed the spice of life—or death, as you prefer. *When I have to choose between two evils,* Mae West had said, *I pick the one I haven't tried yet.* Made sense to him.

And after he'd changed, after he had in fact become a catch-and-release fisherman, there'd been a point when it seemed to him as though he'd had a divine hand keeping him safe all those years. Who was to say that there was not a purpose to it all, and a guiding force running the universe? He'd been spared so that he could—do what? Catch and release?

It hadn't taken him long to decide that was nonsense. He'd killed all those girls because he'd wanted to—or needed to, whatever. And he'd stopped killing because he no longer needed or wanted to kill, was in fact better served by, well, catching and releasing.

So how many had there been? The simple answer was that he did not know, and had no way of knowing. He had never taken trophies, never kept souvenirs. He had memories, but it had become virtually impossible to distinguish between recollections of actual events and recollections of fantasies. One memory was as real as another, whether it had happened or not. And, really, what difference did it make?

He thought of that serial killer they'd caught in Texas, the idiot who kept finding new killings to confess to and leading the authorities to more unmarked graves. Except some of the victims turned out to have been killed when he was in custody in another state. Was he conning them, for some inexplicable reason? Or was he simply remembering—vividly, and in detail—acts he had not in actuality committed?

HE DIDN'T MIND THE rain. His had been a solitary childhood, and he'd grown into a solitary adult. He had never had friends, and had never felt the need. Sometimes he liked the illusion of society, and at such times he would go to a bar or restaurant, or walk in a shopping mall, or sit in a movie theater, simply to be among strangers. But most of the time his own company was company enough.

One rainy afternoon he picked a book from the shelf. It was *The Compleat Angler,* by Izaak Walton, and he'd read it through countless times and flipped through it many times more. He always seemed to find something worth thinking about between its covers.

God never did make a more calm, quiet, innocent recreation than angling, he read. The line resonated with him, as it always did, and he decided the only change he could make would be to the final word of it. He preferred fishing to angling, fisherman to angler. Stephen Leacock, after all, had observed that angling was the name given to fishing by people who couldn't fish.

On the first clear day, he made a grocery list and went to the mall. He pushed a cart up one aisle and down the next, picking up eggs and bacon and pasta and canned sauce, and he was weighing the merits of two brands of laundry detergent when he saw the woman.

He hadn't been looking for her, hadn't been looking for anyone. The only thing on his mind was detergent and fabric softener, and then he looked up and there she was.

She was beautiful, not young-pretty like the hitchhiker or slutty-available like Marni the barfly, but genuinely beautiful. She could have been an actress or a model, though he somehow knew she wasn't.

Long dark hair, long legs, a figure that was at once athletic and womanly. An oval face, a strong nose, high cheekbones. But it wasn't her beauty he found himself responding to, it was something else, some indefinable quality that suddenly rendered the Tide and the Downy, indeed all the contents of his shopping cart, entirely unimportant.

She was wearing slacks and an unbuttoned long-sleeved canvas shirt over a pale blue T-shirt, and there was nothing terribly provocative about her outfit, but it scarcely mattered what she wore. He saw that she had a long shopping list she consulted, and only a few items already in her cart. He had time, he decided, time enough to wheel his cart to the bank of cashiers and pay cash for his groceries. That was better than simply walking away from the cart. People tended to remember you when you did that.

He loaded the bags of groceries back into his cart, and on the way to his SUV he turned periodically for a look at the entrance. He stowed the bags in back, got behind the wheel, and found a good spot to wait for her.

He sat there patiently with the motor idling. He wasn't paying attention to the time, was scarcely conscious of its passage, but felt he'd be comfortable waiting forever for the doors to slide open and the woman to emerge. The impatient man was not meant for fishing, and indeed waiting, patient passive waiting, was part of the pleasure of the pastime. If you got a bite every time your hook broke the water's surface, if you hauled up one fish after another, why, where was the joy? Might as well drag a net. Hell, might as well toss a grenade into a trout stream and scoop up what floated to the surface.

Ah. There she was.

"I'M A FISHERMAN," HE SAID.

These were not the first words he spoke to her. Those were, "Let me give you a hand." He'd pulled up behind her just as she was about to put her groceries into the trunk of her car, and hopped out and offered his help. She smiled, and was about to thank him, but she never had the chance. He had a flashlight in one hand, three C batteries in a hard rubber case, and he took her by the shoulder and swung her around and hit her hard on the back of the head. He caught her as she fell, eased her down gently.

In no time at all she was propped up in the passenger seat of his SUV, and her groceries were in her trunk and the lid slammed shut. She was out cold, and for a moment he thought he might have struck too hard a blow, but he checked and found she had a pulse. He used duct tape on her wrists and ankles and across her mouth, fastened her seat belt, and drove off with her.

And, as patiently as he'd waited for her to emerge from the supermarket, he waited for her to return to consciousness. *I'm a fisherman,* he thought, and waited for the chance to say the words. He kept his eyes on the road ahead, but from time to time he shot her a glance, and her appearance never changed. Her eyes were shut, her muscles slack.

Then, not long after he'd turned onto a secondary road, he sensed that she was awake. He looked at her, and she looked the same, but he could somehow detect a change. He gave her another moment to listen to the silence, and then he spoke, told her that he was a fisherman.

No reaction from her. But he was certain she'd heard him.

"A catch-and-release fisherman," he said. "Not everybody knows what that means. See, I enjoy fishing. It does something for me that nothing else has ever done. Call it a sport or a pastime, as you prefer, but it's what I do and what I've always done."

He thought about that. What he'd always done? Well, just about. Some of his earliest childhood memories involved fishing with a bamboo pole and baiting his hook with worms he'd dug himself in the backyard. And some of his earliest and most enduring adult memories involved fishing of another sort.

"Now I wasn't always a catch-and release fisherman," he said. "Way I saw it back in the day, why would a man go to all the trouble of catching a fish and then just throw it back? Way it looked to me, you catch something, you kill it. You kill something, you eat it. Pretty clear cut, wouldn't you say?"

Wouldn't you say? But she wouldn't say anything, couldn't say anything, not with the duct tape over her mouth. He saw, though, that she'd given up the pretense of unconsciousness. Her eyes were open now, although he couldn't see what expression they may have held.

"What happened," he said, "is I lost the taste for it. The killing and all. Most people, they think of fishing, and they somehow manage not to think about killing. They seem to think the fish comes out of the water, gulps for air a couple of times, and then obligingly gives up the ghost. Maybe he flops around a little first, but that's all there is to it. But, see, it's not like that. A fish can live longer out of water than you'd think. What you have to do, you gaff it. Hit it in the head with a club. It's quick and easy, but you can't get around the fact that you're killing it."

He went on, telling her how you were spared the chore of killing when you released your catch. And the other unpleasant chores, the gutting, the scaling, the disposal of offal.

He turned from a blacktop road to a dirt road. He hadn't been down this road in quite a while, but it was as he remembered it, a quiet path through the woods that led to a spot he'd always liked. He quit talking now, letting her think about what he'd said, letting her figure out what to make of it, and he didn't speak again until he'd parked the car in a copse of trees, where it couldn't be seen from the road.

"I have to tell you," he said, unfastening her seat belt, wrestling her out of the car. "I enjoy life a lot more as a catch-and-release fisherman. It's got all the pleasure of fishing without the downside, you know?"

He arranged her on the ground on her back. He went back for a tire iron, and smashed both her kneecaps before untaping her ankles, but left the tape on her wrists and across her mouth.

He cut her clothing off her. Then he took off his own clothes and folded them neatly. Adam and Eve in the garden, he thought. Naked and unashamed. *Lord, we fished all night and caught nothing.*

He fell on her.

BACK HOME, HE LOADED his clothes into the washing machine, then drew a bath for himself. But he didn't get into the tub right away. He had her scent on him, and found himself in no hurry to wash it off. Better to be able to breathe it in while he relived the experience, all of it, from the first sight of her in the supermarket to the snapped-twig sound of her neck when he broke it.

And he remembered as well the first time he'd departed from the catch-and-release pattern. It had been less impulsive that time, he'd thought long and hard about it, and when the right girl turned up—young, blond, a cheerleader type, with a turned-up nose and a beauty mark on one cheek—when she turned up, he was ready.

Afterward he'd been upset with himself. Was he regressing? Had he been untrue to the code he'd adopted? But it hadn't taken him long to get past those thoughts, and this time he felt nothing but calm satisfaction.

He was still a catch-and-release fisherman. He probably always would be. But, for God's sake, that didn't make him a vegetarian, did it?

Hell, no. A man still had to have a square meal now and then.

POLKA DOTS AND MOONBEAMS

•

Jeffrey Ford

HE CAME FOR HER AT SEVEN in the Belvedere convertible, top down, emerald green, with those fins in the back, jutting up like goalposts. From her third-floor apartment window, she saw him pull to the curb out front.

"Hey, Dex," she called, "where'd you get the submarine?"

He tilted back his homburg and looked up. "All hands on deck, baby," he said, patting the white leather seat.

"Give me a minute," she said, laughed, and then blew him a kiss. She walked across the blue braided rug of the parlor and into the small bathroom with the water-stained ceiling and cracked plaster. Standing before the mirror, she leaned in close to check her makeup—enough rouge and powder to repair the walls. Her eye shadow was peacock blue, her mascara indigo. She gave her girdle a quick adjustment through her dress, then smoothed the material and stepped back to take it all in. Wrapped in strapless black, with a design of small white polka dots, like stars in a perfect universe, she turned in profile and inhaled. "Good Christ," she said and exhaled. Passing through the kitchenette, she lifted a silver flask from the scarred tabletop and shoved it into her handbag.

Her heels made a racket on the wooden steps, and she wobbled for balance just after the first landing. Pushing through the front door, she stepped out into the evening light and the first cool breeze in what seemed an eternity. Dex was waiting for her at the curb, holding the passenger door open. As she approached, he tipped his hat and bent slightly at the waist.

"Looking fine there, madam," he said.

She stopped to kiss his cheek.

The streets were empty, not a soul on the sidewalk, and save for the fact that here and there in a few of the windows of the tall, crumbling buildings they passed a dim yellow light could be seen, the entire city seemed empty as well. Dex turned left on Kraft and headed out of town.

"It's been too long, Adeline," he said.

"Hush now, sugar," she told him. "Let's not think about that. I want you to tell me where you're taking me tonight."

"I'll take you where I can get you," he said.

She slapped his shoulder.

"I want a few cocktails," she said.

"Of course, baby, of course. I thought we'd head over to the Ice Garden, cut the rug, have a few, and then head out into the desert after midnight to watch the stars fall."

"You're an ace," she said and leaned forward to turn on the radio. A smoldering sax rendition of "Every Time We Say Goodbye," like a ball of wax string unwinding, looped once around their necks and then blew away on the rushing wind.

She lit them each a cigarette as the car sailed on through the rising night. An armadillo scuttled through the beams of the headlights fifty yards ahead, and the aroma of sage vied with Adeline's orchid scent. Clamping his cigarette between his lips, Dex put his free hand on her knee. She took it into her own, twining fingers with him. Then it was dark, the asphalt turning to dirt, and the moon rose slow as a bubble in honey above the distant silhouette of hills; a cosmic cream pie of a face, eyeing Adeline's décolletage. She leaned back into the seat, smiling, and closed her eyes. Only a moment passed before she opened them, but they were already there, passing down the long avenue lined with monkey-puzzle trees toward the circular drive of the glimmering Ice Garden. Dex pulled up and parked at the entrance. As he was getting out, a kid with red hair and freckles, dressed in a valet uniform, stepped forward.

"Mr. Dex," he said, "we haven't seen you for a while."

"Take a picture, Jim-Jim," said Dex and flipped a silver dollar in the air. The kid caught it and dropped it into his vest pocket before opening the door for Adeline.

"How's tricks, Jim?" she asked as he delivered her to the curb.

"They just got better," he said and patted his vest.

Dex came around the back of the car, took his date by the arm, and together they headed past the huge potted palms and down a brief tunnel toward a large rectangular patio open to the desert sky and bounded by a lush garden of the most magnificent crystal flora, emitting a blizzard of reflection. At the edge of the high-arching portico, Dex and Adeline stood for a moment, scanning the hubbub of revelers and, at the other end of the expanse of tables and chairs and dance floor, the onstage antics of that night's musical act, Nabob and His Ne'er-do-wells. Above the sea of heads, chrome trombone in one hand, mic in the other, Nabob belted out a jazzed-up version of "Weak Knees and Wet Privates."

A fellow in white tux and red fez approached the couple. He was a plump little man with a pencil mustache; a fifty-year-old baby playing dress-up. Dex removed his homburg and reached a hand out. "Mondrian," he said.

The maitre d' bowed slightly and, raising his voice above the din of merriment, said, "Always a pleasure to have you both back."

Adeline also shook hands.

"You're looking particularly lovely tonight," he said.

"Table for two," said Dex and flashed a crisp twenty under the nose of Mondrian. "Something close to the dance floor."

The plump man bowed again and in his ascent snatched the bill from Dex's hand. "Follow me, my friends," he said, and then turned and made his way slowly in amid the maze of tables and the milling crowd. As they moved through the packed house, Adeline waved hello to those who called her name, and when someone shouted to Dex, he winked, sighted them with his thumb, and pulled an invisible trigger. Mondrian found them a spot at the very front, just to the left of the stage. He pulled out and held Adeline's chair, and once she was seated, he bowed.

"Two gin wrinkles," said Dex, and in an instant the maitre d' vanished back into the crowd.

Adeline retrieved two cigarettes from her purse and lit them on the small candle at the center of the table. Dex leaned over and she put one between his lips. She drew on the other.

"How does it feel to be back in action?" he asked her.

She smiled broadly, blew a stream of smoke, and nodded. "It always feels right, the first couple of hours on the loose. I'm not thinking about anything else at this moment," she said.

"Good," he said and removed his hat, setting it on the empty chair next to him.

The music stopped then and was replaced by the chatter and laughter of the crowd, the clink of glasses and silverware. Nabob jumped down from the band platform, hit the ground, and rolled forward to spring upright next to Dex.

"Dexter," he said.

"Still sweating out the hits," said Dex and laughed as he shook hands with the bandleader.

"Bobby, aren't you gonna give me a kiss?" said Adeline.

"I'm just savoring the prospect," he said and swept down to plant one on her lips. The kiss lasted for a while before Dex reached his leg around the table and kicked the performer in the ass. They all laughed as Nabob moved around the table and took a seat.

Folding his willowy arms in front of him, the bandleader leaned forward and shook his thin head. "You two out for the stars tonight?" he asked.

"And then some," said Adeline.

"So fill me in," said Dex.

"Well, same old same old as usual, you know. And Killheffer's been waiting for you to return."

A waitress appeared with two gin wrinkles—liquid pink ice and the Garden's own bathtub blend of gin. The glasses caught the light and revealed tiny bubbles rising from a fat red cherry. Dex slipped the young woman a five. She smiled at him before leaving the table.

"Fuck Killheffer," said Dex, lifting his drink to touch glasses with Adeline.

"He's been in here almost every night, sitting back in the corner, slapping beads on that abacus of his and jotting numbers in a book," said Nabob.

"Killheffer's solid fruitcake," said Adeline.

"A strange fellow," said Nabob, nodding. "One slow night a while back, and most nights are slow when you fine folks aren't here, he bought me a drink and explained to me how the world is made of numbers. He said that when the stars fall it means everything is being divided by itself. Then he blew a smoke ring off one of his cigars. 'Like that,' he said and pointed at the center."

"Did you get it?" asked Adeline.

Nabob laughed and shook his head. "Jim-Jim makes more sense."

"If he shows that shit-eating grin in here tonight, I'll fluff his cheeks," said Dex.

Adeline took a drag of her cigarette and smiled. "Sounds like boy fun. I thought you were here to dance and drink."

"I am, baby. I am," said Dex and finished the rest of his wrinkle, grabbing the cherry stem between his teeth. When he brought the glass away, the fruit hung down in front of his mouth. Adeline leaned over, put one arm around his shoulder and her lips around the cherry. She ate it slowly, chewing with only her lips before it all became a long kiss.

When they finished, Nabob said, "You're an artist, Miss Adeline."

Dex ordered another round of wrinkles. They talked for a few minutes about the old days, distant memories of bright sun and blue skies.

"Break's over," said Nabob, quickly killing the rest of his drink. "You two be good."

"Do 'Name and Number,'" called Adeline as the bandleader bounded toward the stage. With a running start, he leaped into the air, did a somersault, and landed, kneeling next to his mic stand. He stood slowly, like a vine twining up a trellis.

Dex and Adeline applauded, as did the rest of the house when it saw the performer back onstage. The willowy singer danced with himself for a moment before grabbing the mic. The Ne'er-do-wells took their places and lifted their instruments.

"Mondrian, my good man. Turn that gas wheel and lower the lights," said Nabob, his voice echoing through the garden and out into the desert.

A moment later the flames of the candles in the center of each table went dimmer by half. "Ooooh," said Nabob and the crowd applauded.

"Lower," he called to the maitre d'.

Mondrian complied. Whistles and catcalls rose out of the dull amber glow of the Ice Garden. The baritone sax hit a note so low it was like a tumbleweed blowing in off the desert. Then the strings came up, there was a flourish of piccolo and three sliding notes from Nabob's chrome T-bone. He brought the mouthpiece away, snapped his fingers to the music, and sang:

"My dear, you tear my heart asunder
When I look up your name and number
Right there in that open book
My flesh begins to cook
It's all sweetness mixed with dread

And then you close your legs around my head
As I look up your name and number . . ."

As Nabob dipped into the second verse, Dex rose and held his hand out to Adeline. He guided her through the darkness to the sea of swaying couples. They clutched each other desperately, legs between legs, lips locked, slowly turning through the dark. Within the deep pool of dancers there were currents of movement that could not be denied. They let themselves be drawn by the inevitable flow as the music played on.

When the song ended, Adeline said, "I have to hit the powder room."

They left the dance floor as the lights came up and walked toward the huge structure that held the casino, the gaming rooms, the pleasure parlors of the Ice Garden. Three stories tall, in the style of a Venetian palace, it was a monster of shadows with moonlight in its eyes. At the portico that led inside, Dex handed her a twenty and said, "I'll see you back at the table."

"I know," she barely managed and kissed him on the cheek.

"You okay?" he asked.

"Same old same old," she said and sighed.

He was supposed to laugh but only managed a smile. They turned away from each other. As he skirted the dance floor on the return journey, Dex looked up at Nabob and saw the performer, midsong, flash a glance at him and then nod toward the table. There was Killheffer, sporting a tux and his so-called smile of a hundred teeth, smoking a Wrath Majestic and staring into the sky.

Arriving at the table, Dex took his seat across from Killheffer, who, still peering upward, said, "Gin wrinkles, I presumed."

Dex noticed the fresh round of drinks, and reached for his.

"The stars are excited tonight," said Killheffer, lowering his gaze.

"Too bad I'm not," said Dex. "What's it gonna be this time, Professor? Russian roulette? One card drawn from the bottom of a deck cut three ways? The blindfolded knife thrower?"

"You love to recall my miscalculations," said Killheffer. "Time breaks down, though, only through repetition."

"I'm fed up with your cockeyed bullshit."

"Well, don't be, because I tell you I've got it. I've done the math. How badly do you want out?"

"Want out?" said Dex. "I don't even know how I got in. Tell me again you're not the devil."

"I'm a simple professor of circumstance and fate. An academic with too strong an imagination."

"Then why that crazy smile? All your antics? That cigar of yours smells like what I vaguely remember of the ocean."

"I've always been a gregarious fellow and prized a good cigar. The hundred-tooth thing is a parlor trick of multiplication."

"I'm so fucking tired," Dex said.

Killheffer reached into his jacket pocket and brought forth a hypodermic needle. He laid it on the table. "That's the solution," he said.

The large hypo's glass syringe contained a jade green liquid.

Dex stared at it and shook his head. Tears appeared in the corners of his eyes. "Are you kidding? That's it? That's the saddest fucking thing I've ever seen."

"You have to trust me," said Killheffer, still smiling.

"If you haven't noticed, we're here again. What is it? Poison? Cough syrup? Junk?"

"My own special mixture of oblivion; a distillation of equations for free will. I call it 'Laughter in the Dark,'" said the professor, proudly smoothing back his slick black hair.

Dex couldn't help but smile. "You're a malicious crackpot, but okay, let's get on with it. What's the deal this time?"

"Mondrian is, right at this moment, upstairs, on the third floor, in Sizzle Parlor number four, awaiting a female associate of mine who has promised him exotic favors, but unfortunately will never deliver. Instead, you will arrive. I want him dead." Killheffer hurriedly tamped out his cigar and snapped his fingers to the passing cigarette girl. She stopped next to Dex and opened the case that hung by a strap around her shoulders. There were no cigarettes, just something covered by a handkerchief.

"You think of everything," said Dex and reached in to grab the gun. He stood and slipped it into the waist of his pants. "How do I collect?"

"The cure will be delivered before the night is through," said the professor. "Hurry, Mondrian can only forgo his beloved tips for so long."

"What do you have against him?" Dex asked as he lifted his hat off the chair beside him.

"He's a computational loop," said Killheffer. "A real zero-sum game."

At the head of the long, dark hallway on the third floor of the pavilion, Dex was stopped by the night man, an imposing fellow with a bald head and a sawed-off shotgun in his left hand.

"What's news, Jeminy?" said Dex.

"Obviously, you are, Dex. Looking for a room?"

He nodded.

"Ten dollars. But for you, for old times' sake, ten dollars," said Jeminy and laughed.

"You're too good to me," said Dex, a ten spot appearing in his hand. "The lady'll be along any minute."

"Sizzle Parlor number five," the big man said, his voice echoing down the long hall. "Grease that griddle, my friend."

"Will do," said Dex and before long slowed his pace and looked over his shoulder to check that Jeminy had again taken his seat facing away, toward the stairwell. He passed door after door, and after every six a weak gas lamp glowed on either wall. As he neared parlor number four, he noticed the door was open a sliver, but it was dark inside. Brandishing the gun, he held it straight up in front of him.

Opening the door, he slipped inside, and shut it quietly behind him. Moonlight shone in through one tall, arched window, but Dex could only make out shadows. He scanned the room, and slowly the forms of chairs, a coffee table, a vanity, and, off to the side of the room, a bed became evident to him. Sitting up on the edge of that bed was a lumpen silhouette, atop it, the telltale shape of the fez.

"Is it you, my desert flower?" came the voice of Mondrian.

Dex swiftly crossed the room. When he was next to the figure, and had surmised where his victim's left temple might be, he cocked the gun's hammer with his thumb and wrapped his index finger around the trigger. Before he could squeeze off the shot, though, the slouched bag of shadow that was Mondrian lunged into him with terrific force. Dex, utterly surprised that the meek little fellow would have the gumption to attack, fell backward, tripping on the rug, the gun flying off into the dark. He tried to get to his feet, but the maitre d' landed on him like nine sandbags, one hand grabbing his throat. No matter how many times Dex managed a punch to Mondrian's face, the shadow of the fez never toppled away. They rolled over and over and then partially into the moonlight. Dex saw the flash of a blade above him, but his arms were now pinned by his assailant's knees. Unable to halt the knife's descent, he held his breath in preparation for pain. Then the lights went on, there was a gunshot, and his attacker fell off him.

Dex scrabbled to his feet and turned to find Adeline, standing next to the open door, the muzzle of the gun still smoking. From down the hall, he heard Jeminy blow his whistle, an alert to the Ice Garden's force of leg breakers.

"Nice shot, baby," he said. "Kill the lights and close the door."

She closed the door behind her, but didn't flip the switch. "Look," she said to Dex, pointing with the gun at the floor behind him. He turned and saw the hundred-tooth smile of Killheffer. The fez was secured around the professor's chin by a rubber band. A bullet had left a gaping third eye in his forehead.

"The rat fuck," said Dex. He leaned over, grabbed his hat where it had fallen, and then felt through Killheffer's jacket pockets. All he came up with was a cigar tube, holding a single Wrath Majestic. He slipped it into his inside jacket pocket.

"They're coming," said Adeline. She hit the lights. There was the sound of running feet and voices in the hallway. "They're going door-to-door."

"We'll shoot our way out," said Dex.

Adeline was next to him. She whispered in his ear, "Don't be a jackass, we'll take the fire escape."

Dex moved toward the window. Adeline slipped off her heels.

Somehow Mondrian had known to call the car up, because when Dex and Adeline arrived in front of the Ice Garden, breathless, scuff marks on their clothes, the Belvedere was there, top down and running, Jim-Jim holding Adeline's door.

"I like your shoes," said the boy, pointing to her bare feet.

"My new fashion, Jim," said Adeline.

Dex moved quickly around the car. Mondrian was there to open the door for him. As Dex slid in behind the wheel, he said, "No hard feelings about tonight," and flashed a tip to cover the intended homicide. Mondrian bowed slightly and snatched the bill.

"Ever at your service," said the maitre d'. "Safe journey." He shut the car door.

Dex took a silver dollar out of his pocket, hit the gas, and flipped the coin back over the car. Jim-Jim caught it and before he could stash it in his vest pocket, the Belvedere was no more than two red dots halfway down the avenue of monkey-puzzle trees.

"My feet are killing me," said Adeline as they screeched out of the entrance to the Ice Garden and onto the desert highway.

"You are one hell of a shot," he said.

"Lucky," she said, her voice rising above the wind.

"I'll cherish the moment."

"All well and good," said Adeline, "but what's his game this time?"

"Laughter in the dark," said Dex and cut the wheel hard to the right. Adeline slid toward him and he wrapped his arm around her shoulders. The car left the road and raced along an avenue of moonlight, plowing through tumbleweeds, trailing a plume of dust across the desert. Adeline switched on the radio and found Dete Walader, crooning "I Remember You."

They lay on a blanket beneath shimmering stars. A light breeze blew over them. Here and there, the dark form of a cactus stood sentry. Ten yards away, the radio in the Belvedere played something with strings. Adeline took a sip from her silver flask and handed it to Dex. He flicked the butt of the Majestic off into the sand, and took a drink.

"What is this stuff?" he asked, squinting.

"My own special mixture of oblivion," she said.

"That's Killheffer's line," he said. "Did you see him tonight?"

She nodded and laid her cheek against his chest. "In the ladies' room; he was in the stall next to the one I chose, waiting for me."

"He gets around," said Dex, "'cause he was at our table when I got back to it."

"He whispered from the other stall that he wanted me to kill Mondrian. I said I wouldn't, but then he said he had the solution and was willing to trade me for the murder. I told him I wanted to see it. The next thing, the door to my stall flew open and he was standing there. I almost screamed. I didn't know what to do. I was on the toilet, for criminy sake. He had that stupid smile on his face, and he pulled down his zipper."

Dex rose to one elbow. "I'll kill him," he said.

"Too late," said Adeline. "He reached into his pants and pulled out this big hypodermic needle with green juice in it. He said, 'You see the tip at the end of that needle? Think of that as the period at the end of your interminable story. Do you want out?' I just wanted to get rid of him, so I nodded. He handed me a gun and told me Mondrian was in Sizzle Parlor number four."

A long time passed in silence.

"But, in the end, you decided to off Mondrian?" said Dex.

"I guess so," said Adeline. "What else is there to do when we come to the Ice Garden but fall in with Killheffer's scheme? Mondrian might as well be made of papier-mâché and that's the long and short of it. He's polite, but, sure, I'd clip him for the possibility of a ticket out."

"I'd miss you," said Dex.

"I wouldn't leave you here alone," she said. "I was getting the needle for you."

"You didn't think of using it yourself? Baby, I'm touched."

"Well, maybe once when I realized that if it worked, you wouldn't come for me anymore and I'd spend each go-round in that crappy apartment building back in dragsville watching the plaster crack."

"I was ready to blow Mondrian's brains out for you too," he said. "I can see how stale it's getting for you."

"You never thought of yourself?" she asked.

Dex sat up and pointed into the distance at a pair of headlights. "Let's get the guns," he said. He stood and helped her up. She found her underwear a few feet away and slipped them back on.

"Who do you think it is?" she asked, joining him at the car.

He handed her a pistol. "Ice Garden thugs," he said.

When the approaching car came to a halt a few feet from the blanket, Dex reached over the side of the Belvedere and hit the lights, to reveal a very old black car, more like a covered carriage with a steering wheel and no horse. The door opened and out stepped Mondrian. He carried an open umbrella and a small box. Taking three furtive steps forward, he called out, "Mr. Dexter."

"Expecting rain, Mondrian?" said Dex.

"Stars, sir. Stars."

Adeline laughed from where she was crouched behind the Belvedere.

"A package for the lady and gentleman," said Mondrian.

"Set it down at your feet, right there, and then you can go," said Dex.

Mondrian set the package on the sand, but remained standing at attention over it.

"What are you waiting for?" asked Dex.

Mondrian was silent, but Adeline whispered, "He wants a tip."

Dex fired two shots into the umbrella. "Keep the change," he called.

Mondrian bowed, said, "Most generous, sir," and then got back in the car. As the maitre d' pulled away, Adeline retrieved the package. Dex met her back on the blanket where she sat with the box, an eight-inch cube wrapped in silver paper and a red bow, like a birthday present, on her lap.

"It could be a bomb," he said.

She hesitated for an instant, and said, "Oh, well," and tore the wrapping off. Digging her nails into the seam between the cardboard flaps, she pulled back on both sides, ripping the top away. She reached in and retrieved Killheffer's hypodermic needle. She put her hand back into the box and felt around.

"There's only one," she said.

"Now you know what his game is," said Dex.

She held it up in the moonlight, and the green liquid inside its glass syringe glowed. "It's beautiful," she said with a sigh.

"Do it," said Dex.

"No, you," she said and handed it to him.

He reached for it, but then stopped, his fingers grazing the metal plunger. "No," he said and shook his head. "It was your shot."

"It probably won't even work," she said and laid it carefully on the blanket between them, petting it twice before withdrawing her hand.

"We'll shoot dice," said Dex, running his pinky finger the length of the needle. "The winner takes it."

Adeline said nothing for a time, and then she nodded in agreement. "But first a last dance in case it works."

Dex got up and went to the car to turn the radio up. "We're in luck," he said, and the first notes of "Polka Dots and Moonbeams" drifted out into the desert. He slowly swayed his way back to her. She smoothed her dress, adjusted her girdle, and put her arms around him, resting her chin on his shoulder. He held her around the waist and they turned slowly, wearily, to the music.

"So, we'll shoot craps?" she whispered.

"That's right," he said.

Three slow turns later, Adeline said, "Don't think I don't remember you've got that set of loaded dice."

Dex put his head back and laughed, and, as if in response, at that very moment, the stars began to fall, streaking down through the night, trailing bright streamers. First a handful and then a hundred and then more let go of their hold on the firmament and leaped. Way off to the west, the first ones hit with a distant rumble and firework geysers of flame. More followed, far and near, and Dex and Adeline kissed amid the conflagration.

"Pick me up at seven," she said, her bottom lip on his earlobe, and held him more tightly.

"I'll be there, baby," he promised, "I'll be there."

With the accuracy of a bullet between the eyes, one of the million heavenly messengers screeched down upon them, a fireball the size of the Ice Garden. The explosion flipped the Belvedere into the air like a silver dollar and turned everything to dust.

LOSER

•

Chuck Palahniuk

THE SHOW STILL LOOKS EXACTLY LIKE when you were sick with a really high fever and you stayed home to watch TV all day. It's not *Let's Make a Deal*. It's not *Wheel of Fortune*. It's not Monty Hall, or Pat Sajak. It's that other show where the big, loud voice calls your name in the audience, says to "Come on down, you're the next contestant," and if you guess the cost of Rice-A-Roni, then you fly round-trip to live for a week in Paris.

It's *that* show. The prize is never anything useful, like okay clothes or music or beer. The prize is always some vacuum cleaner or a washing machine, something you might maybe get excited to win if you were, like, somebody's maid.

It's Rush Week, and the tradition is everybody pledging Zeta Delt all take this big chartered school bus and need to go to some TV studio and watch them tape this game show. Rules say, all the Zeta Delts wear the same red T-shirt with, printed on it, the Greek Zeta Delta Omega deals, silk-screened in black. First, you need to take a little stamp of Hello Kitty, maybe half a stamp, and wait for the flash. It's like this little paper stamp printed with Hello Kitty you suck on and swallow, except it's really blotter acid.

All you do is, the Zeta Delts sit together to make this red patch in the middle of the studio audience and scream and yell to get on TV. These are not the Gamma Grab'a Thighs. They're not the Lambda Rape'a Dates. The Zeta Delts, they're who everybody wants to be.

How the acid will affect you—if you're going to freak out and kill yourself or eat somebody alive—they don't even tell you.

It's traditional.

Ever since you were a little kid with a fever, the contestants they call down to play this game show, the big voice always calls for one guy who's a United States Marine wearing some band uniform with brass buttons. There's always somebody's old grandma wearing a sweatshirt. There's an immigrant from some place where you can't understand half of what he says. There's always some rocket scientist with a big belly and his shirt pocket stuck full of pens.

It's just how you remember it, growing up, only now—all the Zeta Delts start yelling at you. Yelling so hard it scrunches their eyes shut. Everybody's just these red shirts and big, open mouths. All their hands are pushing you out from your seat, shoving you into the aisle. The big voice is saying your name, telling you to come on down. You're the next contestant.

In your mouth, the Hello Kitty tastes like pink bubblegum. It's the Hello Kitty, the popular kind, not the strawberry flavor or the chocolate flavor somebody's brother cooks at night in the General Sciences Building where he works as a janitor. The paper stamp feels caught partway down your throat, except you don't want to gag on TV, not on recorded video with strangers watching, forever.

All the studio audience is turned around to see you stumble down the aisle in your red T-shirt. All the TV cameras zoomed in. Everybody clapping exactly the way you remember it. Those Las Vegas lights, flashing, outlining everything onstage. It's something new, but you've watched it a million-zillion times before, and just on automatic you take the empty desk next to where the United States Marine is standing.

The game show host, who's not Alex Trebek, he waves one arm, and a whole part of the stage starts to move. It's not an earthquake, but one whole wall rolls on invisible wheels, all the lights everywhere flashing on and off, only fast, just blink, blink, blink, except faster than a human mouth could say. This whole big back wall of the stage slides to one side, and from behind it steps out a giant fashion model blazing with about a million-billion sparkles on her tight dress, waving one long, skinny arm to show you a table with eight chairs like you'd see in somebody's dining room on Thanksgiving with a big cooked turkey and yams and everything. Her fashion-model waist, about as big around as somebody's neck. Each of her tits, the size of your head. Those flashing Las Vegas kind of lights blinking all around. The big voice saying who made this table, out of what kind of wood. Saying the suggested retail price it's worth.

To win, the host lifts up this little box. Like a magician, he shows

everybody what's underneath—just this whole *thing* of bread in its naturally occurring state, the way bread comes before it's made into anything
you can eat like a sandwich or French toast. Just this bread, the whole way
your mom might find it at the farm or wherever bread grows.

The table and chairs are totally, easily yours, except you have to guess
the price of this big bread.

Behind you, all the Zeta Delts crowd really close together in their
T-shirts, making what looks like one giant, red pucker in the middle of
the studio audience. Not even looking at you, all their haircuts are just
huddled up, making a big, hairy center. It's like forever later when your
phone rings, and a Zeta Delt voice says what to bid.

That bread just sitting there the whole time. Covered in a brown crust.
The big voice says it's loaded with ten essential vitamins and minerals.

The old game show host, he's looking at you like maybe he's never,
ever seen a telephone before. He goes, "And what do you bid?"

And you go, "Eight bucks?"

From the look on the old grandma's face, it's like maybe they should
call some paramedics for her heart attack. Dangling out of one sweatshirt
cuff, this crumpled scrap of Kleenex looks like leaked-out stuffing, flapping
white, like she's some trashed teddy bear somebody loved too hard.

To cut you off using some brilliant strategy, the United States Marine,
the bastard, he says, "Nine dollars."

Then to cut him off, the rocket science guy says, "Ten. Ten dollars."

It must be some trick question, because the old grandma says, "One
dollar and ninety-nine cents," and all the music starts, loud, and the lights
flash on and off. The host hauls the granny up onto the stage, and she's
crying and plays a game where she throws a tennis ball to win a sofa and
a pool table. Her grandma face looks just as smashed and wrinkled as that
Kleenex she pulls out from her sweatshirt cuff. The big voice calls another
granny to take her place, and everything keeps rushing forward.

The next round, you need to guess the price of some potatoes, but like
a whole big thing of real, alive potatoes, from before they become food, the
way they come from the miners or whoever that dig potatoes in Ireland or
Idaho or some other place starting with an *I*. Not even made into potato
chips or French fries.

If you guess right, you get some big clock inside a wood box like a Dracula coffin standing on one end, except with these church bells inside the

box that ding-ding whatever time it is. Over your phone, your mom calls it a *grandfather clock*. You show it to her on video, and she says it looks cheap.

You're onstage with the TV cameras and lights, all the Zeta Delts call-waiting you, and you cup your phone to your chest and go, "My mom wants to know, do you have anything nicer I could maybe win?"

You show your mom those potatoes on video, and she asks: Did the old host guy buy them at the A&P or the Safeway?

You speed-dial your dad, and he asks about the income-tax liability.

Probably it's the Hello Kitty, but the face of this big Dracula clock just scowls at you. It's like the secret, hidden eyes; the eyelids open up, and the teeth start to show, and you can hear about a million-billion giant, alive cockroaches crawling around inside the wood box of it. The skin of all the supermodels goes all waxy, smiling with their faces not looking at anything.

You say the price your mom tells you. The United States Marine says one dollar more. The rocket science guy says a dollar higher than him. Only, this round—you win.

All those potatoes open their little eyes.

Except now, you need to guess the price of a whole cow full of milk in a box, the way milk comes in the kitchen fridge. You have to guess the cost of a whole thing of breakfast cereal like you'd find in the kitchen cabinet. After that, a giant deal of pure salt the way it comes from the ocean only in a round box, but more salt than anybody could eat in an entire lifetime. Enough salt, you could rim approximately a million-billion margaritas.

All the Zeta Delts start texting you like crazy. Your in-box is piling up.

Next come these eggs like you'd find at Easter, only plain white and lined up inside some special kind of cardboard case. A whole, complete set of twelve. These really minimalist eggs, pure white . . . so white you could just look at them forever, only right away you need to guess at a big bottle like a yellow shampoo, except it's something gross called cooking oil, you don't know what for, and the next thing is you need to choose the right price of something frozen.

You cup one hand over your eyes to see past the footlights, except all the Zeta Delts are lost in the glare. All you can hear is their screaming different prices of money. Fifty thousand dollars. A million. Ten thousand. Just loony people yelling just numbers.

Like the TV studio is just some dark jungle, and people are just some monkeys just screeching their monkey sounds.

The molars inside your mouth, they're grinding together so hard you can taste the hot metal of your fillings, that silver melting in your back teeth. Meantime, the sweat stains creep down from your armpit to your elbow, all black-red down both sides of your Zeta Delt T-shirt. The flavor of melted silver and pink bubblegum. It's sleep apnea only in the day, and you need to remind yourself to take the next breath . . . take another breath . . . while the supermodels walking on sparkly high heels try pimping the audience a microwave oven, pimping a treadmill while you keep staring to decide if they're really good-looking. They make you spin this doohickey so it rolls around. You have to match a bunch of different pictures so they go together perfect. Like you're some white rat in Principles of Behavioral Psychology 201, they make you guess what can of baked beans costs more than another. All that fuss to win something you sit on to mow your lawn.

Thanks to your mom telling you prices, you win a thing like you'd put in a room covered in easy-care, wipe-clean, stain-resistant vinyl. You win one of those deals people might ride on vacation for a lifetime of wholesome fun and family excitement. You win something hand painted with the Old World charm inspired by the recent release of a blockbuster epic motion picture.

It's the same as when you felt sick with a high fever and your little-kid heart would pound and you couldn't catch your breath, just from the idea that somebody might take home an electric organ. No matter how sick you felt, you'd watch this show until your fever broke. All the flashing lights and patio furniture, it seemed to make you feel better. To heal you or to cure you in some way.

It's like forever later, but you win all the way to the Showcase Round.

There, it's just you and the old granny wearing the sweatshirt from before, just somebody's regular grandma, but she's lived through world wars and nuclear bombs, probably she saw all the Kennedys get shot and Abraham Lincoln, and now she's bobbing up and down on her tennis-shoe toes, clapping her granny hands and crowded by supermodels and flashing lights while the big voice makes her the promise of a sports utility vehicle, a wide-screen television, a floor-length fur coat.

And probably it's the acid, but it's like nothing seems to add up.

It's like, if you live a boring-enough life, knowing the price of Rice-A-Roni and hot dog wieners, your big reward is you get to live for a week in some hotel in London? You get to ride on some airplane to Rome. Rome, like, in Italy. You fill your head full of enough ordinary junk, and your payoff is giant supermodels giving you a snowmobile?

If this game show wants to see how smart you really are, they need to ask you how many calories in a regular onion–cheddar cheese bagel. Go ahead, ask you the price of your cell phone minutes any hour of the day. Ask you about the cost of a ticket for going thirty miles over the speed limit. Ask the round-trip fare to Cabo for spring break. Down to the penny, you can tell them the price of decent seats for the Panic at the Disco reunion tour.

They should ask you the price of a Long Island iced tea. The price of Marcia Sanders's abortion. Ask about your expensive herpes medication you have to take but don't want your folks to know you need. Ask the price of your History of European Art textbook, which cost three hundred bucks—fuck you very much.

Ask what that stamp of Hello Kitty set you back.

The sweatshirt granny bids some regular amount of money for her showcase. Just like always, the numbers of her bid appear in tiny lights, glowing on the front of her contestant desk where she stands.

Here, all the Zeta Delts are yelling. Your phone keeps ringing and ringing.

For your showcase, a supermodel rolls out five hundred pounds of raw beefsteak. The steaks fit inside a barbecue. The barbecue fits onboard a speed boat that fits inside a trailer for towing it that fits a massive fifth-wheel pickup truck that fits inside the garage of a brand-new house in Austin. Austin, like, in Texas.

Meantime, all the Zeta Delts stand up. They get to their feet and step up on their audience seats cheering and waving, not chanting your name, but chanting, "Zeta Delt!" Chanting, "Zeta Delt!" Chanting, "Zeta Delt!" loud enough so it records for the broadcast.

It's probably the acid, but—you're battling some old nobody you've never met, fighting over shit you don't even want.

Probably it's the acid, but—right here and now—fuck declaring a business major. Fuck General Principles of Accounting 301.

Stuck partway down your throat, something makes you gag.

And on purpose, by accident, you bid a million, trillion, gah-zillion dollars—and ninety-nine cents.

And everything shuts down to quiet. Maybe just the little clicking sounds of all those Las Vegas lights blinking on and off, on and off. On and off.

It's like forever later when the game show host gets up too close, standing at your elbow, and he hisses, "You can't do that." The host hisses, "You have to play this game to win . . ."

Up close, his host face looks cracked into a million-billion jagged fragments only glued back together with pink makeup. Like Humpty Dumpty or a jigsaw puzzle. His wrinkles, like the battle scars of playing his same TV game since forever started. All his gray hairs, always combed in the same direction.

The big voice asks—that big, deep voice booming out of nowhere, the voice of some gigantic giant man you can't see—he demands, can you please repeat your bid?

And maybe you don't know what you want out of your life, but you know it's *not* a grandfather clock.

A million, trillion . . . you say. A number too big to fit on the front of your contestant desk. More zeroes than all the bright lights in the game show world. And probably it's the Hello Kitty, but tears slop out both your eyes, and you're crying because for the first time since you were a little kid you don't know what comes next, tears wrecking the front of your red T-shirt, turning the red parts black so the Greek Omega deals don't make any sense.

The voice of one Zeta Delt, alone in all that big, quiet audience, he yells, "You suck!"

On the little screen of your phone, a text message says, "Asshole!"

The text? It's from your mom.

The sweatshirt grandma, she's crying because she won. You're sobbing because—you don't know why.

It turns out the granny wins the snowmobiles and the fur coat. She wins the speedboat and the beefsteaks. The table and chairs and sofa. All the prizes of both the showcases, because your bid was way, way too high. She's jumping around, her bright-white false teeth throwing smiles in every direction. The game show host gets everybody started clapping their hands, except the Zeta Delts don't. The family of the old granny climbs up onstage—all the kids and grandkids and great-grandkids of hers—and they wander over to touch the shiny sports utility vehicle, touch the supermodels. The granny plants red lipstick kisses all over the fractured pink face of the game show host. She's saying, "Thank you." Saying, "Thank you." Saying, "Thank you," right up to when her granny eyes roll up backward inside her head, and her hand grabs at the sweatshirt where it covers her heart.

SAMANTHA'S DIARY

•

Diana Wynne Jones

Recorded on BSQ SpeekEasi Series 2/89887BQ and discovered in a skip in London's Regent Street

December 25, 2233

TIRED TODAY AND HAVING a lazy time. Got back late from Paris last night from Mother's party. My sister is pregnant and couldn't go (besides, she lives in Sweden) and Mother insisted that *one* of her daughters was there to meet our latest stepfather. Not that I did meet him particularly. Mother kept introducing me to a load of men and telling me how rich each of them was: I think she's trying to start me on her own career, which is, basically, marrying for money. Thanks, Mother, but I earn quite enough on the catwalk to be happy as I am. Besides, I'm having a rest from men since I split up with Liam. The gems of Mother's collection were a French philosopher, who followed me around saying *"La vide cc n'est pas le nknt,"* (clever French nonsense meaning "The void is not nothing," I think), a cross-eyed Colombian film director who kept trying to drape himself over me, and a weird millionaire from goodness knows where with diamante teeth. But there were others. I was wearing my new Stiltskins, which caused me to tower over them. A mistake. They always knew where I was. In the end I got tired of being stalked and left. I just caught the midnight bullet train to London, which did not live up to its name. It was late and crowded out and I had to stand all the way.

My feet are killing me today.

Anyway I have instructed Housebot that I am Not At Home to anyone or anything and hope for a peaceful day. Funny to think that Christmas Day used to be a time when everyone got together and gave each other presents. Shudder. Today we think of it as the most peaceful day of the year. I sit in peace in my all-white living room—a by-product of Mother's career, come to think of it, since my lovely flat was given to me by my last-stepfather-but-one—no, last-but-two now, I forgot.

Oh damn! Someone rang the doorbell and Housebot *answered* it. I know I told it not to.

Did I say we don't give Christmas presents now? Talk about famous last words. Housebot trundled back in here with a *tree* of all things balanced on its flat top. Impossible to tell what *kind* of tree, as it has no leaves, no label to say who sent it, nothing but a small wicker cage tied to a branch with a fairly large brown bird in it. The damn bird pecked me when I let it out. It was not happy. It has gone to earth under the small sofa and left droppings on the carpet as it ran.

I thought Christmas trees were supposed to be green. I made Housebot put the thing outside on the patio, beside the pool, where it sits looking bare. The bird is hungry. It has been trying to eat the carpet. I went on the Net to see what kind of bird it is. After an hour of trying, I got a visual that suggests the creature is a partridge. A game bird apparently. Am I supposed to *eat* it? I know they used to eat birds at Christmas in the old days. Yuk. I got on the Net again for partridge food. "Sorry, dear customer, but there will be no deliveries until the start of the Sales on December 27, when our full range of luxury avian foods will again be available at bargain prices." Yes, but what do I do *now*?

Oh hooray. Housebot has solved the problem by producing a bowl of tinned sweet corn. I shoved it under the sofa and the creature stopped its noise.

Do trees need feeding?

December 26, 2233

I DO NOT BELIEVE this! *Another* tree has arrived with *another* partridge in a cage tied to it. This time I went haring to the front door to make them take it away again, or at least make whoever was delivering it tell me where the things were coming from. But all the man did was shove a birdcage into my hands with two pretty white pigeons in it and go away. The van he drove off in was unlabelled. I raged at Housebot for opening the door, but that does no good. Housebot only has sixty sentences in its repertoire and just kept saying, "Madam, you have a delivery," until I turned its voice off.

We have had a partridge fight under the sofa.

I took the pigeon cage outside onto the patio and opened it. But *will* those birds fly away! I seem to be stuck with them too. At least they will eat porridge oats. The partridges won't. We have run out of tinned sweet corn.

I give up. I'm going to spend the rest of the day watching old movies.

Liam called. I asked him if he had had the nerve to send me four birds and two trees. He said, "What are you talking about? I only rang to see if you'd still got my wristwatch." I hung up on him. Oaf.

December 27, 2233

THE SALES START TODAY! I was late getting off to them because of the beastly bird food. When I brought up Avian Foodstuffs, I found to my disgust that the smallest amount they deliver is in twenty-kilo bags. Where would I put all that birdseed? I turned the computer off and went out to the corner shop. It was still closed. I had to walk all the way to Carnaby Street before I found anything open and then all the way back carrying ten tins of sweet corn. I had promised to meet Carla and Sabrina in Harrods for coffee and I was so late that I missed them.

Not a good day. *And* I couldn't find a single thing I wanted in the Sales.

I came home—my Stiltskins were killing me—to find, dumped in the middle of my living room, yet another tree with a partridge tied to it, a second cage of two white pigeons and a large coop with three different birds in it. It took me a while to place these last, until I remembered a picture book my second stepfather had given me when I was small. Under H for Hen there was a bird something like these, except that one was round and brown and gentle looking. Not these. Hens they may be, but they have mean witchy faces, ugly speckled feathers and a floppy red bit on top that makes them look like some kind of alien. When I got home, they were engaged in trying to peck one another naked. The room was full of ugly little feathers. I shrieked at Housebot and then made it take the lot out onto the patio, where I made haste to let the beastly hens out. They ran around cackling and pecking the partridges, the potted plants and the three trees. They were obviously hungry. I sighed and got on to Avian Foodstuffs again. Problems there. Food for which kind of bird? they queried. Hens,

I tapped in. Pigeons. Partridges. They have just delivered three twenty-kilo sacks. They are labelled differently, but they look suspiciusly the same inside to me. I know because I opened all three and scattered a heap from each around the patio—and another heap indoors because I have had to rescue the partridges. They all eat all kinds.

Exhausted after this. I phoned Carla and Sabrina. Sabrina was useless. She had just found some Stiltskins half price in pink and couldn't think of anything else except should she buy them. "Toss a coin," I told her. Carla was at least sympathetic. "Help!" I told her. "I'm being stalked by a flutter that keeps sending me birds."

"Are you sure it isn't one of Liam's practical jokes?" Carla asked. Shrewd point. He probably rang with that nonsense about his watch just to make sure I was home. "And haven't you told your Housebot thingy not to let any of this livestock in?" Carla said.

"I have, I *have!*" I cried out. "But the darn thing takes not the blindest bit of notice!"

"Reprogramme it," Carla advised. "It must have slipped a cog or something."

Or Liam reprogrammed it, I thought. So I spent an hour with the manual, pushing buttons, by which time I was so livid that I rang Liam. Got his answering service. Typical! I left an abusive message—which he probably won't hear because of Housebot trying to clean up feathers and making the howling noise it does when it chokes—but it relieved my feelings anyway.

December 28, 2233

I SPENT A GLORIOUS morning at the Sales and came back with six bags of Wonderful Bargains, to find I have four parrots now. *Plus* one more partridge (and tree), two more pigeons and three more of those unspeakable hens. Housebot has ignored my attempt at programming as if I'd never tried. The patio is now a small forest full of droppings. The pigeons sit on the trees and the hens rush about below. Indoors are four scuttling partridges and four of those large rings on sticks where parrots are supposed to perch, not that they do. The red one has taken a liking to my bedroom. The green one flies about all the time, shouting swearwords, and the multicoloured two perch anywhere so long as it isn't their official perches. *I* have put those in the closet because Housebot stops whenever it runs into one. I have ordered a twenty-kilo sack of Avian Feed (parrots), which is actually different from the others and which the parrots mostly consume from saucers on the kitchen table. I walk about giving a mad laugh from time to time. I am inured. I am resigned.

No I am NOT!

Someone has taught those damn parrots to shout, "Samantha! I *love* you!" They do it all the time now.

I put on my most austerely beautiful clothes and my Stiltskins and stormed round to Liam's flat. He looked terrible. He was in his night-clothes. He hadn't shaved or combed his curls and I think he was drunk. His flat was just as terrible. I saw it because as soon as he opened the door I marched in with Liam backing in front of me, shouting at the top of my voice. I admit that the nightclothes made me angrier still because it was obvious to me he had a woman in there. But he hadn't actually. He was just lying about. He said, "Just shut up and tell me what you're yelling about." So I did. And he laughed. This made me furious. I yelled, "You are stalking me with *birds!*" and to my great surprise I burst into tears.

To my further surprise, Liam was almost nice about it. He said, "Now look, Sammy, have you any idea how much parrots cost?" I hadn't. He told me. It was a lot. "And before you get suspicious that I know," he said, "I only know because I did an article on them last month. Right? Since when did I have enough money for four parrots? And I don't even know where you buy hens, let alone partridges. So it's somebody else doing this to you, not me. He has to be a rich practical joker, and he has to know how to get at your Housebot to make it ignore your orders and let these birds in. So think about all the rich men you know and then go and yell at the likely ones. Not me."

I gave in. "So I've walked all this way for nothing," I said. "And my feet hurt."

"That's because you wear such silly shoes," he said.

"I'll have you know," I said, "that these are the very latest Stiltskins. They cost me thousands."

He laughed, to my further indignation, and told me, "Then go home in a taxi."

While I was waiting for the taxi, Liam put his arm round me—in an absentminded way, as if he had forgotten we weren't still together—and said, "Poor Sammy. I've had a thought. What kind of trees are they?"

"How should I know?" I said. "They haven't any *leaves*."

"That is a problem," Liam said. "Can you do me a favour and let me know if what your stalker sends next is something quite valuable?"

"I might," I said, and then the taxi came. I don't like these latest taxis. A mechanical tab comes out of the meter that says TIP and it's always huge. But it was probably worth it to know that Liam hasn't been doing this to me.

December 29, 2233

WHATEVER IDEA LIAM HAD, he was *quite right*! The usual tree and avians started arriving, one more partridge, more hens, more pigeons and four more parrots, noisy ones. I left Housebot, who had traitorously let them in, to deal with the damn creatures—although I have to feed the things because I can't get Housebot to get it through its circuitry that living things have to eat: Housebot simply goes round clearing up the piles of birdseed unless I order it to stop. Anyway, I left it shunting coops and the latest tree onto the patio and set off for the Sales. I was halfway down the steps outside when a courier arrived and made me sign for a smallish package.

Someone's sent me a *book* now! I thought disgustedly as I went back indoors. I nearly didn't open it, but, because of what Liam had said, I thought I might as well. What are valuable books? I thought as I tore off wrapping. Antique Bibles? First editions of *Winnie the Pooh*? But it wasn't a book. A book-size jewel case fell on the floor. I picked that up quickly before Housebot could clear it away. I gasped a bit when I opened it. There were five rings in it, all of them very flashy and valuable looking. One bulged with diamonds—or what looked like diamonds—and the rest looked like sapphires, emeralds and equally valuable stones, all in gold settings. And there was a note on top, not in real handwriting, if you see what I mean, but in that kind of round, careful writing that shop assistants use when you ask them to include a message. It said: "From your ardent admirer. Marry me."

"*Blowed* if I will!" I said aloud.

The rings are all too small. I think that proves it wasn't Liam. He once bought me an engagement ring, after all, and he knows that my fingers are rather wide at the base. Unless he's being very cunning, of course. Whoever sent the rings seems to have very flashy taste. They all reminded me so much of the kind of glass-and-plastic rings that people give you when you are a little girl that I took the whole case of them with me when I went out to the Sales and had them checked out by a jeweller. And they are real. I could buy five more pairs of Stiltskins if I sold them. Well!

I meant to tell Liam, but I met Carla in Oxford Street and I forgot. When I told her, she wanted to know if I was thinking of marrying the unknown stalker. "No way!" I told her. "My mother probably would, though."

December 30, 2233

OH MY GOD! I have six geese now. As well as another tree, another partridge, further pigeons, more hens and four extra parrots (making twelve of them and bedlam). I couldn't believe these geese. I got to the door just as a whole team of men finished handing them indoors. The last one rode in on top of Housebot. They are *big* birds and not friendly. At least they are too large to attack the partridges under the sofa, but five of them went out onto the patio and started subduing the hens at once. The shrieks and cackling out there actually drowned out the yells from the parrots. But one goose stayed indoors and seems to have gone broody on the sofa cushions. She stretched out a long, angry neck and tried to peck me when I made an effort to persuade her to join the rest outside. So there she sits, large, boat shaped and white, with her yellow beak swivelling about to make sure I don't disturb her and her shoe-button eyes glaring unnervingly.

The only good thing about this morning was that the same courier turned up with another parcel of rings. He is a nice young man. He seems awed by me. He said hesitantly while I was signing for the delivery, "Excuse me, miss, but aren't you on that media clothes show? *Catwalk?*" I said yes, I was, but we weren't filming at the moment. He sort of staggered away, thoroughly impressed.

The rings today are all antique fancy gold. With the same message as yesterday. Liam couldn't have afforded any of this, even if he mortgaged his flat, his pay and his soul. I forgive him.   ⸺

And I supposed I should feed the geese. I got on to Avian Foodstuffs again and they sent round a waterproof sack of slimy green nibbles. The geese don't seem to care for them. They ate all the hen food instead. The hens protested and got gone for again. To shut them all up, I tipped out one whole sack of hen food in the corner of the patio and this just caused another furious battle. Then it rained and the geese all came indoors. The beam that opens and shuts the sliding doors to the patio is set low so that Housebot can get out there to clean the pool, and it turns out to be just goose height.

I then discovered that geese are the most incontinent creatures in the universe. My living space is now covered with lumps of excrement, and the geese waddle through it, tramping it about with their large triangular feet. You interfere with them at your peril. I cracked and phoned Liam.

He said, "Don't call me. Your phone is probably bugged, if your Housebot is. Meet me at the café on the corner."

How unwelcoming can you get? To make it worse, that cafe is the one where we always used to meet when we were together. But I ground my teeth, got into rainwear and went.

He was sitting outside in the rain. He looks rather good in rainwear. He had even got me the right kind of coffee. He said, "What is it now? Geese?"

I was flabbergasted. "How did you know?"

"And five gold rings yesterday and today?" he said.

"Yes, but all too small," I said.

"Ah," he said, looking pleased with himself. "Then you have an admirer who is not only rich hut mindlessly romantic. He is sending you items from an old song—it used to be very popular two hundred years ago—called 'The Twelve Days of Christmas.'"

"Then whoever he is, he hasn't a *notion* how angry he's making me!" I said.

"The idiot thinks he's wooing you," Liam said. "He probably belongs to one of those societies where they trail about in medieval clothes, or armour and so forth. But he's also up to date enough to tamper with your Housebot and probably bug your phone. So think of any of the rich men you know who fits this description and then you'll have him. Come on. Think."

I had been trying to think. But you try thinking with a row of parrots sitting on the rail of your bed and the rest swooping about shouting that they love you. I had made no progress. I sat and watched raindrops plop into my coffee and thought hard. I do know a lot of rich men. You do, in my trade. But they were all mostly media men and those are *not* romantic.

A more cynical lot you can't imagine. Unless I had annoyed one of them of course . . . And most of the clothes designers are gay.

"Oh," said Liam. "My other conjecture is that he's thoroughly unattractive. I suspect he's used to having to pay a lot to get women interested. Rather pathetic really."

I instantly thought of the truly unattractive set of fellows Mother had introduced me to on Christmas Eve. "That's *it!*" I cried out. "Bless you, Liam! I'll phone Mother this evening."

"I don't think it's your mother doing it," he said.

"No, no," I said and explained. He agreed that I might be on the right track and we talked it over for a while. Then he said, "By the way, the trees will be pear trees," and handed me a list. "So you'll know what to expect next," he told me and got up and left. Just like that.

I was too angry to look at the list. I wish I had.

December 31, 2233, New Year's Eve

I'M GOING TO THREE parties today, so I'm getting out of my bird-infested flat as soon as I can. But I did ring Mother. I raved at her rather. She may have thought I was insane at first, but when I calmed down and described the geese—by the way, the one on the sofa had laid an egg when I got back—she began to see I might be having real trouble. She said, in the cautious, respectful way she always talks about money, "Well, you *might* be talking about Franz Dodeca, I suppose. Not that he would do a thing like that, of course. He owns Multiphones and SpeekEasi and Household Robotics and he's a multimillionaire and he's naturally very much respected."

"Which is he?" I asked. "Of the freaks you introduced to me."

"Not *freaks*, darling," she said reproachfully. "He was the one with the charming diamante teeth."

I thought grimly of this Dodeca, a short fat man in an unbecoming pin-striped suit. A pale freckled creature, I recalled, with thin reddish hair scraped back over his freckled scalp. He kept baring those dreadful glittering teeth at me in creepy smiles. And this idiot owns my diary, my phone and my Housebot! I hoped he swallowed one of his teeth and choked. "Tell him," I said to Mother, "to stop sending me *birds*. Tell him he hasn't got a chance. Tell him he's destroyed his already nonexistent chances by stalking me this way. Tell him no and *go away!*"

Mother demurred. I could tell she was reluctant to pass up the chance of all that money in the family. But after I had told her at least ten times that there was absolutely *no chance* of my marrying this idiot, even if he owned the *universe,* she said, "Well, darling, I'll phone him and try to put it tactfully."

If she did phone dear Franz, she has had no effect. The swans arrived this morning, seven of them. Along with six more geese, et cetera, et cetera. At least I got five more gold rings. They came with a note of dreadful pleading, signed, "Your eternally loving Franz," which looked odd in round shop-assistant writing. I suppose Mother must have phoned the man, since he seems to know that his cover is now blown. But it doesn't seem to have stopped him.

The swans had obviously been drugged. The delivery crew carried them in big drooping armfuls, through the living room and onto the patio, where they carefully wedged them into the pool. The geese waddled in after. There are now twelve of them and they're laying eggs everywhere. As if it wasn't enough to be overrun with hens—also laying—and a new set of green screaming parrots. The swans were just waking up when I left. Housebot tried to make me an omelette before I went and I nearly threw up.

January 1, 2234, New Year's Day

THANK HEAVENS! EVEN THE Dodeca millions can't make anyone in this country work on New Year's Day. No further birds arrived. Nothing came. Relief! Or it would be if the swans didn't fight the geese all the time. And I realised when I got in around four this morning that the place smells. Horribly. Of bird droppings, rotting seeds and old feathers. Housebot can't keep up with the cleaning.

I shall have to stop wearing my Stiltskins. My feet are killing me after last night. One of my big toes has gone kind of twisted. I have very hazy memories of the fun, though I do recall that I ran into Liam at the Markhams' fireworks party and, besides jeering at my Stiltskins, he wanted to know if I'd consulted his list yet. I said I didn't want to know. I told him about dear Franz too—I think. He was, I dimly remember, insistent that I throw away my phone and scrap Housebot. The man has no *idea!*

But this memory has made me realise that I will almost certainly get more swans and more geese tomorrow. I can't rely on Mother to stop them. There is no more room in the patio pool. But it has occurred to me that the big house next door, which belongs to my last-stepfather-but-two, has a large garden with an ornamental as-it-were lake in it. I shall phone Stepdaddy Five. As far as I know, he's still in a hut in Bali, recovering from having been married to Mother.

I got through to him eventually. He was, as ever, sweet about it all. "Isn't that just like your mother!" he said. "I know Franz Dodeca slightly. He's a total obsessive, too rich for his own good. Come here to Bali and I'll undertake to keep him off you."

Well, I couldn't do that. It strikes me as incest. Instead I asked him to lend me the garden of his house next door. He agreed like a shot and gave me the entry code at once. But he warned me that his caretaker gardener might not be pleased. He said he would phone this Mr. Wilkinson and explain. "And keep me posted," he said. "Nothing happens here in Bali. It suits me, but I like a hit of distant action from time to time."

January 2, 2234

JUST AS WELL I made that arrangement with Stepdaddy Five. They brought yesterday's swans et cetera today, plus today's lot, making fourteen inert, heavy floppy swans and twelve more geese. I showed the lot through Stepdaddy Five's front door and out to the lake in his garden. The geese seemed to like it there. When the trees and the pigeons and the hens came, I showed them out there too. But the parrots had to stay with me because they were not hardy enough, they said. At least I got ten more gold rings.

We are getting seriously short of bird food. I went round to the corner shop, but they don't open till tomorrow. Avian Foodstuffs are on holiday for the week. Again.

I don't believe this! The swans were not all. I was just about to cross the road from the corner shop when I saw, trudging and bawling down the street, a whole herd of cows. Eight of them anyway. They were being driven by eight young women who, to do them justice, were looking a bit self-conscious about it. People in cars and on the pavements were stopping to stare. Some folk had followed them from Picadilly, apparently. You don't often see cows in London these days.

My stomach felt queer. I knew they were for me. And they were. Honestly, how can this Dodeca even imagine I might want eight cows? Cows are not in the least romantic. Their noses run and they drop cowpats all the time as they walk. They dropped more cowpats through Stepdaddy Five's nice hallway as I showed the lot of them out into his garden. I said to the girls, "If you want to stay, this house has fourteen bedrooms and there's a pizza takeaway down the road. Feel free." I was feeling more than a little light-headed by then. The parrots don't help.

Now it's got worse. Mr. Wilkinson arrived half an hour after the cows and bawled me out for allowing a herd of cows to trample his lawn. I said I would get rid of them as soon as I could. I was going to phone Mother and extract this Dodeca's phone number from her and then phone him and tell him to come and take his livestock *away*. And see how *he* liked it. Before I could, though, a severe woman with a mighty bosom turned up on the doorstep, saying she was from the Bird Protection Trust and that my neighbours across the street had reported me for cruelty to birds. They had, she said, counted one hundred and seven various birds being delivered to my flat—*busybodies!*—where they were certainly overcrowded. I was to release them to better quarters, she said, or be liable for prosecution.

After Mr. Wilkinson, she was the *last straw*. I told her to get the hell out.

January 3, 2234

NO, THE LAST STRAW was today. I did phone Mother last night and she did, after a lot of squirming, give me Dodeca's private number. The trouble was that I didn't know what to *say*, and all these parrots make it so difficult to *think*—not to speak of yet another swan versus goose fight erupting every five minutes. My God those birds can be vicious! Then I sat on an egg when I started to phone Dodeca and gave up. I said I'd do it today.

Today started with those cowgirls coming round here whining and whingeing. There were beds but no sheets or blankets next door, they said, and it was not what they were used to. And where did they put the twenty gallons of milk? I said pour it away, why not? And they said it was a waste. Anyway, I got rid of them in the end, but only by ordering a stack of sheets and blankets online, which cost a bomb.

Then the bird deliveries began. By then we were almost out of bird feed, so I ushered this lot, swans included, into Stepdaddy Five's garden and raced off to the corner shop. They only had canary food, so I bought all they had of that. I was staggering towards my flat with it when I saw an entirely new sort of van drawing up and Housebot, that traitor, blandly opening my front door to it. The men in it began unloading and putting together a large number of frameworks. I crossed the road and asked them what the hell they were doing.

They said, "Out of the way, miss. We have to get all these into this flat here."

I said, "But what are they?"

"Trampolines, miss," they said.

This caused me to bolt into my flat and race about scattering canary food and looking for that list Liam gave me. I found it just as they manoeuvered the first trampoline in. There were supposed to be nine of them. How they thought they were going to fit them in I have no idea. As I opened the list, one of the men got attacked by the broody goose on the sofa and they all went outside to let it settle down. Liam had written, "Ninth day: Nine lords a-leaping; Tenth day: Ten ladies dancing; Eleventh day: Eleven pipers piping . . ."

I didn't read any more. I gave a wild wail and raced into my bedroom, where all the parrots seemed to have congregated, and to shrieks of "I love you, Samantha," I packed all the parcels of rings into my handbag for safety and raced out again to the nearest public phone, praying it wouldn't have been vandalised.

It wasn't. I got through to Liam. "What is it now?" he said grumpily.

"Liam," I said, "I've got nine trampolines now. Is it really true that I'm going to get ballet dancers and skirling Scotsmen next?"

"Pretty certainly," he said, "if you got milkmaids yesterday. Did you?"

"Yes," I said. "Liam, I have had enough."

"What do you expect me to do about it?" he said.

"Marry me," I said. "Take me away from all this."

There was a dreadful, long silence. I thought he had hung up on me. I wouldn't have blamed him. But at length he said, "Only if you can assure me that I'm not just an escape for you."

I assured him, hand on heart. I told him that the mere thought of Franz Dodeca had made me realise that Liam was the only man for me. "Otherwise I'd get on a plane and go to my sister in Sweden," I said. "Or maybe to Bali, to Stepdaddy Five."

"All right," he said. "Are you coming round here at once?"

"Quite soon," I said. "I have to fix Dodeca first." We then exchanged a surprising number of endearments before I rang off and raced back to my flat for what I sincerely hope was the last time.

I got back just as a minibus drove up and unloaded half a dozen fit-looking young men in scarlet robes and coronets and three more middle-aged ones, who looked equally fit. Most of them were carrying bottles of champagne and clearly looking forward to some fun. They all poured into my flat ahead of me. I had to sidle among them and past the men squeezing the last trampoline in and past several enraged geese and terrified partridges to get to my phone—a phone dear Franz was certainly bugging. While I punched in his number, the chaps all climbed on the trampolines and began solemnly bouncing up and down. One of the geese accidentally joined them. I had to put my hand over one ear to detect that I had got Dodeca's answering service. Good.

"Franz, dear," I said after the beep. "I'm *so* grateful for all the things you've been sending me. You've really gone to my heart. Why don't you come here and join me in my flat? Come soon. And then we'll see." And I rang off, with the delightful thought of dear Franz arriving and the traitor Housebot letting him in among all this.

More than all this it would be, I discovered as I left. Another herd of cows was coming down the street, lowing and cowpatting as it came. From the other direction, I could see the big lady from the Birds Protection, or whatever it was, advancing. She seemed to have a policeman with her. And Mr. Wilkinson was just storming out of Stepdaddy Five's front door. I ran the other way, past the herd of cows. And who should I see but the nice courier lad just getting out of his van with a fifth parcel of rings.

I stopped him. "You know me, don't you?" I said. "Can I sign for them now and save you coming to my door?" He innocently did let me and I raced away with the parcel. "I've brought you a dowry!" I said to Liam as I arrived—

"No, Liam, don't! I haven't finished yet!"

A male voice: "Don't be stupid, Sam. You know he'll be listening in. Do you want him to know where we are? I'm going to throw this away before you tell him any more."

The diary ends here.

LAND OF THE LOST

•

Stewart O'Nan

SHE WAS A CASHIER AT A BILO in Perry whose marriage had long since broken up. Soon after that her two boys moved out of the house, leaving Ollie, her German shepherd, as her sole companion. From the beginning she followed the case in the paper and on TV, absorbing it like a mystery, discussing it with her coworkers and customers—so much so that her manager had to ask her to stop. Early on she visited the Web site and left messages of support in the guest book, from one mother to another, but after James Wade confessed that he'd buried the girl somewhere west of Kingsville, she began keeping a file. At night when she couldn't sleep she sat up in bed and went over the transcripts and the mother's map, convincing herself it was possible. She couldn't believe a feeling so strong could be mistaken.

She didn't tell anyone what she was doing—she wasn't stupid. The first time was the hardest because she felt foolish. In the privacy of her garage, while Ollie looked on, she stocked the trunk of her car with a shovel, a spade, a dry-cell flashlight and a pair of work gloves. She opened the door and he leaped into the backseat, capering from window to window, frantic just to be going somewhere.

"All right, calm down," she said. "It's not playtime."

Searching on foot took longer than she thought. They came across nothing more sinister than a rotting seagull, but she wasn't disappointed. Bushwhacking through the overgrown no-man's-land behind the commercial strip on Route 302 was an adventure, and looking gave her a sense of accomplishment. They could cross this location off and move on to the next one.

Later she added more serious gear like bolt cutters and a lightweight graphite walking stick recommended by professionals, whose Web sites she treated like the Bible. She religiously documented everything, taking videos of any ground they disturbed, writing up her field notes as soon as they got home.

As fall came on she rearranged her shifts, working nights so she could take advantage of the daylight. In a couple of weeks the ground would be frozen and she'd have to shut down until spring. It was then, when she was feeling rushed, that she discovered a U-Store-It outside Mentor with a stockade fence and a dirt road running through the pines behind it. Across the raw lumber, kids had sprayed their illegible fluorescent-red names.

She walked Ollie along the fence until he stopped, sniffing at a weedy mound. She pulled him away twice, and both times he came back to the same spot. "Good boy," she said, giving him a treat, and looped his leash around a tree.

She prodded the mound with her walking stick. The dirt was sandy and loose, and she went back to her car for the shovel.

She dug her first hole deep, then shallow ones every three feet. She was out of shape, and had to dip her head and wipe her face on her shoulder. It was cool out, and when she stopped for a drink of water the sweat on her neck made her shiver. By the time she reached the middle of the fence, the sky was starting to get dark. At the four corners of the self-storage, high floodlights popped on, buzzing and drawing bugs, throwing weird shadows. She checked her cell phone—it was almost five. She needed to go home and get ready for work. Rather than leave the site unguarded over-night she decided to call the FBI.

They told her it was too late in the day. They'd send someone out to talk to her tomorrow.

When she complained to her older son, he asked how long she'd been doing this.

The agent they sent asked the same question. He looked over her binders and the picture of the girl on the mantel and the big map tacked up in the kitchen.

"I'm just trying to help," she said. "If it was one of my kids, I'd want everybody to pitch in."

"I would too," the agent said soothingly, as if it was common sense.

The next day they took her out to the site in an unmarked Suburban to watch a backhoe dig a trench along the fence line. Agents in windbreakers and latex gloves sifted the dirt through metal screens, then spread it on tarps for the dogs. A project like this would have taken her weeks, and she was glad she'd called. She imagined the girl's mother hearing the news. She didn't care about getting the credit. It was enough to know the girl was finally home.

They found nothing. Just dirt. Worms. It had all been a coincidence. As the agent said, there was graffiti on everything these days.

Meaning she was crazy.

Dropping her off, he thanked her. "I know your heart was in the right place."

Was it? She could admit that at least part of the reason she was searching for a stranger's daughter was that no one else needed her. Just Ollie.

She promised her sons to take a break after that. She took down the map and stored the picture in a drawer and watched the last weeks of fall pass.

Honoring her pledge was easier in the winter. She used the time to rethink her strategy and stockpile supplies. Some sites recommended a pitchfork to turn the soil, others a pickax. On paper, again and again, she rearranged her trunk, as if she were traveling cross-country. She enrolled Ollie in an online course for sniffer dogs, practicing with scented rags in the backyard. He didn't always get them right away, and stood looking at her as if she might give him a hint.

"Do you want to pass or not?" she asked. "Or am I just wasting my time?"

She kept an eye on the Web site, and cruised the chat groups for news. She was afraid one day the page would come up and say she'd been found, but month after month, nothing changed. It had been two and a half years. Besides the family, she might be the only person looking for her.

In March the ground thawed and she tacked up the map. She'd turned her older boy's room into a command center, emptying his desk and filling the drawers with her notebooks. On a brand-new corkboard she posted her schedule. Four days a week she'd search, weather permitting. She'd been too impatient in the fall, letting her emotions get the best of her. She'd actually expected to find the girl her first time out, as if she were psychic. She needed to be calm and methodical. If she was going to succeed, it would be because she knew how to work.

Ollie just liked riding in the car and going for walks. He had his certificate, but the death scent made him sneeze. The smells that interested him came from other dogs, and he immediately covered them with his own, lifting his leg and making her wait. As spring turned to summer the only thing he'd discovered was a bee's nest, provoking a swarm and earning him a bump on the nose. He would have stayed and tried to fight them if she hadn't dragged him away.

She made the mistake of telling her younger son, who told her older son, who called and said he thought they agreed she was going to stop.

"I don't see why you're so upset," she said.

"I'm worried about you. Do you understand why?"

"No."

"That's why," he said.

After that, every time he called, he made a point of asking how the search was going.

She refused to lie.

"The same," she said.

"What does that mean?"

It meant she was ranging farther and farther west, devoting whole weeks to a single exit off the interstate, tromping the buggy jungles behind truck stops and fireworks outlets, breaking ground by every stockade fence she came across, graffitied or not. Her knees creaked, her arms ached, and then at work she had to lean over the conveyor and lift a gallon of milk into someone's cart, and she thought maybe he was right. She was too old to be doing this.

There was always the possibility James Wade had been lying. As her map filled with pins, she tried not to let it bother her.

In August, jumping a drainage ditch, she twisted her ankle and missed three weeks, ruining her schedule and giving her son a new excuse to badger her. To catch up she went out five days a week, but felt like she was rushing, cutting corners. The weather was mild, Indian summer lingering deep into October. If it held up (and the Weather Channel said there was a chance), she'd have a shot at finishing.

One bright afternoon she was outside Fairport Harbor, behind a Ryder truck center, when Ollie stopped and lay down in a shallow trough filled with pine duff. He rested his head on his paws and flattened his ears back as if he were being punished. It wasn't anything she'd taught him.

"Come on, get up." She whistled and clapped, and still he didn't budge.

She had to coax him away with a treat and tie him to a tree, and even then he hunkered down, cowering.

The Ryder place wasn't a self-storage, and the fence, though heavily tagged, was chain link with green plastic slats, but she went to get the video camera anyway.

The trough was tub shaped, around five feet long, and sunk a few inches below the ground around it. She brushed away the leaves and pine needles and laid the pitchfork beside it for scale, narrating as she panned along the fence. "November third, 2008, 1:27 P.M."

When she'd gotten enough coverage, she set down the camera and took up the pitchfork. She dug into the very center of the trough, jabbing the prongs through the crust, pushing it deeper with her foot, pulling back on the handle so the ground cracked and broke around the tines. She stuck it in again, levering open a hole.

Behind her Ollie whined.

"Shush," she said.

The third time she dug down and yanked back, the pitchfork snagged on a swath of fabric.

It was discolored with mud and stank of mildew, but was unmistakably a piece of green nylon, a wisp of white batting poking from a hole.

She set aside the pitchfork, tossed away her gloves and tugged at the piece, pulling another couple inches through the dirt. It was the shell of a sleeping bag, she could see the thick seam of the zipper. With a finger she wiped at the crumbling mud, revealing rusty teeth.

Thank God, she thought. What would Brian say now?

As long as she'd waited for this moment, she didn't want to see what was inside. The thing to do was stop and call someone, but after last year, she couldn't. She knelt beside the hole, digging it free with her bare hands. This time she would make sure. Then everyone would know she wasn't crazy.

LEIF IN THE WIND

•

Gene Wolfe

"HE'S BEEN OUT THERE," ENA SAID, "for an hour and fifty-two minutes. It took him twenty-eight to nail that plate back down. I've been trying to get him to come back in ever since."

Brennan rubbed his chin. It was a big one, and required quite a bit of rubbing. "He answers you? He replies?"

"Sometimes. Not always."

"But he's conscious?"

"I think so."

"Fugue state?"

Ena shrugged.

"Talk to him."

"I'll try." Ena's gesture switched on the mike. "This is Ena again, Leif. Brennan is here with me now. What are you doing?"

"Watching the sunrise, Ena. The planetary shadow is fading. Fading... This sun appears behind the horizon curve, just peeping out past it now. I can feel the first breezes of its solar wind."

Brennan tried to make his voice soft. "You can't possibly feel a solar wind, Leif. You're suited up."

"I feel it."

Ena said, "Please come back, Leif. We've completed the survey, done everything we were supposed to do, and—"

Brennan interrupted her. "The job's finished, Leif. There's no life down there. We have rock samples, cores, the works. Habitable planet, no life. Seed it and there could be colonies here in two hundred years. Maybe less."

Leif said nothing.

Ena said, "I've never begged a man for anything—"

"Birds. I see birds."

Brennan snorted. "You don't see birds, damnit! There aren't any, and if there were, you couldn't see them from up here."

Ena said, "Think of me, Leif—if you won't think of yourself, at least think of me. The trip home will take fifteen more years. What if Brennan dies?"

Silence.

"Walt died. So did Barbara and Alaia. Brennan could die, too. I'd try to take the ship home all by myself, and I'd go insane. I couldn't bear it. You know what the tests showed—nobody could." She paused, waiting. "Think of me if you won't think of yourself."

Leif exclaimed, "You should see these birds! The detail! The colors! The combs and crests and wattles!"

Brennan said, "You're dreaming them, Leif."

"I couldn't dream anything like this. It isn't in me. It isn't in anybody. They're so big, and they get smaller as they come closer. Smaller and smaller, like jewels."

Ena looked at Brennan, expecting him to reply, and saw that he was suiting up. She switched off her mike. "Are you going out there after him?"

"If I have to, yes."

"I know you could outwrestle him, but can you catch him?"

"I'll have to."

She switched her mike back on. "Leif, I'm offering everything I've got. I'll be your slave if you'll just come back." She gulped, and wondered whether her mike had picked it up. "I'll do your details, all of them, and mine, too. We'll be heroes when we get home, and I'll give you a bath first, and clean and press your uniform. I'll shine your boots and polish your brass. You said I was beautiful once, remember? Wouldn't you like a beautiful slave?"

Brennan muttered, "Did he really?"

"I'll—sleep with you like you wanted, Leif. You can do whatever you like with me, and I'll do whatever you tell me to. Please?"

Leif said, "They're nesting in me, all the beautiful birds. Perching on nerve fibers, sipping from tiny veins, Ena. Fluttering and singing. This is how a tree feels in summer."

Wearily, Ena switched off her mike. "He doesn't care about me."

"He doesn't care about us," Brennan told her. "Not now he doesn't."

Leif said, "The wind murmurs in my branches, and the birds nest there." He sounded rapturous. Ena's screen showed a silver starfish, arms wide, legs spread, face invisible behind the glare of sunlight on his visor. Slowly, the starfish revolved, rolling like a wheel.

She heard the airlock open. "You're going after him?"

Brennen stepped into the airlock. "Wish me luck."

"I do," she said. The airlock closed, and she added, "I wish you both luck. I hope you don't kill each other."

Still later: "Most of all I wish me luck."

Was there nothing she could do but sit and watch? She unsnapped her belt, floated up, and pushed off.

Walt should have looked just as she remembered him from last time—so quickly frozen that no big crystals had formed, eyes shut, and very, very dead.

He did not. Dead, yes, but still *there*. So quickly frozen, she thought, that his soul had not had time to leave his body. Brennan thought it might be possible to reanimate him back on earth, and Brennan might be right.

Walt's eyes were not completely shut. Surely they had been before?

Surely. But Walt was peeking out like one who feigns sleep.

"I may sleep with Leif if Brennan brings him back. I'll have to sleep with Brennan. You're dead, Walt." Ena paused. "You're dead for now, anyway. I won't be cheating on you."

From behind a plastic shield as clear as air, Walt watched her in silence.

"You understand, don't you?" She began to close the lid. "Besides, I—we're not all that different from you, we women."

She returned to the bridge, floating along ovoid black corridors that should have echoed but did not. It had been wrong to silence them, she thought. The sound absorption was too good, it worked too well. Ghosts whispered in the black corridors now, Alaia's ghost and Barbara's.

Walt's ghost.

On her screen, Brennan had a line around Leif's waist and was playing it out behind him as he returned to the ship. Brightly lit by rising Beta Andromedae, the slack orange line traced fantastic loops and whorls against the still-dark planet they orbited. Ena switched on her mike. "Did he give you any trouble, Brennan?"

"Not a bit."

Changing viewpoints, she watched Brennan enter the airlock, turn, and begin hauling Leif in. No resistance, but . . . She inserted a sedative cap in the injector. Leif, she told herself, was not particularly strong. And pushed aside the knowledge that all psychotics were.

Inside, he removed his helmet without assistance. His expression was rapt, his eyes elsewhere. The neck was one of the best places.

Leif relaxed, swaying, and Brennan said, "That was probably a good idea."

"It can't hurt." Ena was opening Leif's suit.

"I'm full of birds," Leif told her.

"I see."

"They're nesting in me. Have I mentioned that?"

Absently, she nodded.

"We are their trees. That's why there are no trees down there. We trees have just arrived." Leif paused. "I would like to sit down."

"No reason not to," Brennan told him. "Step out of the boots and I'll put you in a chair."

When Leif did not move, Brennan lifted him out, the magnetic boot soles holding them to the deck. When Brennan had Leif in his console seat, Ena belted him in.

The first jump covered four thousandths of one light-year; recharging for the next would take thirty-six hours.

"Are we going home?" Leif asked. He sounded sleepy, and had not touched the buckle that held him in his seat.

Brennan said, "Right." He was refolding Leif's suit.

"You'll have to walk in the spinner," Ena told Leif, "just like Brennan and me. Just like you did on the trip out. Can you do it?"

Leif seemed not to have heard her.

"Two hours a day," Brennan said. "If you don't, your legs will break when we get home."

Ena was inspired. "Your limbs, Leif. That's your arms and your legs. You know what happens when limbs break."

Leif stared at her. "The nests fall down."

"Exactly!"

"I'm going into the spinner now." Leif released his buckle. "Three hours. Three hours every day for me. I won't forget."

When Leif had gone, Brennan chuckled, wrapped Ena in his arms, and kissed her. When they parted, he whispered, "You were always the smartest woman on board."

They were recharging for the fourth jump when Ena heard the first bird, its clear trills carried through the ventilation system. A twenty-minute search found it in Specimen Storage number 3, where it had nested among her neatly labeled sacks of rocks.

It was somewhat larger than a crow, and was not (she decided) exactly as a bird should be. That sinuous neck, armored in diamond scales, might have belonged to a snake; the sides of its long, curved beak were toothed like the blades of saws. It spread its wings when she approached, threatening her with retractile claws that sprouted from their forward edges.

"I don't want to hurt you," Ena said softly. "Really, I don't. You're very, very valuable to all three of us. You're an alien life-form, you see." It was difficult to remain calm.

The bird rattled its feathers—a warning buzz, loud and abrupt.

She kicked off from a specimen bag, backing away. "I'm going to bring you something to eat. I don't know what you'll like, so I'll try several things." Could it eat their food?

Brennan was checking the recharge readings. "Pile's running good," he told her. "Next jump should be right on schedule."

"Leif's birds are real." She had drifted over to her console.

"Are you kidding me?"

Seeing his skepticism, she nodded. "Sure. But don't you hear that noise? Listen. I think it's coming through the vents."

After a moment he left his seat and kicked off, stopping aft vent. Ena smiled to herself.

"That's a bearing getting ready to fail. Probably one of the fans. I'll see to it."

As he shot out into the corridor, she called, "Good luck!"

She was checking the pile herself when Leif wandered in. "Do you need me?"

"Not really." She smiled. "The best thing you could do right now is to shower and put on a clean uniform. Will you do that? For me?"

Leif nodded.

"Thank you! I really appreciate it. Put the one you're wearing in the laundry, and I'll see to it. Don't forget to empty the pockets."

"There's nothing in there." Leif seemed to wait for her to speak. "All right, I'll empty them anyway."

It was almost time for the jump when Brennan returned. "There's a bird on the ship!"

"No shit?" Ena feigned surprise.

He grabbed at a handy conduit and swung to a stop, panting. "Sweetheart, you ought to see it! It's taller than I am."

"If you're going to sniff solvents," Ena said icily, "I don't want you to call me sweetheart. Cut it out. Cut it out right now. This is the only warning you'll get."

"It's down on H Deck. Come on, I'll show you."

"One of us has to stay on the bridge, and since you've been sniffing, it had better be me."

"Leif can do it."

"Leif isn't around, and God only knows what he'd do if he were alone here."

"It's real. Do I have to take a picture?"

Feeling almost sorry for him, she shook her head. "No. No, you don't, Brennan. Catch it and throw it off the ship. It'll be out in space somewhere, and I can pick it up in my viewer."

"Don't you understand what this means?"

"Yes. It means that Leif can infect others with his hallucinations. Or else you've been sniffing. I like the second one better."

"I'm going to catch it," Brennan told her. "Catch it and confine it. Then I'm going to show it to you. Don't jump without me. You're not qualified."

"You mean I don't have the paper. By this time I know how to do it as well as you do."

"Don't jump!"

Then he was gone. Ena smiled to herself as she tried to track him through the surveillance cameras. When FULL CHARGE appeared on her upper-left screen, she jumped.

A DAY AND MORE passed before Brennan returned. Ena slept on the bridge, tethered to a hatch handle and hanging weightless among 552 instruments. Leif wandered in and volunteered to bring her food and water. She was using the surveillance cameras to search for Brennan when Brennan touched her shoulder.

"You jumped—I felt it." He was trying hard to look severe, but could only look haggard and triumphant.

"Sure," Ena said. "I knew you would. I jumped, and that's why the pile's burning and power's flickering. I don't know what that vibration is, but it darned near—"

"Very funny." Brennan belted himself into his console seat. He studied the screen, clicked twice, and studied it again.

"Did you catch the bird?"

"I did." Brennan nodded. "I got a number three cargo net and rigged it up to close when the bird tried to get through. When it was ready, I drove the bird in front of me with a welding torch."

"Where is it now?"

He sighed. "Empty ration locker, or I hope it is. It may still be tangled in the net. I don't know."

"We can't keep it there for fifteen years."

"Right. We'll let it out, v-tape it, kill it, v-tape it some more, strip the bones and save them." Under his breath he added, "If it has bones."

Ena said, "Tissue specimens, too. Maybe we should freeze the head."

"Yeah."

"There's something you're not telling me."

"It tried . . . Tricks. You wouldn't believe me."

"You didn't believe *me* when I told you Leif's birds were real."

Brennan straightened up. "I'm still not sure you were right. Maybe I caught a delusion. You want to fetch the 'corder?"

"Somebody's supposed to stay on the bridge."

"Leif. I'll get him."

This time she offered no objection.

The green food lockers were on C Deck. Brennan caught the handle of one in Aisle 10. "This is it. I'm going to level with you, sweetheart. I don't think it's still in here, but this is where I put it. I threw it in and locked the door." He took the key from his pocket, a strip of plastic no larger than a paper clip.

Ena sighed. "Walt was supposed to have those. Keep us from eating too much."

"Walt's dead."

She nodded. "So now I can eat all I want."

"With three gone, it won't matter. Don't worry about it."

"So I ought to eat too much. Bored people always eat too much."

Watching her, Brennan nodded. "That was why Walt kept the keys."

"But I don't. I don't eat enough. I keep driving myself to eat. Or try to, anyway. All my uniforms are loose." She paused. "Aren't you going to open it?"

"In a minute, maybe. Boredom makes people eat—you're right about that. Depression keeps them from eating. Get somebody depressed enough, and she'll starve herself to death. You tried to bribe Leif with sex. I heard you."

Slowly Ena nodded.

"I'm not going to say I don't want sex. It would be a lie, and you'd know it was a lie. Every man wants sex, but that's not the only thing I want. I want you to love me. I want you to love me the way you loved Walt. Okay, I want it for my own selfish reasons. Hell yes, I do. But I want it for your sake, too."

Brennan paused. "For a second there you were trying to smile. I wish you'd made it."

She said, "So do I."

"When I kissed you, up on the bridge, you kissed back."

She nodded.

"So there's hope for us."

" 'Hope is the thing with feathers.' " Ena waited for Brennan to speak. When he did not, she added, "That's Emily Dickinson."

"Yeah, I know." Brennan pulled himself toward the food locker. "You want me to show you the bird and quit talking about all this, because it bothers you. I've got it. Only it might help you, too, so I've got to keep it up. You think I don't miss Barbara? You think I don't wake up when the cabin's dark, wondering if she's asleep? I need you almost as much as you need me. You don't have to believe that."

"What I believe doesn't matter."

"The hell it doesn't! I need you, and that's why I'll never quit. You'll see, and Ena . . ."

"What?"

"We'll get back home alive. Both of us."

She kissed him, and it was like—yet not quite like—their kiss on the bridge.

"I don't think the bird's still in here," Brennan said rather later. "Not really. It was too tricky for that."

"We didn't think they could nest in Leif either."

"Yeah. What the hell are they? Devils? They can't be angels."

Ena said, "I don't think we've got the word. Or the concept either. We'll have to develop them."

"Maybe. If we can."

Brennan opened the locker, and something smaller than a bee flew out. "It got out," he said. "Some way it got out. Where the hell did it go?"

" 'They get smaller as they come closer.' "

"What's that supposed to mean?"

"What it says, perhaps. Leif said it before you pulled him in."

Brennan rubbed his jaw. Rather to her surprise, Ena discovered that she enjoyed watching him rub his jaw.

"Mine didn't get smaller when I was chasing it."

Ena nodded. "It wasn't coming closer. You were, or you were trying to."

They jumped.

"Sonofabitch! Did you feel that?"

"Yes." She discovered that she was holding his arm, and let go. "Yes, I did. It was Leif, up on the bridge."

"Sure. Had to be." Brennan glanced at his watch. "He went the minute recharge was complete."

She nodded. "Now we'll have to see in which direction."

THEY HELD A TRIAL the next day, a kangaroo court with Leif tied into his seat. "I'm the prosecutor," Brennan explained. Brennan no longer sounded, or looked, angry, but his voice was deadly serious. "You're the defendant and the counsel for the defense, too. Ena's the judge. She and I think that will be fair. What you think doesn't matter. I'm going to put the case against you. You'll be given an opportunity to rebut it. Ena will decide on your penalty."

"If any," Ena said.

"She'll decide your penalty, if there is one. Do you understand?"

"I didn't want to hurt any of you," Leif said. He might have been talking to himself. "I just wanted to go back. Fuel's forty-seven percent surplus. Food's—"

Brennan raised his fist and looked at Ena.

She shook her head. "We used to be friends, Leif. I'd like us to be friends again. Like us to be friends right now."

"All right."

"Good. This is a trial. I am your judge. Do you understand that?"

"I'm not stupid. I just want to go back."

"I know. Brennan?"

"He sabotaged our mission. Not by some accident. Not even by inattention. He did it deliberately. He brought his damned birds in. We don't know how many there are, but there's a lot. You and I will have to round them up and kill them. It may take years, and we may never catch them all."

Leif started to speak, but Brennan silenced him. "He negated our last jump, and he'll be a danger to us, and to the mission, for the next fifteen years. Say that we let him live. We'll have to lock him up and feed him, just you and me, on top of all our other duties. We'll have to make sure he stays locked up, because we can't trust him out for a minute. One of us will have to walk with him in the spinner, and that will have to be me, because he might jump you. If—"

"I might jump you, too," Leif said.

"Sure." Brennan grinned. "Want to try?"

"He will try," Ena said thoughtfully. "He might even succeed, if he catches you off guard. Now stop arguing with him."

She pointed to Leif. "You're to be quiet until it's your turn to talk. We'll tape your mouth if we have to."

Brennan cleared his throat. "You're right. I don't think he'd succeed, but he'll try. Sooner or later, he'll try to jump me. If he does succeed, the mission is shot. Finished. Ruined. Six lives and billions of dollars, all wasted."

Ena nodded.

"That's not the only danger. This ship wasn't built as a prison. No matter where we lock him up, he'll have years to try to figure some way out. I've never wanted to kill anybody, and God knows I don't want to kill Leif. We're going to have to do it just the same. Can we keep him sedated for fifteen years? Have you got enough dope for that?"

Ena shook her head.

"For one year?"

"We might keep him lightly sedated for a year or more. Not for two."

"How do you know lightly would be enough?"

"I don't," Ena said.

Brennan sighed. "Okay, you've got my case. Can he be killed, legally? I don't know and you don't either, but we both doubt it. So I'm not asking you to kill him or even help me to. I'll do it alone. I'll stick him in the airlock without a suit, and we'll write it up in the log. Maybe they'll try me for murder when we get home. Maybe they won't. I'll take my chances. Now let's hear Leif."

"I didn't endanger the mission," Leif began. "I've explained that already. There's plenty of food and plenty of fuel. The air plant's running fine. What I tried to do would have delayed the ship's return to earth by a few days. No more than that. You two are perfectly capable of taking the ship back. If you were to die, it's perfectly capable of taking itself back. The six of us were put on board to take care of emergencies, and because we'd be needed once the ship got to Beta Andromedae. We've done all that, or at least we've done it as well as three people could, taking pix, measuring the magnetic field, mapping, and all the rest of it."

"You finished?" Brennan asked.

"No. You blame me for bringing the birds. If what you say were correct—it's not, but if it were—I'd deserve a medal. Neither of you found alien life. Not a speck. Not a trace. I found it, and returned to the ship with live specimens. You won't concede a thing, I know. But if your accusation were correct, that would be the fact and I would be a hero."

Ena said, "You say it's not."

"I do. The birds came into me while I was suited up, out in space. I told you they were there."

Reluctantly, Ena nodded.

"I didn't want to come back onto the ship, infected as I was. Brennan forced me to. If bringing my birds onto the ship was a crime, Brennan is the criminal. Not me."

"You're the one who sabotaged our mission," Brennan said.

Ena raised her hand. "We've heard the accusation and Leif's defense. I don't want to get into it again."

Leif said, "You promised me a chance to defend myself. I have one more thing to say. It will take less than a minute. May I do it?"

She nodded. "Go ahead."

"Brennan threatens me with death. Surely you can see that I wanted to return to Beta Andromedae so that I could die there. I'll suit up and go out again. You need only let me do it. Put a K beside my name in the log, and note that I was a suicide. It will be true, and if either of you is accused of my murder a veriscope reading will prove your innocence."

Ena smiled. "Brennan?"

"I'm willing if you are."

"I'm not. Not as it stands. You'll have to do us a service first, Leif. Go through the ship and collect the birds. All of them. Get them back inside you. They went in once, and I think they'll go in again if you approach them right. Do it, and we'll go back as you ask and put you out."

HE HAD SPREAD HIMSELF like a starfish, and the birds had flown. All of them—or nearly all. Now he blew like a dry leaf in the solar wind, revolving like a cartwheel.

His air was running out. His body would die; and that which would not die would be free at last, free to rove the universe and beyond.

Death waited beside him, warm and dark and friendly, and Leif could hardly wait.

IN HER CABIN, ENA smiled to herself as she shook the small brown bottle. She had caught the faint fragrance of Brennan's aftershave when he relieved her on the bridge. He could not possibly have brought enough to last for half the voyage; thus he had hoarded some and was using it now.

The odor haunted her, delightful and unidentifiable. What aftershave had Walt used, what cologne? She had known those things once, but they were gone and only the memory of Brennan's faint fragrance remained. Russian leather? Spice? Neither seemed correct.

Turning the bottle over in her hand, she reread the label she had read so often since finding the bottle in a food locker: VANILLA EXTRACT.

She would smell like a cookie.

Opening the bottle, she applied the thin brown liquid it contained to five strategic spots.

Brennan would welcome her return. They would kiss, and she would unbutton his shirt. And then—

She interrupted the daydream to listen. A bird sang in her right wrist.

UNWELL

·

Carolyn Parkhurst

I WAS FEELING A BIT UNWELL, so I called Yvonne to come and sit with me. I believe that sisters have a responsibility to look out for one another, even though that doesn't seem to be a popular view with everybody these days. I think that if more people would take their family responsibilities more seriously, then the world wouldn't be in the kind of trouble . . . But the phone was ringing.

"Hello," said Yvonne.

"Yvonne, I need you to come over this afternoon. I'm not well."

I heard her sigh on the other end; I don't believe she even tried to mask it. "Is it really important, Arlette? I've got a million wedding things to do."

"Oh, the wedding. Is that coming up soon?"

"It's Saturday, Arlette, and you know it."

"Well, I hope I'll be able to make it. I've been feeling weak all day, and I'm not at all sure I'll be myself by Saturday."

"Arlette, please don't start . . ."

"Well, it's hardly my fault if I'm ill. But perhaps if I had a little help . . ."

There was a long silence. I could just see her on the other end, wearing that outlandish engagement ring on her finger. A woman her age. "All right," she said. "I'll get Arthur to do some of my errands for me. I'll be over in half an hour."

We hung up, and I leaned back against my bed pillows, well pleased.

THE FACT IS, THIS should by all rights be my wedding. Yvonne and I met Arthur at the same time, and it was clear from the beginning that I was the one he was interested in. It used to be, in biblical times, and I believe some other notable points in history, that if there were two unmarried sisters, the younger one wasn't allowed to be married before the elder. It was illegal. If the younger sister tried to break the rules and run off and get married anyway, they'd put her to death. I should tell that to Yvonne. They'd cut her head right off. It was just the way it was.

We met Arthur on a seniors' cruise that Yvonne took me on in honor of my seventieth birthday. It was her idea, and not a very good one, I must say—the room was cramped, the food was terrible, and most of the other passengers were pathetic old bores. When Yvonne gave me the tickets, she had said, "Who knows? Maybe we'll meet a couple of nice widowers," but there were three women for every man, and what men there were were bald, toothless and demented. I actually saw one of them trying to eat soup with his fingers. So when Arthur walked into the dining room, tall and unstooped, with his full head of silver hair gleaming in the light from the nautical-themed chandeliers, all the old biddies in the room seemed to sit up a little straighter. And when he sat down next to me, I thought, Watch me. I am going to charm the pants off this man. So I started up a conversation about current events—test him, I thought, see if he's still in possession of a fully functioning mind—and he seemed to be able to talk about something more than what kind of medication he was taking, which automatically made him a better dining companion than anyone else at the table. He and I chatted and laughed all through the meal, and Yvonne just sort of melted into the upholstery, as usual. It's always been that way; there's a softness to her, a sleepiness, that I can't stand. If it weren't for me, the world would have eaten her up long ago.

So Yvonne sat quietly and picked her way through her prime rib—no appetite on that girl, never has been—while I began laying the groundwork for my grand seduction. Things were going quite well, and I was sure I had him in my pocket. Arthur and Arlette, my mind kept singing, Arthur and Arlette. I was ecstatic, and God knows I deserve some happiness. Yvonne knows how lonely I've been since my Stephen passed away. She doesn't mind being alone; she's used to it. But I was made to be married, and in my mind I already had the church decorated, the flowers arranged artfully on the tables.

And then at the end of the meal, something odd happened. Arthur rose from his seat, helped me out of my chair and said, looking right at me, "Might I interest you in a walk in the moonlight, Yvonne?"

I felt a little prick of acid in my stomach, and my whole body tightened.

I saw Yvonne raise her head hopefully, but I shot her a look. "Well," I said to Arthur tartly, "I'd be a lot more interested if you tried calling me by the right name."

For an instant, Arthur's face turned cool as he flicked his eyes between me and Yvonne. Then he widened his eyes in a gentlemanly show of shock and proceeded to fall all over himself apologizing. "I'm so sorry," he said. "I must have misheard the introductions. So Yvonne is your sister?"

"That's right," I said. I drew my wrap around me, closing myself up. It'd take a little more wooing to make up for a flub like that.

"Please forgive me," he said. And then, as if this had anything to do with anything, "You two look so much alike."

Well, that was a fatal misstep on his part. Our whole lives, Yvonne and I have been told we look like twins, but I don't see it myself. I don't see it at all. True, we're only thirteen months apart—and oh! how often I've wished I could go back and recapture the glory of those precious thirteen months when it was only me!—and we have similar coloring, but my features are much more graceful. Any person who thinks that comparing me to Yvonne is a compliment has a lot to learn. And the lessons might as well begin as soon as possible.

"Sorry," I said, my voice as icy as the wretched frozen swan sculpture defiling the buffet. "But I'm feeling a bit tired this evening, and I think I'll pass on your kind invitation." And I swept off to bed, my dowdy sister in tow.

My plan was to keep Arthur at arm's length for another half day or so, and then gradually let him win me over again through much hard work and flattery. But at breakfast the next morning, I could see I'd made a tactical error. Arthur ignored me completely and began doting on Yvonne as if she were some rare bird he'd been hoping to spot for years. By midmorning, they were heading to the onboard casino together; by late afternoon, they'd signed up for a ballroom dancing lesson. And I was left sitting on my deck chair, stewing in my fury, watching the waves pass me by.

TRUTH BE TOLD, THIS is not the first time Yvonne and I have found ourselves in a situation like this. When I first met my late husband Stephen—I was twenty-one at the time, and Yvonne was twenty—he was already dating Yvonne. She and I were both working in our father's bakery, which I thought was a pleasant enough thing to do while I was waiting to find a husband. But it wasn't enough for Yvonne, and she'd started taking classes at a local college. She wanted to become a librarian—like you need to go to school to learn how to say "shhh." Well, none of us knew anything about it till later, but apparently there was a young man who rode the bus at the same time as Yvonne, and the two of them used to look at each other over the tops of their books as they rode. And one or the other of them would smile a little, and then they'd get all embarrassed and look away. Quite a romance, wasn't it, all that reading and looking away—*Casablanca* it was not. Finally, after a year of this—yes, it took a full year for one of those ninnies to make a move—the young man moved over to sit next to Yvonne and say hello. They became inseparable after that, riding the bus together and talking about books. The young man's name was Stephen, and he was a poet. At least, that's what he said; the truth was, he was an accountant with ambitions to be a poet.

Anyway, she brought him home one night to have dinner with Mother and Father and me, and you could have knocked me over with a feather. Here I'd been flirting with every man who came into the bakery, while mousy little Yvonne bent her head over her books, and she'd found a man all by herself.

So Yvonne brings this man home, this shy, gawky man who spent a year trying to get up the courage to say hello, and we all sat in the parlor and looked at him. And I'll tell you, he was handsome. He had these big eyes, like a doe, and his legs were so long, they stretched way out to the center of the room. But I watched him and Yvonne watching each other, two little mice peeping out of their holes, and I thought this boy needs a woman who will turn him into something. Someone lively and bold, not timid like Yvonne. I looked at their future together, and I saw a lifetime of quiet nights, sitting side by side, waiting to see which one of them would gather the courage to say, "Would you like milk in your tea?" Reading books together—that's exactly the kind of thing they would have done. It made me want to yawn. This Stephen, he needed a woman who could teach him how to have fun, a woman who wasn't afraid to speak her mind. Stephen and I were meant to be together, I could see it right away. Didn't we deserve some happiness? And what would Yvonne do with a man like that, anyway? Yvonne had her studies, her solitary pursuits. She was always happiest on her own. And so, for the sake of us all, I set out to save Stephen from Yvonne.

It was harder than I expected. He had become quite enamored of her, for reasons I never could quite imagine. I tried all the more subtle forms of flirtation—never were more gloves dropped in a young man's path, never were a young lady's shoulders more often proclaimed to be chilly—but they went right over his head. And then one day, I got a little help from fate. The three of us were supposed to go to a nearby lake together for a picnic—by this point, I'd insinuated myself into most of Stephen and Yvonne's activities—but Yvonne got sick and couldn't go. Stephen was all ready to cancel the whole thing, but I put on a sad face and told him I'd spent all morning in the kitchen, cooking up my special deviled eggs, and why couldn't the two of us have a nice day? And Yvonne, predictably, took my side and told us to go and have a good time. Really, that woman never knows when to stand up for herself. So Stephen and I went to the lake ourselves, and I made sure we found a nice, secluded spot. We spent the afternoon sitting in the shade of a lovely weeping willow tree, and we just had a wonderful time, talking and laughing. Later, Yvonne would ask me how I could do such a thing to her, but at the time, it didn't feel like Yvonne had anything to do with it at all. We were falling in love, that's all there is to it. I'd sneaked some of Father's whiskey into the picnic basket, and neither Stephen nor I was much of a drinker, so we both got a bit tipsy, and when a sudden thunderstorm forced us to take shelter in the backseat of his car, we just did what came naturally. Our love was a force of nature, I always said.

Of course, there were tears and accusations, but a month later, when I told Stephen I was pregnant, it just seemed like it would be for the best if the two of us got married. And by the time I realized that I'd gotten my dates confused and I wasn't pregnant at all, we were already back from our honeymoon.

For a while, Yvonne kept herself away from our door, and she and Stephen seemed a bit awkward whenever they were near each other, but I made it clear that I wouldn't have the two of them tiptoeing around over some little doomed infatuation, and they got the picture pretty quick.

Stephen and I had a good marriage. At first, he wasn't the kind of husband I'd hoped he would be, but with my guidance, he began to take shape. I got him to give up his poetry and his reading, and all the other silly things he liked to fill his time with, and to concentrate on his career instead. Within a few years, he'd risen through the ranks of his firm, and we had enough money to make a nice life for ourselves. Stephen lost the

boyishness and softness he'd had when I married him, and it pleased me to
see the hard edges he developed in their place. We tried for a while to have
children, but we never could—some problem with my uterus that I'm sure
you don't want to hear about—and if I'm being honest with myself, I think
it's probably just as well. I'm not really the maternal type.

It was a few years after we got married that Mother gave me the
Christmas ornaments. Mother had quite an artistic eye, and her Christmas
tree was always breathtaking. Over the years, she'd amassed a beautiful
collection of ornaments, some of them quite valuable, and I know Yvonne
had always hoped they'd pass to her someday. I think she was quite hurt
that Mother chose to give them to me, but it was fast becoming clear that
her role was going to be that of maiden aunt, hovering at the edges of our
family Christmases, and it just wouldn't have made any sense for her to
have them. Mother was a practical woman, and she saw this as well as I
did. She knew it was the way of the world, and there was nothing you or
I could do about it. But Yvonne never could see things that were plain to
everybody else, and I know she took it as a slight. Honestly, it's forty-five
years later, and I don't think she's gotten over it yet.

That first Christmas we had the ornaments, I had a big party for the
whole family. I made a beautiful ham dinner, and we all sat beneath my
perfect Christmas tree and opened gifts. Stephen played the piano—now
there was one hobby I approved of—and we sang carols late into the night.
After everyone left, Yvonne offered to stay late and clean up a little, since
I'd done all the work of the party, and I agreed to her kind offer. I went up
to bed, leaving Yvonne in the kitchen and Stephen still sitting at the piano,
picking out tunes.

It must have been two hours later when I woke up and discovered
that Stephen wasn't in bed with me. The lights were still on downstairs,
and I crept down to the living room. Stephen and Yvonne were sitting
on the couch together. They had their arms around each other, and they
were looking deep into each other's eyes, their foreheads touching. She
was stroking the back of his neck and speaking to him in a low voice. In
the instant before the floorboards creaked and they looked up and saw me,
I heard her say two words to him. I heard her say, "Leave her."

Then, like I said, there was the business of the floorboards, and the
two of them snapped their heads around like they'd been caught stealing,
which, in a way, they had.

"Get out of my house," I roared, and for a minute I wasn't sure which of them I was talking to. They just sat there, frozen. I plucked one of the ornaments from the tree, a little white porcelain angel, and threw it at them with the newfound strength of a woman betrayed. It hit the wall over their heads and landed on the floor, chipping one of its wings, but it didn't break. It was made of harder stuff than I'd thought.

Stephen didn't leave me, of course. What a thought. Say what you will about him, he took his responsibilities seriously. I think he knew he had it pretty good with me. Really, not so much changed after that; I got a new fur coat out of it, and a trump card to play in every argument we ever had. And when Yvonne came around, sniffling and saying her sorries, I welcomed her back with open arms. Friends close, enemies closer. But I made sure that she and Stephen never had a single minute alone together, not a single moment in thirty years. When Stephen was lying in his hospital bed, two hours away from dying, he asked me if he could have a few minutes to say good-bye to her alone, and you know what I said? No. I said no. Simple as that.

IT WAS THE PICTURES that got me thinking. I don't know if you've ever been on a cruise—if you haven't, don't waste your money—but one of the many irksome things they do is take endless pictures of you and then try to sell you prints. There's a whole hallway dedicated to displaying these souvenir masterpieces, and you have to go through and pick your face out of the crowd. It's quite depressing, actually, the sameness of all the photos. Here's the whole herd of cattle, walking up the gangplank; here they are stuffed into their ill-fitting evening wear, posing next to the poor captain, who has to hear the same jokes over and over again—"If you're here, who's driving the ship?" And it turns out you're just like the rest of them, smiling for the camera and trying to look like you're having fun. No, I wasn't going to spend a penny on their pictures.

But with Yvonne spending every waking moment with Arthur (only her waking moments, mind you—the one wild week of her life, and she's too much of a prude to have any fun), I found myself with some spare time. And so I took a walk down the hall of farm animals to try to pinpoint the moment when my sister's betrayal began. Look—here are Yvonne and Arlette arriving together, looking as happy as two sisters can be. Here's

Arthur, arriving all by his lonesome. Here are Yvonne and Arlette against a splashy Caribbean backdrop; here they are against a sprinkle of fake stars. And then—here it is, right before your eyes!—Arlette standing by herself on Formal Night, dressed in her prettiest clothes, and there are Yvonne and Arthur posed together like some old married couple at their golden anniversary party. Look at them together. You can see right away they don't match. At least, I thought, with no small amount of glee, at least the picture didn't come out well; Arthur had turned his head at the moment the shutter snapped, so you can hardly even tell it's him. And that's when I noticed something odd. I looked back through all the earlier photos, and I noticed there wasn't a single one of Arthur's face. It would seem that for some reason he didn't want his picture taken. And that's when I thought, This is a man with something to hide.

I was concerned for Yvonne's welfare, of course. You wouldn't know it from the way she dresses or the way she decorates her home, but Yvonne has quite a bit of money. None of us ever expected it, of course—librarians barely make enough to keep themselves in books and donations to public TV stations. But there was a man who used to come into the library where she worked, a little old man who liked to come in each morning to read the paper. And I guess he was sweet on Yvonne. Not that anything ever came of it—story of Yvonne's life, or so everyone thought before Arthur—but I guess they used to talk to each other, and she'd bend the rules for him and let him drink his coffee while he read, as long as he wasn't too obvious and didn't spill. She used to tell me about this man, about how he'd point out articles she might be interested in, and how after a while he started bringing a cup of coffee for her too, and I'd say, "You're living a movie-star life, Yvonne. The thrills never stop." But then one day, the man died in his sleep, and he left Yvonne almost five million dollars. You'd think a man with that much money could've afforded his own newspaper subscription, but anyway. Of course, it was a big surprise to everyone, and there were stories about Yvonne in all the papers. She told the reporters, "Oh, it won't change my life," just like those lottery winners who go out and buy helicopters the next day, but for her it was really true. She kept her job at the library, and she still gets her hair cut at the six-dollar place like some no-class nonmillionaire. Pathetic.

So when I saw the way Arthur kept hiding his face in all those pictures, at first I thought he just didn't want to be seen with Yvonne and her six-dollar hair. But when I noticed that he was doing the same thing in all the earlier pictures, the pre-let's-trample-on-Arlette-and-her-big-soft-heart pictures, I realized what was going on. It wasn't that he didn't want to be seen with Yvonne; he just didn't want to be seen, period.

WHEN WE GOT HOME—never have I been so happy to put my feet on dry land—I decided I was going to find out what Arthur's story was. It was easier than you'd think. I sat down and watched that *America's Most Wanted* show, and I found out they had one of those Web sites. So I turned on the computer Yvonne gave me for my birthday last year, and I had a look around. And wouldn't you know it, I found Arthur in an hour. His real name isn't Arthur, it turns out. It's Martin Edward Jaffe, and he's wanted in connection with the disappearance of a woman he married in Denver. A wealthy woman, a whirlwind courtship. It's such an old story it's almost boring. Honestly, could Yvonne be any more naive? I sent away to Denver for a copy of a newspaper article that had his picture in it, and I waited for the right moment to bring it to Yvonne's attention.

AFTER HANGING UP THE phone with Yvonne, I settle myself against the pillows, and I wait to see whether or not today is going to be the day. It takes her more than an hour to arrive, which is not a point in her favor— honestly, she only lives five minutes away—and at first, I think maybe I won't tell her at all. Serves her right, I think, she's digging her own grave. But when you get right down to it, I'm a big softie, and she is my only sister. Still, it's not an easy thing to bring up; it would kill her to have to cancel the wedding at this late date, poor thing. She's happier than I've seen her in years, and who am I to take that away from her? So while she's downstairs heating up some broth for me, I take the box of Christmas ornaments out of the closet. Inside, wrapped in old newspaper, are all the foolish pieces of glass and glitter she seems to care so much about. God knows why I've held on to them this long. I take one out and unwrap it; it's the little white angel with the chip in its wing. I place the angel on the newspaper clipping from Denver and wrap it up tight, then bury it deep in the box. I hear Yvonne coming up the stairs, and I quickly close the box and get back into bed.

Yvonne comes into the room with a tray of soup and crackers. I can see she's brought saltines instead of Ritz, and I almost decide to call off the whole plan and leave her to find out about Arthur for herself. But I take a deep breath and remind myself that she's my sister. And in any case, she's already seen the box in the middle of the floor.

She sets the tray down on the bed and points at the box. "What's this?" she asks, even though it's clearly marked and she's seen it a hundred times before. Really, she is the most infuriating creature. Arthur doesn't know what he's gotten himself into.

But I smile and make my voice as sugary as the icing on the tacky wedding cake she's sure to have on Saturday. "A wedding gift," I say. "I know how you've always wanted these." She gets that look on her face that I've always hated, a sort of tentative, frightened joy, like a dog taking meat from a hand she knows might hit her.

"Arlette, really?" she says. She sounds like she might cry, and I feel like pinching her.

"Well, I expect I'll be coming over to your house for Christmas from now on. It just makes sense."

"Oh, Arlette!" she cries and throws her arms around me, nearly upsetting my bowl of broth. "That's why you made me come over here today, isn't it? You're the sweetest sister a person could have!"

"You always could see right through me," I say and bite into a saltine.

I watch as she picks the box up to carry it down to her car, chattering away about some nonsense or other. I think about the picture of Arthur hidden deep inside, his lying face wrapped around a ruined angel. She'll find it at Christmastime, if her eyes are sharp. And if anything should happen before then, I can hardly be held accountable. I've done everything I can.

And if, God forbid, anything should happen before then, I'm prepared to take the situation into my own hands. I have no doubt that, with a little bit of guidance, Arthur could become the kind of husband I deserve.

A LIFE IN FICTIONS

●

Kat Howard

HE WROTE ME INTO A STORY AGAIN.

I told him to stop doing that, after we broke up. In fact, it was one of the reasons that we broke up. I mean, being a muse is all well and good until you actually become one.

The first time it happened, I was flattered. And it wasn't like my normal life was so great that I was going to miss it, you know? So getting pulled into that world—a world he had written just for me, where I was the everything, the unattainable, the ideal—it was pretty powerful.

When he finished the story, and I came back to the real world, the first thing I did was screw him until my thighs ached. It was our first time together. He said it was the best sex of his life.

When I asked him if someone had ever fallen into a story that he had written before, he said not that he knew of. Oh, sure, he had based characters on people he knew, stolen little bits of their lives. A gesture, a phrase, a particular color of eye or way of walking. The petty thievery all writers commit.

I asked what he had done differently this time.

"I was falling in love with you, I guess. You were all I could think of. So when I wrote Marah, there you were in my head. Always."

I hadn't fallen into the story right away, and I didn't know what happened in the parts where Marah didn't appear. Reading the finished draft was this weird mix of déjà vu and mystery.

Apparently inspired by my real-world sexual abandon, the next thing he wrote me into was an erotic novella. Ali was a great deal more flexible than I was, both physically and in her gender preferences.

I really enjoyed that story, but one night I tried something in bed that Ali thought was fun but that he thought was beyond kinky. After that, the only sex scenes he wrote me into involved oral sex.

Men can be so predictable, even when they are literary geniuses.

Maybe especially then.

The next time he wrote me into something, I lost my job. It was a novel, what he was working on then, and when he was writing Nora, I would just disappear from my life as soon as he picked up his pen. For days, or even weeks at a time, when the writing was going well.

He said he didn't know what happened to me during those times. He would go to my apartment, check on things, water my plants. When he remembered. When he wasn't so deep in the writing that nothing outside registered.

I was always in his head during those times, he said, at the edges of his thoughts. As if that should reassure me.

It happened faster. He would begin to write, and I would be in the story, and I would stay there until he was finished.

The more I lived in his writing, the less I lived in the real world, and the less I remembered what it was like to live in the real world, as a real person, as me.

When the writing was going well, I would be surrounded by the comfortable, warm feeling that someone else knew what was going on, was making all the decisions, was the safety net under the high wire. Everything was gauzy, soft focus, fuzzed at the periphery.

I could have an adventure without worrying about the consequences. After all, I was always at the edges of his thoughts.

Until the day I wasn't. Everything froze, and I was in a cold, white room, full of statues of the people I had been talking to.

I walked from person to person, attempting to start conversations, but nothing happened. Walked around the room again, looking for a way out, but there was nothing. Solid white walls, floor, ceiling. It was a large room, but I could feel the pressure of the walls against my skin.

I walked to the center of the room, and sat, cross-legged, on the floor. Waiting.

Have you ever had your mind go blank? That space between one thought and the next when your brain is just white noise, when there is not one thought in your head—do you remember that feeling?

Imagine that absence extending forever. There's no way of escaping it, because you don't know—not don't remember, don't know—what you were thinking about before your brain blanked out, and so you don't know what to do to get it started again. There's just nothing. Silence. White.

And there's no time. No way of telling how long you sit in that vast, claustrophobic white room, becoming increasingly less.

I never was able to figure out how long I waited there. But suddenly I was in a room I had never seen before, back in the real world, and he was there.

There were wrinkles at the corners of his eyes, and gray threading through his hair. Writer's block, he explained to me. He had tried to write through it, work on other projects, but nothing helped. Finally, that morning, he had abandoned the novel as unworkable.

I asked if he had tried to bring me back, while he was stuck.

He hadn't really thought of it.

That was when I broke up with him.

He had, I discovered, become quite successful while I was away. A critical darling, praised especially for the complexity, the reality, of his female characters.

Speaking of Marah in an interview, he described her as his one lost love. The interviewer found it romantic.

I found the interviewer tiresome. Being lost was not romantic at all.

Parts of me stayed lost, or got covered over by all those other women I had been for him. Sure, they were me, but they were his view of me, exaggerated, slightly shifted, truth told slanted.

I would turn up a song on the radio, then remember that it was Ali who liked gypsy punk. I abandoned my favorite bakery for two weeks when I convinced myself that I had Fiona's gluten allergy.

For three months, I thought my name was Marah.

During all of this, there were intervals of normalcy. But I still felt the tugs as he borrowed little pieces of me for his fictions. I would lose my favorite perfume, or the memory of the first time I had my heart broken. Tiny bits of myself that would slough away, painlessly. Sometimes they would return when he wrote "The End." More often, they did not.

I reminded him that he had promised not to write about me anymore. He assured me he hadn't meant to. It was just bits, here and there. He'd be more careful. And really, I ought to be flattered.

But then a week of my life disappeared. I loved that short story, and Imogen was an amazing character, the kind of woman I wished I was. That wasn't the point.

The point was, he had stolen me from myself again. I was just gone, and I didn't know where I went. And there were more things about myself that I had forgotten. Was green really my favorite color?

I flicked on the computer, started typing madly. Everything I could remember about myself. But when I looked over the file, there were gaps that I knew I had once remembered, and duplications of events.

Panting, I stripped off my clothing and stared at myself, hoping that my body was more real than my mind. But was that scar on my knee from falling off my bike when I was twelve, or from a too-sharp rock at the beach when I was seventeen. Was that really how I waved hello? Would I cry at a time like this?

Anyone would, I supposed.

I tried to rewrite myself. I scoured boxes of faded flower petals, crumpled ticket stubs, paged obsessively through old yearbooks. Called friend after friend to play do you remember.

When I remembered enough to ask. To know who my friends were.

It didn't work. Whatever gift he had or curse that I was under that let him pull me into his stories, it was a magic too arcane for me to duplicate.

And still, the gaps in my life increased. New changes happened. I woke one morning to find my hair was white. Not like an old woman's, but the platinum white of a rock star or some elven queen.

I didn't dye it back.

There was a collection published of his short fiction. He appeared on Best Of lists, and was shortlisted for important literary prizes.

I forgot if I took milk in my coffee.

He called, asked to see me. Told me he still loved me, was haunted by memories of my skin, my voice, my scent. I missed, I thought, those things, too. So I told him yes.

It took him a moment to recognize me, he said, when I walked across the bar to meet him. Something was different. I told him I didn't know what that might be.

He ordered for both of us. I let him. I was sure he knew what I liked.

There was a story, he explained. He thought maybe the best thing he would ever write. He could feel the electricity of it crackle across his skin, feel the words that he would write pound and echo in his brain.

He had an outline that I could look at, see what I thought. He slid a slim folder across the table.

I wondered aloud why, this time, he would ask permission. This one was longer. An epic. He wasn't sure how long it would take him to write it. And after what had happened the last time, when I had . . . Well. He wanted to ask.

I appreciated the gesture.

I drummed my fingers across the top of the folder, but did not open it.

A waiter discreetly set a martini to the right of my plate. Funny. I had thought that it was Madeleine who drank martinis. But I sipped, and closed my eyes in pleasure at the sharpness of the alcohol.

I said yes.

To one more story, this masterpiece that I could see burning in his eyes. But I had a condition.

Anything, he said. Whatever I needed.

I wanted him to leave me in the story when he was finished.

He told me he had wondered if I might ask for that. I was surprised he hadn't known. He nodded agreement, and that was settled.

We talked idly through dinner. Occasionally his eyes would unfocus, and I could see the lines of plot being woven together behind them.

I wondered what he would name me this time, almost asked, then realized it didn't matter. Then realized I wasn't even sure what my own name was anymore. Grace, maybe? I thought that sounded right. Grace.

He started scribbling on the cover of the folder while we were waiting for the check. I watched him write.

"Rafe fell in love with her voice first, tumbled into it when she introduced herself as . . ."

LET THE PAST BEGIN

•

Jonathan Carroll

EAMON REILLY WAS HANDSOME AND SLOPPY. He seemed to know every-one, even waitresses in restaurants. When he walked in the door, they beamed and began seriously flirting the minute he sat down at their table. I saw this happen several times at different places, places none of us had ever been to before. I asked if he knew these women but he always said no.

Eamon wore his heart on his sleeve and it worked. People cared about him even when he was being impossible, which was pretty often. He drove an old, badly neglected Mercedes that was filthy inside and out. Whenever you rode in it, he had to move stuff off the passenger's seat and throw it in the back. Sometimes you couldn't believe what was there—a metal dows-ing rod; a box of diapers (he was single); a jai alai *xistela;* or once a very inti-mately autographed, badly wrinkled photo of a famous movie actress. He wrote everything in block letters so precise that you might have guessed it came from a typewriter. He kept a detailed daily diary but no one ever saw what was in it, although he carried the book around with him everywhere. His love life was a constant disaster and we wondered why no woman ever stayed with him for very long.

He had once been together with my girlfriend Ava for a couple of weeks. But she was no help when I finally got up the nerve to ask why she broke up with him. "We didn't fit."

"And?"

"And nothing. Some people just don't fit together in certain configu-rations. There are people you can be good friends with, but if you turn it into lovers, the mix is wrong or toxic or . . . something. For me, Eamon is a good guy to hang around with but he wasn't a good boyfriend."

"Why?"

She narrowed her eyes, which is usually the sign a topic is closed and

Ava doesn't want to talk about it anymore. But this time was different. "Sit down."

"What?"

"Sit down. I'm going to tell you a story. It's kind of long."

I did as I was told. When Ava tells you to do something, you do it because, well, because she's Ava. The woman likes dessert, foreign politics, the truth, working in perilous situations, and wonder, not necessarily in that order. She's a journalist who goes on assignment to extremely dangerous places around the world like Spinkai Raghzai, Pakistan, or Sierra Leone. You see her on the TV news holding down her hair or helmet as a military helicopter takes off nearby, leaving her and a small camera crew in some forward armed outpost or barren village that was attacked by rebels the night before. She is fearless, self-confident, and impatient. She is also pregnant, which is why she's home these days. We're pretty sure the child is mine but there is a chance that it might be Eamon's.

I've known Ava Malcolm twelve years and loved her for about eleven of them. During those eleven years, she expressed virtually no interest in me save for an occasional late-night telephone call from unimaginable places like Ouagadougou or Aleppo. The reception on these calls was invariably bad and scratchy. More often than not until the birth of satellite telephones, somewhere in the middle of these chats the line would suddenly go dead, as if it had grown tired of our gabbing and wanted to go to sleep.

Later she admitted that for a while she thought I was gay. But when she came back from some assignment at the end of the world and saw I was living with Jan Schick, it put an end to my gay days in Ava Malcolm's mind.

But poor Jan didn't stand a chance. I always assumed I would only get to love Ava from a distance, be grateful for any time she gave me, and go on admiring this brave talented woman as she went about living her larger-than-life life.

Then she got shot. The bitter irony is that it did not happen in some far-flung flyblown, 130-degree-in-the-shade hellhole where the bad guys rode in on animals instead of tanks. It happened at a convenience store four blocks from her New York apartment. A quick trip to the market for a bottle of red wine and a bag of Cheez Doodles coincided with a dunce named Leaky trying to rob his first store with a gun he later said went off accidentally, twice. One of those bullets nicked Ava's shoulder. But since it came from a Glock G36 subcompact pistol, being "nicked" was an understatement. It probably would not have happened if she'd dropped to the floor like the rest of the people in the store as soon as Leaky started screaming. But Ava being Ava, she wanted to see what was going on, so she just stood there until the gun went off while pointed roughly in her direction.

Ava saw many terrible things in her years as a reporter but had always escaped being hurt. However, as is often the case with people who have been seriously injured, it traumatized her. When she got out of the hospital, she "traveled, screwed men, and hid for a year." Her words.

"I came out of the hospital with my arm in a sling and my ass on fire. I was about 142 percent crazy, I'll say that. I wanted to live life twice as hard afterward—see twice as many things, and have as many men as I could. I'd come this close to dying and the only sure thing I learned from the experience was I wanted *more*: more life, more sex, more new places . . .

"So I used up all the frequent-flyer miles I'd accrued over the years in my job. When they were gone, I called in every favor I had due from people who could get me where I wanted to go. I spent a lot of time in southwestern Russia because that area was like the new Wild West, what with all the oil money and exploration going on down there.

"It was in Baku that I met the Yit."

This was typical Ava storytelling. On her TV reports she gave you relevant information in perfect sound bites and was crystal clear about it. Yet in person she often got so carried away telling you a story or personal anecdote that she overlooked the fact you might not know Baku or, like most people on planet earth, what a "Yit" was.

"Please explain the last two terms."

"Azerbaijan," she said impatiently. "Baku is the capital of Azerbaijan."

"Okay, that's Baku. What's a Yit?"

"A *djelloum*."

"What's a jell-loom?"

"A Yit is another word for a *djelloum*—kind of like a fortune-teller but more shamany. It's a sort of combo fortune-teller and sage. But in Azerbaijan, women are *djelloum*, not men. Which is interesting because it's a very macho, male-oriented society otherwise."

"Okay—Baku, and a Yit."

She leaned over and kissed me on one side of my mouth. "I like how you stop me and ask for clarification. Most people just let me rattle on."

"Proceed."

"Okay. So at the end of the trip I wanted to spend some time in Baku because one of my favorite novels, *Ali and Nino*, takes place there. The book makes the city sound like one of the most romantic places on earth. It isn't, but that's beside the point.

"I was visiting a section called Sabunçu. My guide was Magsud, an Azeri fluent in English who we'd used before when I was there on assignment for the network. So I knew the guy pretty well. He knew the sort of things I liked and was interested in. This time, because I wasn't working, I hired him just to show me around.

"When we got to Sabunçu, Magsud said one of the most famous *djelloum* in Russia lived in that part of the city. Would I be interested in visiting her? Things like palmists, astrology, and tarot card readings are like crack for chicks. Seers, shamans, psychics—lead us to 'em. So I said sure, I'd love to meet a Yit.

"Her name was Lamiya, which is Azeri for 'educated.' She lived in a small apartment in one of those soulless 1950s, gray-cement Communist public-housing projects where every building looks exactly the same and you can easily get lost. I think there were two rooms in the place but we only saw the living room, which was dark even in the middle of the day. Lamiya sat on a couch. Next to it was a baby bassinet. The whole time we were there she kept one hand inside the bassinet, as if she were touching the baby to keep it quiet.

"After we sat down, she asked Magsud if I knew about *lal bala*, which means the silent child. He said no. She told him to explain it to me before she went any further. Of course I didn't understand them because they were speaking Azeri. But I did see him grimace when she finished, like it was going to be tough explaining this in a way that I'd comprehend.

"While Magsud explained *lal bala* to me, Lamiya kept her hand constantly inside the bassinet. I didn't know why until later." Ava stopped speaking and just stared at me for a few moments. I think she was gathering her energy to go on to the difficult part.

"Now I'm going to tell you the story exactly as it happened. You can believe it or not, but just know that I do with all my heart because of what Lamiya told me about myself. Details and facts no one on earth could know but me. *No one,* do you understand? Not my parents, or my sister, no one. But Lamiya knew. She rattled off the most intimate things about me like she was reading them from a list.

"Let me first explain the silent child. According to legend, there are three of them in Russia at all times. When one dies another is immediately born to replace it. It's kind of like the succession of the Dalai Lama in Tibet: a silent child chooses its mother before it's born."

"What do you mean, before it's born? Before the *child* is born?"

"Yes. Lamiya said she knew she'd have a silent child the moment she first sensed she was pregnant. So when hers was born, she wasn't surprised or upset to see it."

"Why would you be upset to see your own baby? Was there something wrong with it?"

Ava looked apprehensive, as if hesitant to tell what must be said next. "The child is not alive. I mean, it's half alive—half alive and half dead; it lives half in this world and half in the other world too."

"What 'other world'?"

"The afterlife. The baby's half alive and half dead, as I said. It never ages. It lives a certain number of years; they never know how many it'll be. That's different for each child. The day it dies, it looks exactly the same as it did on the day it was born, although some of these children live for decades. It never moves, eats, or breathes. It never opens its eyes. But its heart beats, and most important, it's an oracle.

"After she's told you secret things about yourself that absolutely convinces you beyond a doubt that she's genuine, you're allowed to ask the mother two questions. You can ask anything—about the past, about the future, anything you want. As long as she's touching her silent child, she will answer them. But you are only allowed to ask two."

"What did you ask?"

Ava shook her head. "I won't tell you. But part of—" She stopped, got up, and walked to the window. I sat still, waiting for some sign about what to do—go to her, sit, talk, keep quiet . . .

Touching the window glass, she slid her fingers in a long arc across the condensation there. I could almost feel the cold wetness under my own fingertips. What she said next took me completely off guard.

"Did Eamon Reilly ever tell you about his past? About his childhood?"

"*Eamon?* What does he have to do with this?"

"A lot." Ava began rubbing both hands back and forth very fast on the glass, as if trying to erase something. Then she turned to face me. "Just go along with me on this—it's all of a piece. Did you ever talk to him about his past?"

"No."

"Eamon's father was a pilot. He terrorized his family for years, beat them all up and did many other terrible things— a genuine sadist. One of his favorite tortures was to fly really low back and forth over their house in a small plane when he knew everyone was home. Eamon said it was so frightening that the kids and their mother used to all hide under the beds or in the cellar because they were sure one day he'd crash the plane into the house and kill them."

"What happened to him?"

"The guy was also a drunk who luckily drove his car off a bridge one day and died."

"Jesus! So that's why Eamon has . . . what, *issues*?"

"Yes. Once I got so fed up with the way he was behaving that I slapped him. Only then did he tell me some of the stories and details of his childhood. Finally I began to understand why he is the way he is. It doesn't make him any less exasperating, but boy, with that background . . ."

"Terrible. Poor guy."

"Yeah. I don't know if that's the whole reason for him being so peculiar, but it's gotta contribute."

Crossing my arms over my chest, I asked, "But what does it have to do with the silent child?"

"One of the things Lamiya told me was that I'm part of a curse."

I slowly uncrossed my arms and then didn't know what to do with them. "What do you mean, you're *cursed*?" My voice sounded both skeptical and desperate at the same time. How useless your hands and voice are at moments like that. They're all just in the way; none of them knows what to do or how to behave in a crisis that's suddenly dropped on you in the form of one word—like "cursed," or "dead," or "cancer."

She shook her head. "No, I'm *part* of a curse. But I guess in some ways I am because of the role I play in this.

"Lamiya said that after I returned to America I'd get pregnant, which I *have*. But my child will be cursed to live exactly the same life as its father whether it wants to or not. Only some unimportant details will be different." She stopped and said nothing else but continued staring straight at me. I think she was letting her words sink in.

"She didn't say who the father would be?"

"No, she wouldn't. She said whoever made me pregnant, they'd be the one carrying the curse."

"So that could be me too, Ava."

"Yes it could, you're right. We'll find out with a DNA test, but I wanted to talk to you first before I did it. You're obviously a big part of this."

"Yeah, I *guess*," I said cynically and meanly, although I didn't want to. I never wanted to be mean to her, but why was she telling me this now? Why not before?

More silence.

"I love you Ava, but this is nuts, absolutely nuts. It sounds like one of the Arabian Nights—the silent child, a *djelloum,* a curse . . . How can you know it's true?"

"Because of the things that have happened since I saw her. Things Lamiya said *would* happen. Every single one of them has taken place: the pregnancy, my affair with Eamon, and most of all *you*."

"What do you mean, me?"

At that moment the washing machine that had been chugging along in the background chose to *ping* and stop. Ava went silent and didn't look like she was going to answer my question anytime soon. I made a face and walked across the room to get the laundry. Opening the door to the machine, I bent down to pull the wet wash out.

"Ava?"

"What?"

"Your washing machine is full of letters." I pulled out a large white wet K and laid it across my palm. After looking at it, I held it up for her to see. About ten inches long, it appeared to be made of wet cloth. I looked in the machine again and saw that instead of clothes, it was full of a droopy pile of wet capital block letters.

Ava did not seem surprised. In fact, she nodded when I held up the K.

"I put them in there."

"You put them—where's our laundry?"

"In the bathroom."

"But why? Why did you do that? What are they? What are they for?"

"Take out four more. Don't look at which ones—just reach in and take out four. I'll tell you why when you're done."

I wanted to say something but didn't. Reaching into the washing machine, I plunged my hand into the large, soft, wet heap of cloth letters like I was choosing numbers for bingo. When I had four, Ava told me to lay them out together on the floor so that they spelled something. The letters were K, V, Q, R, and O.

"They can't spell anything because there's only one vowel."

She was far enough away so she couldn't see what they were. "Tell me which ones you chose."

"K, V, Q, R, and O."

She slapped both hands down on her lap. "Those were the same letters Eamon chose."

"*What?* Eamon did this too? You also had him take wet letters out of the washing machine?" I realized my voice was way up there, close to shouting.

"Yes, it was a test for both of you. I knew what the answer was going to be, but I had to do it anyway." The tone of her voice said this was no big deal—why was I making such a fuss?

A test using wet letters from the washing machine? Eamon had done it too? The silent child. A Yit. A curse. For the first time in all the years I had known her, I looked at Ava now like she might be the enemy.

"DO YOU THINK AVA'S CRAZY?"

"Of course she's crazy. Why do you think I left her?"

"*You* left her? She said it was just the opposite—she left you."

Eamon snorted and pulled his earlobe. "Do you know the saying—never fall in love with a psychiatrist because they're the craziest people of all? Well, let me amend that to war correspondents too. Never fall in love with a war correspondent either. They've seen too many really bad things. All that pain and death gets into their bones and screws up their heads. Ava's gyroscope is bent, man.

"Did she tell you her story about the silent child? Is that why you're here?" He didn't wait for me to answer. He picked up his vodka and took a sip as if he already knew what I'd say. "That was all right. It was a mad thing, but at least it was entertaining. It was a really good story. But then came those letters in the washing machine, and then the frozen animals—"

"What frozen animals?"

He slapped my shoulder. "She hasn't done that to you yet? Ah, more surprises in store for you there, pal! The longer you hang out with Ava, the funner she gets. I left after the frozen animals. That was it for me. Phew."

"But what if the child really is yours?"

Eamon put his chin in his hand and looked at the floor. "Then I'll do everything I can to make sure Ava and the baby are comfortable and well cared for. But I won't live with that woman. Nope. She's as crazy as they come." He spoke calmly and with resolution. He'd obviously thought all this through and was now at peace with his decisions.

"But wait, Eamon. Just for a minute imagine that what she said was true *is* true. What if you are the father, and the kid is cursed to live your life?"

"Nothing's the matter with my life. I have a good one."

"What about your father and the things he did to your family?"

"Yes, that stuff was terrible, but I don't plan on doing the same things to my family if I end up having one someday." He smiled at me. "I also don't have a pilot's license, so you don't have to worry that I'm going to fly over Ava's house and dive-bomb it.

"And by the way, what about *your* dad? Was he a good man? What if you're the father of her kid? Does she have anything to worry about with you?"

"I never knew my father. He left my mother when I was two."

"Well, there you go! I'm sorry to hear that, but in a way it means you could be more dangerous than me if there really is a curse. Because you don't know what kind of guy your father was, or is. He could be much worse than my old man."

We looked at each other and our silence said we agreed on what he had just said.

Eamon chuckled and shook his head. "Poor Ava—in a worst-case scenario, if that curse *is* true, she may be doomed either way: me with my monster dad, and you with your mystery dad who could be Jack the Ripper."

I said weakly, "But maybe my father's a great guy."

"Great guys don't abandon their families."

"You abandoned Ava."

His voice dropped to a low grumble. "She's not my family. I never said I wanted to be a father."

Sometimes people say things, often inadvertently, that make up your mind for you. The moment after Eamon said he didn't want to be a father, it clicked in my mind that I *did* want to be the father to Ava's child—more than anything else in the world. It was as simple as that. I loved her and yearned to be her partner for the rest of my life if she'd have me. I didn't care if her child was Eamon's and I didn't care if there was a curse. Most important, I didn't even care if Ava Malcolm was as crazy as a fly in a jar. I wanted to be with her and would do anything to make that happen.

When I told Eamon that, he raised one arm and crossed the air with it, as if he were a priest giving me a blessing. "I don't know if you're an idiot, a masochist, or the greatest guy on earth. You know people don't get better as we get older—we just get more of who we are. If Ava's crazy now, she's only going to get crazier."

"I know. But maybe she's not."

"True, maybe she's not. But the alternative to her being crazy is that there really *is* a curse and you're going to have to face a whole different bunch of crap. Either way, you're in the hot seat."

"Maybe but maybe not. You know she's going to the hospital today to get the results of the DNA test."

Eamon, took a deep breath and let it out in one hard *hush*. "Call me and let me know the results, will you?"

"I will." I put out my right hand and we shook for a long time.

He smiled. "You're a good guy, you really are. Sticking by Ava like that, no matter what? That's stand-up stuff."

"Eamon, before I go, tell me about these frozen animals you mentioned before."

"No, you don't need to hear about that now. Maybe it was just a thing she did to me. Forget I even told you." He patted me on the shoulder again and walked out of the bar.

When I got back to Ava's apartment, she wasn't there, so I let myself in. On a table in the hallway, impossible to miss, was a sheaf of papers with a yellow note on top. In large black letters it said PLEASE READ. I picked up the papers and saw there was more written in smaller letters on the note.

"This is the DNA report. It says that neither you nor Eamon are the father of my child. I'm a coward and don't have the nerve to be here when you learn that. I'm going to spend the afternoon with my sister and will be back later. Please be here then so we can at least talk about it. I'm so sorry that I lied to you about not being with other men. There have been others since you and I got together.

"Whether it makes any difference to you or not now, I wasn't lying about Lamiya and the curse. I don't know who the father is, although until today I was certain it was either you or Eamon. But Lamiya *was* real. The curse is real. My deepest love and affection for you is real. Please be here later. I don't deserve that, but I can ask."

Stunned, I tried to look at the other papers in the sheaf but everything was numbers and graphs and at the end a summary I couldn't understand because my brain was flying south fast and had no more room in it.

Still in my coat, I walked into the living room with the papers in hand and sat down on the couch. The couch where we'd had so many good talks and sex and silent, contented times sitting together and reading or just being. I tried to look at the papers again but it was not possible, so I leaned forward to toss them on the coffee table in front of the couch.

A large-format book of photographs I had never seen before was there. The title of the book was *Freeze Frame,* and every picture inside it was a striking rendering of dead animals, fish, and reptiles . . . the whole animal kingdom, frozen. Every single picture was of dead frozen creatures—on their backs, their sides, on ice in markets, on empty snowy roads where they'd obviously been hit and killed by passing cars. The book was gorgeous, poignant, and macabre all at the same time. As I leafed through it, I kept thinking of Eamon's question about whether I had encountered Ava's frozen animals yet. Was this what he was talking about, this book? Or was there more?

I'd looked at perhaps ten of the photos before I came to the marked page. A green Post-it note was at the top, bent over onto the page by constant use. The photograph was unlike any of the others in the book. It was of a woman dressed in black holding an infant in her arms. It is snowing—the world around her is white. She and the child are the only color there. But the child, or what little we can see of it because the woman is holding it so that it looks like she is hiding it from the photographer, looks dead and so white in her arms that it could be frozen too, like all of the other subjects in the book.

But what is most arresting about the photograph is the look on the woman's face. She is totally serene. If she *is* holding a dead child, she has risen beyond her grief into something holy or inhuman. She is at peace, or a kind of transcendent madness that has given her peace. The image was so powerful and beautiful—there is no other word for it—

that I stared at it for what must have been a solid minute. Only after that hypnotic first impression had passed did I look at the bottom of the page where the credits for the pictures all were. The photographer's name was not listed, but the location where it had been taken was Sabunçu, Baku, Azerbaijan.

THE THERAPIST

•

Jeffery Deaver

One

I MET HER BY CHANCE, in a Starbucks near the medical building where I have my office, and I knew at once she was in trouble.

Recognizing people in distress was, after all, my profession.

I was reading over my patient notes, which I transcribe immediately after the fifty-minute sessions (often, as now, fortified by my favorite latte). I have a pretty good memory, but in the field of counseling and therapy you must be "completely diligent and tireless," the many-syllabled phrase a favorite of one of my favorite professors.

This particular venue is on the outskirts of Raleigh in a busy strip mall and, the time being ten thirty A.M. on a pleasant day in early May, there were many people inside for their caffeine fixes.

There was one empty table near me but no chair, and the trim brunette, in a conservative dark blue dress, approached and asked if she could take the extra one at my table. I glanced at her round face, *Good Housekeeping* pretty, not *Vogue*, and smiled. "Please."

I wasn't surprised when she said nothing, didn't smile back. She just took the chair, spun it around, clattering, and sat. Not that it was a flirtation she was rejecting; my smile obviously hadn't been more than a faint pleasantry. I was twice her age and resembled—surprise, surprise—a balding, desk- and library-bound therapist. Not her type at all.

No, her chill response came from the trouble she was in. Which in turn troubled *me* a great deal.

I am a licensed counselor, a profession in which ethics rules preclude me from drumming up business the way a graphic designer or personal trainer might do. So I said nothing more but returned to my notes, while she pulled a sheaf of papers out of a gym bag and began to review them, urgently sipping her drink but not enjoying the hot liquid. I was not surprised. With aching eyes, head down, I managed to see that it was a school lesson plan she was working on. I believed it was for seventh grade.

A teacher . . . I grew even more concerned. I'm particularly sensitive to emotional and psychological problems within people who have influence over youngsters. I myself don't see children as patients—that's a specialty I've never pursued. But no psychologist can practice without a rudimentary understanding of children's psyches, where are sowed the seeds of later problems my colleagues and I treat in our adult practices. Children, especially around ten or eleven, are in particularly susceptible developmental stages and can be forever damaged by a woman like the teacher sitting next to me.

Of course, despite all my experience in this field, it's not impossible to make bum diagnoses. But my concerns were confirmed a moment later when she took a phone call. She was speaking softly at first, though with an edge in her voice, the tone and language suggesting the caller was a family member, probably a child. My heart fell at the thought that she'd have children of her own. I wasn't surprised when after only a few minutes her voice rose angrily. Sure enough, she was losing control. "You did what? . . . I told you not to, under any circumstances . . . Were you just not listening to me? Or were you being stupid again? . . . All right, I'll be home after the conference . . . I'll talk to you about it then."

If she could have slammed the phone down instead of pushing the disconnect button, I'm sure she would have done it.

A sigh. A sip of her coffee drink. Then back to angrily jotting notes in the margins of the lesson plan.

I lowered my head, staring at my own notes. My taste for the latte was gone completely. I tried to consider how to proceed. I'm good at helping people and I enjoy it (there's a reason for that, of course, and one that goes back to my own childhood, no mystery there). I knew I could help her. But it wasn't as easy as that. Often people don't know they need help and even if they do they resist seeking it. Normally I wouldn't worry too much about a passing encounter like this; I'd give a person some time to figure out on their own that they needed to get some counseling.

But this was serious. The more I observed, the more clear the symptoms. The stiffness of posture, the utter lack of humor or enjoyment in what she was doing with her lesson plan, lack of pleasure in the drink, the anger, the twitchy obsessive way she wrote.

And the eyes. That's what speaks the most, to me at least.

The eyes . . .

So I decided to give it a try. I stood to get a refill of latte and, walking back to my table, I dropped a napkin onto hers. I apologized and collected it. Then laughed, looking at her handiwork.

"My girlfriend's a teacher," I said. "She absolutely hates lesson plans. She's never quite sure what to do with them."

She didn't want to be bothered, but even people in her state acknowledge some social conventions. She looked up, the troubled eyes a deep brown. "They can be a chore. Our school board insists."

Clumsy, but at least it broke the ice and we had a bit of a conversation.

"I'm Martin Kobel."

"Annabelle Young."

"Where do you teach?"

It was in Wetherby, a good-size town in central North Carolina about an hour from Raleigh. She was here for an education conference.

"Pam, my girlfriend, teaches grade school. You?"

"Middle school."

The most volatile years, I reflected.

"That's the age she's thinking of moving over to. She's tired of six-year-olds . . . You put a lot into that," I said, nodding at the plan.

"I try."

I hesitated a moment. "Listen, kind of fortuitous I ran into you. If I gave you our phone number and you've got a few minutes—I mean, if it's no imposition—would you think about giving Pam a call? She could really use some advice. Five minutes or so. Give her some thoughts on middle school."

"Oh, I don't know. I've only been a teacher for three years."

"Just think about it. You seem like you know what you're doing." I took out a business card.

Martin J. Kobel, MS, MSW
Behavioral Therapy
Specialties: Anger Management and Addiction

I wrote "Pam Robbins" on the top along with the home phone number.

"I'll see what I can do." She slipped the card in her pocket and turned back to her coffee and the lesson plan.

I knew I'd gone as far as I could. Anything more would have seemed inappropriate and pushed her away.

After fifteen minutes, she glanced at her watch. Apparently whatever conference she was attending was about to resume. She gave a chill smile my way. "Nice talking to you."

"The same," I said.

Annabelle gathered the lesson plan and notes and stuffed them back into her gym bag. As she rose, a teenage boy eased past and jostled her inadvertently with his bulky backpack. I saw her eyes ripple with that look I know so well. "Jesus," she whispered to him. "Learn some manners."

"Hey, lady, I'm sorry—"

She waved a dismissing hand at the poor kid. Annabelle walked to the counter to add more milk to her coffee. She wiped her mouth and tossed out the napkin. Without a look back at me or anyone she pointed her cold visage toward the door and pushed outside.

I gave it thirty seconds then also stopped at the milk station. Glancing into the hole for trash, I spotted, as I'd half expected, my card, sitting next to her crumpled napkin. I'd have to take a different approach. I certainly wasn't going to give up on her. The stakes for her own well-being and of those close to her were too high.

But it would require some finesse. I've found that you can't just bluntly tell potential patients that their problems are the result not of a troubled childhood or a bad relationship, but simply because an invisible entity had latched onto their psyches like a virus and was exerting its influence.

In a different era, or in a different locale, someone might have said that the teacher was possessed by a demonic spirit or the like. Now we're much more scientific about it, but it's still wise to ease into the subject slowly.

ANNABELLE YOUNG HAD COME under the influence of a neme.

The term was first coined by a doctor in Washington, D.C. James Pheder was a well-known biologist and researcher. He came up with the word by combining "negative" and "meme," the latter describing a cultural phenomenon that spreads and replicates in societies.

I think a reference to meme—"m" version—is a bit misleading, since it suggests something rather more abstract than what a neme really is. In my lengthy book on the subject, published a few years ago, I define a neme as "a discrete body of intangible energy that evokes extreme emotional responses in humans, resulting in behavior that is most often detrimental to the host or to the society in which he or she lives."

But "neme" is a convenient shorthand and every therapist or researcher familiar with the concept uses it.

The word is also beneficial in that it neutrally describes a scientific, proven construct and avoids the historical terms that have muddied the truth for thousands of years. Words like ghosts, spirits, Rudolf Otto's numinous presences, revenants, Buddhism's hungry ghosts, rural countrysides' white ladies, Japanese yurei, demons. Dozens of others.

Those fictional legends and superstitions were largely the result of the inability to explain nemes scientifically in the past. As often happens, until a phenomenon is rationally explained and quantified, folklore fills the gaps. The old belief, for instance, in spontaneous generation—that life could arise from inanimate objects—was accepted for thousands of years, supported by apparently scientific observations, for instance, that maggots and other infestations appeared in rotting food or standing water. It was only when Louis Pasteur proved via controlled, repeatable experiments that living material, like eggs or bacteria, *had* to be present for life to generate that the old view fell by the wayside.

Same thing with nemes. Framing the concept in terms of ghosts and possessing spirits was a convenient and simple fiction. Now we know better.

Growing up, I'd never heard of these things that would later be labeled nemes. It was only after a particular incident that I became aware: the deaths of my parents and brother.

You could say that my family was killed by one.

When I was sixteen we went to one of Alex's basketball games at our school. At some point my father and I hit the hot dog stand. The father of a player on the opposing team was standing nearby, sipping a Coke and watching the game. Suddenly—I can still remember it perfectly—the man underwent a transformation, instantly shifting from relaxed and benign to tense, distracted, on guard. And the eyes . . . there was no doubt that they changed. The very color seemed to alter; they grew dark, malevolent. I knew something had happened, something had possessed him, I thought at the time. I felt chilled, and I stepped away from him.

Then the man suddenly grew angry. Furious. Something on the court set him off. A foul maybe, a bad call. He screamed at Alex's team, he screamed at our coach, at the ref. In his rage, he bumped against my father and dropped his soda, spilling it on his shoes. It was his fault but he seemed to blame my father for the mishap. The men got into an argument, though my father soon realized that the man was out of control, consumed by this odd rage, and ushered us back to the bleachers.

After the game I was still troubled but assumed the matter was over. Not so. The man followed us out into the parking lot and, screaming, bizarrely challenged my father to a fight. The man's wife was crying, pulling him back and apologizing. "He's never behaved like this, really!"

"Shut up, bitch," he raged and slapped her.

Shaken, we climbed into the car and drove off. Ten minutes later, driving down I-40, we were sitting in troubled silence when a car veered over three lanes. The man from the game swerved right toward us, driving us off the road.

I remember seeing his face, twisted with anger, over the steering wheel.

In court he tearfully explained that he didn't know what happened. It was like he was possessed. That defense didn't get him very far. He was found guilty of three counts of first-degree manslaughter.

After I got out of the hospital following the crash, I couldn't get out of my head the memory of what had happened to the man. How clear it was to me that he'd changed, in a flash. It was like flipping a light switch.

I began reading about sudden changes in personality and rage and impulse. That research led eventually to the writings of Dr. Pheder and other researchers and therapists. I grew fascinated with the concept of nemes, considered a theory by some, a reality by others.

As to their origin, there are several theories. I subscribe to one I found the most logical. Nemes are vestiges of human instinct. They were an integral part of the psychological makeup of the creatures in the chain that led to Homo sapiens and were necessary for survival. In the early days of humanoids, it was occasionally necessary to behave in ways we would consider bad or criminal now. To commit acts of violence, to be rageful, impulsive, sadistic, greedy. But as societies formed and developed, the need for those darker impulses faded. The governing bodies, the armies, the law enforcers took over the task of our survival. Violence, rage, and the other darker impulses became not only unnecessary but were counter to society's interests.

Somehow—there are several theories on this—the powerful neuro impulses that motivated those dark behaviors separated from humans and came to exist as separate entities, pockets of energy, you could say. In my research I found a precedent for this migration: the same thing happened with telepathy. Many generations ago, psychic communication was common. The advent of modern communication techniques eliminated the need for what we could call extrasensory perception, though many young children still have documented telepathic skills. (However, it's interesting that with the increased use of cell phones and computers by youngsters, incidents of telepathy among young people are dramatically decreasing.)

But whatever their genealogy, nemes exist and there are millions of them. They float around like flu viruses until they find a vulnerable person and then incorporate themselves into the psyche of their host ("incorporate" is used, rather than a judgmental term like "infest" or "infect," and never the theologically loaded "possess"). If someone is impulsive, angry, depressed, confused, scared—even physically sick—nemes will sense that and make a beeline for the cerebrum cortex, the portion of the brain where emotion is controlled. They usually avoid people who are emotionally stable, strong willed, and have high degrees of self-control, though not always.

Nemes are invisible, like electromagnetic waves and light at the far end of the spectrum, though it's sometimes possible to tell they're nearby if you hear distortion on a cell phone, TV, or radio. Usually, the host doesn't sense the incorporation itself; they only experience a sudden mood swing. Some people can outright sense them. I'm one of these, though there's nothing "special" about me. It's simply like having acute hearing or good eyesight.

Do nemes think?

They do, in a way. Though thought is probably the wrong word. More likely they're like insects, with a sense of awareness and instinct. Survival is very strong within them, too. There's nothing immortal about nemes. When their host passes away, they seem to dissipate also. I myself don't believe they communicate with one another, since I've never seen any evidence that they do.

This isn't to minimize the damage they can do, of course. It's significant. The rage, the impulsive behavior that arises from incorporation leads to rape, murder, physical and sexual abuse, and more subtle harm like substance overuse and verbal abuse. They also affect the physiology and morphology of the host's body itself, as a series of autopsies several years ago proved.

After my devastating personal encounter with nemes, I decided I wanted to work in a field that would help minimize the damage they could do. I became a therapist.

The thrust of my approach is behavioral. Once you're under the influence of a neme, you don't "cast it out," as a practitioner (now former) unfortunately joked at a psychotherapy conference in Chicago some years ago. You treat the symptoms. I concentrate on working with my patients to achieve self-control, using any number of techniques to avoid or minimize behaviors that are destructive to them or others. In most cases it doesn't even matter that the patient knows he or she is a host for a neme (some patients are comfortable with the reality, and others aren't). In any case, the methods I use are solid and well established, used by all behavioral therapists, and by and large successful.

There've been occasional defeats, of course. It's the nature of the profession. Two of my patients, in which very potent nemes had incorporated, killed themselves when they were simply unable to resolve the conflict between their goals and the neme-influenced behavior.

There's also something that's been in the back of my mind for years: risk to myself. My life has been devoted to minimizing their effectiveness and spread and so I sometimes wonder if a neme senses that I'm a threat. This is probably according them too much credit; you have to guard against personifying them. But I can't help but think back to an incident several years ago. I was attending a psychology conference in New York City and was nearly mugged. It was curious since the young attacker was a model student at a nice high school near my hotel. He'd never been in trouble with the police. And he was armed with a long knife. An off-duty policeman happened to be nearby and managed to arrest him just as he started after me with the weapon.

It was late at night and I couldn't see clearly, but I believed, from the boy's eyes, that he was being influenced by a neme, motivated by its own sense of survival to kill me.

Probably not. But even if there was some truth to it, I wasn't going to be deterred from my mission to save people at risk.

People like Annabelle Young.

THE DAY AFTER RUNNING into her in Starbucks, I went to the North Carolina State University library and did some research. The state licensing agencies' databases and ever-helpful Google revealed that the woman was thirty years old and worked at Chantelle West Middle School in Wetherby County. Interestingly, she was a widow—her husband had died three years ago—and, yes, she had a nine-year-old son, probably the target of her anger on the phone. According to information about the school where she taught, Annabelle would generally teach large classes, with an average of thirty-five students per year.

This meant that she could have a dramatic and devastating impact on the lives of many young people.

Then too was the matter of Annabelle's own well-being. I was pretty sure that she'd come under the influence of the neme around the time her husband died; a sudden personal loss like that makes you emotionally vulnerable and more susceptible than otherwise. (I noted too that she'd gone back to work around that time, and I wondered if her neme sensed an opportunity to incorporate within someone who could influence a large number of equally vulnerable individuals, the children in her classes.)

Annabelle was obviously a smart woman and she might very well get into counseling at some time. But there comes a point when the neme is so deeply incorporated that people actually become accustomed or addicted to the inappropriate behaviors nemes cause. They don't *want* to change. My assessment was that she was past this point. And so, since I wasn't going to hear from her, I did the only thing I could. I went to Wetherby.

I got there early on a Wednesday. The drive was pleasant, along one of those combined highways that traverse central North Carolina. It split somewhere outside of Raleigh and I continued on the increasingly rural branch of the two, taking me through old North Carolina. Tobacco warehouses and small industrial-parts plants—most of them closed years ago—but still squatting in weeds. Trailer parks, very unclosed. Bungalows and plenty of evidence of a love of Nascar and Republican party lines.

Wetherby has a redeveloped downtown, but that's just for show. I noted immediately as I cruised along the two-block stretch that nobody was buying anything in the art galleries and antiques stores, and the nearly empty restaurants, I suspected, got new awnings with new names every eight months or so. The real work in places like Wetherby got done in the malls and office parks and housing developments built around new golf courses.

I checked into a motel, showered, and began my reconnaissance, checking out Chantelle Middle School. I parked around the time I'd learned classes were dismissed but didn't catch a glimpse of Annabelle Young.

Later that evening, about seven thirty, I found her house, four miles away, a modest twenty-year-old colonial in need of painting, on a cul-de-sac. There was no car in the drive. I parked under some trees and waited.

Fifteen minutes later a car pulled into the drive. I couldn't tell if her son was inside or not. The Toyota pulled into the garage and the door closed. A few minutes later I got out, slipped into some woods beside the house, and glanced into the kitchen. I saw her carting dishes inside. Dirty dishes from lunch or last night, I assumed. She set them in the sink and I saw her pause, staring down. Her face was turned away but her body language, even from this distance, told me that she was angry.

Her son appeared, a skinny boy with longish brown hair. *His* body language suggested that he was cautious. He said something to his mother. Her head snapped toward him and he nodded quickly. Then retreated. She stayed where she was, staring at the dishes, for a moment. Without even rinsing them she stepped out of the room and swept her hand firmly along the wall, slapping the switch out. I could almost hear the angry gesture from where I was.

I didn't want to talk to her while her son was present, so I headed back to the motel.

The next day I was up early and cruised back to the school before the teachers arrived. At seven fifteen I caught a glimpse of her Camry arriving and watched her climb out and stride unsmilingly into the school. Too many people around and she was too harried to have a conversation now.

I returned at three in the afternoon and when Annabelle emerged followed her to a nearby strip mall, anchored by a Harris-Teeter grocery store. She went shopping and came out a half hour later. She dumped the plastic bags in her trunk. I was going to approach her, even though a meeting in the parking lot wasn't the most conducive place to pitch my case, when I saw her lock the car and walk toward a nearby bar and grill.

At three thirty she wouldn't be eating lunch or dinner and I knew what she had in mind. People influenced by nemes often drink more than they should, to dull the anxiety and anger that come from the incorporation.

Though I would eventually work on getting her to cut down on her alcohol consumption, her being slightly intoxicated and relaxed now could be a big help. I waited five minutes and followed. Inside the dark tavern, which smelled of Lysol and onions, I spotted her at the bar. She was having a mixed drink. Vodka or gin, it seemed, and some kind of juice. She was nearly finished with her first and she waved for a second.

I sat down two stools away and ordered a Diet Coke. I felt her head swivel toward me, tilt slightly as she debated whether she'd seen me before, and turn back to her drink. Then the pieces fell together and she faced me again.

Without looking up I said, "I'm a professional counselor, Ms. Young. I'm here only in that capacity. To help. I'd like to talk to you."

"You . . . you followed me here? From Raleigh?"

I made a show of leaving money for the soda to suggest that I wasn't going to stay longer than necessary, trying to put her at ease.

"I did, yes. But please, you don't need to be afraid."

Finally I turned to look at her. The eyes were just as I expected, narrow, cold, the eyes of somebody else entirely. The neme was even stronger than I'd thought.

"I'm about five seconds away from calling the police."

"I understand. But please, listen. I want to say something to you. And if you want me to leave, I'll head back to Raleigh right now. You can choose whatever you want."

"Say it and get out." She took another drink.

"I specialize in treating people who aren't happy in life. I'm good at it. When I saw you the other day in Starbucks, I knew you were exactly the sort of patient who could benefit from my expertise. I would like very much to help you."

No mention of nemes, of course.

"I don't need a shrink."

"I'm actually not a shrink. I'm a psychologist, not a doctor."

"I don't care what you are. You can't . . . can't you be reported for this, trying to drum up business?"

"Yes, and you're free to do that. But I thought it was worth the risk to offer you my services. I don't care about the money. You can pay me whatever you can afford. I care about helping you. I can give you references and you can call the state licensing board about me."

"Do you even have a girlfriend who's a teacher?"

"No. I lied. Which I'll never do again . . . It was that important to try to explain how I can help you."

And then I saw her face soften. She was nodding.

My heart was pounding hard. It had been a risk, trying this, but she was going to come around. The therapy would be hard work. For both of us. But the stakes were too high to let her continue the way she was. I knew we could make significant progress.

I turned away to pull a card from my wallet. "Let me tell you a—"

As I looked back, I took the full tide of her second drink in the face. My eyes on fire from the liquor and stinging juice, I gasped in agony and grabbed bar napkins to dry them.

"Annie, what's wrong?" the bartender snapped, and through my blurred vision I could just make out his grabbing her arm as she started to fling the glass at me. I raised my own arm to protect myself.

"What'd he do?"

"Fuck you, let go of me!" she cried to him.

"Hey, hey, take it easy, Annie. What—?"

Then he ducked as she launched the glass at *him*. It struck a row of others; half of them shattered. She was out of control. Typical.

"Fuck you both!" Screaming. She dug a bill out of her purse and flung it onto the bar.

"Please, Ms. Young," I said, "I can help you."

"If I see you again, I'm calling the police." She stormed out.

"Listen, mister, what the hell d'you do?"

I didn't answer him. I grabbed some more napkins and, wiping my face, walked to the window. I saw her stride up to her son, who was standing nearby with a book bag. So this was the rendezvous spot. I wondered how often he'd had to wait outside for mom while she was in here getting drunk. I pictured cold January afternoons, the boy huddled and blowing breath into his hands.

She gestured him after her. Apparently there'd been something else on the agenda for after school, and, disappointed, he lifted his arms and glanced at the nearby sports store. But the shopping was not going to happen today. She stormed up and grabbed him by the arm. He pulled away. She drew back to slap him, but he dutifully walked to the car. I could see him clicking on his seat belt and wiping his tears.

Without a glance back at the bartender, I too left.

I walked to the car to head back to the motel to change. What had happened was discouraging, but I'd dealt with more difficult people than Annabelle Young. There were other approaches to take. Over the years I've learned what works and what doesn't; it's all part of being a therapist.

THE NEXT MORNING AT six I parked behind Etta's Diner, in a deserted portion of the lot. The restaurant was directly behind Annabelle's house. I made my way up the hill along a path that led to the sidewalk in her development. I had to take an oblique approach; if she saw me coming she'd never answer the door, and that would be that.

The morning was cool and fragrant with the smells of pine and wet earth. Being spring, the sky was light even at this early hour and it was easy to make my way along the path. I wondered how different Annabelle's life had been before her husband died. How soon the neme had incorporated itself into her afterward. I suspected she'd been a vivacious, caring mother and wife, completely different from the enraged out-of-control woman she now was becoming.

I continued to the edge of the woods and waited behind the house in a stand of camellias with exploding red blossoms. At about six thirty her son pushed out the front door, carting a heavy book bag, and strolled to the end of the cul-de-sac, presumably to catch his bus.

When he was gone, I walked to the porch and climbed the stairs.

Was I ready? I asked myself.

Always those moments of self-doubt, even though I'd been a professional therapist for years.

Always, the doubts.

But then I relaxed. My mission in life was to save people. I was good at that task. I knew what I was doing.

Yes, I was ready.

I rang the doorbell and stepped aside from the peephole. I heard the footsteps approach. She flung the door open and had only a moment to gasp at the sight of the black stocking mask I was wearing and the lengthy knife in my gloved hand.

I grabbed her hair and plunged the blade into her chest three times, then sliced through her neck. Both sides and deep, so the end would be quick.

Lord knew I didn't want her to suffer.

Two

THE JOB OF MAKING sure that Martin Kobel was either put to death or sentenced to life in prison for the murder of Annabelle Young fell to Glenn Hollow, the Wetherby County prosecutor.

And it was a job that he had embraced wholeheartedly from the moment he got the call from county-police dispatch. Forty-two years old, Hollow was the most successful prosecutor in the state of North Carolina, judging in terms of convictions won, and judging from the media since he had a preference for going after violent offenders. A mark of his success was that this was to be his last year in Wetherby. He'd be running for state attorney general in November and there wasn't much doubt he'd win.

But his grander plans wouldn't detract from his enthusiastic prosecution of the murderer of Annabelle Young. In big cities the prosecutors get cases tossed onto their desks along with the police reports. With Glenn Hollow it was different. He had an honorary flashing blue light attached to his dash and, ten minutes after getting the call about the homicide, he was at Ms. Young's house while the forensic team was still soaking up blood and taking pix.

He was now walking into the Wetherby County Courthouse. Nothing Old South about the place. It was the sort of edifice you'd find in Duluth or Toledo or Schenectady. One story, nondescript white stone, overtaxed air-conditioning, scuffed linoleum floors, and greenish fluorescents that might engender the question, "Hey, you feeling okay?"

Hollow was a lean man, with drawn cheeks and thick black hair close to a skullish head—defendants said he looked like a ghoul; kinder reports, that he resembled Gregory Peck in *Moby Dick*, minus the beard. He was somber and reserved and kept his personal life far, far away from his professional life.

He now nodded at the secretary in the ante-office of Judge Brigham Rollins's chambers.

"Go on in, Glenn."

Inside were two big men. Rollins was midfifties and had a pitted face and the spiky gray hair of a crew cut neglected a week too long. He was in shirtsleeves, though noosed with a tie, of course. He wore plucky yellow suspenders that hoisted his significant tan pants like a concrete bucket under a crane. Gray stains radiated from under his arms. As usual the judge had doused himself with Old Spice.

Sitting opposite was Bob Ringling—the circus jokes all but dead after these many years of being a defense lawyer in a medium-size town, and, no, there was no relation. Stocky, with blondish brown hair carefully trimmed, he resembled a forty-five-year-old retired army major—not a bad deduction, since Fayetteville wasn't terribly far away, but, like the circus brothers, not true.

Hollow didn't like or dislike Ringling. He was fair, though abrasive, and he made Hollow work for every victory. Which was as it should be, the prosecutor believed. God created defense lawyers, he'd said, to make sure the system was fair and the prosecution didn't cheat or get lazy. After all, there *was* that one-in-a-hundred chance that the five-foot-eight black gangbanger from Central High presently in custody wasn't the same five-foot-eight black gangbanger from Central High who actually pulled the trigger.

Judge Rollins closed a folder that'd he'd been perusing. He grunted. "Tell me where we are with this one, gentlemen."

"Yessir," Hollow began. "The state is seeking special-circumstances murder."

"This's about that teacher got her throat slit, right?"

"Yessir. In her house. Broad daylight."

A distasteful grimace. Not shock. Rollins'd been a judge for years.

The courthouse was on the crook of Route 85 and Henderson Road. Through one window you could see Galloway-belted cows grazing. They were black and white, vertically striped, precise, as if God had used a ruler. Hollow could look right over the judge's shoulder and see eight of them, chewing. Out the other window was a T.J. Maxx, a Barnes & Noble, and a multiplex under construction. These two views pretty much defined Wetherby.

"What's the story behind it?"

"This Kobel, a therapist. He was stalking her. They met at a Starbucks when she was in Raleigh at an educational conference. Got witnesses say he gave her his card but she threw it out. Next thing he tracked her down and shows up in Wetherby. Got into a fight at Red Robin, near Harris-Teeter. She threw a drink in his face. One witness saw him park at Etta's, the diner, the morning she was killed—"

"Tonight's corned beef," the judge said.

"They do a good job of that," Ringling added.

True, they did. Hollow continued, "—and he hiked up into those woods behind her place. When she opened the door, he killed her. He waited till her boy left."

"There's that, at least," Rollins grumbled. "How'd the boys in blue get him?"

"Unlucky for him. Busboy on a smoke break at Etta's saw him coming out of the forest, carrying some things. The kid found some blood near where he'd parked. Called the police with the make and model. Kobel'd tossed away the knife and mask and gloves, but they found 'em. Fibers, DNA, fingerprints on the *inside* of the gloves. People always forget that. They watch *CSI* too much . . . Oh, and then he confessed."

"*What?*" the judge barked.

"Yep. Advised of rights, twice. Sang like a bird."

"Then what the hell're you doing here? Take a plea and let's get some real work done."

The judge glanced at Ringling, but the defense lawyer in turn cast his eyes to Hollow.

Rollins gripped his ceramic coffee mug and sipped the hot contents. "What isn't who telling who? Don't play games. There's no jury to impress with your clevers."

Ringling said, "He's completely insane. Nuts."

A skeptical wrinkle on the judge's brow. "But you're saying he wore a mask and gloves?"

Most insane perps didn't care if they were identified and didn't care if they got away afterward. They didn't wear ninja or hit-man outfits. They were the sort who hung around afterward and fingerpainted with the blood of their victims.

Ringling shrugged.

The judge asked, "Competent to stand trial?"

"Yessir. We're saying he was insane at the time of commission. No sense of right or wrong. No sense of reality."

The judge grunted.

The insanity defense is based on one overriding concept in jurisprudence: responsibility. At what point are we responsible for acts we commit? If we cause an accident and we're sued in civil court for damages, the law asks, would a reasonably prudent person have, say, driven his car on a slippery road at thirty-five miles per hour? If the jury says yes, then we're not responsible for the crash.

If we're arrested for a crime, the law asks, did we act knowingly and intentionally to break a law? If we didn't, then we're not guilty.

There are, in fact, two ways in which sanity arises in a criminal court. One is when the defendant is so out of it that he can't participate in his own trial. That U.S. Constitution thing: the right to confront your accusers.

But this isn't what most people familiar with *Boston Legal* or *Perry Mason* think of as the insanity defense and, as Bob Ringling had confirmed, it wasn't an issue in *State v. Kobel.*

More common is when defense lawyers invoke various offshoots of M'Naughten rule, which holds that if the defendant lacked the capacity to know he was doing something wrong when he committed the crime, he can't be found guilty. This isn't to say he's going scot-free; he'll get locked up in a mental ward until it's determined that he's no longer dangerous.

This was Bob Ringling's claim regarding Martin Kobel.

But Glenn Hollow exhaled a perplexed laugh. "He wasn't insane. He was a practicing therapist with an obsession over a pretty woman who was ignoring him. Special circumstances. I want guilty, I want the needle. That's it."

Ringling said to Rollins, "Insanity. You sentence him to indefinite incarceration in Butler, Judge. We won't contest it. No trial. Everybody wins."

Hollow said, "Except the other people he kills when they let him out in five years."

"Ah, you just want a feather in your cap for when you run for AG. He's a media bad boy."

"I want justice," Hollow said, supposing he was sounding pretentious. And not caring one whit. Nor admitting that, yeah, he did want the feather, too.

"What's the evidence for the looney tunes?" the judge asked. He had a very different persona when he was in chambers compared with when he was in the courtroom, and presumably different yet at Etta's Diner, eating corned beef.

"He absolutely believes he didn't do anything wrong. He was saving the children in Annabelle's class. I've been over this with him a dozen times. He *believes* it."

"Believes what exactly?" the judge asked.

"That she was possessed. By something like a ghost. I've looked it up. Some cult thing on the Internet. Some spirit or something makes you lose control, lose your temper and beat the crap out of your wife or kids. Even makes you kill people. It's called a neme." He spelled it.

"Neme."

Hollow said, "I've looked it up too, Judge. You can look it up. We all can look it up. Which is just what Kobel did. To lay the groundwork for claiming insanity. He killed a hot young woman who rejected him. And now he's pretending he believes in 'em to look like he's nuts."

"If that's the case," Ringling said gravely, "then he's been planning ever since he was a teenager to kill a woman he met two weeks ago."

"What's that?"

"His parents died in a car crash when he was in high school. He had a break with reality, the doctors called it. Diagnosed as a borderline personality."

"Like my cousin," the judge said. "She's awkward. The wife and I never invite her over, if we can avoid it."

"Kobel got involuntary commitment for eight months back then, talking about these creatures that possessed the driver who killed his family. Same thing as now."

"But he had to go to shrink school," the judge pointed out. "He graduated. That's not crazy in my book."

Hollow leaped in with, "Exactly. He has a master's in psychology. One in social work. Good grades. Sees patients. And he's written books. For God's sake."

"One of which I happen to have with me and which I will be introducing into evidence. Thank you, Glenn, for bringing it up." The defense law-yer opened his briefcase and dropped a 10-pound stack of 8½-by-11 sheets on the judge's desk. "*Self*-published, by the way. And written by hand."

Hollow looked it over. He had good eyes but it was impossible to read any of the text except the title because it was in such tiny handwriting. There had to be a thousand words per page, in elegant, obsessive script.

Biblical Evidence of Malevolent
Emotional ENERGY Incorporated into Psyches
By Martin Kobel
© *All rights reserved*

"All rights reserved?" Hollow snorted. "Who's going to plagiarize this crap? And what's with the capitalization?"

"Glenn, this is one of about thirty volumes. He's been writing these things for twenty years. And it's the smallest one."

The prosecutor repeated, "He's faking."

But the judge was skeptical. "Going back all those years?"

"Okay, he's quirky. But this man is dangerous. Two of his patients killed themselves under circumstances that make it seem like he sug-gested they do it. Another one's serving five years because he attacked Kobel in his office. He claimed the doctor provoked him. And Kobel broke into a funeral home six years ago and was caught fucking around with the corpses."

"What?"

"Not that way. He was dissecting them. Looking for evidence of these things, these nemes."

Ringling said happily, "There's another book he wrote on the autopsy. Eighteen hundred pages. Illustrated."

"It wasn't an autopsy, Bob. It was breaking into a funeral home and fucking around with corpses." Hollow was getting angry. But maybe it's just a neme, he thought cynically. "He goes to conferences."

"Paranormal conferences. Wacko conferences. Full of wackos just like him."

"Jesus Christ, Bob. The people who cop insanity pleas're paranoid schizos. They don't bathe, they take Haldol and lithium, they're delusional. They don't go to fucking Starbucks and ask for an extra shot of syrup."

Hollow had used the *f* word more times today than in the past year.

Ringling said, "They kill people because they're possessed by ghosts. That's not sane. End of story."

The judge lifted his hand. "You gentlemen know that when the earth was young, Africa and South America were right next to each other. I mean, fifty feet away. Think about that. And here you are, same thing. You're real close, I can tell. You can work it out. Come together. There's a song about that. It's in your interest. If we go to trial, you two're doing all the work. All I'm gonna be doing is saying 'sustained' and 'overruled.'"

"Bob, he killed that girl, a schoolteacher. In cold blood. I want him away forever. He's a danger and he's sick . . . What I can do, but only this, I'll go with life. Drop special circumstances. But no parole."

The judge looked expectantly toward Bob Ringling. "That's something."

"I knew it'd come up," Ringling said. "I asked my client about it. He says he didn't do anything wrong and he has faith in the system. He's convinced there're these things floating around and they glom onto you and make you do bad stuff. No, we're going for insanity."

Hollow grimaced. "You want to play it that way, you get your expert and I'll get mine."

The judge grumbled. "Pick a date, gentlemen. We're going to trial. And, for Christ sake, somebody tell me, what the hell is a neme?"

THE PEOPLE OF THE *State of North Carolina v. Kobel* began on a Wednesday in July.

Glenn Hollow kicked it off with a string of witnesses and police reports regarding the forensic evidence, which was irrefutable. Bob Ringling let most of it go and just got a few errant bits of trace evidence removed, which Hollow didn't care about anyway.

Another of Hollow's witnesses was a clerk from Starbucks in Raleigh, who testified about the business card exchange. (Hollow noted the troubled looks on the faces of several jurors and people in the gallery, leaving them wondering, he supposed, about the wisdom of affairs and other indiscreet behavior in places with observant baristas.)

Other witnesses testified about behavior consistent with stalking, including several who'd seen Kobel in Wetherby on the days before the murder. Several had seen his car parked outside the school where Anna-belle Young taught. If there's any way to put your location on record, it's to be a middle-aged man parked outside a middle school. Eight concerned citizens gave the police his tag number.

The busboy at Etta's Diner gave some very helpful testimony with the help of a Spanish translator.

As for Kobel himself, sitting at the defense table, his hair was askew and his suit didn't fit right. He frantically filled notebook after notebook with writing like ant tracks.

Son of a bitch, thought Hollow. It was pure performance, orches-trated by Bob Ringling, Esq., of course, with Martin Kobel in the role of schizophrenic. Hollow had seen the police interview video. On screen the defendant had been well scrubbed, well spoken, and no twitchier than Hollow's ten-year-old Lab, known to take naps in the middle of tornados.

Any other case, the trial would've been over with on the second day—with a verdict for the People, followed by a lengthy appeal and an uncom-fortable few minutes while the executioner figured out which was the better vein, right arm or left.

But there was more, of course. Where the real battle would be fought.

Ringling's expert psychiatrist testified that the defendant was, in his opinion, legally insane and unable to tell the difference between right and wrong. Kobel honestly believed that Annabelle Young was a threat to stu-dents and her son because she was infested by a neme, some spirit or force that he truly believed existed.

"He's paranoid, delusional. His reality is very, very different from ours," was the expert's conclusion.

The shrink's credentials were good, and since that was about the only way to attack him, Hollow let him go.

"Your Honor," Ringling next said. "I move to introduce defense exhib-its numbers one through twenty-eight."

And wheeled up to the bench—literally, in carts—Kobel's notebooks and self-published treatises on nemes, more than anybody could possibly be interested in.

A second expert for the defense testified about these writings. "These are typical of a delusional mind." Everything Kobel had written was typi-cal of a paranoid and delusional individual who had lost touch with reality.

He stated that there was no scientific basis for the concept of neme. "It's like voodoo, it's like vampires, werewolves."

Ringling tried to seal the deal by having the doctor read a portion from one of these "scientific treatises," a page of utterly incomprehensible nonsense. Judge Rollins, on the edge of sleep, cut him off. "We get the idea, Counselor. Enough."

On cross-examination, Hollow couldn't do much to deflate this testimony. The best he could do was: "Doctor, do you read the Harry Potter books?"

"Well, as a matter of fact, yes, I have."

"The fourth was my favorite. What was yours?"

"Umm, I don't know really."

"Is it possible," the prosecutor asked the witness, "that those writings of Mr. Kobel are merely attempts at writing a novel? Some big fantasy book."

"I . . . I can't imagine it."

"But it's possible, isn't it?"

"I suppose. But I'll tell you, he'll never sell the movie rights."

Amid the laughter, the judge dismissed the witness.

There was testimony about the bizarre autopsy, which Hollow didn't bother to refute.

Bob Ringling also introduced two of Kobel's patients, who testified that they had been so troubled by his obsessive talk about these ghosts or spirits inhabiting their bodies that they quit seeing him.

And then Ringling had Kobel himself take the stand, dressed in the part of a madman in his premeditatedly wrinkled and dirty clothes, chewing his lip, looking twitchy and weird.

This idea—insane in its own right—was a huge risk, because on cross-examination Hollow would ask the man point-blank if he'd killed Annabelle Young. Since he'd confessed once, he would have to confess again—or Hollow would read the sentence from his statement. Either way the jury would actually hear the man admit to the crime.

But Ringling met the problem head-on. His first question: "Mr. Kobel, did you kill Annabelle Young?"

"Oh, yes, of course I did." He sounded surprised.

A gasp filled the courtroom.

"And why did you do that, Mr. Kobel."

"For the sake of the children."

"How do you mean that?"

"She was a teacher, you know. Oh, God! Every year, thirty or forty students, impressionable young people, would come under her influence. She was going to poison their minds. She might even hurt them, abuse them, spread hatred." He closed his eyes and shivered.

And the Academy Award for best performance on the part of a crazed murder suspect goes to . . .

"Now, tell me, Mr. Kobel, why did you think she would hurt the children?"

"Oh, she'd come under the influence of a neme."

"That's what we heard a little about earlier, right? In your writings?"

"Yes, in my writings."

"Could you tell us, briefly, what a neme is?"

"You could call it an energy force. Malevolent energy. It attaches to your mind and it won't let go. It's terrible. It causes you to commit crimes, abuse people, fall into rages. A lot of temper tantrums and road rage are caused by nemes. They're all over the place. Millions of them."

"And you were convinced she was possessed?"

"It's not possession," Kobel said adamantly. "That's a theological concept. Nemes are purely scientific. Like viruses."

"You think they're as real as viruses?"

"They are! You have to believe me! They are!"

"And Ms. Young was being influenced by nemes."

"One, just one."

"And was going to hurt her students."

"And her son. Oh, yes, I could see it. I have this ability to see nemes. I had to save the children."

"You weren't stalking her because you were attracted to her?"

Kobel's voice cracked. "No, no. Nothing like that. I wanted to get her into counseling. I could have saved her. But she was too far gone. The last thing I wanted to do was kill her. But it was a blessing. It really was. I had to." Tears glistened.

Oh, brother . . .

"Prosecution's witness."

Hollow did the best he could. He decided not to ask about Annabelle Young. Kobel's murdering her was no longer the issue in this case. The whole question was Kobel's state of mind. Hollow got the defendant to admit that he'd been in a mental hospital only once, as a teenager, and hadn't seen a mental health professional since then. He'd taken no antipsychotic drugs. "They take my edge off. You have to be sharp when you're fighting nemes."

"Just answer the question, please."

Hollow then produced Kobel's tax returns for the past three years.

When Ringling objected, Hollow said to Judge Rollins, "Your Honor, a man who files a tax return is of sound mind."

"That's debatable," said the ultraconservative judge, drawing laughter from the courtroom.

Oh, to be on the bench, thought Glenn Hollow. And maybe after a few years' stint as the attorney general I will be.

Rollins said, "I'll let 'em in."

"These are your returns, aren't they, sir?"

"I guess. Yes."

"They indicate you made a fair amount of money at your practice. About forty thousand dollars a year."

"Maybe. I suppose so."

"So despite those other two patients who testified earlier, you must have a much larger number of patients you treat regularly and who are satisfied with your services."

Kobel looked him in the eyes. "There're a lot of nemes out there. Somebody's gotta fight 'em."

Hollow sighed. "No further questions, Your Honor."

The prosecutor then called his own expert, a psychiatrist who'd examined Kobel. The testimony was that, though quirky, he was not legally insane. He was well aware of what he was doing, that he was committing a crime when he killed the victim.

Ringling asked a few questions, but didn't belabor the cross-examination.

Toward the end of the day, during a short break, Glenn Hollow sneaked a look at the jury box; he'd been a prosecutor and a trial lawyer for a long time and was an expert not only at the law but at reading juries.

And, goddamn it, they were reacting just the way Bob Ringling wanted them to. Hollow could tell they hated and feared Martin Kobel, but because he was such a monster and the things he was saying were so bizarre, he couldn't be held to the jury's standards of ethics and behavior. Oh, Ringling had been smart. He wasn't playing his client as a victim, he wasn't playing him as somebody who'd been abused or suffered a traumatic childhood (he barely referred to the deaths of Kobel's parents and brother).

No, he was showing that this *thing* at the defense table was not even human.

Like his expert said, "Mr. Kobel's reality is not *our* reality."

Hollow stretched his skinny legs out in front of him and watched the tassels on his loafers lean to the side. I'm going to lose this case, he reflected. I'm going to lose it. And that son of a bitch'll be out in five or six years, looking for other women to stalk.

He was in despair.

Nemes . . . shit.

Then the judge turned away from his clerk and said, "Mr. Hollow? Shall we continue with your rebuttal of Mr. Ringling's affirmative defense?"

It was then that a thought occurred to the prosecutor. He considered it for a moment and gasped at where the idea led.

"Mr. Hollow?"

"Your Honor, if possible, could we recess until tomorrow? The prosecution would appreciate the time."

Judge Rollins debated. He looked at his watch. "All right. We'll recess until nine A.M. tomorrow."

Glenn Hollow thanked the judge and told his young associates to gather up the papers and take them back to the office. The prosecutor rose and headed out the door. But he didn't start sprinting until he was well out of the courthouse; he believed that you never let jurors see anything but your dignified self.

AT A LITTLE AFTER nine the next morning, Glenn Hollow rose to his feet. "I'd like to call to the stand Dr. James Pheder."

"Objection, Your Honor." Bob Ringling was on his feet.

"Reasons?"

"We received notice of this witness last night at eight P.M. We haven't had adequate time to prepare."

"Where were you at eight?"

Ringling blinked. "Well, Your Honor, I . . . the wife and I were out to dinner."

"At eight *I* was reading documents in this case, Mr. Ringling. And Mr. Hollow was—obviously—sending you notices about impending witnesses. Neither of us were enjoying the buffet line at House O'Ribs."

"But—"

"Think on your feet, Counselor. That's what you get paid those big bucks for. Objection overruled. Proceed, Mr. Hollow."

Pheder, a dark-complexioned man with a curly mop of black hair and a lean face, took the oath and sat.

"Now, Mr. Pheder, could you tell us about your credentials?"

"Yessir. I have degrees in psychology and biology from the University of Eastern Virginia, the University of Albany, and Northern Arizona University."

"All of which are accredited four-year colleges, correct?"

"Yes."

"And what do you do for a living?"

"I'm an author and lecturer."

"Are you published?"

"Yessir. I've published dozens of books."

"Are those self-published?"

"Nosir. I'm with established publishing companies."

"And where do you lecture?"

"All over the country. At schools, libraries, bookstores, private venues."

"How many people attend these lectures?" Hollow asked.

"Each one is probably attended by four to six hundred people."

"And how many lectures a year do you give?"

"About one hundred."

Hollow paused and then asked, "Are you familiar with the concept of neme?"

"Yessir."

"Is it true that you coined that term?"

"Yessir."

"What does it refer to?"

"I combined the words 'negative' and 'meme.' 'Negative' is just what it sounds like. 'Meme' is a common phenomenon in society, like a song or catchphrase, that captures the popular imagination. It spreads."

"Give us the gist of the concept of neme, that's *n-e-m-e*, if you would."

"In a nutshell?"

"Oh, yessir. I got Cs in science. Make it nice and simple."

Nice touch, Hollow thought of his improvisation. Science.

Pheder continued. "It's like a cloud of energy that affects people's emotions in destructive ways. You know how you're walking down the street and you suddenly feel different? For no reason at all. Your mood swings. It could be caused by any number of things. But it might be a neme incorporating itself into your cerebrum."

"And you say, 'negative.' So nemes are bad?"

"Well, bad is a human judgment. They're neutral, but they tend to make us behave in ways society characterizes as bad. Take a case of swimming in the ocean. Sharks and jellyfish aren't bad; they're simply doing what nature intended, existing. But when they take a bite out of us or sting us, we call that bad. Nemes are the same. They make us do things that to them are natural but that we call evil."

"And you're convinced these nemes are real?"

"Oh, yessir. Absolutely."

"Are other people?"

"Yes, many, many are."

"Are these people scientists?"

"Some, yes. Therapists, chemists, biologists, psychologists."

"No further questions, Your Honor."

"Your witness, Mr. Ringling."

The defense lawyer couldn't, as it turned out, think on his feet, not very well. He was prepared for Hollow to introduce testimony by experts attacking his client's claim of insanity.

He wasn't prepared for Hollow to try to prove nemes were real. Ringling asked a few meaningless questions and let it go at that.

Hollow was relieved that he hadn't explored Pheder's history and credentials in other fields, including parapsychology and pseudoscience. Nor did he find the blog postings where Pheder claimed the lunar landings were staged in a film studio in Houston, or the ones supporting the theory that the Israelis and President George Bush were behind the 9/11 attacks. Hollow had particularly worried that Pheder's essay about the 2012 apocalypse might surface.

Dodged the bullet there, he thought.

Ringling dismissed the man, seemingly convinced that the testimony had somehow worked to the defense's advantage.

This concluded the formal presentations in the case and it was now time for closing statements.

Hollow had been writing his mentally even as he'd fled the courthouse yesterday, in search of Pheder's phone number.

The slim, austere man walked to the front of the jury box and, a concession to camaraderie with the panel, undid his suit jacket's middle button, which he usually kept snugly hooked.

"Ladies and gentlemen of the jury. I'm going to make my comments brief, out of respect to you and respect to the poor victim and her family. They—and Annabelle Young's spirit—want and deserve justice, and the sooner you provide that justice, the better for everyone.

"The diligent law officers involved in this case have established beyond a reasonable doubt that Martin Kobel was, in fact, the individual who viciously and without remorse stabbed to death a young, vibrant schoolteacher; widow; and single mother, after stalking her for a week, following her all the way from Raleigh, spying on her, and causing her to flee from a restaurant while she waited to meet her son after school. Those facts are not in dispute. Nor is there any doubt about the validity of Mr. Kobel's confession, which he gave freely and after being informed of his rights. And which he repeated here in front of you.

"The only issue in this case is whether or not the defendant was insane at the time he committed this heinous crime. Now, in order for the defendant to be found not guilty by reason of insanity, it must—I repeat, *must*—be proven that he did not appreciate the difference between right and wrong at the time he killed Annabelle. It must be proven that he did not understand reality as you and I know it.

"You have heard the defendant claim he killed Annabelle Young because she was infected by forces called nemes. Let's think on that for a moment. Had Mr. Kobel been convinced that she was possessed by aliens from outer space or zombies or vampires, maybe that argument would have some validity. But that's not what he's claiming. He's basically saying that she was infected by what he himself described as a virus . . . not one that gives you a fever and chills but one that makes you do something bad."

A smile. "I have to tell you, when I first heard this theory, I thought to myself, brother, that's pretty crazy. But the more I thought about it, the more I wondered if there wasn't something to it. And in the course of this trial, listening to Mr. Kobel and Dr. Pheder and spending all last night reading through Mr. Kobel's lengthy writing, I've changed my mind . . . I too now believe in nemes."

The gasp throughout the courtroom was loud.

"I'm convinced that Martin Kobel is right. Nemes exist. Think about it, ladies and gentlemen: what else can explain the random acts of violence and abuse and rage we find in people who were previously incapable of them."

Yes . . . some of the jurors were actually nodding. They were with him!

Hollow's voice rose. "Think about it! Disembodied forces of energy that affect us. *We* can't see them but doesn't the moon's gravitation affect us? Doesn't radiation affect us? We can't see them either. These nemes are the perfect explanation for behaviors we otherwise would find impossible to understand.

"There was a time when the concept of flight by airplane would have been considered sorcery. The same with GPS. The same with modern medical treatments. The same with lightbulbs, computers, thousands of products that we now know are rooted in scientific fact but when first conceived would seem like black magic."

Hollow walked close to the rapt members of the jury. "But . . . but . . . if that's the case, if nemes exist, as Mr. Kobel and I believe, then that means they're part of the *real* world. They are part of *our* society, our connection with one another, for good or for bad. Then to say that Annabelle Young was infected with one is exactly the same as saying that she had a case of the flu and might infect other people. Some of those infected people, the elderly or young, could die. Which would be a shame, tragic . . . But does that mean it would be all right to preemptively murder her to save those people? Emphatically no! That's not the way the world works, ladies and gentlemen. If, as I now believe, Annabelle Young was affected by these nemes, then as a trained professional, Martin Kobel's responsibility was to get her into treatment and help her. Help her, ladies and gentlemen. Not murder her.

"Please, honor the memory of Annabelle Young. Honor the institution of law. Honor personal responsibility. Find the defendant in this case sane. And find him guilty of murder in the first degree for taking the life of a young woman whose only flaw was to be sick, and whose only chance to get well and live a content and happy and productive life was snatched from her grasp by a vicious killer. Thank you."

His heart pounding, Glenn Hollow strode to the prosecution table through an utterly quiet courtroom, aware that everyone was staring at him.

He sat. Still, no voices, no rustling. Nothing. Pin-drop time.

After what seemed like an hour, though it was probably only thirty seconds, Bob Ringling rose, cleared his throat, and delivered his closing statement. Hollow didn't pay much attention. And it seemed no one else did either. Every soul in the courtroom was staring at Glenn Hollow, and, the prosecutor believed, replaying in their minds what was the most articulate and dramatic closing argument he'd ever made. Turning the whole case on its ear at the last minute.

If, as I now believe, Annabelle Young was affected by these nemes, then as a trained professional, Martin Kobel's responsibility was to get her into treatment and help her. Help her, ladies and gentlemen. Not murder her.

Glenn Hollow was inherently a modest man but he couldn't help but believe he'd pulled off the coup of his career.

And so it was a surprise, to say the least, when the good men and woman on the jury panel rejected Hollow's argument completely and came back with a verdict finding Martin Kobel not guilty by reason of insanity after one of the shortest deliberations in Wetherby County history.

Three

I AVOIDED THE SUNROOM as much as I could.

Mostly because it was full of crazy people. Lip-chewing, Haldol-popping, delusional crazies. They smelled bad, they ate like pigs at a trough, they screamed, they wore football helmets so they didn't do any more damage to their heads. As if that were possible. At my trial I was worried that I was overacting the schizo part. I shouldn't have worried. My performance in the courtroom didn't come close to being over the top.

The Butler State Hospital doesn't include the words "for the criminally insane" in the name because it doesn't need to. Anybody who sees the place will get the idea pretty fast.

The sunroom was a place to avoid. But I'd come to enjoy the small library and this was where I'd spent most of my time in the past two months since I was committed here.

Today I was sitting in the library's one armchair, near the one window. I usually vie for the chair with a skinny patient, Jack. The man was committed because he suspected his wife of selling his secrets to the Union army—which would've been funny except that as punishment for her crime he tortured her for six hours before killing and dismembering her.

Jack was a curious man. Smart in some ways and a true expert on Civil War history. But he'd never quite figured out the rules of the game: that whoever got into the library first got the armchair.

I'd been looking forward to sitting here today and catching up on my reading.

But then something happened to disrupt those plans. I opened this morning's paper and noticed a reference to the prosecutor in the case against me, Glenn Hollow, whose name, I joked with my attorney Bob Ringling, sounded like a real estate development. Alarming Ringling somewhat since I wasn't sounding as crazy as he would have liked—because, of course, I'm not.

The article was about party officials pulling all support for Hollow's bid for attorney general. He'd dropped out of the race. I continued to read, learning that his life had fallen apart completely after failing to get me convicted on murder one. He'd had to step down as county prosecutor and no law firm in the state would hire him. In fact, he couldn't find work anywhere.

The problem wasn't that he'd lost the case, but that he'd introduced evidence about the existence of spirits that possessed people and made them commit crimes. It hadn't helped that he was on record as stating that nemes were real. And his expert was a bit of a crackpot. Though I still hold that Pheder's a genius. After all, for every successful invention, da Vinci came up with a hundred duds.

In fact, Hollow's strategy *was* brilliant and had given me some very uncomfortable moments in court. Bob Ringling, too. Part of me was surprised that the jury hadn't bought his argument and sent me to death row.

These revelations were troubling and I felt sorry for the man—I never had anything personal against him—but it was when I read the last paragraph that the whole shocking implication of what had happened struck home.

Before the Kobel trial, Hollow had been a shoo-in to become the attorney general of the state. He had the best conviction record of any prosecutor in North Carolina, particularly in violent crimes such as rape and domestic abuse. He actually won a premeditated murder case some years ago for a road rage incident, the first time any prosecutor had convinced a jury to do so.

Reading this, I felt like I'd been slugged. My God . . . My God . . . I literally gasped. I'd been set up.

It was suddenly clear. From the moment Annabelle Young had sat next to me in Starbucks, I was being suckered into their plan. The nemes . . . they knew I'd take on the mission of trying to become her therapist. And they knew that I'd see that the neme within her was so powerful and represented such a danger to those around her that I'd have to kill her. (I'd done this before, of course; Annabelle was hardly the first. Part of being a professional therapist is matching the right technique to each patient.)

And where did the nemes pick their host? In the very county with the prosecutor who represented perhaps the greatest threat to them. A man who was winning conviction after conviction in cases of impulsive violence—locking away some of their most successful incarnations in the country: abusers, rapists, murderers . . .

Well, that answered the question that nobody had been able to answer yet: yes, nemes communicate.

Yes, they plot and strategize. Obviously they'd debated the matter. The price to eliminate Glenn Hollow was to get me off on an insanity plea, which meant that I would be out in a few years, and back on the attack, writing about them, counseling people to guard against them.

Even killing them if I needed to.

So, they'd decided that Glenn Hollow was a threat to be eliminated.

But not me. I'd escaped. I sighed, closing my eyes, and whispered, "But not me. Thank God, not me."

I saw a shadow fall on the newspaper on my lap. I glanced up to see my fellow patient Jack staring down at me.

"Sorry, got the chair first today," I told him, still distracted by the stunning understanding. "Tomorrow . . ."

But my voice faded as I looked into his face.

The eyes . . . the eyes.

No!

I gasped and started to rise, shouting for a guard, but before I could get to my feet, Jack was on me, "My chair, you took my chair, you took it, you took it! . . ."

But then, as the razor-sharp end of the spoon he clutched slammed into my chest again and again, it seemed that the madman began to whisper something different. My vision going, my hearing fading, I thought perhaps the words slipping from these dry lips were, "Yes you, yes you, yes you . . ."

PARALLEL LINES

•

Tim Powers

IT SHOULD HAVE BEEN THEIR BIRTHDAY TODAY. Well, it was still hers, Caroleen supposed, but with BeeVee gone the whole idea of "birthday" seemed to have gone, too. Could she be seventy-three on her own?

Caroleen's right hand had been twitching intermittently since she'd sat up in the living room daybed five minutes ago, and she lifted the coffee cup with her left hand. The coffee was hot enough but had no taste, and the living room furniture—the coffee table, the now-useless analog TV set with its forlorn rabbit-ears antenna, the rocking chair beside the white-brick fireplace, all bright in the sunlight glaring through the east window at her back—looked like arranged items in some kind of museum diorama; no further motion possible.

But there was still the gravestone to be dealt with, these disorganized nine weeks later. Four hundred and fifty dollars for two square feet of etched granite, and the company in Nevada could not get it straight that Beverly Veronica Erlich and Caroleen Ann Erlich both had the same birth date, though the second date under Caroleen's name was to be left blank for some indeterminate period.

BeeVee's second date had not been left to chance. BeeVee had swallowed all the Darvocets and Vicodins in the house when the pain of her cancer, if it had been cancer, had become more than she could bear. For a year or so she had always been in some degree of pain—Caroleen remembered how BeeVee had exhaled a fast *whew!* from time to time, and the way her forehead seemed always to be misted with sweat, and her late-acquired habit of repeatedly licking the inner edge of her upper lip. And she had always been shifting her position when she drove, and bracing herself against the floor or the steering wheel. More and more she had come to rely—both of them had come to rely—on poor dumpy Amber, the teenager who lived next door. The girl came over to clean the house and fetch groceries, and seemed grateful for the five dollars an hour, even with BeeVee's generous criticisms of every job Amber did.

But Amber would not be able to deal with the headstone company. Caroleen shifted forward on the daybed, rocked her head back and forth to make sure she was wearing her reading glasses rather than her bifocals, and flipped open the brown plastic phone book. A short silver pencil was secured by a plastic loop in the book's gutter, and she fumbled it free—

—And her right hand twitched forward, knocking the coffee cup right off the table, and the pencil shook in her spotty old fingers as its point jiggled across the page.

She threw a fearful, guilty glance toward the kitchen in the moment before she remembered that BeeVee was dead; then she allowed herself to relax and looked at the squiggle she had drawn across the old addresses and phone numbers.

It was jagged, but recognizably cursive letters:

Ineedyourhelpplease

It was, in fact, recognizably BeeVee's handwriting.

Caroleen's hand twitched again, and scrawled the same cramped sequence of letters across the page. She lifted the pencil, postponing all thought in this frozen moment, and after several seconds her hand spasmed once more, no doubt writing the same letters in the air. Her whole body shivered with a feverish chill and she thought she was going to vomit; she leaned out over the rug, but the queasiness passed.

She was sure that her hand had been writing this message in the air ever since she had awakened.

Caroleen didn't think BeeVee had ever before, except with ironic emphasis, said *please* when asking her for something.

She was remotely glad that she was sitting, for her heart thudded alarmingly in her chest and she was dizzy with the enormous thought that BeeVee was not gone, not entirely gone. She gripped the edge of the bed, suddenly afraid of falling and knocking the table over, rolling into the rocking chair. The reek of spilled coffee was strong in her nostrils.

"Okay," she whispered. "Okay!" she said again, louder. The shaking in her hand had subsided, so she flipped to a blank calendar page at the back of the book and scrawled *OKAY* at the top of the page.

Her fingers had begun wiggling again, but she raised her hand as if to wave away a question, hesitant to let the jiggling pencil at the waiting page just yet.

Do I want her back, she thought, *in any sense?* No, not *want,* not *her,* but—in these past nine weeks I haven't seemed to exist anymore, without her paying attention, any sort of attention, to me. These days I'm hardly more than an imaginary friend of Amber's next door, a frail conceit soon to be outgrown, even by her.

She sighed and lowered her hand to the book. Over her *OKAY* the pencil scribbled,

Iambeevee

"My God," Caroleen whispered, closing her eyes. "You think I need to be told?"

Her hand was involuntarily spelling it out again, breaking the pencil lead halfway through but continuing rapidly to the end, and then it went through the motions three more times, just scratching the paper with splintered wood. Finally her hand uncramped.

She threw the pencil on the floor and scrabbled among the orange plastic prescription bottles on the table for a pen. Finding one, she wrote, *What can I do? To help*

She wasn't able to add the final question mark because her hand convulsed away from her again, and wrote,

touseyourbodyinvitemeintoyourbody

and then a moment later,

imsorryforeverythingplease

Caroleen watched as the pen in her hand wrote out the same two lines twice more, then she leaned back and let the pen jiggle in the air until this bout, too, gradually wore off and her hand went limp.

Caroleen blinked tears out of her eyes, trying to believe that they were caused entirely by her already-sore wrist muscles. But—for BeeVee to apologize, to her . . . ! The only apologies BeeVee had ever made while alive were qualified and impatient: *Well, I'm sorry if . . .*

Do the dead lose their egotism? wondered Caroleen, their onetime need to limit and dominate earthly households? BeeVee had maintained Caroleen as a sort of extended self, and it had resulted in isolation for the two of them; if, in fact, they had added up to quite as many as two during the last years. The twins had a couple of brothers out there somewhere, and a least a couple of nieces, and their mother might even still be alive at ninety-one, but Caroleen knew nothing of any of them. BeeVee had handled all the mail.

Quickly she wrote on the calendar page, *I need to know—do you love me?*

For nearly a full minute she waited, her shoulder muscles stiffening as she held the pen over the page; then her hand flexed and wrote,

yes

Caroleen was gasping and she couldn't see the page through her tears, but she could feel her hand scribbling the word over and over again until this spasm, too, eventually relaxed.

Why did you have to wait, she thought, *until after you had died to tell me?*

But *use your body, invite me into your body.* What would that mean? Would BeeVee take control of it, ever relinquish control?

Do I, thought Caroleen, *care, really?*

Whatever it might consist of, it would be at least a step closer to the wholeness Caroleen had lost nine weeks ago.

Her hand was twitching again. She waited until the first couple of scribbles had expended themselves in the air before touching the pen to the page. The pen wrote,

yesforever

She moved her hand aside, not wanting to spoil that statement with echoes.

When the pen had stilled, Caroleen leaned forward and began writing, *Yes, I'll invite you,* but her hand took over and finished the line with

exhaustedmorelater

Exhausted? Was it strenuous for ghosts to lean out or in or down this far? Did BeeVee have to brace herself against something to drive the pencil?

But, in fact, Caroleen was exhausted, too—her hand was aching. She blew her nose into an old Kleenex, her eyes watering afresh in the menthol-and-eucalyptus smell of Ben Gay, and lay back across the daybed and closed her eyes.

A SHARP KNOCK AT the front door jolted her awake, and though her glasses had fallen off and she didn't immediately know whether it was morning or evening, she realized that her fingers were wiggling, and had been for some time.

She lunged forward and with her left hand wedged the pen between her twitching right thumb and forefinger. The pen began to travel lightly over the calendar page. The scribble was longer than the others—with a pause in the middle—and she had to rotate the book to keep the point on the page until it stopped.

The knock sounded again, but Caroleen called, "Just a minute!" and remained hunched over the little book, waiting for the message to repeat.

It didn't. Apparently she had just barely caught the last echo—perhaps only the end of the last echo.

She couldn't make out what she had written. Even if she'd had her glasses on, she'd have needed the lamplight, too.

"Caroleen?" came a call from out front. It was Amber's voice.

"Coming." Caroleen stood up stiffly and hobbled to the door. When she pulled it open, she found herself squinting in the noon sunlight that filtered through the avocado tree branches.

The girl on the doorstep was wearing sweatpants and a huge T-shirt and blinking behind her gleaming round spectacles. Her brown hair was tied up in a knot on top of her head. "Did I wake you up? I'm sorry." She was panting, as if she had run over here from next door.

Caroleen felt the fresh air—smelling of sun-heated stone and car exhaust—cooling her sweaty scalp. "I'm fine," she said hoarsely. "What is it?" Had she asked the girl to come over today? She couldn't recall doing it, and she was tense with impatience to get back to her pen and book.

"I just—" said Amber rapidly—"I liked your sister, well, you know I did really, even though—and I—could I have something of hers, not like valuable, to remember her by? How about her hairbrush?"

"You want her hairbrush?"

"If you don't mind. I just want something—"

"I'll get it. Wait here." It would be quicker to give it to her than to propose some other keepsake, and Caroleen had no special attachment to the hairbrush—her own was a duplicate anyway. She and BeeVee had, of course, matching everything—toothbrushes, coffee cups, shoes, wristwatches.

When Caroleen had fetched the brush and returned to the front door, Amber took it and went pounding down the walkway, calling "Thanks!" over her shoulder.

Still disoriented from her nap, Caroleen closed the door and made her way back to the daybed, where she patted the scattered blankets until she found her glasses and fitted them on.

She sat down, switched on the lamp, and leaned over the phone book page. Turning the book around to follow the newest scrawl, she read,

bancaccounts
getmyhairbrushfromhernow

"Sorry, sorry!" exclaimed Caroleen; then in her own handwriting, she wrote, *I'll get it back.*

She waited, wondering why she must get the hairbrush back from Amber. Was it somehow necessary that all of BeeVee's possessions be kept together? Probably, at least the ones with voodoo-type identity signatures on them—DNA samples, like hair caught in a brush, dried saliva traces on dentures, Kleenex in a forgotten wastebasket. But—

Abruptly her chest felt cold and hollow.

But this message had been written down *before* she had given Amber the hairbrush. And Caroleen had been awake only for the last few seconds of the message transmission, which, if it had been like the others, had been repeating for at least a full minute before she woke up.

The message had been addressed to Amber next door, not to her. Amber had read it somehow and had obediently fetched the hairbrush.

Could all of these messages have been addressed to the girl?

Caroleen remembered wondering whether BeeVee might have needed to brace herself against something in order to communicate from the far side of the grave. Had BeeVee been bracing herself against Caroleen, her still-living twin, in order to talk to Amber? Insignificant *Amber*?

Caroleen was dizzy, but she got to her feet and padded into the bedroom for a pair of outdoor shoes. She had to carry them back to the living room—the bed in the bedroom had been BeeVee's, too, and she didn't want to sit on it in order to pull the shoes on—and on the way she leaned into the bathroom and grabbed her own hairbrush.

DRESSED IN ONE OF her old church-attendance skirts, with fresh lipstick, and carrying a big embroidered purse, Caroleen pulled the door closed behind her and began shuffling down the walk. The sky was a very deep blue above the tree branches and the few clouds were extraordinarily far away overhead, and it occurred to her that she couldn't recall stepping out of the house since BeeVee's funeral. She never drove anymore—Amber was the only one who drove the old Pontiac these days—and it was Amber who went for groceries, reimbursed with checks from Caroleen . . . and the box of checks came in the mail, which Amber brought in from the mailbox by the sidewalk. If Caroleen alienated the girl, could she do these things herself? She would probably starve.

Caroleen's hand had begun wriggling as she reached the sidewalk and turned right, toward Amber's parents' house, but she resisted the impulse to pull a pen out of her purse. *She's not talking to* me, she thought, blinking back tears in the sunlight that glittered on the windshields and bumpers of passing cars; she's talking to stupid *Amber.* I won't *eavesdrop.*

Amber's parents had a Spanish-style house at the top of a neatly mowed sloping lawn, and a green canvas awning overhung the big arched window out front. Even shading her eyes with her manageable left hand Caroleen couldn't see anyone in the dimness inside, so she huffed up the widely spaced steps, and while she was catching her breath on the cement apron at the top, the front door swung inward, releasing a puff of cool floor-polish scent.

Amber's young, dark-haired mother—Crystal? Christine?—was staring at her curiously. "It's . . . Caroleen," she said, "right?"

"Yes." Caroleen smiled, feeling old and foolish. "I need to talk to Amber." The mother was looking dubious. "I want to pay her more, and see if she'd be interested in balancing our, my, checkbook."

The woman nodded, as if conceding a point. "Well, I think that might be good for her." She hesitated, then stepped aside. "Come in and ask her. She's in her room."

Caroleen got a quick impression of a dim living room with clear plastic covers over the furniture, and a bright kitchen with copper pans hanging everywhere. Amber's mother then knocked on a bedroom door and said, "Amber honey? You've got a visitor," then pushed the door open.

"I'll let you two talk," the woman said, and stepped away toward the living room.

Caroleen stepped into the room. Amber was sitting cross-legged on a pink bedspread, looking up from a cardboard sheet with a rock, a pencil, and BeeVee's hairbrush on it. Lacy curtains glowed in the street-side window, and a stack of what appeared to be textbooks stood on an otherwise bare white desk in the opposite corner. The couple of pictures on the walls looked like pastel blobs. The room smelled like cake.

Caroleen considered what to say. "Can I help?" she asked finally.

Amber, who had been looking wary, brightened and sat up straight. "Shut the door."

After Caroleen had shut the door, Amber went on, "You know she's coming back?" She waved at the cardboard in front of her. "She's been talking to me all day."

"I know, child."

Caroleen stepped forward and leaned down to peer at the cardboard, and saw that the girl had written the letters of the alphabet in an arc across it.

"It's one of those things people use to talk to ghosts," Amber explained with evident pride. "I'm using the rock crystal to point to the letters. Some people are scared of these things, but it's one of the good kinds of crystals."

"A Ouija board."

"That's it! She made me dream of one over and over again just before the sun came up, because this is her birthday. Well, yours, too, I guess. At first I thought it was a hopscotch pattern, but she made me look closer till I got it." She pursed her lips. "I wrote it by reciting the rhyme, and I accidentally did *H* and *I* twice, and left out *J* and *K*." She pulled a sheet of lined paper out from under the board. "But it was only a problem once, I think."

"Can I see? I, uh, want this to work out."

"Yeah. She won't be gone. She'll be in me, did she tell you?" She held out the paper. "I drew in lines to break the words up."

"Yes. She told me." Caroleen slowly reached out to take the paper from Amber, and then held it up close enough to read the penciled lines:

I/NEED/YOUR/HELP/PLEASE
Who R U?
I/AM/BEEVEE
How can I help U?
I/NEED/TO/USE/YOUR/BODY/INVITE/ME/IN/TO/YOUR/BODY
IM/SORRY/FOR/EVERY/THING/PLEASE
R U an angel now? Can U grant wishes?
YES
Can U make me beautiful?
YES/FOR/EVER
OK. What do I do?
EXHAUSTED/MORE/LATER
BV? It's after lunch. Are U rested up yet?
YES
Make me beautiful.
GET/MY/HAIRBRUSH/FROM/MY/SISTER
Is that word "hairbrush"?
YES/THEN/YOU/CAN/INVITE/ME/IN/TO/YOU
How will that do it?
WE/WILL/BE/YOU/TOGETHER
+ what will we do?
GET/SLIM/TRAVEL/THE/WORLD
Will we be rich?
YES/I/HAVE/BANC/ACCOUNTS GET/MY/HAIRBRUSH/FROM/
HER/NOW
I got it.
NIGHT/TIME/STAND/OVER/GRAVE/BRUSH/YR/HAIR/INVITE/
ME/IN

"That should be B-A-N-K, in that one line," explained Amber helpfully. "And I'll want to borrow your car tonight."

Not trusting herself to speak, Caroleen nodded and handed the paper back to her, wondering if her own face was red or pale. She felt invisible and repudiated. BeeVee could have approached her own twin for this, but her twin was too old; and if she did manage to occupy the body of this girl—a more intimate sort of twinhood!—she would certainly not go on living with Caroleen. And she had eaten all the Vicodins and Darvocets.

Caroleen picked up the rock. It was some sort of quartz crystal.

"When . . . " she began in a croak. She cleared her throat and went on more steadily, "When did you get that second-to-last message? About the bank accounts and the hairbrush?"

"That one? Uh, just a minute before I knocked on your door."

Caroleen nodded, wondering bleakly if BeeVee had even known that she was leaving *her* with carbon copies—multiple, echoing carbon copies—of the messages.

She put the crystal back down on the cardboard and picked up the hairbrush. Amber opened her mouth as if to object, then subsided.

There were indeed a number of white hairs tangled in the bristles.

Caroleen tucked the brush into her purse.

"I need that," said Amber quickly, leaning forward across the board. "She says I need it."

"Oh, of course, I'm sorry." Caroleen forced what must have been a ghastly smile, and then pulled her own hairbrush instead out of the purse and handed it to the girl. It was identical to BeeVee's, right down to the white hairs.

Amber took it and glanced at it, then laid it on the pillow, out of Caroleen's reach.

"I don't want," said Caroleen, "to interrupt . . . you two." She sighed, emptying her lungs, and dug the car keys out of her purse. "Here," she said, tossing them onto the bed. "I'll be next door if you . . . need any help."

"Fine, okay." Amber seemed relieved at the prospect of her leaving.

CAROLEEN WAS AWAKENED THE next morning by the pain of her sore right hand flexing, but she rolled over and slept for ten more minutes before the telephone by her head conclusively jarred her out of the monotonous dream that had occupied her mind for the last hour or so.

She sat up, wrinkling her nose at the scorched smell from the fireplace and wishing she had a cup of coffee, and still half-saw the Ouija board she'd been dreaming about.

She picked up the phone, wincing. "Hello?"

"Caroleen," said Amber's voice, "nothing happened at the cemetery last night, and BeeVee isn't answering my questions. She spelled stuff out, but it's not for what I'm writing to her. All she's written so far this morning is—just a sec—she wrote, uh, '*You win—you'll do—we've always been a team, right—*' Is she talking to you?"

Caroleen glanced toward the fireplace, where last night she had burned—or charred, at least—BeeVee's toothbrush, razor, dentures, curlers, and several other things, including the hairbrush. And today she would call the headstone company and cancel the order. BeeVee ought not to have an easily locatable grave.

"Me?" Caroleen made a painful fist of her right hand. "Why would she talk to me?"

"You're her twin sister, she might be—"

"BeeVee is dead, Amber, she died nine weeks ago."

"But she's coming back. She's going to make me beautiful! She said—"

"She can't do anything, child. We're better off without her."

Amber was talking then, protesting, but Caroleen's thoughts were of the brothers she couldn't even picture anymore, the nieces she'd never met and who probably had children of their own somewhere, and her mother who was almost certainly dead by now. And there was everybody else, too, and not a lot of time.

Caroleen was resolved to learn to write with her left hand, and, even though it would hurt, she hoped her right hand would go on and on writing uselessly in the air.

At last she stood up, still holding the phone, and she interrupted Amber: "Could you bring back my car keys? I have some errands to do."

THE CULT OF THE NOSE

•

Al Sarrantonio

FIRST MENTION OF THE CULT in the literature is found in a tract of the Germanic heretic Jacobus Mesmus, which I have dated to somewhere near 1349 A.D.; it mentions, amidst an account of an outbreak of plague in the town of Breece, that "a band of townsfolk had spied this day two figures, a man and a woman, prancing gaily on the outskirts of the village, wearing the feared Nose. They were driven out with fire clubs and a hail of stones." Mesmus goes on to say that the appearance of figures wearing the Nose continues—sometimes there are two figures mentioned, sometimes three: a man, woman and small child; the text is partly destroyed and confusing—throughout the reign of the plague, abruptly terminating with the last case of the disease, although there is one cloudy passage toward the end of the treatise (which, as a sidelight, deals mainly with weather) mentioning that a "nosed person" was spotted in the church bell tower intermittently for some time afterward.

There is, actually, a case for the Cult's being traced to well before this time; scant evidence and brief mentions exist that might date it to the Egyptian dynastic era. There is a legend that one of the noses itself was found in the burial chamber of Ramses II, though there is no surviving physical evidence or corroborating testimony to support this.

After Jacobus Mesmus, accounts of the Cult become more frequent. A figure wearing the Nose appears in one of Brueghel's triptychs; there are several appearances of Cult members in the work of Bosch, as might be expected. There is also, curiously, an appearance of a figure bearing the Nose in a little-known (and by reason of the appearance of the adornment, thought to be spurious) painting by Pierre-Auguste Renoir: a tiny grinning figure, peeking out from behind a child holding a red parasol, is seen wearing a Nose utilizing a strap to keep it upon its face. The story is that the young girl in the painting was the daughter of M. Ebrezy, a prominent minister, and that the girl died mysteriously soon after posing for the artist.

There are mentions of the Nose in the works of Maupassant; Emily *and* Charlotte Brontë; and, in the Americas, Hawthorne and, quite often, in the later works of Twain.

There is a false, and dangerously misleading, conception that the Nose is a modern concoction, that it was not only invented for the foolish pleasure of children and childlike adults, but that it was promoted for this use alone, and for the further and more arcane uses to which it is currently being put by the modern Cult. It must be understood that the Nose is not only an ancient instrument, but that its use can be traced back nearly to the dawn of recorded history (see my opening remarks). The Nose has doubtless gone through periods—it might be hypothesized that these periods were ones of relative calm and social and religious stability—where it has been relegated to the position of toy. It has been determined, though, that these times of tranquility have always been rather brief, and, further, that the Nose has always regained its position of mysterious authority—and of feared nebulosity.

Such a period is, of course, where we find ourselves at the moment.

I might add at this point that my interest in the Cult is not a recently flowering one; I have been gathering references to it and carefully formulating my theories for many years.

FOR THE RECORD, MY interest was sparked during the waning months of the free world's involvement in the Vietnam War. At that time I was a special attaché aligned with a covert arm of American intelligence, checking black-and-white photographs taken by spies and insurgents behind Communist lines—these were photos smuggled out of prisoner-of-war camps and such. I might also add that this was a period in which I was seeking to forget an unfortunate incident in my personal life: my young spouse, understandably lonely due to my lengthy absence, took up with another man and had a child by him. I sought solace by immersing myself in my work.

I began to notice in some of the photos I handled a recurring and curious phenomenon. Here and there, tucked in a corner or peering out from behind a barracks, was a peculiar figure wearing what seemed to be a false nose upon its face. Often the figure was identifiably male; at other times it appeared to be a female, or even a child. Many prisoners of war at that time, due to malnutrition and concurrent emaciation, were barely identifiable by their gender—or their age—so it must be remembered that any sort of positive identification was difficult. Many of the nose-wearing figures appeared beside, or within (though they were apparently not dead) mass graves.

I put these photographs aside, thinking that, though there was little here to interest my superiors, there might yet be something to investigate further.

I began to dream of figures, birdlike, resembling Bosch's horrid hell beasts, wearing false, beaklike noses.

My collection of photographs grew. I realized that as the scenes of horror increased—by this time we were receiving covert daily pictures from death camps holding Americans and Vietnamese Buddhists—the number of nose-bearing figures increased. In one photograph—one I keep to this day folded in my wallet—a man, woman and child, in a long line of tired and bleakly hopeless prisoners, most of them in tatters of clothes hanging on barely enough bones to stand, being led meekly to an open pit by machine gun–bearing guards, have turned their faces toward the camera, three in a row, and are smiling a death's-head smile. There seems to be a bit more meat on their bones than on those in front and in back of them.

They each wear the Nose.

OTHER ACTIVITIES SOON SAVED me from complete absorption in the manner of these curious photographs, and it was not until well after the war's resolution, after I had settled in Montreal, far away from my ex-wife, her son and husband (who traveled extensively) that I came across a small bundle of the grainy pictures in a box (the above-mentioned photo was among them) and all of my former interest was rekindled. I began to search other sources—having a bit of influence, due to my war service, in being able to access materials not easily available by the public—and began to come across other photos taken in other sectors of the war in which figures bearing the Nose appeared.

I then broadened my research, and found similar artifacts among

World War II memorabilia. I came across one precious bit of evidence (alas, recently lost to fire) that depicted a Third Reich rally in which two separate nosed figures could plainly be discerned. I remember this photo clearly, because one of the figures stood a few scant feet from Hitler himself, and grinned maliciously at the camera.

Eventually, my interest once again waned, until I picked up one morning in 1979 a London newspaper that contained a news-service photo on the front page presenting the dead body of the assassinated president of South Korea, Park Chung Hee. To the right of the body, barely visible in the deep background, was a figure with the Nose on its face.

I immediately researched other photos that were taken at the time but came up with nothing useful.

However, another reference turned up in a photograph of a train derailment that killed forty-five passengers in Ohio the same week: among the twisted metal a head could be seen poking through with the false appendage attached to it by a thin silver strap. The figure it belonged to, which was surrounded by dead commuters, was clearly alive.

I began to comb picture morgues and newspaper files, turning up hundreds of photos with similar figures in them. Most depicted disasters or near disasters; I began to notice that the number—and demeanor—of the figures often depended on the amount of destruction that surrounded them. Their faces glowed with pleasure in ratio to the amount of mayhem and carnage. This was by no means a strictly quantifiable thing, but the correlation, in general, seemed to exist.

Most of these photos, unfortunately, have also been destroyed by fire.

I began to notice small, easily missed references to the Nose, or the Cult of those wearing the Nose, in literature, and naturally broadened my research to include that area also, as I have already mentioned.

I had apparently stumbled onto something that had gone nearly undetected by the general populace, something that had stayed just outside the general consciousness since the beginning of recorded history. Here was a sect so arcane, nefarious and secret (a kind of truly devilish Freemasonry?) that no more than widely scattered references to it remained, or had ever existed. There were no prime source materials; the only evidence to point to its existence were the photos few and far between and a symbol—the Nose—so thoroughly steeped in the general notion of tomfoolery as to virtually ensure safety from detection.

The next step, of course, was to search for the modern remnants of the Cult.

My task of discovery proved to be a long and difficult one. It would take me days to recount the numerous blind alleys and dead ends I encountered; the false leads, misinformation (deliberate, some of it), the intrigue, deception, the attempts (yes) on my life. For years, I meticulously pored over each scrap of evidence that might at last lead me to the discovery of the true aspect of the Cult.

Eventually, despite all attempts to stop me, I succeeded.

IN THE SPRING OF this year my obsession led me to Paris, where I hoped to meet with a man under the pyramidic shadow of the Eiffel Tower. I was to wait at a certain café until three o'clock in the afternoon, and then I was to ask the waiter to change my table to the one next to mine. It was a half-gray, half-sunny day in early April; there were breezes in the air that gave hope of a coming warmth mixed with the threat of a quick return to a latent wet winter. I had a coat and muffler on, and a black bowler hat. I carried a folded umbrella. In these things, too, I had followed instructions. I felt like a figure model in a painting by Magritte, felt I should somehow be floating in midair above the redbrick shop across the street, stiff and sharp as a cardboard cutout. Three o'clock came. I changed my table, tipped my waiter for his trouble and waited. Nothing happened. I bought a paper from a passing vendor, unfolded it before me and began to read. This kind of thing had happened too many times before; I would wait another ten minutes and then make my way, undaunted, back to my hotel. On the front page of the paper was a picture of a man with a black bowler hat on and a false nose. I heard the sound of the metal chair at the table I had just vacated scrape across the patio floor and the man in the photo, in the flesh, sat down across from me. He wore the Nose. The photo in the paper, I now saw, had been pasted on.

"You follow instructions, I see," he said in clipped, neutral English, the schoolroom English taught all over the world. He did not wait for me to answer, but held out an envelope.

"Take this and continue to follow instructions."

In the envelope was a ticket to a baseball game in New York City.

Two days hence found me in crowded Yankee Stadium. The seat

beside me remained empty for eight full innings; by this time the home team had a commanding lead and many of the spectators had left. I took little notice when the seat was finally occupied by a young boy who had, I surmised, come down from higher, cheaper seats; it was happening all around me.

It was only when he turned toward me that I saw that, under his ball cap, the boy wore the Nose. He smiled crookedly, handed me another envelope and slipped away.

The next weeks found me at a succession of similar rendezvous in public locations—theaters, restaurants, the London Zoo and Piccadilly Circus, a San Francisco streetcar. Always the pattern was the same. A messenger, identified by the Nose, approached and handed me an envelope with a ticket, or a short, untraceable note in it.

I always did as I was told. My obsession had become a compulsion: I was determined to find the source of the mystery.

I began to see false noses everywhere—in lines, in food markets, rising suddenly out of a mass of people on a street as if the wearer had put a box down and stepped up on it to elevate himself above those around him. My dreams were haunted. I would wake in the middle of the night calling for the Nose to confront me and be done with it. I had visions of my father and mother bathing me as a young boy, bending down over my shallow tub and splashing water on me, laughing. They wore the Nose—golden versions of it, tied with bright red ribbons behind their heads. One morning in Seattle, Washington, sick from lack of sleep, I hallucinated a man into my hotel bedroom doorway who bore a silver Nose in a tin box. The man himself had no face, only a blank oval of flesh.

And then, abruptly, on the same day as this hallucination, the Cult finally made its secrets known to me.

AFTER THE VISION DISSIPATED I spent the entire morning in the bath. My eyes were tightly closed; I sought a wakeful kind of sleep.

There came a knock at my hotel room door. I ignored it. The knock was repeated.

I called out tentatively, fearfully.

I was answered by a trill of tinkling, insubstantial laughter from the behind the door, which I had left unlocked. I stepped dripping from the bath into the living area in time to see the doorknob turning. I waited for the man with no face to reveal himself again.

The door opened to reveal an empty hallway.

I dressed quickly, in my Magritte outfit—black bowler, umbrella, black laced shoes—and put my research material hurriedly into my briefcase, snapping it closed with a jerk. As I did so a picture, the one depicting the führer and his nosed shadow, dropped out, to the floor. I retrieved it, and now saw that there were more cultish figures in the frame than I had at first noticed.

The platform on which Hitler stood was filled by figures with noses on.

I shoved the picture back into my case and closed it. I took the morning paper from the table by the door. The front-page photograph was of a gangster who had been drowned in his own bathtub—what looked like a false nose floated on the water near the submerged face.

On a hunch, I moved to the window, and just caught sight of a man, woman and child disappearing into the entrance to the hotel, eight floors below. I was plainly visible, but they did not peer back up at me.

I straightened my tie. On a hunch, I turned back to the window and there, sure enough, were the man, woman and child. They had retreated from the front entrance to the curb and stood staring up at me expectantly. The child waved.

He was the boy I had seen at the baseball park, with the crooked smile.

The man was the same one I had seen under the shadow of the Eiffel Tower.

The woman looked familiar also.

The three of them wore the Nose.

They reentered the hotel and I turned quickly from the window and set my briefcase by the doorway.

On the table where the newspaper had been was a can of fluid. I unscrewed its top carefully, avoiding the sharp industrial smell, and began to splash its contents around the room. When the can was empty I placed it by the briefcase. I removed a cigarette lighter from my coat pocket and casually flipped it open.

Flame burst up unexpectedly, burning my finger, and I was forced to drop the lighter. It did not go out, but instead fell into the liquid.

The fire before me burst to hot life. I was blinded momentarily. When

I regained my sight the room was filling rapidly with smoke. I could hear voices beginning to build outside the window on the street, a few cries of alarm.

The man, woman and child, wearing their Noses, had somehow made their way into the room, and stood smiling at me as they quickly bound one another with ropes.

Gasping, I groped for the door, yanked it open and lurched out into the hallway and down the fire stairs. I stopped before the door to the street to brush and straighten my clothes.

I heard screams behind me. Like the tinderbox it was, the cheap hotel was exploding into roaring flames.

I eased open the door to the street. Television crews had already arrived with cameras; one of those pictures would undoubtedly grace tomorrow's front page. I reached inside my coat to make sure that my ticket home to Montreal was in place. It was. Many of the reporters and spectators on the street wore Noses. A woman, wearing the Nose, fell, screaming, on fire, to the pavement in front of me. She was the one I had seen in my hotel room. Her hands were still bound behind her.

It was at that point that I realized with shock that I had left my brief-case behind.

I turned and, though a wall of flames met me, I went back.

AS YOU CAN IMAGINE, it is very painful for me in this condition. I cannot see through these bandages; I have not been told if I will have my sight back when they are removed.

And now, to my horror, I find my testimony on the Cult of the Nose disputed.

The literary references to the Cult are real, though they are scattered with the loss of my notes and would have to be researched once more. Other documentation exists; since the destruction of my valuable material it would have to be reassembled. I am told that my one remaining photograph, which was in my wallet, and which the unesteemed prosecutor contends I snapped myself, that of the man, woman and child in line, has been tampered with, and so cannot be used as evidence in my defense: the death camp has somehow been doctored into an amusement park, and now only the child wears the true Nose. The others bear noses that, oddly, have been drawn on with a felt-tip pen, and it appears that whoever did take the photograph was hiding in a hedge, since there are branches and small leaves visible in the forefront.

Obviously, I have been the victim of fraud and chicanery.

But this does not discourage me.

Nothing does.

Why?

Because I possess the most revealing bit of evidence proving the existence of the Cult of the Nose.

I know, without a shred of doubt, that it exists.

How?

It is obvious.

Because:

Despite all of the testimony that has been given against me here today; despite all of the lies and accusations; despite the spurious contention by the unesteemed prosecutor that I set the blaze in that ramshackle hotel deliberately, in order to murder my ex-wife, her son and husband, merely because she left me to have another man's child while I was overseas, which, the unesteemed prosecutor contends, caused me to become obsessed, to track them for months, even years and, eventually, to murder them; despite all of this, I know that if my bandages were removed; if my ruined and melted face were restored and my eyes made whole; if I could look through the inches of useless salve and acres of white gauze that enfold my head—I know with certainty that if I could do these things I would see, upon the face of each of the twelve of you who have given me this sentence of death, the Adornment of which I have so eloquently spoken.

HUMAN INTELLIGENCE

•

Kurt Andersen

HE FOUND IT ALMOST PHYSICALLY PAINFUL TO LIE, which was unfortunate for someone who had spent most of his life as a spy.

Back when everything was proceeding according to plan, year after
year after year, he had gotten a little sloppy, allowing bystanders to see the
aircraft in flight, sometimes even announcing to children and their childlike parents who he was and where he lived. What did it matter, back then?
Besides, he told himself, his openness created a rapport with the natives.
But mainly it relieved his loneliness.

When people asked his occupation, his standard answer for a long
time had been "a writer" or "an anthropologist." But lately, once again,
he was responding to such questions with a more dangerous version of
the truth. These gestures toward self-revelation felt exciting, like precur-
sors to intimacy. But he never put himself in real jeopardy. In America
in the twenty-first century, who was going to be anything but charmed
and amused by a well-dressed, well-groomed, intelligent, alert, friendly
old Anglo-Saxon-looking gentleman who made a fantastic remark or two?
"I'm a spy," he'd started telling the curious with a smile and a wink, "here
on a long-term intelligence-gathering operation. But it's super-top-secret,
so if you don't mind, that's really all I can say about it."

He had looked like an old man even when he was younger because,
early on, before he took up the posting, he'd grown a full beard to conceal
the purple cross-hatching of surgical scars on his chin and upper neck.
Now that he was genuinely elderly, it pleased him that appearance and
reality had come into sync. He looked old and, by any standard, he was
old. One less lie to live.

Of course, if he told the whole truth, anyone but a lunatic would consider him a lunatic. Then the authorities would be notified, and even in this

comparatively enlightened era he would lose his freedom for the rest of his life. The project to which he'd devoted such vast time and effort—dutifully, yes, but with enthusiasm as well—would be for naught.

On the other hand, with the passing years that downside calculus had changed. Incarceration and 24/7 gawking would be unpleasant, no doubt, but the rest of his life was looking like a manageably brief time.

As for aborting the operation, he doubted that anyone at headquarters was any longer aware of him or his mission—if headquarters still existed. Doing his job had become easier and easier over the years, especially with television and the Internet—although, of course, the promiscuous availability of information also tended to make his job moot. Maybe the project was already for naught.

Yet he had continued to adhere to the four main directives of the contingency plan, almost as articles of faith: remain at the last position reported to headquarters, maintain all necessary discretion and secrecy, continue to chronicle the people and their society to whatever extent possible, and await retrieval. "Retrieval" is the closest English translation of the word in the orders, not "rescue," a bit of stoic bureaucratese he had come to resent ever since the crash. (Had he gone native? Probably.)

So here he was, living in a city now a thousand times larger than when he arrived, chronicling and waiting, chronicling and waiting, chronicling and still waiting.

After he read *End Game* and *Waiting for Godot* at the Chicago Public Library one pleasantly frigid afternoon near the end of December 1959, he wrote a long, effusive fan letter to Samuel Beckett in Paris, describing the two plays as "perhaps the most profound works of literature since Shakespeare." Discovering them, he gushed, had "made this Christmas one of my merriest ever." In response he received a curt, generic form letter, mimeographed, which struck him as almost funny. Since the stranding, he has not been an outwardly jovial man, but he's never lost his sense of humor. By nature and by training, he takes the long view.

And so he was more intrigued than anxious when the little light on the remote beacon had, for the first time ever, started flashing. He wasn't sure exactly when the flashing began, because he kept the device hidden at the back of a high shelf in his bedroom closet. He'd been checking it only once every month or so, grudgingly, feeling like a chump each time he lifted it down, pushed the test button, for the ten thousandth time heard the beep confirming that it worked and the connection was secure—*Takes a Licking and Keeps on Ticking! Nothing Outlasts the Energizer Bunny!*—and then, after waiting ten seconds for the flashing signal that never came, put the thing back up on the shelf.

Until the remarkable evening of September 16, 2007, when he first saw the throb of purple light and shouted so loudly that his young downstairs neighbor called up to see if he was all right. According to the contingency-plan instructions, the light on his box could flash in one or more of nine different colors, each color corresponding to a particular alert condition. Purple means that sensors on the exterior of the station, 2,400 miles away, are now exposed to sunlight.

When the station was set up all those years ago, covered by dozens of feet of ice even at the height of summer, its secrecy seemed guaranteed. Nobody else, not Peary or Amundsen or Byrd or free-ranging Inuits, had traveled so far north. But for the last several decades, more of the Arctic ice had been melting each summer—and in 2007 the summer melt radically spiked, turning a third of the polar ice cap into open sea. The top of the station, a 150-foot oval of tubing and tanks suspended just beneath the water's surface, must be visible. And now there are permanent research stations scattered all over the high Arctic, and surveillance satellites shooting high-resolution pictures of every rod and furlong of the no-longer-trackless wastes.

What was taking them so long to find it? Seasonal ice may still grow back to hide the base in winter, but for each of the last three summers he has waited for the news bulletins (HIGH-TECH "ATLANTIS" FOUND NEAR NORTH POLE) and the resulting global hysteria. He does worry that the discovery will discombobulate people en masse—the "unforeseeable cultural and ontological impacts," as headquarters' boilerplate put it. But he also has a hopeful hunch that a critical, controlling fraction of humanity had matured, and would, after some initial breathlessness, learn to accommodate the new facts.

Selfishly, he's also eager to see pictures of the station again after all this time, to compare his hazy memories with fresh digital images. And although it felt vaguely insubordinate (to whom?), or even traitorous (to what?), he was excited by the prospect of everyone on earth learning all at once the truth that he alone had known for so long.

———

AS HER FLIGHT FROM Oslo approaches O'Hare, Nancy Zuckerman thinks once again of the cliché uttered sooner or later by everyone who spends time in Svalbard, including herself: *This is what it must be like to live on another planet.* NASA actually runs a research station on the other side of the North Pole, in the Canadian Arctic, where they simulate the conditions of a Martian space colony.

She had always liked spending time outdoors, and when she was seven could stick a live worm on a fishing hook and set up a tent herself. But it was the second *Indiana Jones* sequel, which came out the summer she turned eight, that decided her on becoming an explorer when she grew up. In earlier generations, adults would have smiled at a little *girl* who said she wanted to be an explorer. But at the turn of the twenty-first century in Boulder, Colorado, adults smiled and patronized little Nancy Zuckerman not because of her gender but because her cute dream job no longer existed.

Fortunately, she was both collegial and self-reliant, a cheerful team player as well as a cheerfully independent loner. "If I could be a super-hero," she used to say, "I'd be totally willing to be like a second-string member of X-Men or the Justice League." And so science in general and her chosen field in particular—exploration geophysics, specializing in the Arctic—suited her. She hadn't minded spending the last year and a half on a postdoc in Longyearbyen, a town in the Svalbard islands, northernmost Norway, 1,200 miles up from Oslo and 600 miles below the North Pole. It was and it wasn't a fortress of solitude. Her fellow researchers and faculty were a cosmopolitan, caffeinated assortment of English speakers from all over the world, chatty good company for the six months of perpetual sunlight. And Einar, a single young coal miner who'd grown up in Svalbard and had no idea how handsome he was, made the six months of subzero darkness tolerable, even though (or maybe because) he spoke very little English. She played squash, she swam in the indoor pool, she took pictures.

She was attached to one team drilling experimental wells to store captured CO_2 in a sandstone aquifer, and part of another project testing the feasibility of thickening the polar cap by pumping seawater onto the ice and letting it freeze. Good data had been collected. Techniques had been refined. Reasonable progress had been made. It wasn't heroic exploration of the kind she'd imagined as a kid, but as she approached thirty she had made her peace with the exigencies of incremental science and the real world.

Or so she had thought until a few weeks ago. She was five days into an excursion aboard the university's sixty-eight-foot research vessel, the *Dauntless*, taking a group of new undergraduates on a tour of the southern edge of the ice cap. Around two A.M. on the morning of July 11, unable to sleep, she'd gotten up and taken one of the motorboats out alone to cruise close to the ice, looking for polar bears to photograph. It was warm, 46°F, the sky almost cloudless, and, of course, the sun high in the sky. The sea was calm. Thirty yards from the ice, at the mouth of a recently formed inlet, she cut the motor and let herself drift along, sitting cross-legged on the deck at midships, watching, camera and long lens at the ready. She was exploring. A half hour passed. Some terns flew over, but she saw no seals and no bears.

When she heard and felt the thud, she figured she'd struck a chunk of submerged ice. As she stood to investigate, the boat rocked freely in the water even though it was stuck more or less in place, knocking against some underwater structure to its left and its right. It was as if the boat had slid into a marina slip.

What the fuck?

She started probing underwater with the tip of an oar blade, and a foot and a half beneath the surface found not ice, but what felt like pipe, a big pipe, a pipe with a diameter—she scraped and stroked the hard surface—of several feet. She climbed over to the starboard side to probe some more, and found an apparently identical pipe, running parallel to the other. The distance between them was ten, maybe twelve feet.

Completely bizarre.

A sunken ship? Even the fleeting thought made her feel childish and silly. The water was a mile deep. No way a wreck could float to the surface, and ditto for stray lengths of oil or gas pipeline. Unless, *shit*, she'd discovered some hitherto unknown shoal or reef in the Arctic Ocean! She had discovered *something*. More to the point, *she* had *discovered* something.

Kneeling on the deck, she started to use the oar as a push pole, levering it against the underwater pipe on the port side to propel the boat back—shove, coast a couple of yards, shove, coast—toward the opening through which she must have drifted.

But then, abruptly, the dinghy stopped moving, caught between the mysterious pipes. The pipes didn't run parallel, it turned out, but came together at an angle, and she was now wedged near their apex. She stood.

The boat barely budged. She tried and failed to pole herself forward. She was stuck fast. Crouching and leaning out next to the raised motor, she stuck the oar into the water directly behind the boat—and found another smooth, hard underwater surface. But this was different, not a pipe but some kind of funnel. She used both hands to plunge the oar straight down into the funnel's neck.

She gasped as she felt the blade end of the oar being smartly, mechanically grabbed, then slowly pulled into the water another foot. She let go. The oar's hand grip protruded straight up between waves. She stared down, bewildered.

Then she was shocked beyond belief, and terrified. The ocean beneath the boat and in a long, narrow strip beyond began to churn, forming into a 100-foot-long tubular wave—but the very opposite of a breaking surf, for this wave had depth instead of height, its crest not a peak but a trough ten feet below the water's surface. She thought of her mother and brothers, of her late father, and of the fact that she wouldn't get any credit at all for discovering this freakish inverted tsunami before it killed her.

But the boat wasn't swamped or sucked under, and the upside-down wave, instead of crashing, just kept rolling and rolling. In other words, a ten-foot-wide ditch had formed in the sea, with ten-foot sides of smooth water and a sloshing, foamy bottom. Nancy Zuckerman was sitting in a boat suspended by metal pincers—the two big pipes, now fully exposed—at the top of this perfect, impossible ditch.

As in Exodus 14, the waters of the sea had been divided, the waters being a wall on her right hand and on her left. But even at that supremely dreamlike moment, Nancy Zuckerman's faith in reason and science was unshaken. Miracles are a function of ignorance, inexplicability a temporary condition. By some mechanical means, a hundred thousand gallons of seawater were being sucked away to form a semicylindrical void. It was amazing, but it was also like one of the rides at Water World, off I-25 in Denver.

She had the presence of mind to push the button on her GPS, and press again to record the reading: longitude 14° 48' 53" east, latitude 86° 19' 27" north.

And then she was vindicated—although also freshly terrified—when a rubbery blue sleeve rose from the pit beneath the boat and wrapped itself tightly around the hull with a vacuum-packing *thrrrooooop*. Definitely a machine at work, not God or Satan. As the dinghy started moving smoothly and slowly into the slot in the sea, she considered escape—she might be able to dive out past the edge of the slot and swim away, might make it to the ice and pull herself out of the water before hypothermia set in, might be rescued by searchers from the *Dauntless* after they discovered her and the dinghy missing. But curiosity kept her in the boat. As the machine moved her down into the mists and darkness, Nancy was careful to notice everything she heard and saw and smelled. She was an explorer.

TWELVE DAYS AGO, HIS beacon—now out of the closet and sitting on the coffee table in the living room—had started alternating a chartreuse throb with each purple one. Chartreuse meant that someone had entered the station. And the station's mapping console, assuming it still worked, would give the intruders the precise location of the remote beacon. He thought of getting rid of the device, leaving it on the El or heaving it into the Chicago River, to put the hounds off his scent. But then he admitted, once and for all, that he wants to be tracked down. He craves being found.

And so he has gotten all his documents and images in order, the entire chronicle. He has packed a suitcase, and straightened up the apartment. He has been watching cable news and surfing the Web constantly. Surely it is only a matter of time.

But he's surprised when the front-door buzzer buzzes. He had expected helicopters and floodlights and grappling hooks and special-ops troopers in black visors and haz-mat suits bursting through the doors and windows with automatic weapons and gas canisters, and had even practiced dropping to the floor and putting his hands over his head. The Obamas' Hyde Park house is ten minutes from his apartment, which he'd figured would make the brouhaha all the more spectacular. As he stands at the intercom speaker, he looks out the window down at Kimbark Avenue: cars driving past, people strolling by and hanging out as on any summer afternoon, no evacuation of the block, no emergency vehicles, no perimeter secured.

The doorbell buzzes again. He wonders if it's the UPS guy.

"Yes?"

"Hello?" A woman, sounding tentative.

"Yes?"

"I'm looking for someone who, um, also lives at 86 degrees, 19 minutes, 27 seconds north?"

He grins, and buzzes her in.

Opening the apartment door, he's surprised all over again: she's alone, apparently unarmed, and very young. She extends her right hand.

"I'm Nancy Zuckerman."

"Hello. I'm Nicholas Walker."

"I'm a scientific researcher," she says. "From the Arctic."

"Really?" He smiles, and motions her inside. "So am I! How very fortunate. For the both of us."

THEY SIT. SHE SETS aside the cardigan he'd handed her, and explains herself in a nervous rush. Why she had been in the Arctic, how she happened to drift over the station and accidentally jimmy the entry system with her oar. How she'd figured, at first, that it must be some military facility, American or Russian or Chinese, but then, as she spent hours exploring the interior—the peculiar materials and shapes and technology interfaces, the very peculiar quality of artificial light, the unrecognizable written language, the images displayed—how she had developed a new hypothesis. How she had photographed everything, including the mapping console with its one, tiny blinking light in the middle of North America, and then, on her computer back in Longyearbyen, had transposed a longitude and latitude grid over her image to find the precise location of the blinking light—41 degrees, 47 minutes, 54.1475 seconds north and 87 degrees, 35 minutes, 41.7095 seconds west, South Kimbark Avenue between 53rd and 54th Streets, Chicago. How she had taken a few things from the station—including a small plastic picture of him, which she had just shown to a lady downstairs in order to find his apartment. She hands him the picture.

"My goodness," he says, "I was young. So young!" He puts the picture down and turns to look at her. They've talked for ten minutes, yet she hasn't asked where he's from or what he's doing here. Which is fine by him. He's in no particular hurry.

She's a little flummoxed. "I have to tell you I am incredibly excited. This is beyond surreal. It's like I'm having a stroke, or been drugged, or gone to heaven. It's—it's a new category of excitement." She takes a deep breath. "I'm also scared."

"Scared? Of me? Oh, don't be. No, no, no."

"No, scared that I haven't *told* anyone about any of this—not my colleagues, not my bosses, not any government people, not my mom, no one. I don't know what the rules are, but I sure as shit haven't followed them."

How interesting. "Why have you kept it secret?" He knows about keeping secrets.

"Well, I guess possibly I worried that . . . no, I'll tell you why. Because I want to be the one who gets to *reveal* it, to tell the whole story. To be, you know, 'the discoverer.' Like Columbus or Magellan or Galileo or Einstein. I'm sorry—do you know who they are?"

He smiles. "Yes."

"Before the rest of the world finds out and rushes in and pushes me out of the way, I want to learn as much as I can. I want to be *the expert.*"

He likes this girl. He will give her the gift she wants.

"Oh, *Jesus.*" She reaches into a bag, searching for her two tape recorders. "May I record our conversation?"

"Of course." He spots something in the bag. "You found the gold? At the station?"

She blushes, and pulls out a half-pound golden cylinder the size of a lipstick. "You can have it back. I took one, as a research sample."

He strokes the ingot with one finger. "And you said you saw images at the station?"

"Projected on those big spherical monitors in the, like, office."

"To the left and straight back as you entered?"

"Hundreds of pictures on those monitors, 3-D photographs, in color, of huts and houses and towns and farm animals and pots and carts and soldiers and children and temples, it looked like from all over the world, Europe, Asia, Africa—"

He hates to seem smug, which he's afraid is about to become his default affect, but he can't suppress a knowing smile, and interrupts her. "I know. I took them."

"Shot from overhead, mostly, I guess with a very long lens?"

"Intelligence gathering is supposed to be clandestine. And I tried to minimize the Hawthorne effect—people behaving differently when they know they're being watched."

"A lot of the images look extremely old. Unbelievably old. Not the *pictures,* I mean, but the people and buildings and so on."

"They are."

She hesitates before asking the next question. "So, you were tak-ing photographs all over the world before . . . before photography was invented?" This is precisely what she'd hypothesized, that he must be at least two hundred years old. *Incredible.*

"And moving pictures as well—videos, more or less. From when I arrived until the day the camera was destroyed. By the time the technol-ogy existed . . . indigenously, it seemed pointless for me to start up again."

"May I ask your age?"

This time it's he who pauses, anticipating her reaction. "The station was established in 429, CE."

She stares, saying nothing. Her skepticism races to catch up with her astonishment.

He restates his answer, trying to help her register the fact. "I arrived fifteen hundred and eighty-one years ago."

"You're *sixteen hundred* years old?"

"Eighteen hundred and seven. Which is fairly ancient even on my planet."

Finally, she thinks, *yes: "on my planet."* It had seemed impossible, but it also seemed like the only plausible explanation. She tries not to hyperven-tilate. "Where—what planet are you from?"

"We call it"—for an instant his voice slips into an inhuman half hiss, half buzz—"Vrizhongil"—and then back to English with no trace of an accent: "It's a moon, really, which orbits a large planet. Which orbits our sun, of course. About sixty-two light-years away. Very close by, in the scheme of things. But far enough, it turns out, that it made me expendable."

Nancy says nothing, and continues to stare. Can this be happening? Can all of this possibly be real?

He had imagined this encounter hundreds of times, thousands, even rehearsed it. "You're wondering if I'm insane, I expect. Well, there have been moments over the years when I've begun wondering that very thing: Am I mad? Is this story—spy from another planet stationed on Earth and abandoned by his superiors, almost two thousand years old, undersea polar base—is this all delusion, some sorry old man's schizophrenic gib-berish? And when I've reached those moments of existential crisis, this is one of the things I do, to prove to myself that I'm sane, that I am who I believe I am."

He picks up a pair of nail scissors from the coffee table and jabs hard into the palm of his right hand. His blood is a kind of Day-Glo orange, and as it drips from his hand onto the table it sizzles and burns the wood like acid.

"Of course," he says, grabbing a tissue to wipe his hand and the wood, "a skeptic would think this is a trick, some theatrical special effect. But you, Ms. Zuckerman, you have seen the Arctic station. And you found my picture there."

"Yes."

"So given the evidence, perhaps I don't need to perform any further mortifications to establish my bona fides." He's smiling. He really does not want to remove his eyes from their sockets, or show her that he has a bifurcated phosphorescent penis and no anus at all.

"I believe you," she tells him.

He explains that his government established a system to monitor civilizations on planets feasible for Vrizhongilians to reach, and that Earth was one of those 116 designated planets when he embarked on his 83-year-long flight here. The big ship carried four other intelligence agents headed for four other planets in the vicinity, along with their terrestrial stations in prefabricated pieces and individual expeditionary aircraft. A reconnaissance probe was sent to the surface to photograph humans, so that the necessary reconstructive surgery—remodeling ears, removing external neck cartilage, giving his skin a convincingly soft texture and pinkish tint, and so on—could be performed by doctors aboard the mother ship. His station was installed beneath the polar ice. And, voilà, he was on his own.

Sending a message between Earth and Vrizhongil took sixty-two years, so communication was impractical. He spent six weeks each year doing the field work—flying around the world, observing human settlements, taking pictures, making videos, scribbling notes—and the rest of his time organizing and distilling his material.

"Huh," she says.

"What?"

"That's so much time for assembling and editing."

"Well, yes. Our productivity problem. You see, we sleep twenty or twenty-one hours a day. It's the single thing I envy most about you. About people here, I mean." Eating and digestion, he did not add, were what he found monstrous about humans. No doubt all intelligent species have their horrific and pathetic outliers, the psychopaths and murderers, the self-mutilators and televangelists. But on Earth, *every single person* chews food and swallows and shits, and it still disgusts him.

Once each century, he says, a mother ship would visit to resupply him and take back home a copy of his meticulous multimedia chronicle of another Earth century. And by the way—every one of his first six chronicles received the highest possible rating from headquarters.

"So your people, back on your planet, were only seeing your reports of life on Earth a hundred years after the fact."

"Or longer."

"And you wouldn't hear back from them for another hundred years after that."

He shrugs. "The speed of light is the speed of light."

At the end of his standard eight hundredth tour of duty, which fell in the thirteenth century, he was to have been replaced by a young agent, and return to Vrizhongil for a headquarters job for another five hundred years before retiring. But no mother ship arrived in 1229. No mother ship ever showed up again. He's been waiting ever since. And he never retired. The chronicle, he tells her, "is rather absurdly up to date."

He explains that his people possess, by human standards, an uncanny ability to learn languages, so that during his biannual field expeditions, the northern hemisphere in December and the southern in June, he could move among people incognito. When he was threatened with harm or capture, he protected himself with a weapon, a long wand, which temporarily paralyzed every creature ("except, oddly, marsupials") within 200 feet. He used the weapon, according to his records, 373 times in 1,442 years.

Quite often, however, when his aircraft hovered for long periods at very low altitudes, people saw it and became alarmed. To demonstrate his peaceful intentions, he would give away tokens, beads and bits of gold.

"The way that poll takers," he says, a little defensively, "offer small cash payments in exchange for participating in a survey. It was one of our standard protocols."

"And the station was established in the Arctic," she asks, "for secrecy's sake?"

He nods. "Yes, and for my personal comfort as well. Vrizhongil is a cold planet. During these hellish months," he says, nodding toward the windows, "I give thanks every day for the invention of air-conditioning." Outside it was almost ninety degrees, but Nancy had put on his sweater.

"The region of my birth is considered warm, and temperatures there are the equivalent of Fairbanks. Or were, anyway."

"But so—why are you here now, in Chicago? Why aren't you in the Arctic?"

"Because it's my kind of town?"

She doesn't get the joke.

"An accident," he says. He was wrapping up one of his annual northern field surveys, having just revisited and filmed the large Indian city of Cahokia, at the confluence of the Mississippi and Illinois rivers. Flying north, back toward the station, he suddenly lost power, and crash-landed in Lake Michigan. He managed to get gold, as well as the paralyzer, video equipment, and portable beacon—he touched the blinking device on the table—into the emergency raft. His aircraft sank.

"Our orders were unequivocal—remain as close as possible to one's last position and wait for . . . rescue. Besides, back then I had no means of returning to the Arctic. So I built a home in the woods and coexisted with the natives. Every so often I brandished the paralyzer to reestablish my bona fides." He smiles. "And I'm afraid I never disabused them of their 'White God from the Heavens' idea."

"But what about, you know, the Europeans, the settlers?"

"They came later. Much later." He pauses, possibly for dramatic effect. "Three hundred and fifty-six years later. I crashed in February 1317. When the French arrived, fortunately, they ignored the stories the Indians told about me. I was just another supernatural character in one of the savages' supernatural myths. Fiction."

"So for food, you hunted and gathered?"

"I don't eat. As such. My body absorbs nutrients from the air." This tangent makes him dread that she will ask to use his bathroom. He has no toilet paper.

He tells her about moving into Chicago not long after it was founded, about buying what he needed with pieces of his gold, about working at odd jobs in order to conserve the gold, about losing his video camera and paralyzer in the great fire of 1871, about the difficulty of employment in this era of income taxes and Social Security and government IDs. He has, of course, never sought medical care from a physician, and has kept changing residences so that neighbors don't get too curious about why he doesn't seem to age, or die. This is his fourteenth apartment. But except for the years he spent up in Winnetka, from the 1940s through the 1960s, in order to experience suburban life firsthand—"Once an anthropologist, always an anthropologist"—he has lived in Chicago since 1837.

They had talked for more than three hours, and Nicholas had awoken three hours before she arrived. He's getting drowsy.

"You've told me almost nothing about your planet," she says. "Your people, your history. We have so much to talk about. So much."

"We do indeed. But if you don't mind, perhaps we can finish for the day and continue our conversation tomorrow?"

"Oh, yes, of course, yes, absolutely." But what if he runs away? What if he dies overnight? Then she reassures herself. She had today's recordings. She'd taken pictures of him. She'd photographed the station, and knows its location exactly. Everything would be okay. She reaches over and touches his shoulder.

"Thank you. This is so extraordinary, I can't . . . words really don't . . . *thank* you."

"I'm pleased, too. Extraordinarily pleased that it was *you* who made the discovery. I'm very, very lucky."

"*You're* lucky? Well, this is—I mean, I've won the lottery to end all lotteries, right? It's Christmas in July!"

He chuckles, and the chuckle becomes, as he sits back, a full-throttle guffaw.

She's horrified. Is he about to tell her that this has all been a practical joke, a hoax? That he's an actor in some incredibly elaborate reality show?

"I'm sorry," he says finally, still chuckling. "My fatigue has ruined my manners. I'm so sorry."

"What?"

"There's another part of the story you need to know. I was going to save it for tomorrow. But now that I've upset you, that won't do."

He begins by describing his aircraft in more detail than he had before: small, just twenty-six feet long, a large transparent canopy, landing rails instead of wheels, and a thicket of navigational probes extending from the front of the fuselage.

"When the people of the north, the Nordics and the Lapps and the rest, saw me flying, cruising at low altitudes through their midwinter skies nine hundred years ago, eleven hundred years ago, what do you suppose they thought they were seeing?"

Nancy shakes her head. She has no idea what he's getting at.

"A *flying sleigh,* driven by a large bearded man who had given them gifts."

"Oh my God."

"And a flying sleigh pulled by what? By nothing? Literally unimaginable, so the array of antennae on the nose of the aircraft appeared to them as—what?"

"Oh my God."

"Antlers, on a team of flying reindeer."

"Oh my *God.*" She's had three weeks to get used to the idea that she'd discovered an extraterrestrial base, and that she might actually find a creature from another planet. But this—*meeting Santa Claus*—is almost too shocking to process.

"When people would ask my name, I gave the one I'd always used, adapted to the local language—Nikolaos, Nikola, Nicholas. And when they asked where I lived, I saw no reason to conceal the truth—'beyond the mountains of Korvatunturi,' I told them, 'near the top of the world.' Although I don't believe I ever said, 'At the North Pole.'"

WHEN SHE ARRIVES THE next afternoon, he doesn't answer the buzzer. Oh, *Christ,* no. She presses again. As she's about to press a third time she hears his voice over the speaker.

"Nancy? Very sorry! Come right up."

Has she ever been so thrilled? He's still here, still friendly, his windows still improbably frosty. And she sees he has been scanning through his documentary videos. He invites her to sit next to him on the sofa and watch on a small, black spherical device that reminds her of Magic 8-Ball.

"I'm afraid I've never figured out a way to hook it up to the television," he tells her as he touches the Play button.

"Holy Christ, they've got *sound!*" Nancy says, embarrassing herself. "Excuse me. I'm an idiot. Of course they have sound."

She sees aerial panoramas of Lakota Indians chasing a bison over a cliff in the Sand Hills, junks and gondolas on the Tigris in Baghdad, China's Great Wall half built. She watches and listens to slightly furtive-looking shots inside a bustling Viking tavern in northern England, men packing a piece of bronze statuary into a crate in eleventh-century Benin, a mock sea battle at the Colosseum in Rome, a smiling toddler in Edo speaking Japanese directly to the camera, a tall beardless man delivering a speech in Chicago in the summer of 1858. "Yes," he tells her, "Abraham Lincoln."

She is wonderstruck. She could keep watching forever. But after yesterday she's more conscious of the time. Before long, he would get sleepy again.

"I want to discuss with you, Nicholas, exactly how you'd like us to proceed."

"We can watch some more of this footage. We can talk. As you wish."

"I mean longer term. I'll do whatever you say. If you want, I could take you back up to the station, and you could see if the people on Vreez-honk, Vreez . . . I'm sorry. You could see if your headquarters has sent any messages to you, there, during the last seven hundred years. And couldn't you send them a message?"

"And then wait 124 years for a reply? If there's anyone there to reply." He shakes his head. If he could cry, he might cry.

She says nothing for a few seconds. "Well, if I have your permission to tell your story to the world—I mean, if you prefer that I wait until after you, after you're *gone* to reveal everything, posthumously, I would completely understand. If you want to maintain your privacy, I mean."

"Thank you. *Thank* you. But while I am very old, it's true, I might have another thirty or forty or fifty years left. Vrizhongilians have lived to be two thousand."

"Good!"

"But I think you would find it a great burden and disappointment to be obliged wait that long, would you not? And when someone else stumbles across the station in the meantime?" He leans forward. "I'm tired of keeping my secret. All right, Nancy? I'm ready." He'd thought about saying, "All right, Ms. Zuckerman, I'm ready for my close-up," but figured she probably wouldn't get it.

She wipes away tears. "I thought I was going to have to convince you."

"You know, my dear, I've had more than enough time to consider this."

He lays out his thinking, his concerns, his plan. The biggest problem, he believes, will be persuading the world that the Arctic station is not some kind of military base, that no invasion of Earth is imminent. Before anything becomes public, he thinks it might make sense to get Rupert Murdoch on board, possibly even offer him some kind of media exclusive, in order to keep Fox News from terrifying Americans unnecessarily. Nancy thinks he's joking. He assures her he is not.

"Now I know this will sound corny in the extreme. Especially given the 'Santa' business. But I believe the best way for us to create goodwill from the outset is to describe what I have in mind as, quote, 'Gifts to the People of Earth.'"

He will hand over his chronicle—all 2.4 million words he has written and, "far more interesting, I should think," all 73,496 of hours of video that he shot on every continent but Antarctica in every year from the early fifth century to the late nineteenth century.

He will tell everything he knows about life in our part of the Milky Way, corroborated by the library of text and images stored at the station. "It's all badly out of date, of course," he says, "but it's better than nothing."

And he will give to the people of Earth his surviving pieces of technology—in particular the batteries that power the video player and portable beacon and Arctic station, all still operating 1,581 years after installation. "I should think," he says, "that some bright scientists somewhere will be able to reverse-engineer them."

As she wonders how many billions of dollars his Vrizhongilian batteries might be worth, she feels a jolt of self-loathing. "This is going to be unbelievable, Nicholas."

He smiles. "Let's hope not."

"I mean, this will be the biggest thing . . . *ever.*"

"I suppose. I do hope that people, anyway most people, will be glad to learn, finally, definitively, that they're not alone in the universe." *Because,* he thinks to himself, *I know I am inexpressibly happy that my loneliness is finally about to end.*

"Nicholas?"

"Yes?"

"May I hug you?"

STORIES

•

Michael Moorcock

THIS IS THE STORY OF MY FRIEND Rex Fisch who blew out his complicated brains in his Lake District library all over his damned books one Sunday afternoon last September. Naturally the place was a horror to clean,
but Rex never really cared much about the mess he left in his wake. What
pissed me off was the waste: each blasted cell was a story he'd never tell;
a story no one else would ever tell. Rex knew how to hurt himself and
the old friends who loved him. Only a few of us are now left. Cancer took
Hawthorn, Hayley, Slade and Allard that same year. The first three had
shared digs with Rex when he first lived in London. It didn't seem fair of
the bastard to deliberately deplete what remained of our joint memory.

As I said at his funeral Rex had more fiction in him than could ever
come out, no matter how long he'd lived. A superb raconteur, he produced
stories in every form, from dry, funny narrative verse to self-dramatising
social lies. Novels, plays, short stories, comic strips, operas, movies, RPGs:
throughout his career he was never stuck for a narrative. In that respect we
were pretty much alike and shared a kind of discomfort at our own facility.
We both identified with Balzac, sharing a fascination for Jacques Collin, his
sinister and ubiquitous many-named master villain who set out to ruin La
Torpille in *Splendeurs et misères des courtisanes*. Rex discovered that most
people prefer a good story and a bit of conventional prejudice to honest
ambiguity; they made their most profound life decisions based on tales
they saw in the tabloids or on reality TV. That didn't stop Rex telling the
truth when it frequently occurred to him. Truth was always in there somewhere, even when he thought he was lying. For all his later right-wing
posturing, he had, like Balzac, a way of tapping into poor peoples' dreams
and understanding what they wanted most in the world. I envied him his
empathy, if not his ambition. There was one story he couldn't write. I think

it was what we were all waiting for and which might have brought him the literary recognition he longed for. But he believed *Paris Review* editors could "smell the pulp writer on you," while as an editor I rejected stories because I could smell *Paris Review* on them. I believed we were too good for the reviews even when we appeared in them. The conventions of genre were staler in literary writing than Harlequin romances: exactly why Rex turned out to be the writer we most needed on *Mysterious*.

We were both six-two and shared the same colouring and humour, though Rex was already balding. I guess our differences came from our backgrounds. I was a Londoner. Rex had been born and raised in Wrigley, Texas, pop. 1,204, about forty miles from Waco. He'd believed everything they told him until he went to Austin where he found out how to doubt his small-town certainties, trading them for the snobberies of the UT literary enclave. Dumping his provincialism a little late, he never lost his reverence for academia. Furiously cynical, he was determined to tell readers what fools they were to believe his stories. Despite this, he seemed oddly innocent when he turned up in London fresh from the UT campus via Spain, with the remnants of his jaundice, an uncompleted creative-writing degree and a few sales to the American crime and sci-fi digests, to be disgusted by our rates, even lower than the U.S., but delighted when we bought whatever he wrote, at whatever length he did it. When we met we were both twenty-five. Literary powers like Julie Mistral had already called him the James M. Cain of his generation. Angus Wilson had compared me to Gerald Kersh and Arnold Bennett.

The "digests" were the pulps' attempts to look more sophisticated, with abstract expressionist covers and cooler titles, but I had grown up reading the real pulps with their powerful pictures and raving shout lines (*Donna was a dame who dared to be different—Kelly was a cop who craved to kill!*). The quality of the fiction didn't alter, just the presentation.

I found it hard to come in at the end of that era, working on the Falcon and Sexton Blake Library, but it had proved one thing to me. There were no such things as pulp writers. Bad writers like Carroll John Daly and brilliant ones like Dashiell Hammett just happened to write for the pulps. Mostly their reputation had to do with context. Jack Trevor Story would write a novel for Sexton Blake then, with minor modifications, turn it into a novel for Secker and Warburg.

By the time I took it over, Hank Janson's *Mystery Magazine* was about the last of the UK thriller digests and I had some crackbrained notion to lift it away from genre altogether and make it into something addressing the widest possible readership. By 1964 there were few short story mags left and most of those were generic. They ran romances, military adventures, mysteries and sci-fi. To get published and paid you had to adapt your work, usually by inserting a clunky rationalised plot. That way you earned a bit as you learned a bit. We didn't want to write what we called Englit-fic: the styles and themes of which came out of universities in sad imitation of the great modernists. We wanted to write something that had the vitality of good commercial fiction and the subtle ambition of good literary fiction, reflecting the sensibilities and events of our times: stuff that would get us high with the sense of enthusiasm and engagement of Proust or Faulkner but with the disciplined vitality of genre fiction pulsing from every page.

A few of us talked about a "two-way street" to reunite junk, middle-brow and highbrow fiction. Some people out there had to be as frustrated as us, dissatisfied by pretty much everything on offer, literary or commercial. For ages people had discussed the "two cultures." We might just be the guys to unite them: writing for a reader who knew a bit about poetry, painting and physics, enjoyed Gerald Kersh, Elizabeth Bowen and Mervyn Peake, merging realism with grotesquerie and doing it elegantly, eloquently. By 1963 we were publishing a few examples in the digests and with Billy Allard and Harry Hayley, my two closest writer friends; we made plans for a "slick" quarto magazine bringing together designers, artists, scientists, poets, but of course the cost of the art paper alone made publishers shake their heads.

Then Len Haynes, the decent old drunk who ran it forever, proposed that I take over *Janson's* when he retired to live with his daughter in Majorca.

Married less than a year, Helena Denham and I lived in Colville Terrace, still Rackman's Notting Hill fiefdom. We'd had our first daughter, Sara, and Helena, beautiful as ever with her pageboy chestnut hair framing a heart-shaped face, was furiously pregnant with Cass, our second. I'd been fired from *Liberal Topics*, the party magazine whose wages I'd taken in spite of promising Winston Churchill, when I was eleven, never to become a Liberal. So I needed Janson's money. More important, it would be a chance to do what we'd been saying we should do for so long. I talked it over with Helena and the others.

When I went back to Dave and Howard Vasserman, the publishers, I made only three conditions: that I decide policy, that they let me change the title gradually and if our circulation went up they give me the paper and size I wanted. I would help them get mainstream distribution with their more upmarket titles. I convinced them I could make their imprint respectable enough to be taken on by the high-street retailers. Then I got my friends busy. We lacked a decent designer but I did my best. Our first issue would not merely offer a manifesto, we would attempt to demonstrate policy—and we'd have a lot of illustrations, one of the secrets, in my experience, of a successful periodical. They were Jack Hawthorn's job.

Hayley started finishing a novella he'd been talking about, a weird thing in which the detective's dreams informed his case. Allard began writing us a new serial, full of brooding metaphysical imagery borrowed from Dali and Ernst. Helena finished her alternate-world Nazi creeper. I drafted my editorial about pulp influences on William Burroughs, and Burroughs gave us a chapter from his new book. American beats and British pop artists had something in common with noir movies, our other great enthusiasm. Allard produced a guest editorial arguing that "the space age" needed a new lexicon, new literary ideas. I did a short under a regular pseudonym and the rest came from Janson's stable of favourites.

All three of us were English but had known little conventional upbringing. Hayley had been orphaned by a buzz bomb, taken a job on a local paper before being conscripted into the RAF, studied metaphysics at Oxford where he'd met Allard who'd been raised in occupied France with an Anglo-Jewish mother who'd been on one of the last transports to Auschwitz, worked for the Resistance as a kid then come home not to prewar Mayfair fantasy but despairing suburban austerity, the world Orwell captured. After his conscription served in the RAF, he did physics at Oxford, where he met Harry. They both dropped out after a few terms, writing features and noirish sci-fi stories for mags like *Authentic* or *Vargo Statten's*. Allard was qualified to fly obsolete prop planes, Hayley was a qualified radio operator and I'd done a couple of miserable ATC years before they abolished conscription about a nanosecond before I was due to be drafted, edited juvenile story papers, trade mags and Sexton Blake, so I had loads of editorial experience but little formal education.

We'd spent half our lives in the pub discussing why modern fiction was crap and why it needed an infusion of the methods and concerns of popular fiction, all of us having sold a bit to the surviving thriller and science fantasy pulps. I think we felt we knew what we were talking about, having been raised in the social margins, thanks to one trick of fate or another, and loved surrealism, absurdism, French new wave movies as well as Pound, Eliot, Proust and the rest. In common with a few other restless autodidacts of our day we loved anything containing Gabin's smoking .38, Mitchum's barking .45 or Widmark's glittering knives, all mixed up with Brecht and Weill, Camus' Fascist *Caligula* screaming "I'm still alive" and the black bars crossing the faces of Sartre's *Huis Clos,* emphasizing the prisons in which we place ourselves. Into that mix we threw James Mason in *Odd Man Out,* Harry Lime, Gerald Kersh's *Night and the City,* Bester's *Demolished Man,* Bradbury's *Fahrenheit 451,* Household's *Rogue Male,* Lodwick's *Brother Death.* We'd met the likes of Francis Bacon, Somerset Maugham and Maurice Richardson at the Colony, read Beckett, Miller and Durrell in Olympia Press and generally got our education from the best novelists, journalists and artists of our day. Allard liked Melville more than I did, Hayley preferred Kafka and I loved Meredith. We were agreed that their lessons needed to be brought back into contemporary culture via the popular arts. Borges, too, though his stuff was only just being done into English via Ferlinghetti's City Lights press. We also thought that fiction should be able to carry as many narratives per paragraph as possible, using techniques borrowed from absurdism, futurism and combined with new ideas of our own. We'd thought there were hundreds of writers dying for the chance to do the same as us, but though a lot more readers welcomed what we made of *Mysterious,* contributors were slow in coming.

By 1965 we'd at least laid the foundations of the two-way street. Pop art came one way, pulp the other. The Beatles and Dylan were doing the sound track. They broke new ground and got paid for it, but most people had no real idea what we meant when we talked about combining "high" and "low" arts, in spite of the two cultures being as popular a subject in features pages as the big bang and planet-size computers. We wanted to rid pop fiction of its literalism, taking exaggeration for granted in ambitious work, but were only slowly developing a critical vocabulary, trying to bring a deeper seriousness to the novel, but were still frustrated, reckoning we were still missing a piece in the equation. Whittling the title slowly down to one word hadn't been enough. We needed writers desiring to emulate modern classicism to help build a genuine bridge able to take the weight of our two-way traffic.

It took Rex turning up in 1965 to show us what we needed to convince readers and writers of our authority. Like Allard or Hayley, he wrote better than any other contemporary I knew. His sardonic style was deceptively simple. He, too, was a Balzac fan with a special love of Jacques Collin/ Vautrin. We were almost exactly the same age. Like me, he'd supported himself since the age of sixteen. He'd climbed out of a family of father-dominated German Catholic drunks, dropping out of the University of Texas after selling a few stories to the digests which got him a couple of book contracts to fund the trip to Europe he felt was the next rung on his career ladder, which he planned with his friend Jake Slade, a fellow Texan Catholic and a master ironist.

I was only familiar with Rex's world through what little fiction I'd read of Jim Thompson or what he'd described himself in *Paine in Congress* or *The Clinic*. I'd certainly never been to Texas and only knew Manhattan. Jake's stories had never seen print; they were dry, sly and ticking with the energy of unexploded bombs. Rex's were like Henry James on speed. Quick-mouthed contemporary clarity; good fast fiction fresh off the calendar and with plenty of class. Rooted in our familiar world.

Jake and Rex had planned to write a mystery together in Spain, travel around Europe for a while, then return either to Austin or to New York. But they hadn't anticipated catching jaundice from bad acid in Spain and having to stay with friends in London until they could finish the book. Rex, having read about us in Juliette Masters's *NYT* column, came to see me in the hope of raising some living money. He also brought some of Jake's manuscripts and I immediately knew we were in luck. Neither had come from populist traditions but they thirsted for pulp. They brought the best academic ambitions to the subject matter we featured. They were exactly what I'd been looking for, roaring down from the other end of the two-way street and bringing a bunch of new writers and readers after them. Two for the price of one. Murder and the human soul. The face of society and the fabric of the future. Their intensity and intelligence lacked the hesitancy or vulgarity I'd rejected when posh literary agents thought they'd found somewhere to dump their clients' awful bits of generic slumming, neither did they stink of the creative-writing class.

Sociable, a little formal, a knowing catalyst, Rex introduced me to friends he had known at UT, including the talented fine artists Peggy Zorin, Jilly Cornish and her husband, Jimmy, as well as others who were yet to leave Texas en route for *Mysterious* and London. At last we had a full set of talented contributors who could give us a substantial inventory, interacting with increased gravity, attracting other writers who added superb stories to our contents list, the best anyone had read in ages, combining a sophistication and vitality taken for granted today but representing a quantum jump at the time and making us the most celebrated fiction magazine of our day. The debate was suddenly over. We could demonstrate everything we'd discussed. That was what Rex Fisch did for *Mysterious* and the rough-and-ready movement we'd always denied was a movement. We entered a golden age. Almost every story we published was anthologized. A good many won prizes.

I knew of course that our little revolution would collapse rapidly once we achieved what we hoped for and our individual careers were made. Real life grew darker after those good years. The first tragedy was Jane Allard's death on a trip back to the family home near Nantes. Billy moved to Streatham to bring up his kids. We drove over with our own to visit from time to time. Next, Rex took part in a poetry tour with several well-known poets, including the notoriously omnisexual Spike Allison. He came back gay (no surprise to his friends) and monstrously troubled about it after Spike dumped him on their return to London. Our relationships were only just surviving the divorces, rearrangements and general infighting. People join revolutions until they get what they want as individuals, then start quarrelling over the spoils, however imaginary. I was surprised by how many of our friendships remained intact. Writing mostly nonfiction, Jake settled down with a local girl, Daisy Angelino, in Portobello Road, near our offices. Rex met Chick Archer, who was from Maine, at an S & M bar in Paris. They fell in love, travelled for a few years, then bought their lovely freezing old house in the English Lakes. The place couldn't be more Wordsworthy with its hard, driving cloud banks bringing relentless rain, rewarding you with bursts of sunshine, the whole fell moving like a living body in its contours and shadows, over which Rex presided with a rather proprietorial air at his huge sitting-room windows. Sometimes the wind bawled against the long scar of Wattendale Edge, creating waves across the black tarn. You can see those landscapes, beautifully drawn by Chick in their *Mary Stone* comic. They're still syndicated. Almost nobody knew Rex wrote that great, gritty newspaper strip which made them more money than anything else and which explained why their home smelled so strongly of well-loved wealth.

Rex and I still made each other laugh uncontrollably, much to Chick's silent disgust. This of course drove the sadistic Rex to increase Chick's discomfort. I suspect that's why we didn't get invited up so often. Harry went to live in Ireland with his Dublin-born wife, to look after her mother who lived on a miserable council estate just outside Cork. Stuck there, Harry grew increasingly depressed and began a long book on Nietschze. I saw him occasionally when he came to do research at the British Library. Jimmy and Jill Cornish settled near the old mill in Tufnell Hill. He wrote reviews, criticism for the *LRB* and nonfiction guides. She produced commercial posters to supplement her gallery shows. Others continued to get novels published and exhibitions arranged with increased success. Pete Bates disappeared on a cycling holiday in France. His bike was found at the bottom of a sea cliff in Brittany. Other good writers and artists came and went. Charlie Ratz joined us as our designer. I performed and made records with the Deep Fix.

I thought we were extending the '60s golden age but really it was the end. I continued to publish *Mysterious* but now it was edited by others as affairs and relationships collapsed dramatically across four continents. Gender roles rolled in every possible direction. Stable quartets became full orchestras; ramshackle duets became rock-solid trios. If you visited friends in San Francisco, you needed a complicated chart to know who was with whom, why, when and where. As he and Rex settled in to do the old Alan Bennetts, Chick now wore the slightly self-conscious air of a resting chorus boy down from London for the weekend. Rex had exchanged his Texan brogue for a rather attractive Cowardian drawl which disappeared on the few occasions he phoned home. Chick's tones grew increasingly clipped. They were models of moral righteousness, so thoroughly faithful that when AIDS came it gave them no hint of anxiety. They adopted a very superior attitude to everyone else, of course. And particularly, it turned out, to me. With three much-loved offspring to care for, I weakly divorced Helena, married again and moved across the street with my child bride, Jenny.

Though I had suffered with Rex through his sexual transition and every minor treachery practiced on and by him, he chose to see my breakup with Helena as perhaps the most infamous deed since Eddie's in *Death of the Heart*. My separation from Helena was reasonably amicable, I thought. I was still supporting everyone. I'd done it pretty straightforwardly. But the first time I took Jenny up to Wattendale to see them and a group of friends they'd invited, I thought the murmured commentary from Rex would never end. If Kim and Di Stanley hadn't as usual conned me into giving them a lift up from Bury I would have gone back on the Saturday morning. I was furious and very close to ending our friendship on the spot.

Jenny talked me out of it. "I love hearing you and Rex tell your stories." She grinned. "You're such great liars."

I hardly saw Rex or Chick for the next three years. Chick sent a card at Christmas with just his signature on it. Jenny sent one from us. But I'd had enough. Rex wasn't the only moody bastard writing for *Mysterious* and I just didn't have the energy to work at anything more. At least he was still sending his stuff in, via Charlie Ratz, the new editor. Charlie still saw him regularly. His parents had retired to a massive house outside Keswick, only a couple of miles from Rex and Chick. Whenever Charlie returned to London, he had a new story or two with him. Or Jake Slade would go up and bring something back.

Rex knew the prestige of publishing in the mag. The public saw no ruptures. We were getting more praise than was probably healthy. In fact, a critic brought about our reconciliation. Julie Mistral, the *NYT* reviewer who had been our early champion, now lived about half the year in England. She threw one of her so-called A-list parties and we were all invited. The party was held in the huge rundown hotel restaurant she rented.

Jenny and I were amongst the first to arrive. Rex and Chick were already there, sipping Jacquesson from dusty flutes. Rex spotted me, came over and greeted us with all his old, amused affection. The Great Big Hi as Jake called it. We were embraced. We were kissed. We were mystified.

I was wise enough not to ask how or why this had happened but Jenny found out later from Chick. Rex had come across a review written by Helena for *Tribune*, which had a circulation of about twenty. She had failed to praise *Lost Time Serenade*, Rex's Proustian parody, as much as Rex felt it should be praised. It wasn't a bad review, given I knew she'd found the whole thing pretentious and unworthy of such a good writer, but with Rex you were expected as a friend either to praise him to the skies or not review him at all. Now I knew why Helena hadn't been invited and since I'd never made that particular error of diplomacy I was back in favour again. Then Chick came up and gave me that look of wordless disgust, which was his way of maintaining friendships when Rex blew hot and cold. I was still unsure of him. I was a bit unsure of everything, in fact, because Jenny was just getting into what she'd call her experimental phase, which would enliven our sex life and destroy our marriage. Fourteen years younger than me, she felt she hadn't experienced enough of the world.

I have to admit our sexual experiments were funny to me at first. There's not a lot of sexual pleasure to be got from hopping shouting around your bedroom having failed to wallop your wife's bottom and whacked your own leg instead. I had no instinct for it. Eventually though I was able to play the cruel Sir Charles with reasonable skill. A bit like faking an orgasm.

Ever since we'd been together Jenny had a fantasy about me watching one of my friends fuck her. There were a thousand scenarios in her little head and scarcely one in mine. I think I used up all my stories while I was working. I didn't dream either. I needed a rest from tale spinning at the end of the day. But I did my best. I hated to disappoint her.

I had an idea of the scenario she planned one evening when Rex turned up holding a bottle of Algerian red in one hand and his dripping cap and overcoat in the other, beaming. "Hi!" A wild giggle at his own physical discomfort. Charming. On his best and happiest behaviour. He embraced us in his soft gigantic arms. He had some meetings with Universal Features and wanted to stay for a bit. I thought the evening was to be a celebration of our reborn friendship. Jenny was all over him, flirting like a fag hag, bringing Rex out all atwitter. So we dined. While I washed up, she whispered in his ear.

It turned out Jenny loved threesomes but mostly with her looking on frigging herself blind while waiting to get fucked by the least exhausted bloke. Mostly that was me, as Rex jerked off. That image is no more appealing to me than to you. After three or four nights and days of this, I realised that Rex was getting most of his buzz from knowing Chick had no suspicion of what he was up to.

Of course, to add to his own wicked relish Rex told Chick what he'd done with us. He had to. He never could resist a good story, particularly if he was telling it. Our few nights of passionless sex had become a means of manipulating Chick. This time Chick cut us.

Inevitably Jenny and I grew further apart as our games got more fantastic. Rex had already been through all that with Chick in Paris. Real-life fantasies are distractions for a working writer. Years before Rex told me that himself. "It's as bad as going to law. The story starts to take over.

Like falling in love. All sentimentality and melodrama. The scenarios are repetitive, conventional. All they offer are the comforts of genre." He was right. Sex games are more boring than an Agatha Christie novel.

Anyway Jenny, despite our investment in special clothing and sex aids, wasn't getting a big enough buzz out of my efforts. It's like horror movies or superhero comics, you either stop and give them a rest or you have to keep heightening the action. Even if the games didn't bore me, our widening circle of acquaintances did. I wasn't finding enough time alone. Individuals, couples, whole fucking communes got involved. If they gave me a good paragraph or two, I wouldn't have minded so much, but there was an infantile sameness about their scenarios. Jenny and I were driven further apart by what the courts call intimacy. I tried to get to see Rex and Chick on their own, desperately needing to find out how they had rescued themselves from the crack of the crop, the smell of damp leather, the spell of repetition. Did you just grow out of it? Sometimes Jenny seemed to be flagging until some fresh variation on a familiar theme perked her up again. She was a natural addict. I've never been seriously addicted to anything. So I started trying to get her off the habit. It didn't work. She made excuses, started doing stuff in secret. I hate ambiguity in my day-to-day life. There's enough in my work. A writer needs routines and certainties. What can I say? As well as losing real intimacy with old friends, I lost it with Jenny. In a half-arsed attempt to restore our earlier closeness, she told me some of her new adventures. Then I got hooked for a while. I started pumping her for more revelations. She owed me that, I decided. They added nothing but did become pretty chilling. The seduction of underage girls. Things my friends liked to do. It amazed me how so many women took the odd rape for granted. Too many secrets revealed. Friendships frayed. Rex came back in the picture. I moved out.

I took my kids, whom I'd been missing anyway, on a long trip round the USA. It made us feel better. To my relief we grew back together. Feeling my old self I got home, bought a short lease on a little flat in Fulham, just when Notting Hill turned into a gentrified suburb. I saw enough of Jenny to know it was thoroughly over. I didn't like what she'd done to herself. She'd dyed her hair bright blond and her brown eyes had a vaguely dazed, mirrorlike quality, as if they only reflected and no longer saw anything. She'd lost her sense of humour, too, and was into various odd relationships, still searching for the good life. When I shifted the last of my stuff she made a halfhearted attempt to patch things up. She wanted to have a baby, she said, and get back into our old domestic routine. Even while she proposed this deal, a bloke I vaguely knew was sleeping upstairs in what had been our bed, where once, like Proust, I'd done most of my writing. From being a place of concentration in which I conceived stories it had become a place of distraction, where real stories died. I said she could keep the place. All she had to do was pay the mortgage.

"But I love you." She wept. She made an awkward attempt to remind me of the old days. "I love just lying in your arms at night while you tell me a story."

I was sad. "It's too late, Jenny." Those stories were over.

I went up to Windermere, phoned Rex and Chick, but Chick was frosty. Did I know I had almost broken them up? I apologized. I said how much I regretted what had happened. Rex, just as distant and haughty, put the phone down on me. I saw them in Kendal once or twice and in Grasmere. They wouldn't speak to me. Once, over his shoulder, Rex gave me the most peculiar leer. Did he wish we were still deceiving Chick? It made me shudder. Was something wrong with him?

Of course I longed to be back with Helena but she'd settled down with a jolly Scottish chef and was doing her best work. Why would she want to change that?

Even though our pillow talk inspired a couple of shorts, I really hated having been part of Jenny's daisy chain. Some of those people I never wanted to see again, others I needed distance from; I wasn't ready to see Charlie Ratz or Jonny Fowler yet. Pete was still missing in France, presumed dead. I gave up any interest in *Mysterious,* which was now doing fine without me, bought a house near Ingleton, West Yorks, and settled in first with Emma MacEwan, who couldn't stand the rain and cold, and then started seeing a local woman who disapproved of central heating. I desperately hoped to restore my friendship with Rex, even after I met Lucinda, to this day the love of my life. Lu found my obsession weird, I know, until she eventually met Rex in Leeds, at a Ted Hughes literary weekend we'd all been invited to. Lu's teenage daughter loved Rex's work and wanted him to autograph her books. She was too shy to ask him, so Lucy, her fair hair flying and blue eyes blazing, marched up to the table where he was sitting and said: "I gather you're Mike's old friend. Well, I'm his new wife and this is my daughter, who's read most of your work and loves it. I think it's pretty good, too. So what about some autographs and while you're at it why don't you two shake hands?" And, that being just one of her powers, we did.

Later at the bar Rex told me Chick blamed me for the infamous "seduction." At that idea we continued to laugh for the rest of the day, until the next, when Chick turned up, glaring when he saw us, and Lucinda, nearly six feet herself, took him in hand as well. "It's all over," she said. "If you're going to blame anyone, blame that poor, barmy bitch Jenny. She got you all involved in her folly and now look at you." And when Chick grumbled that Rex was still seeing Jenny, which surprised me, Lu said: "Well, she's poison as far as I can tell, and he doesn't need her now he has Mike back." Chick teared up then. He told her I was the best friend Rex had ever had but I had betrayed them both. Which again I admitted. And the following weekend Lu and I went up and stayed with them. On our way home she said: "You two could make Jeremiah roll about on the floor laughing himself sick."

I didn't know why Rex went on seeing Jenny, unless he simply enjoyed wounding Chick. He still had that cruel streak in him. Chick and I talked about it. Chick thought it had to be directed at him, too. He guessed Jenny was a substitute for me, especially when Rex dropped Jenny so soon after we were reconciled. She still phoned him.

I saw Jenny myself a few times after that. She seemed more her old self in some ways. She'd had twins and was living with her mother in Worthing, on the Sussex coast. She had the washed-out look of so many single mothers, said she was happy, if poor, and even suggested my "sexual conservatism" had dulled me down. Next time I bumped into her in Kensington High Street she was again pale, overpainted, dyed up. She looked as if all the vitality had been sucked from her. I thought she was doing junk. Her eyes were back to blank. Was she living in London? Did she have someone? She laughed and looked even more devitalized. "None of your business," she said. I couldn't argue with that.

Of course, I was curious to know what she and Rex had been up to. I guessed she hadn't accepted that he'd dropped her. At a party in Brighton a year or two later she looked worse than ever, clinging to Rupert Herbert, one of those new Low Tories on the *Spectator*. More makeup, too blond and getting through a packet of Gauloises a minute. I did really feel sorry for her. Then Rex turned up and snubbed her so royally he pissed me off, so I made a point of going over to talk to her but she snubbed me in turn. Lucinda came over and murmured "poor bitch" and meant it. Between us the *Mysterious* crew had ruined a nice, unimaginative girl, she thought. Not entirely fair. You could hear Jenny over the general buzz talking about some famous film producer she'd lived with. He'd been the one who bought *The Vices of Tom* from Rex and then turned it into that pot of toss. "The bastard . . . ," she was saying. You could guess the rest. Maybe Lu was right.

For the next ten years or so life settled into routines nobody felt like messing with though Rex grew increasingly unreasoning in his arguments with editors, then publishers, then agents until almost nobody would work with him. His books didn't sell enough for any editor to bother keeping him sweet. He took offence easily and frequently and, through his vengeful verse, publicly. Chick said he could no longer manage him. I would have thought this a good thing. I believed Chick's natural leanings towards convention and literary respectability pushed Rex away from his saving self-mocking vulgarity. Balzac and Vautrin were less his models than Proust or Albertine. His work seemed to apologise for itself. He lost his popular touch without gaining critical prestige. Only *Mary Stone* went on making money for them. His short stories came out less frequently, but he kept his habit of phoning and often reading the whole thing to you. And he still enjoyed inventing a story when he got your answering machine. "Oh, I know what you're doing. You've met that good-looking farmer again and gone badger watching with him." Usually the time would be up before he could complete his fantasy. His new novels tended to peter out after a few chapters. I'd get frustrated and consider continuing them for him. They were wonderful ideas. Occasionally they would reemerge when a way of telling them occurred to him. His aptitude for ironic narrative verse never left him. I'd labour for hours to get anything close to what usually took him minutes. Chick helped him develop his taste for classical music, which is how he came to write his three operas, one of which he based on Kersh's *The Brazen Bull* and another on Balzac's *Illusions Perdue* but he became snobbish about popular music or he'd have written some great lyrics. I used a few of his verses in my own music stuff. I inserted another into one of my hack thrillers, its redeeming feature. His only opera to reach the stage was a version of Firbank's *Cardinal Pirelli*. Rex delighted in upsetting Catholics, although his attacks meant little to most of us.

Then, as we limped into our sixties, we began to suffer from real illnesses, as opposed to passing scares. Rex was diabetic, arthritic. Chick was the first of us to be diagnosed with cancer. I think it was colon, he wouldn't say. Even Rex refused to betray him on that occasion. His surgery seemed to cure him. We heard Jenny survived a stroke. By that time she hardly saw any old friends. When she had an operation, I'm not sure what for. Rex didn't speak of the years when he'd seen her regularly, even as we grew closer than ever, all living up in those northern hills, from Todmorden to Kendal. Harry, of course, was still in Ireland. Billy Allard went to Corfu after his children grew up. Pete continued to be presumed dead. Peggy Zoran returned to New York and was very successful. The Cornishes moved to Kirkby Lonsdale. I had a hernia operation which went wrong. Bad stitching cut off an artery and caused problems in my leg. I couldn't walk or climb anymore. Rex's diabetes was complicated by drinking. Chick successfully got him on the wagon. In 2005, while we were at our place in Paris, I got an e-mail from Rex referring casually to Chick's return to Airedale General, so I phoned the hospital at once. "It's spread a bit," Chick said. "I'll be out in a few days." So we flew home and drove over. Chick had lost a lot of weight. He was ghastly white but Rex pretended nothing was wrong. A lot of surgery was involved. Chick started a short story called "Over the Knife." He showed it to us. Very mystical and sardonic. He got me to ask Jack Hawthorn if he'd take over *Mary Stone,* but Jack wasn't up to it. The next thing we knew he was admitted again and we made the first of several trips to Skipton. Chick was bitter about friends who couldn't find time to visit or phone. "Or send a bloody Hallmark card and a bunch of fucking flowers." Rex, sometimes there when I was, echoed all this. I did what I could to make friends visit. Very few did. People were fighting to keep some sort of income, I suppose. At the hospital we made the usual jokes, complimented Chick on his courage. He found this amusing. "You're just thanking me for not making you feel bad. It's easy to be brave when everyone's attention's focused on you." He could do the best wan smile, remembered Rex, giggling later. Chick asked us to stop sending flowers. The smell reminded him too much of funerals. I remembered my mother making the same complaint.

Rex was still pretty much in denial. Who could blame him? His responses became more and more monosyllabic, either because he didn't want to cry or because he didn't want to be reminded of what was happening. His partner of nearly forty years, however, spoke more freely. He had so little time. Subsequent operations were done to "repair" his intestines.

When he went home he was only there for a matter of weeks, even days, before they sent him back again. Another series of surgeries was proposed but Chick refused any more. He wanted to die with a semblance of dignity. A quietly practicing Anglican for some years, he was ready to go. I asked if he was scared. "In a way," he said, "as if I were going for a job interview." He chiefly needed promises that we'd keep an eye on Rex, make sure he paid bills, had repairs done, all the jobs Chick had taken on so Rex could write without worry. "I know it's hard, but you're the best friends he has." A kind of blackmail. I didn't resent it. He probably said the same to others. "He mustn't start drinking. He won't look after the place unless you pester him. There's still a bit on the mortgage. He'll let the pool go. Make sure he gives you a key. Oh, and he has a gun. Get the bullets if you can. You know what a drama queen he can be." Next time we saw him he had written out a list in his educated American hand. Where the stopcocks were, what needed watering when, the names and numbers of the oil-delivery people, the gas and electricity people, the best plumber, the most reliable electrician. Their handyman, the local rates office: all the details of their domestic lives. We promised to do all we could.

His thin, grey face with its grey toothbrush moustache became earnest. "In spite of anything Rex says?"

We promised.

"Or anything he tells you? Or I tell you?" This was puzzling, but we agreed. Once he had our promises, he drew a long breath. Then: "You know, don't you, what he was doing with Jenny?"

"We don't want to." Lucinda spoke before I could answer. Of course I wanted him to tell me.

"Okay." Chick turned on his pillows. "Probably just as well."

Lu and I drove home in unspeaking silence.

Chick died a few days later. In late August many friends were on holiday and couldn't make it to the funeral. Rex blamed them, of course. If Chick's frail old dad could make the trip, then surely . . . ? I went to stay with him. He was dazed. He'd found Chick's diaries before we could. "I never realised what he gave up. Why he was so unhappy." I pointed out that journals are almost always misleading. We use them to record miseries, frustrations of the moment, anger we don't want to put into the air. We didn't need them when we were content. But he refused to be comforted. He had failed Chick. That's all he had to say. He was drinking again.

Rex was very particular about the funeral, insisting we wear what he called "full mourning," which meant black hats and veils for women, suits and ties for men. There were only seven of us in the Grasmere cemetery where Chick wanted to be buried. Rex bore his grief through his familiar haughty disguise. Lucinda had organized the funeral meats, such as they were. Rex had insisted on everything being simple. Chick had wanted the same. After we had all gone to bed or home, Rex sat down in his study and phoned everyone who hadn't been able to make it. If they didn't pick up, he left messages on their machines. Not the usual whimsical tales. He told them what he and Chick had always said behind their backs about their lack of talent, their ugly child, their gigantic ego, their terrible cooking, their bad taste. When Rex hurt, everyone got hurt. Next day, high on his own vengeance, he told me in a series of vignettes what he'd done. Some of the people phoned me next. Many were in tears. Almost all tried to forgive him. Several wanted to know if he was right. My daughter Cass had given him Helena's regards and been snubbed so badly by Rex she was still crying when she got through to me. She was readier to forgive him than I was.

About a week later, while Lu visited her hypochondriacal mother, I went over to see how Rex was doing. He'd been drinking heavily. "I'm glad you came," he said. "I wanted you to know about a favour I did you a few years back." I cooked us dinner, after which he told me what he'd done for me. He was sure I'd be pleased, he said. I didn't know who he was mocking. Gasping and yelping with pain from the arthritis brought on by the booze, he poked up the fire and poured us cognacs. Then he started with the slow, dramatic relish he reserved for his readings. I suppose you could call it a revenge tale, with all the elements he enjoyed in Balzac and the Jacobeans. Soon after Jenny and I split up, and blaming her for "luring" him into the threesome with which he had taunted Chick, Rex became, in his words, her confessor, suggesting ideas to her for sexual adventures, often helping her make specific contacts and introducing her to what he called his list of "forty famous perverts." He had sometimes accompanied her to dinners and parties, encouraging her to risks she'd never have dared take on her own. "I drove her farther and farther down that road, Mike. You'd have loved it! Whenever she faltered I was there encouraging her to stay the course. I told her heroin wasn't addictive!" (Luckily he'd only been able to persuade her to snort it.) "I convinced her she was a natural whore. I became her best friend, just as Vautrin took Emma under his wing!" That terrible, self-approving chuckle followed as he sat there in his big leather chair overlooking the darkening fell, staring in sardonic satisfaction at the sky, speaking in the tones of measured mockery usually reserved for his satirical verse. "I knew you wanted to do it but couldn't. So I took your revenge *for* you, Mike!"

"Jesus, Rex. She didn't deserve . . . I would never . . ."

"Oh, Mike, you *know* what she deserved. *You'd* never do it, but Vautrin could, eh? I learned the lessons of Balzac better than you ever did!" At that point, as the world grew darker and the fire reflected on his face, he was every inch Balzac's monster, apparently completely mad. I felt physically sick, concerned for his sanity, deeply sorry for Jenny. I wondered if Lucinda had guessed what had gone on. Was that why she had refused to let Chick tell us anything? Rex relished every revelation. Giggling, he explained how he persuaded her to do something particularly demeaning. I was no sadist but of course he was. He could hate women. He went on for ages, offering chapter and verse, names, places, bringing all the horror and misery back. He explained little mysteries, offered anecdotes, consequences, a whole catalogue of betrayal. Chick could not have known the half of it. I wanted to walk out on him there and then but I was too fascinated. Besides, I had promised Chick I would stand by Rex. I couldn't abandon him. This was Rex's way of being my friend. I knew how much he relished revenge. He sincerely believed others merely pretended not to take the same pleasure in it.

I had promised to stay the night. By the time I went to bed, I had nothing to say to him. I knew how kind he could often be, how kind he had been to Jenny. I could hardly imagine such complicated, elaborate cruelty. Around three A.M. I took a couple of sleeping pills and woke up at eight on a wonderful sunny morning. Under a clear grey-blue sky the granite glittered and the grass glowed. Rex was down in the big, stone-flagged kitchen making breakfast. I ate it as if it might be poisoned. Standing in his drive beside my car, I hugged him. "I love you, Rex," I said. And I did, even at that moment, when I could barely look at him. He paused, appearing to consider this. Then he teared up, making that muted humming sound I became used to hearing when he searched for an appropriate word, the little smack of his lips and intake of breath when he'd found it.

"I love you, too," he said at last.

I got home that afternoon. I'd had to pull over twice to collect myself.

Lucinda was still out. I'd hoped so much she would be home before me. The message light was flickering on the phone. I had a sickening premonition something had happened to her. But it was Rex sounding dramatically cheerful, a sure sign he'd been drinking. "Hi, Mike! I know you're off ratting with your friend the vicar and your Jack Russells. Clearly you've no time to spend for poor old Rex . . ." And so on until the machine cut him off. I was relieved I'd taken longer getting home. When Lu finally arrived with fish and chips from the local, she was too full of her own frustrations with her mother to notice my mood so I explained how I was tired from staying up all night with Rex.

We saw a bit more of Rex after that. Because I would never know anything different, I decided to treat most of what he'd told me that night as an elaborate fiction. I was probably right. A couple of months later, as if he had been practicing on me with the Jenny story, he began writing again. At first I was relieved, but we eventually realised he was unable to finish anything. He had lost his gift for narrative, his sense of the future. We did all we could to encourage him, to keep him engaged. The ideas themselves were as brilliant as ever. He phoned to read me a couple of opening paragraphs over the answer machine and they were so good, so typical of Rex at his best, Lucinda wouldn't let me erase them. When I was home he might read several pages, even a chapter. But two chapters were the most he could manage of anything. Chick had always been the one to help with construction. After I stopped editing he wouldn't let me do it anymore. He claimed Chick's diary had left him unable to complete a story. "Maybe because I know how it finishes. How they all finish."

Rex had spent his whole life telling stories. There wasn't much I could say. He was still writing narrative verse and every fortnight or so he would phone again with the start of a new story, still leaving it on the machine if we weren't in.

Then his troubles began to increase. Phoning him I learned how he was threatened by the VAT authorities because of his failure to send in his forms or how a builder had gone off on a second job in the middle of fixing the library roof, how rain was drenching his books. I'd go over and do what I could but eventually I'd have to return home. I felt horribly guilty, recalling my promise to Chick. Not that I failed to remind Rex of what Chick had mentioned, but I couldn't be there the whole time. Often he seemed to resent our help. I suppose the boxed wine he bought by mail order didn't help. He ate a lot, but badly for a diabetic, and for all the various domestic disasters, which his friends coped with pretty well among us, things appeared to improve with time. If anything his grasp on reality seemed to strengthen. He broke down less and began going to a few parties and conferences. He made his peace with the friends he'd insulted and was mostly forgiven. Optimistically, we spoke of him as becoming his old self again. He was introspective in a positive way.

When another August came round he seemed pretty positive. He might start off feeling miserable but conversation soon cheered him up. We'd share a piece of gossip or make fun of a good friend. That was how we were. He joked about Chick, too. I saw that as another sign of healing. Lucinda could always tell who was on the phone because of the laughter. I spoke to him on the first Monday in September. He was drunk, but no more than usual. He'd sent me an e-mail, he said. This was unusual. He hated e-mail as a rule. So I went to my PC and there it was. Rex rarely offered that amount of self-revelation and this had the feel of a continuing conversation, maybe with himself. It knocked me back a bit. So much that I made plans to see him the following weekend. It was as short as it was shocking:

"The story I never wrote was the story of my life, my unhappiness at failing to convince my father of my worth. I tried so hard, but I never had the courage or the method to tell that story. I wrote to impress. The verses always had to be witty, the prose clever. You remember me telling you, when we were young, how scared I was about dropping my guard. Truth wasn't as important as success to me. I needed to impress the people my dad approved of. Nobody else's opinion meant much. Either he saw me in the *Saturday Evening Post* or I simply didn't exist as a writer." I think he'd planned to say more, but that's all there was.

On the Thursday, Jimmy Cornish called and told me Rex was dead. The rest was in the obits. Gone but not forgiven.

I had failed to keep my word to Chick. I hadn't found the bullets. I should have spoken to his accountant. I should have helped him back to AA. I've never understood booze. People have to be rolling in the gutter singing "Nellie Dean" before I get the picture. I missed all the signs and fell down on a solemn promise. Not for the first time. I never gave a promise to a child I couldn't keep, but I made a habit of breaking them to adults. Rex knew exactly what he was doing. I'm not the only survivor still running scenarios through their head. If I'd found the gun and stolen it . . . If I'd checked to see how much he was drinking . . . If I'd listened more closely . . .

Rex wrote some great ghost stories. When it came to haunting his friends, he was a bloody expert. What he'd done to Jenny told me he knew exactly what he was up to. People say all ghost stories are optimistic because they show a belief in life after death. Equally, all artists are optimists because the act of creation is optimistic in itself. Rex's poems and openings are still on our machine. Lu won't erase them. On a bad night I'll pour myself a glass of wine and press the button until I hear his voice. I'll listen to his gentle mockery as he invents an outrageous tale about my getting my toe stuck in the bath's hot tap or being arrested for vagrancy on my way back from a climb. He always gets cut off. If I'm feeling up to it, I'll listen the way you listen to a sweet, familiar tune.

I think that was the real reason why, after Chick's death, Rex never completed anything. There was only one story he really had to tell and from deep habit he had repressed it, choosing suicide rather than write it. "The Story of Rex and Chick." Even under such dreadful stress he couldn't let it come out. He had destroyed Chick's journals to ensure it never would be known. And then he had destroyed himself.

Rather than dwell on that I'll listen to his familiar fantasies once again. Then I'll turn off the machine, curse the bastard for a liar and a coward and a calculating fucking sadist, pick up one of his books and head for bed, glad enough, I guess, that I still have a few stories of my own to tell and some rotten bloody friends to remember.

THE MAIDEN FLIGHT OF MCCAULEY'S
Bellerophon

•

Elizabeth Hand

BEING ASSIGNED TO THE HEAD for eight hours was the worst security shift you could pull at the museum. Even now, thirty years later, Robbie had dreams in which he wandered from the Early Flight gallery to Balloons & Airships to Cosmic Soup, where he once again found himself alone in the dark, staring into the bland gaze of the famous scientist as he intoned his endless lecture about the nature of the universe.

"Remember when we thought nothing could be worse than that?" Robbie stared wistfully into his empty glass, then signaled the waiter for another bourbon and Coke. Across the table, his old friend Emery sipped a beer.

"I liked the Head," said Emery. He cleared his throat and began to recite in the same portentous tone the famous scientist had employed. "Trillions and trillions of galaxies in which our own is but a mote of cosmic dust. It made you think."

"It made you think about killing yourself," said Robbie. "Do you want to know how many times I heard that?"

"A trillion?"

"Five thousand." The waiter handed Robbie a drink, his fourth. "Twenty-five times an hour, times eight hours a day, times five days a week, times five months."

"Five thousand, that's not so much. Especially when you think of all those trillions of galleries. I mean galaxies. Only five months? I thought you worked there longer."

"Just that summer. It only seemed like forever."

Emery knocked back his beer. "A long time ago, in a gallery far, far away," he intoned, not for the first time.

Thirty years before, the Museum of American Aviation and Aerospace had just opened. Robbie was nineteen that summer, a recent drop-out from the University of Maryland, living in a group house in Mount Rainier. Employment opportunities were scarce; making $3.40 an hour as a security aide at the Smithsonian's newest museum seemed preferable to bagging groceries at Giant Food. Every morning he'd punch his time card in the guards' locker room and change into his uniform. Then he'd duck outside to smoke a joint before trudging downstairs for the morning meeting and that day's assignments.

Most of the security guards were older than Robbie, with backgrounds in the military and an eye on future careers with the D.C. police department or FBI. Still, they tolerated him with mostly good-natured ribbing about his longish hair and bloodshot eyes. All except for Hedge, the security chief. He was an enormous man with a shaved head who sat, knitting, behind a bank of closed-circuit video monitors, observing tourists and guards with an expression of amused contempt.

"What are you making?" Robbie once asked. Hedge raised his hands to display an intricately patterned baby blanket. "Hey, that's cool. Where'd you learn to knit?"

"Prison." Hedge's eyes narrowed. "You stoned again, Opie? That's it. Gallery Seven. Relieve Jones."

Robbie's skin went cold, then hot with relief when he realized Hedge wasn't going to fire him. "Seven? Uh, yeah, sure, sure. For how long?"

"Forever," said Hedge.

"Oh, man, you got the Head." Jones clapped his hands gleefully when Robbie arrived. "Better watch your ass, kids'll throw shit at you," he said, and sauntered off.

Two projectors at opposite ends of the dark room beamed twin shafts of silvery light onto a head-shaped Styrofoam form. Robbie could never figure out if they'd filmed the famous scientist just once, or if they'd gone to the trouble to shoot him from two different angles.

However they'd done it, the sight of the disembodied Head was surprisingly effective: it looked like a hologram floating amid the hundreds of back-projected twinkly stars that covered the walls and ceiling. The creep factor was intensified by the stilted, slightly puzzled manner in which the Head blinked as it droned on, as though the famous scientist had just realized his body was gone, and was hoping no one else would notice. Once, when he was really stoned, Robbie swore that the Head deviated from its script.

"What'd it say?" asked Emery. At the time he was working in the General Aviation Gallery, operating a flight simulator that tourists clambered into for three-minute rides.

"Something about peaches," said Robbie. "I couldn't understand, it sort of mumbled."

Every morning, Robbie stood outside the entrance to Cosmic Soup and watched as tourists streamed through the main entrance and into the Hall of Flight. Overhead, legendary aircraft hung from the ceiling. The 1903 Wright Flyer with its Orville mannequin; a Lilienthal glider; the Bell X-1 in which Chuck Yeager broke the sound barrier. From a huge pit in the center of the Hall rose a Minuteman III ICBM, rust-colored stains still visible where a protester had tossed a bucket of pig's blood on it a few months earlier. Directly above the entrance to Robbie's gallery dangled the *Spirit of St. Louis*. The aides who worked upstairs in the planetarium amused themselves by shooting paper clips onto its wings.

Robbie winced at the memory. He gulped what was left of his bourbon and sighed. "That was a long time ago."

"*Tempus fugit*, baby. Thinking of which—" Emery dug into his pocket for a BlackBerry. "Check this out. From Leonard."

Robbie rubbed his eyes blearily, then read.

From: *l.scopes@MAAA.SI.edu*
Subject: *Tragic Illness*
Date: *April 6, 7:58:22 P.M. EDT*
To: *emeryubergeek@gmail.com*

Dear Emery,
I just learned that our Maggie Blevin is very ill. I wrote her at
Christmas but never heard back. Fuad El-Hajj says she was diagnosed
with advanced breast cancer last fall. Prognosis is not good. She is still
in the Fayetteville area, and I gather is in a hospice. I want to make a
visit though not sure how that will go over. I have something I want to
give her but need to talk to you about it.
L.

"Ahhh." Robbie sighed. "God, that's terrible."

"Yeah. I'm sorry. But I figured you'd want to know."

Robbie pinched the bridge of his nose. Four years earlier, his wife, Anna, had died of breast cancer, leaving him adrift in a grief so profound it was as though he'd been poisoned, as though his veins had been pumped with the same chemicals that had failed to save her. Anna had been an oncology nurse, a fact that at first afforded some meager black humor, but in the end deprived them of even the faintest of false hopes borne of denial or faith in alternative therapies.

There was no time for any of that. Zach, their son, had just turned twelve. Between his own grief and Zach's subsequent acting out, Robbie got so depressed that he started pouring his first bourbon and Coke before the boy left for school. Two years later, he got fired from his job with the county parks commission.

He now worked in the shipping department at Small's, an off-price store in a desolate shopping mall that resembled the ruins of a regional airport. Robbie found it oddly consoling. It reminded him of the museum. The same generic atriums and industrial carpeting; the same bleak sunlight filtered through clouded glass; the same vacant-faced people trudging from Dollar Store to Sunglass Hut, the way they'd wandered from the General Aviation Gallery to Cosmic Soup.

"Poor Maggie." Robbie returned the BlackBerry. "I haven't thought of her in years."

"I'm going to see Leonard."

"When? Maybe I'll go with you."

"Now." Emery shoved a twenty under his beer bottle and stood. "You're coming with me."

"What?"

"You can't drive—you're snackered. Get popped again, you lose your license."

"Popped? Who's getting popped? And I'm not snackered, I'm—" Robbie thought. "Snockered. You pronounced it wrong."

"Whatever." Emery grabbed Robbie's shoulder and pushed him to the door. "Let's go."

Emery drove an expensive hybrid that could get from Rockville to Utica, New York, on a single tank of gas. The vanity plate read MARVO and was flanked by bumper stickers with messages like GUNS DON'T KILL PEOPLE: TYPE 2 PHASERS KILL PEOPLE and FRAK OFF! as well as several slogans that Emery said were in Klingon.

Emery was the only person Robbie knew who was somewhat famous. Back in the early 1980s, he'd created a local-access cable TV show called *Captain Marvo's Secret Spacetime,* taped in his parents' basement and featuring Emery in an aluminum foil costume behind the console of a cardboard spaceship. Captain Marvo watched videotaped episodes of low-budget 1950s science fiction serials with titles like *PAYLOA.D.: MOONDUST* while bantering with his copilot, a homemade puppet made by Leonard, named Mungbean.

The show was pretty funny if you were stoned. Captain Marvo became a cult hit, and then a real hit when a major network picked it up as a late-night offering. Emery quit his day job at the museum and rented studio time in Baltimore. He sold the rights after a few years, and was immediately replaced by a flashy actor in Lurex and a glittering robot sidekick. The show limped along for a season then died. Emery's fans claimed this was because their slacker hero had been sidelined.

But maybe it was just that people weren't as stoned as they used to be. These days the program had a surprising afterlife on the Internet, where Robbie's son, Zach, watched it with his friends, and Emery did a brisk business selling memorabilia through his official Captain Marvo Web site.

It took them nearly an hour to get into D.C. and find a parking space near the Mall, by which time Robbie had sobered up enough to wish he'd stayed at the bar.

"Here." Emery gave him a sugarless breath mint, then plucked at the collar of Robbie's shirt, acid green with SMALLS embroidered in purple. "Christ, Robbie, you're a freaking mess."

He reached into the backseat, retrieved a black T-shirt from his gym bag. "Here, put this on."

Robbie changed into it and stumbled out onto the sidewalk. It was mid-April but already steamy; the air shimmered above the pavement and smelled sweetly of apple blossom and coolant from innumerable air conditioners. Only as he approached the museum entrance and caught his reflection in a glass wall did Robbie see that his T-shirt was emblazoned with Emery's youthful face and foil helmet above the words O CAPTAIN MY CAPTAIN.

"You wear your own T-shirt?" he asked as he followed Emery through the door.

"Only at the gym. Nothing else was clean."

They waited at the security desk while a guard checked their IDs, called upstairs to Leonard's office, signed them in and took their pictures before finally issuing each a visitor's pass.

"You'll have to wait for Leonard to escort you upstairs," the guard said.

"Not like the old days, huh, Robbie?" Emery draped an arm around Robbie and steered him into the Hall of Flight. "Not a lot of retinal scanning on your watch."

The museum hadn't changed much. The same aircraft and space capsules gleamed overhead. Tourists clustered around the lucite pyramid that held slivers of moon rock. Sunburned guys sporting military haircuts and tattoos peered at a mockup of a F-15 flight deck. Everything had that old museum smell: soiled carpeting, machine oil, the wet-laundry odor wafting from steam tables in the public cafeteria.

But the Head was long gone. Robbie wondered if anyone even remembered the famous scientist, dead for many years. The General Aviation Gallery, where Emery and Leonard had operated the flight simulators and first met Maggie Blevin, was now devoted to Personal Flight, with models of jet packs worn by alarmingly lifelike mannequins.

"Leonard designed those." Emery paused to stare at a child-size figure who seemed to float above a solar-powered skateboard. "He could have gone to Hollywood."

"It's not too late."

Robbie and Emery turned to see their old colleague behind them.

"Leonard," said Emery.

The two men embraced. Leonard stepped back and tilted his head. "Robbie. I wasn't expecting you."

"Surprise," said Robbie. They shook hands awkwardly. "Good to see you, man."

Leonard forced a smile. "And you."

They headed toward the staff elevator. Back in the day, Leonard's hair had been long and luxuriantly blond. It fell unbound down the back of the dogshit yellow uniform jacket, designed to evoke an airline pilot's, which he and Emery and the other General Aviation aides wore as they gave their spiel to tourists eager to yank on the controls of their Link Trainers. With his patrician good looks and stern gray eyes, Leonard was the only aide who actually resembled a real pilot.

Now he looked like a cross between Obi-Wan Kenobi and Willie Nelson. His hair was white and hung in two braids that reached almost to his waist. Instead of the crappy polyester uniform, he wore a white linen tunic, a necklace of unpolished turquoise and coral, loose black trousers tucked into scuffed cowboy boots, and a skull earring the size of Robbie's thumb. On his collar gleamed the cheap knockoff pilot's wings that had once adorned his museum uniform jacket. Leonard had always taken his duties very seriously, especially after Margaret Blevin arrived as the museum's first curator of Proto-Flight. Robbie's refusal to do the same, even long after he'd left the museum himself, had resulted in considerable friction between them over the intervening years.

Robbie cleared his throat. "So, uh. What are you working on these days?" He wished he wasn't wearing Emery's idiotic T-shirt.

"I'll show you," said Leonard.

Upstairs, they headed for the old photo lab, now an imaging center filled with banks of computers, digital cameras, scanners.

"We still process film there," Leonard said as they walked down a corridor hung with production photos from *The Day the Earth Stood Still* and *Frau Im Mond.* "Negatives, old motion picture stock—people still send us things."

"Any of it interesting?" asked Emery.

Leonard shrugged. "Sometimes. You never know what you might find. That's part of Maggie's legacy—we're always open to the possibility of discovering something new."

Robbie shut his eyes. Leonard's voice made his teeth ache. "Remember how she used to keep a bottle of Scotch in that side drawer, underneath her purse?" he said.

Leonard frowned, but Emery laughed. "Yeah! And it was good stuff, too."

"Maggie had a great deal of class," said Leonard in a somber tone.

You pompous asshole, thought Robbie.

Leonard punched a code into a door and opened it. "You might remember when this was a storage cupboard."

They stepped inside. Robbie did remember this place—he'd once had sex here with a General Aviation aide whose name he'd long forgotten. It had been a good-size supply room then, with an odd, sweetish scent from the rolls of film stacked along the shelves.

Now it was a very crowded office. The shelves were crammed with books and curatorial reports dating back to 1981, and archival boxes holding god knows what—Leonard's original government-job application, maybe. A coat had been tossed onto the floor in one corner. There was a large metal desk covered with bottles of nail polish, and an ancient swivel chair that Robbie vaguely remembered having been deployed during his lunch hour tryst.

Mostly, though, the room held Leonard's stuff: tiny cardboard dioramas, mock-ups of space capsules and dirigibles. It smelled overpoweringly of nail polish. It was also extremely cold.

"Man, you must freeze your ass off." Robbie rubbed his arms.

Emery picked up one of the little bottles. "You getting a manicurist's license?"

Leonard gestured at the desk. "I'm painting with nail polish now. You get some very unusual effects."

"I bet," said Robbie. "You're, like, huffing nail polish." He peered at the shelves, impressed despite himself. "Jeez, Leonard. You made all these?"

"Damn right I did."

When Robbie first met Leonard, they were both lowly GS-1s. In those days, Leonard collected paper clips and rode an old Schwinn bicycle to work. He entertained tourists by making balloon animals. In his spare time, he created Mungbean, Captain Marvo's robot friend, out of a busted lamp and some spark plugs.

He also made strange ink drawings, hundreds of them. Montgolfier balloons with sinister faces; B-52s carrying payloads of soap bubbles; caricatures of the museum director and senior curators as greyhounds sniffing each others' nether quarters.

It was this last, drawn on a scrap of legal paper, which Margaret Blevin picked up on her first tour of the General Aviation Gallery. The sketch had fallen out of Leonard's jacket: he watched in horror as the museum's deputy director stooped to retrieve the crumpled page.

"Allow me," said the woman at the director's side. She was slight, fortyish, with frizzy red hair and enormous hoop earrings, wearing an Indianprint tunic over tight, sky blue trousers and leather clogs. She snatched up the drawing, stuffed it in her pocket, and continued her tour of the gallery. After the deputy director left, the woman walked to where Leonard stood beside his flight simulator, sweating in his polyester jacket as he supervised an overweight kid in a Chewbacca T-shirt. When the kid climbed down, the woman held up the crumpled sheet.

"Who did this?"

The other two aides—one was Emery—shook their heads.

"I did," said Leonard.

The woman crooked her finger. "Come with me."

"Am I fired?" asked Leonard as he followed her out of the gallery.

"Nope. I'm Maggie Blevin. We're shutting down those Link Trainers and making this into a new gallery. I'm in charge. I need someone to start cataloging stuff for me and maybe do some preliminary sketches. You want the job?"

"Yes," stammered Leonard. "I mean, sure."

"Great." She balled up the sketch and tossed it into a wastebasket. "Your talents were being wasted. That looks just like the director's butt."

"If he was a dog," said Leonard.

"He's a son of a bitch, and that's close enough," said Maggie. "Let's go see personnel."

Leonard's current job description read Museum Effects Specialist, Grade 9, Step 10. For the last two decades, he'd created figurines and models for the museum's exhibits. Not fighter planes or commercial aircraft—there was an entire division of modelers who handled that.

Leonard's work was more rarefied, as evidenced by the dozens of flying machines perched wherever there was space in the tiny room. Rocket ships, bat-winged aerodromes, biplanes and triplanes and saucers, many of them striped and polka dotted and glazed with, yes, nail polish in circus colors, so that they appeared to be made of ribbon candy.

His specialty was aircraft that had never actually flown; in many instances, aircraft that had never been intended to fly. Crypto-aviation, as some disgruntled curator dubbed it. He worked from plans and photographs, drawings and uncategorizable materials he'd found in the archives Maggie Blevin had been hired to organize. These were housed in a set of oak filing cabinets dating to the 1920s. Officially, the archive was known as the Pre-Langley Collection. But everyone in the museum, including Maggie Blevin, called it the Nut Files.

After Leonard's fateful promotion, Robbie and Emery would sometimes punch out for the day, go upstairs, and stroll to his corner of the library. You could do that then—wander around workrooms and storage areas, the library and archives, without having to check in or get a special pass or security clearance. Robbie just went along for the ride, but Emery was fascinated by the things Leonard found in the Nut Files. Grainy black-and-white photos of purported UFOs; typescripts of encounters with deceased Russian cosmonauts in the Nevada desert; an account of a Raelian wedding ceremony attended by a glowing crimson orb. There was also a large carton donated by the widow of a legendary rocket scientist, which turned out to be filled with 1950s foot-fetish pornography, and sixteen-millimeter film footage of several pioneers of flight doing something unseemly with a spotted pig.

"Whatever happened to that pig movie?" asked Robbie as he admired a biplane with violet-striped ailerons.

"It's been deaccessioned," said Leonard.

He cleared the swivel chair and motioned for Emery to sit, then perched on the edge of his desk. Robbie looked in vain for another chair, finally settled on the floor beside a wastebasket filled with empty nail polish bottles.

"So I have a plan," announced Leonard. He stared fixedly at Emery, as though they were alone in the room. "To help Maggie. Do you remember the *Bellerophon*?"

Emery frowned. "Vaguely. That old film loop of a plane crash?"

"*Presumed* crash. They never found any wreckage, everyone just assumes it crashed. But yes, that was the *Bellerophon*—it was the clip that played in our gallery. Maggie's gallery."

"Right—the movie that burned up!" broke in Robbie. "Yeah, I remember, the film got caught in a sprocket or something. Smoke detectors went off and they evacuated the whole museum. They got all on Maggie's case about it, they thought she'd installed it wrong."

"She didn't," Leonard said angrily. "One of the tech guys screwed up the installation—he told me a few years ago. He didn't vent it properly, the projector bulb overheated and the film caught on fire. He said he always felt bad she got canned."

"But they didn't fire her for that." Robbie gave Leonard a sideways look. "It was the UFO—"

Emery cut him off. "They were gunning for her," he said. "C'mon, Rob, everyone knew—all those old military guys running this place, they couldn't stand a woman getting in their way. Not if she wasn't air force or some shit. Took 'em a few years, that's all. Fucking assholes. I even got a letter-writing campaign going on the show. Didn't help."

"Nothing would have helped." Leonard sighed. "She was a visionary. She *is* a visionary," he added hastily. "Which is why I want to do this—"

He hopped from the desk, rooted around in a corner, and pulled out a large cardboard box.

"Move," he ordered.

Robbie scrambled to his feet. Leonard began to remove things from the carton and set them carefully on his desk. Emery got up to make more room, angling himself beside Robbie. They watched as Leonard arranged piles of paper, curling eight by tens, faded blueprints, and an old 35-millimeter film viewer, along with several large manila envelopes closed with red string. Finally he knelt beside the box and very gingerly reached inside.

"I think the Lindbergh baby's in there," whispered Emery.

Leonard stood, cradling something in his hands, turned and placed it in the middle of the desk.

"Holy shit." Emery whistled. "Leonard, you've outdone yourself."

Robbie crouched so he could view it at eye level: a model of some sort of flying machine, though it seemed impossible that anyone, even Leonard or Maggie Blevin, could ever have dreamed it might fly. It had a zeppelin-shaped body, with a sharp nose like that of a Lockheed Starfighter, slightly uptilted. Suspended beneath this was a basket filled with tiny gears and chains, and beneath that was a contraption with three wheels, like a velocipede, only the wheels were fitted with dozens of stiff flaps, each no bigger than a fingernail, and even tinier propellers.

And everywhere, there were wings, sprouting from every inch of the craft's body in an explosion of canvas and balsa and paper and gauze. Bird-shaped wings, bat-shaped wings; square wings like those of a box kite, elevators and hollow cones of wire; long tubes that, when Robbie peered inside them, were filled with baffles and flaps. Ailerons and struts ran between them to form a dizzying grid, held together with fine gold thread and monofilament and what looked like human hair. Every bit of it was painted in brilliant shades of violet and emerald, scarlet and fuchsia and gold, and here and there shining objects were set into the glossy surface: minute shards of mirror or colored glass; a beetle carapace; flecks of mica.

Above it all, springing from the fuselage like the cap of an immense toadstool, was a feathery parasol made of curved bamboo and multicolored silk.

It was like gazing at the Wright Flyer through a kaleidoscope.

"That's incredible!" Robbie exclaimed. "How'd you do that?"

"Now we just have to see if it flies," said Leonard.

Robbie straightened. "How the hell can that thing fly?"

"The original flew." Leonard leaned against the wall. "My theory is, if we can replicate the same conditions—the *exact same* conditions—it will work."

"But." Robbie glanced at Emery. "The original didn't fly. It crashed. I mean, presumably."

Emery nodded. "Plus there was a guy in it. McCartney —"

"McCauley," said Leonard.

"Right, McCauley. And you know, Leonard, no one's gonna fit in that, right?" Emery shot him an alarmed look. "You're not thinking of making a full-scale model, are you? Because that would be completely insane."

"No." Leonard fingered the skull plug in his earlobe. "I'm going to make another film—I'm going to replicate the original, and I'm going to do it so perfectly that Maggie won't even realize it's *not* the original. I've got it all worked out." He looked at Emery. "I can shoot it on digital, if you'll lend me a camera. That way I can edit it on my laptop. And then I'm going to bring it down to Fayetteville so she can see it."

Robbie and Emery glanced at each other.

"Well, it's not completely insane," said Robbie.

"But Maggie knows the original was destroyed," said Emery. "I mean, I was there, I remember—she saw it. We all saw it. She has cancer, right? Not Alzheimer's or dementia or, I dunno, amnesia."

"Why don't you just Photoshop something?" asked Robbie. "You could tell her it was an homage. That way—"

Leonard's glare grew icy. "It is not an homage. I am going to Cowana Island, just like McCauley did, and I am going to re-create the maiden flight of the *Bellerophon*. I am going to film it, I am going to edit it. And when it's completed, I'm going to tell Maggie that I found a dupe in the archives. Her heart broke when that footage burned up. I'm going to give it back to her."

Robbie stared at his shoe so Leonard wouldn't see his expression. After a moment he said, "When Anna was sick, I wanted to do that. Go back to this place by Mount Washington where we stayed before Zach was born. We had all these great photos of us canoeing there, it was so beautiful. But it was winter, and I said we should wait and go in the summer."

"I'm not waiting." Leonard sifted through the papers on his desk. "I have these—"

He opened a manila envelope and withdrew several glassine sleeves. He examined one, then handed it to Emery.

"This is what survived of the original footage, which in fact was *not* the original footage—the original was shot in 1901, on cellulose nitrate film. That's what Maggie and I found when we first started going through the Nut Files. Only of course nitrate stock is like a ticking time bomb. So the Photo Lab duped it onto safety film, which is what you're looking at."

Emery held the film to the light. Robbie stood beside him, squinting. Five frames, in shades of amber and tortoiseshell, with blurred images that might have been bushes or clouds or smoke damage, for all Robbie could see.

Emery asked, "How many frames do you have?"

"Total? Seventy-two."

Emery shook his head. "Not much, is it? What was it, fifteen seconds?"

"Seventeen seconds."

"Times twenty-four frames per second—so, out of about four hundred frames, that's all that's left."

"No. There was actually less than that, because it was silent film, which runs at more like eighteen frames per second, and they corrected the speed. So, about three hundred frames, which means we have about a quarter of the original stock." Leonard hesitated. He glanced up. "Lock that door, would you, Robbie?"

Robbie did, looked back to see Leonard crouched in the corner, moving aside his coat to reveal a metal strongbox. He prised the lid from the top.

The box was filled with water—Robbie *hoped* it was water. "Is that an aquarium?"

Leonard ignored him, tugged up his sleeves, then dipped both hands below the surface. Very, very carefully he removed another metal box. He set it on the floor, grabbed his coat, and meticulously dried the lid, then turned to Robbie.

"You know, maybe you should unlock the door. In case we need to get out fast."

"Jesus Christ, Leonard, what is it?" exclaimed Emery. "Snakes?"

"Nope." Leonard plucked something from the box, and Emery flinched as a serpentine ribbon unfurled in the air. "It's what's left of the original footage—the 1901 film."

"That's nitrate?" Emery stared at him, incredulous. "You *are* insane! How the hell'd you get it?"

"I clipped it before they destroyed the stock. I think it's okay—I take it out every day, so the gases don't build up. And it doesn't seem to interact with the nail polish fumes. It's the part where you can actually see McCauley, where you get the best view of the plane. See?"

He dangled it in front of Emery, who backed toward the door. "Put it away, put it away!"

"Can I see?" asked Robbie.

Leonard gave him a measuring look, then nodded. "Hold it by this edge—"

It took a few seconds for Robbie's eyes to focus properly. "You're right," he said. "You can see him—you can see someone, anyway. And you can definitely tell it's an airplane."

He handed it back to Leonard, who fastidiously replaced it, first in its canister and then the water-filled safe.

"They could really pop you for that." Emery whistled in disbelief. "If that stuff blew? This whole place could go up in flames."

"You say that like it's a bad thing." Leonard draped his coat over the strongbox, then started to laugh. "Anyway, I'm done with it. I went into the photo lab one night and duped it myself. So I've got that copy at home. And this one—"

He inclined his head at the corner. "I'm going to take the nitrate home and give it a Viking funeral in the backyard. You can come if you want."

"Tonight?" asked Robbie.

"No. I've got to work late tonight, catch up on some stuff before I leave town."

Emery leaned against the door. "Where you going?"

"South Carolina. I told you. I'm going to Cowana Island, and . . ." Robbie caught a whiff of acetone as Leonard picked up the *Bellerophon*. "I am going to make this thing fly."

"HE REALLY IS NUTS. I mean, when was the last time he even saw Maggie?" Robbie asked as Emery drove him back to the Mall. "I still don't know what really happened, except for the UFO stuff."

"She found out he was screwing around with someone else. It was a bad scene. She tried to get him fired; he went to Boynton and told him Maggie was diverting all this time and money to studying UFOs. Which unfortunately was true. They did an audit, she had some kind of nervous breakdown even before they could fire her."

"What a prick."

Emery sighed. "It was horrible. Leonard doesn't talk about it. I don't think he ever got over it. Over her."

"Yeah, but . . ." Robbie shook his head. "She must be, what, twenty years older than us? They never would have stayed together. If he feels so bad, he should just go see her. This other stuff is insane."

"I think maybe those fumes did something to him. Nitrocellulose, it's in nail polish, too. It might have done something to his brain."

"Is that possible?"

"It's a theory," said Emery broodingly.

Robbie's house was in a scruffy subdivision on the outskirts of Rockville. The place was small, a bungalow with masonite siding, a cracked cinder-block foundation, and the remains of a garden that Anna had planted. A green GMC pickup with an expired registration was parked in the drive. Robbie peered into the cab. It was filled with empty Bud Light bottles.

Inside, Zach was hunched at a desk beside his friend Tyler, owner of the pickup. The two of them stared intently at a computer screen.

"What's up?" said Zach without looking away.

"Not much," said Robbie. "Eye contact."

Zach glanced up. He was slight, with Anna's thick blond curls reduced to a buzz cut that Robbie hated. Tyler was tall and gangly, with long black hair and wire-rimmed sunglasses. Both favored tie-dyed T-shirts and madras shorts that made them look as though they were perpetually on vacation.

Robbie went into the kitchen and got a beer. "You guys eat?"

"We got something on the way home."

Robbie drank his beer and watched them. The house had a smell that Emery once described as Failed Bachelor. Unwashed clothes, spilled beer, marijuana smoke. Robbie hadn't smoked in years, but Zach and Tyler had taken up the slack. Robbie used to yell at them but eventually gave up. If his own depressing example wasn't enough to straighten them out, what was?

After a minute, Zach looked up again. "Nice shirt, Dad."

"Thanks, son." Robbie sank into a beanbag chair. "Me and Emery dropped by the museum and saw Leonard."

"Leonard!" Tyler burst out laughing. "Leonard is so fucking sweet! He's, like, the craziest guy ever."

"All Dad's friends are crazy," said Zach.

"Yeah, but Emery, he's cool. Whereas that guy Leonard is just wack."

Robbie nodded somberly and finished his beer. "Leonard is indeed wack. He's making a movie."

"A real movie?" asked Zach.

"More like a home movie. Or, I dunno—he wants to reproduce another movie, one that was already made, do it all the same again. Shot by shot."

Tyler nodded. "Like *The Ring* and *Ringu*. What's the movie?"

"Seventeen seconds of a 1901 plane crash. The original footage was destroyed, so he's going to restage the whole thing."

"A plane crash?" Zach glanced at Tyler. "Can we watch?"

"Not a real crash—he's doing it with a model. I mean, I think he is."

"Did they even have planes then?" said Tyler.

"He should put it on YouTube," said Zach, and turned back to the computer.

"Okay, get out of there." Robbie rubbed his head wearily. "I need to go online."

The boys argued but gave up quickly. Tyler left. Zach grabbed his cell phone and slouched upstairs to his room. Robbie got another beer, sat at the computer, and logged out of whatever they'd been playing, then typed in MCCAULEY BELLEROPHON.

Only a dozen results popped up. He scanned them, then clicked the Wikipedia entry for Ernesto McCauley.

McCauley, Ernesto (18??–1901) American inventor whose eccentric aircraft, the Bellerophon, allegedly flew for seventeen seconds before it crashed during a 1901 test flight on Cowana Island, South Carolina, killing McCauley. In the 1980s, claims that this flight was successful and predated that of the Wright brothers by two years were made by a Smithsonian expert, based upon archival film footage. The claims have since been disproved and the film record unfortunately lost in a fire. Curiously, no other record of either McCauley or his aircraft has ever been found.

Robbie took a long pull at his beer, then typed in MARGARET BLEVIN.

*Blevin, Margaret (1938–) Influential cultural historian whose
groundbreaking work on early flight earned her the nickname "the
Magnificent Blevin." During her tenure at the Smithsonian's Museum
of American Aeronautics and Aerospace, Blevin redesigned the General
Aviation Gallery to feature lesser-known pioneers of flight, including
Charles Dellschau and Ernesto McCauley, as well as . . .*

"'The Magnificent Blevin'?" Robbie snorted. He grabbed another beer
and continued reading.

*But Blevin's most lasting impact upon the history of aviation was
her 1986 best-seller* Wings for Humanity!, *in which she presents a
dramatic and visionary account of the mystical aspects of flight, from
Icarus to the Wright brothers and beyond. Its central premise is that
millennia ago a benevolent race seeded the earth, leaving isolated
locations with the ability to engender human-powered flight. "We
dream of flight because flight is our birthright," wrote Blevin, and since
its publication* Wings for Humanity! *has never gone out of print.*

"Leonard wrote this frigging thing!"
"What?" Zach came downstairs, yawning.
"This Wikipedia entry!" Robbie jabbed at the screen. "That book was
never a best-seller—she sneaked it into the museum gift shop and no one
bought it. The only reason it's still in print is that she published it herself."
Zach read the entry over his father's shoulder. "It sounds cool."
Robbie shook his head adamantly. "She was completely nuts. Obsessed
with all this New Age crap, aliens and crop circles. She thought that planes
could only fly from certain places, and that's why all the early flights
crashed. Not because there was something wrong with the aircraft design,
but because they were taking off from the wrong spot."
"Then how come there's airports everywhere?"
"She never worked out that part."
"'We must embrace our galactic heritage, the spiritual dimension of
human flight, lest we forever chain ourselves to earth,'" Zach read from
the screen. "Was she in that plane crash?"

"No, she's still alive. That was just something she had a wild hair about. She thought the guy who invented that plane flew it a few years before the Wright brothers made their flight, but she could never prove it."

"But it says there was a movie," said Zach. "So someone saw it happen."

"This is Wikipedia." Robbie stared at the screen in disgust. "You can say any fucking thing you want and people will believe it. Leonard wrote that entry, guarantee you. Probably she faked that whole film loop. That's what Leonard's planning to do now—replicate the footage then pass it off to Maggie as the real thing."

Zach collapsed into the beanbag chair. "Why?"

"Because he's crazy, too. He and Maggie had a thing together."

Zach grimaced. "Ugh."

"What, you think we were born old? We were your age, practically. And Maggie was about twenty years older—"

"A cougar!" Zach burst out laughing. "Why didn't she go for you?"

"Ha ha ha." Robbie pushed his empty beer bottle against the wall. "Women liked Leonard. Go figure. Even your mom went out with him for a while. Before she and I got involved, I mean."

Zach's glassy eyes threatened to roll back in his head. "Stop."

"We thought it was pretty strange," admitted Robbie. "But Maggie was good-looking for an old hippie." He glanced at the Wikipedia entry and did the math. "I guess she's in her seventies now. Leonard's in touch with her. She has cancer. Breast cancer."

"I heard you," said Zach. He rolled out of the beanbag chair, flipped open his phone, and began texting. "I'm going to bed."

Robbie sat and stared at the computer screen. After a while he shut it down. He shuffled into the kitchen and opened the cabinet where he kept a quart of Jim Beam, hidden behind bottles of vinegar and vegetable oil. He rinsed out the glass he'd used the night before, poured a jolt and downed it, then carried the bourbon with him to bed.

THE NEXT DAY AFTER work, he was on his second drink at the bar when Emery showed up.

"Hey." Robbie gestured at the stool beside him. "Have a seat."

"You okay to drive?"

"Sure." Robbie scowled. "What, you keeping an eye on me?"

"No. But I want you to see something. At my house. Leonard's coming over, we're going to meet there at six thirty. I tried calling you but your phone's off."

"Oh. Right. Sorry." Robbie signaled the bartender for his tab. "Yeah, sure. What, is he gonna give us manicures?"

"Nope. I have an idea. I'll tell you when I get there; I'm going to Royal Delhi first to get some takeout. See you—"

Emery lived in a big town house condo that smelled of Moderately Successful Bachelor. The walls held framed photos of Captain Marvo and Mungbean alongside a life-size painting of Leslie Nielsen as Commander J. J. Adams.

But there was also a climate-controlled basement filled with Captain Marvo merchandise and packing material, with another large room stacked with electronics equipment—sound system, video monitors and decks, shelves and files devoted to old Captain Marvo episodes, and dupes of the grade Z movies featured on the show.

This was where Robbie found Leonard, bent over a refurbished Steenbeck editing table.

"Robbie." Leonard waved, then returned to threading film onto a spindle. "Emery back with dinner?"

"Uh-uh." Robbie pulled a chair alongside him. "What are you doing?"

"Loading up that nitrate I showed you yesterday."

"It's not going to explode, is it?"

"No, Robbie, it's not going to explode." Leonard's mouth tightened. "Did Emery talk to you yet?"

"He just said something about a plan. So what's up?"

"I'll let him tell you."

Robbie flushed angrily, but before he could retort there was a knock behind them.

"Chow time, campers." Emery held up two steaming paper bags. "Can you leave that for a few minutes, Leonard?"

They ate on the couch in the next room. Emery talked about a pitch he'd made to revive Captain Marvo in cell-phone format. "It'd be freaking perfect, if I could figure out a way to make any money from it."

Leonard said nothing. Robbie noted that the cuffs of his white tunic were stained with flecks of orange pigment, as were his fingernails. He looked tired, his face lined and his eyes sunken.

"You getting enough sleep?" Emery asked.

Leonard smiled wanly. "Enough."

Finally the food was gone, and the beer. Emery clapped his hands on his knees, pushed aside the empty plates, then leaned forward.

"Okay. So here's the plan. I rented a house on Cowana for a week, starting this Saturday. I mapped it online and it's about ten hours. If we leave right after you guys get off work on Friday and drive all night, we'll get there early Saturday morning. Leonard, you said you've got everything pretty much assembled, so all you need to do is pack it up. I've got everything else here. Be a tight fit in the Prius, though, so we'll have to take two cars. We'll bring everything we need with us, we'll have a week to shoot and edit or whatever, then on the way back we swing through Fayetteville and show the finished product to Maggie. What do you think?"

"That's not a lot of time," said Leonard. "But we could do it."

Emery turned to Robbie. "Is you car roadworthy? It's about twelve hundred miles round-trip."

Robbie stared at him. "What the hell are you talking about?"

"The *Bellerophon*. Leonard's got storyboards and all kinds of drawings and still frames, enough to work from. The Realtor's in Charleston; she said there wouldn't be many people this early in the season. Plus there was a hurricane a couple years ago; I gather the island got hammered and no one's had money to rebuild. So we'll have it all to ourselves, pretty much."

"Are you high?" Robbie laughed. "I can't just take off. I have a job."

"You get vacation time, right? You can take a week. It'll be great, man. The Realtor says it's already in the eighties down there. Warm water, a beach—what more you want?"

"Uh, maybe a beach with people besides you and Leonard?" Robbie searched in vain for another beer. "I couldn't go anyway—next week's Zach's spring break."

"Yeah?" Emery shook his head. "So, you're going to be at the store all day, and he'll be home getting stoned. Bring him. We'll put him to work."

Leonard frowned, but Robbie looked thoughtful. "Yeah, you're right. I hadn't thought of that. I can't really leave him alone. I guess I'll think about it."

"Don't think, just do it. It's Wednesday, tell 'em you're taking off next week. They gonna fire you?"

"Maybe."

"I'm not babysitting some—" Leonard started.

Emery cut him off. "You got that nitrate loaded? Let's see it."

They filed into the workroom. Leonard sat at the Steenbeck. The others watched as he adjusted the film on its sprockets. He turned to Robbie, then indicated the black projection box in the center of the deck.

"Emery knows all this, so I'm just telling you. That's a quartz halogen lamp. I haven't turned it on yet, because if the frame was just sitting there it might incinerate the film, and us. But there's only about four seconds of footage, so we're going to take our chances and watch it, once. Maybe you remember it from the gallery?"

Robbie nodded. "Yeah, I saw it a bunch of times. Not as much as the Head, but enough."

"Good. Hit that light, would you, Emery? Everyone ready? Blink and you'll miss it."

Robbie craned his neck, staring at a blank white screen. There was a whir, the stutter of film running through a projector.

At the bottom of the frame the horizon lurched, bright flickers that might be an expanse of water. Then a blurred image, faded sepia and amber, etched with blotches and something resembling a beetle leg: the absurd contraption Robbie recognized as the original *Bellerophon*. Only it was moving—it was flying—its countless gears and propellers and wings spinning and whirring and flapping all at once, so it seemed the entire thing would vibrate into a thousand pieces. Beneath the fuselage, a dark figure perched precariously atop the velocipede, legs like black scissors slicing at the air. From the left corner of the frame leaped a flare of light, like a shooting star or burning firecracker tossed at the pedaling figure. The pilot listed to one side, and—

Nothing. The film ended as abruptly as it had begun. Leonard quickly reached to turn off the lamp, and immediately removed the film from the take-up drive.

Robbie felt his neck prickle—he'd forgotten how weird, uncanny even, the footage was.

"Jesus, that's some bizarre shit," said Emery.

"It doesn't even look real." Robbie watched as Leonard coiled the film and slid it in a canister. "I mean, the guy, he looks fake."

Emery nodded. "Yeah, I know. It looks like one of those old silents, *The*

Lost World or something. But it's not. I used to watch it back when it ran a hundred times a day in our gallery, the way you used to watch the Head. And it's definitely real. At least the pilot, McCauley—that's a real guy. I got a big magnifier once and just stood there and watched it over and over again. He was breathing, I could see it. And the plane, it's real too, far as I could tell. The thing I can't figure is, who the hell shot that footage? And what was the angle?"

Robbie stared at the empty screen, then shut his eyes. He tried to recall the rest of the film from when it played in the General Aviation gallery: the swift, jerky trajectory of that eerie little vehicle with its bizarre pilot, a man in a black suit and bowler hat; then the flash from the corner of the screen, and the man toppling from his perch into the white and empty air. The last thing you saw was a tiny hand at the bottom of the frame, then some blank leader, followed by the words "The Maiden Flight of McCauley's *Bellerophon* (1901)." And the whole thing began again.

"It was like someone was in the air next to him," said Robbie. "Unless he got only six feet off the ground. I always assumed it was faked."

"It wasn't faked," said Leonard. "The cameraman was on the beach filming. It was a windy day, they were hoping that would help give the plane some lift but there must have been a sudden gust. When the *Bellerophon* went into the ocean, the cameraman dove in to save McCauley. They both drowned. They never found the bodies, or the wreckage. Only the camera with the film."

"Who found it?" asked Robbie.

"We don't know." Leonard sighed, his shoulders slumping. "We don't know anything. Not the name of the cameraman, nothing. When Maggie and I ran the original footage, the leader said 'Maiden Flight of McCauley's *Bellerophon*.' The can had the date and 'Cowana Island' written on it. So Maggie and I went down there to research it. A weird place. Hardly any people, and this was in the summer. There's a tiny historical society on the island, but we couldn't find anything about McCauley or the aircraft. No newspaper accounts, no gravestones. The only thing we did find was in a diary kept by the guy who delivered the mail back then. On May 13, 1901, he wrote that it was a very windy day and two men had drowned while attempting to launch a flying machine on the beach. Someone must have found the camera afterward. Somebody processed the film, and somehow it found its way to the museum."

Robbie followed Leonard into the next room. "What was that weird flash of light?"

"I don't know." Leonard stared out a glass door into the parking lot. "But it's not overexposure or lens flare or anything like that. It's something the cameraman actually filmed. Water, maybe—if it was a windy day, a big wave might have come up onto the beach or something."

"I always thought it was fire. Like a rocket or some kind of flare."

Leonard nodded. "That's what Maggie thought, too. The mailman— mostly all he wrote about was the weather. Which if you were relying on a horse-drawn cart, makes sense. About two weeks before he mentioned the flying machine, he described something that sounds like a major meteor shower."

"And Maggie thought it was hit by a meteor?"

"No." Leonard sighed. "She thought it was something else. The weird thing is, a few years ago I checked online, and it turns out there was an unusual amount of meteor activity in 1901."

Robbie raised an eyebrow. "Meaning?"

Leonard said nothing. Finally he opened the door and walked outside. The others trailed after him.

They reached the edge of the parking lot, where cracked tarmac gave way to stony ground. Leonard glanced back, then stooped. He brushed away a few stray leaves and tufts of dead grass, set the film canister down and unscrewed the metal lid. He picked up one end of the coil of film, gently tugging until it trailed a few inches across the ground. Then he withdrew a lighter, flicked it, and held the flame to the tail of film.

"What the—" began Robbie.

There was a dull *whoosh*, like the sound of a gas burner igniting. A plume of crimson and gold leaped from the canister, writhing in the air within a ball of black smoke. Leonard staggered to his feet, covering his head as he backed away.

"Leonard!" Emery grabbed him roughly, then turned and raced to the house.

Before Robbie could move, a strong chemical stink surrounded him. The flames shrank to a shining thread that lashed at the smoke then faded into flecks of ash. Robbie ducked his head, coughing. He grasped Leonard's arm and tried to drag him away, glanced up to see Emery running toward them with a fire extinguisher.

"Sorry," gasped Leonard. He made a slashing motion through the smoke, which dispersed. The flames were gone. Leonard's face was black with ash. Robbie touched his own cheek gingerly, looked at his fingers, and saw they were coated with something dark and oily.

Emery halted, panting, and stared at the twisted remains of the film can. On the ground beside it, a glowing thread wormed toward a dead leaf, then expired in a gray wisp. Emery raised the fire extinguisher threateningly, set it down, and stomped on the canister.

"Good thing you didn't do that in the museum," said Robbie. He let go of Leonard's arm.

"Don't think it didn't cross my mind," said Leonard, and walked back inside.

THEY LEFT FRIDAY EVENING. Robbie got the week off, after giving his dubious boss a long story about a dying relative down South. Zach shouted and broke a lamp when informed he would be accompanying his father on a trip during his spring vacation.

"With Emery and *Leonard*? Are you fucking *insane*?"

Robbie was too exhausted to fight: he quickly offered to let Tyler come with them. Tyler, surprisingly, agreed, and even showed up on Friday afternoon to help load the car. Robbie made a pointed effort not to inspect the various backpacks and duffel bags the boys threw into the trunk of the battered Taurus. Alcohol, drugs, firearms: he no longer cared.

Instead he focused on the online weather report for Cowana Island. Eighty degrees and sunshine, photographs of blue water, white sand, a skein of pelicans skimming above the waves. Ten hours, that wasn't so bad. In another weak moment, he told Zach he could drive part of the way, so Robbie could sleep.

"What about me?" asked Tyler. "Can I drive?"

"Only if I never wake up," said Robbie.

Around six Emery pulled into the driveway, honking. The boys were already slumped in Robbie's Taurus, Zach in front with earbuds dangling around his face and a knit cap pulled down over his eyes, Tyler in the back, staring blankly, as though they were already on I-95.

"You ready?" Emery rolled down his window. He wore a blue flannel shirt and a gimme cap that read STARFLEET ACADEMY. In the hybrid's passenger seat, Leonard perused a road atlas. He looked up and shot Robbie a smile.

"Hey, a road trip."

"Yeah." Robbie smiled back and patted the hybrid's roof. "See you."

It took almost two hours just to get beyond the gravitational pull of the Washington Beltway. Farms and forest had long ago disappeared beneath an endless grid of malls and housing developments, many of them vacant. Every time Robbie turned up the radio for a song he liked, the boys complained that they could hear it through their earphones.

Only as the sky darkened and Virginia gave way to North Carolina did the world take on a faint fairy glow, distant green and yellow lights reflecting the first stars and a shining cusp of moon. Sprawl gave way to pine forest. The boys had been asleep for hours, in that amazing, self-willed hibernation they summoned whenever in the presence of adults for more than fifteen minutes. Robbie put the radio on, low, searched until he caught the echo of a melody he knew, and then another. He thought of driving with Anna beside him, a restive Zach behind them in his car seat; the aimless trips they'd make until the toddler fell asleep and they could talk or, once, park in a vacant lot and make out.

How long had it been since he'd remembered that? Years, maybe. He fought against thinking of Anna; sometimes it felt as though he fought Anna herself, her hands pummeling him as he poured another drink or staggered up to bed.

Now, though, the darkness soothed him the way those long-ago drives had lulled Zach to sleep. He felt an ache lift from his breast, as though a splinter had been dislodged; blinked and in the rearview mirror glimpsed Anna's face, slightly turned from him as she gazed out at the passing sky.

He started, realized he'd begun to nod off. On the dashboard his fuel indicator glowed red. He called Emery, and at the next exit pulled off 95, the Prius behind him.

After a few minutes they found a gas station set back from the road in a pine grove, with an old-fashioned pump out front and yellow light streaming through a screen door. The boys blinked awake.

"Where are we?" asked Zach.

"No idea." Robbie got out of the car. "North Carolina."

It was like stepping into a twilight garden, or some hidden biosphere at the zoo. Warmth flowed around him, violet and rustling green, scented overpoweringly of honeysuckle and wet stone. He could hear rushing water, the stirring of wind in the leaves, and countless small things—frogs peeping, insects he couldn't identify. A nightbird that made a burbling song. In the shadows behind the building, fireflies floated between kudzu-choked trees, like tiny glowing fish.

For an instant he felt himself suspended in that enveloping darkness. The warm air moved through him, sweetly fragrant, pulsing with life he could neither see nor touch. He tasted something honeyed and faintly astringent in the back of his throat, and drew his breath in sharply.

"What?" demanded Zach.

"Nothing." Robbie shook his head and turned to the pump. "Just—isn't this great?"

He filled the tank. Zach and Tyler went in search of food, and Emery strolled over.

"How you holding up?"

"I'm good. Probably let Zach drive for a while so I can catch some z's."

He moved the car, then went inside to pay. He found Leonard buying a pack of cigarettes as the boys headed out, laden with energy drinks and bags of chips. Robbie slid his credit card across the counter to a woman wearing a tank top that set off a tattoo that looked like the face of Marilyn Manson, or maybe it was Jesus.

"Do you have a restroom?"

The woman handed him a key. "Round back."

"Bathroom's here," Robbie yelled at the boys. "We're not stopping again."

They trailed him into a dank room with gray walls. A fluorescent light buzzed overhead. After Tyler left, Robbie and Zach stood side by side at the sink, trying to coax water from a rusted spigot to wash their hands.

"The hell with it," said Robbie. "Let's hit the road. You want to drive?"

"Dad." Zach pointed at the ceiling. "Dad, look."

Robbie glanced up. A screen bulged from a small window above the sink. Something had blown against the wire mesh, a leaf or scrap of paper.

But then the leaf moved, and he saw that it wasn't a leaf at all but a butterfly.

No, not a butterfly—a moth. The biggest he'd ever seen, bigger than his hand. Its fan-shaped upper wings opened, revealing vivid golden eye-spots; its trailing lower wings formed two perfect arabesques, all a milky, luminous green.

"A luna moth," breathed Robbie. "I've never seen one."

Zach clambered onto the sink. "It wants to get out—"

"Hang on." Robbie boosted him, bracing himself so the boy's weight wouldn't yank the sink from the wall. "Be careful! Don't hurt it—"

The moth remained where it was. Robbie grunted—Zach weighed as much as he did—felt his legs trembling as the boy prised the screen from the wall then struggled to pull it free.

"It's stuck," he said. "I can't get it—"

The moth fluttered weakly. One wing tip looked ragged, as though it had been singed.

"Tear it!" Robbie cried. "Just tear the screen."

Zach wedged his fingers beneath a corner of the window frame and yanked, hard enough that he fell. Robbie caught him as the screen tore away to dangle above the sink. The luna moth crawled onto the sill.

"Go!" Zach banged on the wall. "Go on, fly!"

Like a kite catching the wind, the moth lifted. Its trailing lower wings quivered and the eyespots seemed to blink, a pallid face gazing at them from the darkness. Then it was gone.

"That was cool." For an instant, Zach's arm draped across his father's shoulder, so fleetingly Robbie might have imagined it. "I'm going to the car."

When the boy was gone, Robbie tried to push the screen back into place. He returned the key and went to join Leonard, smoking a cigarette at the edge of the woods. Behind them a car horn blared.

"Come on!" shouted Zach. "I'm leaving!"

"Happy trails," said Leonard.

Robbie slept fitfully in back as Zach drove, the two boys arguing about music and a girl named Eileen. After an hour he took over again.

The night ground on. The boys fell back asleep. Robbie drank one of their Red Bulls and thought of the glimmering wonder that had been the luna moth. A thin rind of emerald appeared on the horizon, deepening to copper then gold as it overtook the sky. He began to see palmettos among the loblolly pines and pin oaks, and spiky plants he didn't recognize. When he opened the window, the air smelled of roses, and the sea.

"Hey." He poked Zach, breathing heavily in the seat beside him. "Hey, we're almost there."

He glanced at the directions, looked up to see the hybrid passing him and Emery gesturing at a sandy track that veered to the left. It was bounded by barbed-wire fences and clumps of cactus thick with blossoms the color of lemon cream. The pines surrendered to palmettos and prehistoric-looking trees with gnarled roots that thrust up from pools where egrets and herons stabbed at frogs.

"Look," said Robbie.

Ahead of them the road narrowed to a path barely wide enough for a single vehicle, built up with shells and chunks of concrete. On one side stretched a blur of cypress and long-legged birds; on the other, an aquamarine estuary that gave way to the sea and rolling white dunes.

Robbie slowed the car to a crawl, humping across mounds of shells and doing his best to avoid sinkholes. After a quarter mile, the makeshift causeway ended. An old metal gate lay in a twisted heap on the ground, covered by creeping vines. Above it a weathered sign clung to a cypress.

WELCOME TO COWANA ISLAND
NO DUNE BUGGIES

They drove past the ruins of a mobile home. Emery's car was out of sight. Robbie looked at his cell phone and saw there was no signal. In the back, Tyler stirred.

"Hey, Rob, where are we?"

"We're here. Wherever here is. The island."

"Sweet." Tyler leaned over the seat to jostle Zach awake. "Hey, get up. "

Robbie peered through the overgrown greenery, looking for something resembling a beach house. He tried to remember which hurricane had pounded this part of the coast, and how long ago. Two years? Five?

The place looked as though it had been abandoned for decades. Fallen palmettos were everywhere, their leaves stiff and reddish-brown, like rusted blades. Some remained upright, their crowns lopped off. Acid-green lizards sunned themselves in driveways where ferns poked through the blacktop. The remains of carports and decks dangled above piles of timber and mold-blackened Sheetrock. Now and then an intact house appeared within the jungle of flowering vines.

But no people, no cars except for an SUV crushed beneath a toppled utility pole. The only store was a modest grocery with a brick facade and shattered windows, through which the ghostly outlines of aisles and displays could still be glimpsed.

"It's like *28 Days*," said Zach, and shot a baleful look at his father.

Robbie shrugged. "Talk to the man from the Starfleet Academy."

He pulled down a rutted drive to where the hybrid sat beneath a thriving palmetto. Driftwood edged a path that led to an old wood-frame house raised on stiltlike pilings. Stands of blooming cactus surrounded it, and trees choked with honeysuckle. The patchy lawn was covered with hundreds of conch shells arranged in concentric circles and spirals. On the deck a tattered red whirligig spun in the breeze, and rope hammocks hung like flaccid cocoons.

"I'm sleeping there," said Tyler.

Leonard gazed at the house with an unreadable expression. Emery had already sprinted up the uneven steps to what Robbie assumed was the front door. When he reached the top, he bent to pick up a square of coconut matting, retrieved something from beneath it, then straightened, grinning.

"Come on!" he shouted, turning to unlock the door; and the others raced to join him.

THE HOUSE HAD LINOLEUM floors, sifted with a fine layer of sand, and mismatched furniture—rattan chairs, couches covered with faded bark-cloth cushions, a canvas seat that hung from the ceiling by a chain and groaned alarmingly whenever the boys sat in it. The sea breeze stirred dusty white curtains at the windows. Anoles skittered across the floor, and Tyler fled shouting from the outdoor shower, where he'd seen a black widow spider. The electricity worked, but there was no air-conditioning and no television, no Internet.

"This is what you get for three hundred bucks in the off season," said Emery when Tyler complained.

"I don't get it." Robbie stood on the deck, staring across the empty road to where the dunes stretched, tufted with thorny greenery. "Even if there was a hurricane—this is practically oceanfront, all of it. Where is everybody?"

"Who can afford to build anything?" said Leonard. "Come on, I want to get my stuff inside before it heats up."

Leonard commandeered the master bedroom. He installed his laptop, Emery's camera equipment, piles of storyboards, the box that contained the miniature *Bellerophon*. This formidable array took up every inch of floor space, as well as the surface of a Ping-Pong table.

"Why is there a Ping-Pong table in the bedroom?" asked Robbie as he set down a tripod.

Emery shrugged. "You might ask, why is there not a Ping-Pong table in all bedrooms?"

"We're going to the beach," announced Zach.

Robbie kicked off his shoes and followed them, across the deserted road and down a path that wound through a miniature wilderness of cactus and bristly vines. He felt light-headed from lack of sleep, and also from the beer he'd snagged from one of the cases Emery had brought. The sand was already hot; twice he had to stop and pluck sharp spurs from his bare feet. A horned toad darted across the path, and a skink with a blue tongue. His son's voice came to him, laughing, and the sound of waves on the shore.

Atop the last dune small yellow roses grew in a thick carpet, their soapy fragrance mingling with the salt breeze. Robbie bent to pluck a handful of petals and tossed them into the air.

"It's not a bad place to fly, is it?"

He turned and saw Emery, shirtless. He handed Robbie a bottle of Tecate with a slice of lime jammed in its neck, raised his own beer and took a sip.

"It's beautiful." Robbie squeezed the lime into his beer, then drank. "But that model. It won't fly."

"I know." Emery stared at where Zach and Tyler leaped in the shallow water, sending up rainbow spray as they splashed each other. "But it's a good excuse for a vacation, isn't it?"

"It is," replied Robbie, and slid down the dune to join the boys.

OVER THE NEXT FEW days, they fell into an odd, almost sleepless rhythm, staying up till two or three A.M., drinking and talking. The adults pretended not to notice when the boys slipped a Tecate from the fridge, and ignored the incense-scented smoke that drifted from the deck after they stumbled off to bed. Everyone woke shortly after dawn, even the boys. Blinding sunlight slanted through the worn curtains. On the deck where Zack and Tyler huddled inside their hammocks, a tree frog made a sound like rusty hinges. No one slept enough, everyone drank too much.

For once it didn't matter. Robbie's hangovers dissolved as he waded into water as warm as blood, then floated on his back and watched pelicans skim above him. Afterward he'd carry equipment from the house to the dunes, where Emery had created a shelter from old canvas deck chairs and bedsheets. The boys helped him, the three of them lugging tripods and digital cameras, the box that contained Leonard's model of the *Bellerophon*, a cooler filled with beer and Red Bull.

That left Emery in charge of household duties. He'd found an ancient red wagon half buried in the dunes, and used this to transport bags of tortilla chips and a cooler filled with Tecate and limes. There was no store on the island save the abandoned wreck they'd passed when they first arrived. No gas station, and the historical society building appeared to be long gone.

But while driving around, Emery discovered a roadside stand that sold homemade salsa in mason jars and sage-green eggs in recycled cardboard cartons. The drive beside it was blocked with a barbed-wire fence and a sign that said BEWARE OF TWO-HEADED DOG.

"You ever see it?" asked Tyler.

"Nope. I never saw anyone except an alligator." Emery opened a beer. "And it was big enough to eat a two-headed dog."

By Thursday morning, they'd carted everything from one end of the island to the other, waiting with increasing impatience as Leonard climbed up and down dunes and stared broodingly at the blue horizon.

"How will you know which is the right one?" asked Robbie.

Leonard shook his head. "I don't know. Maggie said she thought it would be around here—"

He swept his arm out, encompassing a high ridge of sand that crested above the beach like a frozen wave. Below, Tyler and Zach argued over whose turn it was to haul everything uphill again. Robbie shoved his sunglasses against his nose.

"This beach has probably been washed away a hundred times since McCauley was here. Maybe we should just choose a place at random. Pick the highest dune or something."

"Yeah, I know." Leonard sighed. "This is probably our best choice, here."

He stood and for a long time gazed at the sky. Finally he turned and walked down to join the boys.

"We'll do it here," he said brusquely, and headed back to the house.

Late that afternoon they made a bonfire on the beach. The day had ended gray and much cooler than it had been, the sun swallowed in a haze of bruise-tinged cloud. Robbie waded into the shallow water, feeling with his toes for conch shells. Beside the fire, Zach came across a shark's tooth the size of a guitar pick.

"That's probably a million years old," said Tyler enviously.

"Almost as old as Dad," said Zach.

Robbie flopped down beside Leonard. "It's so weird," he said, shaking sand from a conch. "There's a whole string of these islands, but I haven't seen a boat the entire time we've been here."

"Are you complaining?" said Leonard.

"No. Just, don't you think it's weird?"

"Maybe." Leonard tossed his cigarette into the fire.

"I want to stay." Zach rolled onto his back and watched as sparks flew among the first stars. "Dad? Why can't we just stay here?"

Robbie took a long pull from his beer. "I have to get back to work. And you guys have school."

"Fuck school," said Zach and Tyler.

"Listen." The boys fell silent as Leonard glared at them. "Tomorrow morning I want to set everything up. We'll shoot before the wind picks up too much. I'll have the rest of the day to edit. Then we pack and head to Fayetteville on Saturday. We'll find some cheap place to stay, and drive home on Sunday."

The boys groaned. Emery sighed. "Back to the salt mines. I gotta call that guy about the show."

"I want to have a few hours with Maggie." Leonard pulled at the silver skull in his ear. "I told the nurse I'd be there Saturday before noon."

"We'll have to leave pretty early," said Emery.

For a few minutes nobody spoke. Wind rattled brush in the dunes behind them. The bonfire leaped then subsided, and Zach fed it a knot of driftwood. An unseen bird gave a piping cry that was joined by another, then another, until their plaintive voices momentarily drowned out the soft rush of waves.

Robbie gazed into the darkening water. In his hand, the conch shell felt warm and as silken as skin.

"Look, Dad," said Zach. "Bats."

Robbie leaned back to see black shapes dodging sparks above their heads.

"Nice," he said, his voice thick from drink.

"Well." Leonard stood and lit another cigarette. "I'm going to bed."

"Me, too," said Zach.

Robbie watched with mild surprise as the boys clambered to their feet, yawning. Emery removed a beer from the cooler, handed it to Robbie.

"Keep an eye on the fire, compadre," he said, and followed the others.

Robbie turned to study the dying blaze. Ghostly runnels of green and blue ran along the driftwood branch. Salt, Leonard had explained to the boys, though Robbie wondered if that was true. How did Leonard know all this stuff? He frowned, picked up a handful of sand and tossed it at the feeble blaze, which promptly sank into sullen embers.

Robbie swore under his breath. He finished his beer, stood, and walked unsteadily toward the water. The clouds obscured the moon, though there was a faint umber glow reflected in the distant waves. He stared at the horizon, searching in vain for some sign of life, lights from a cruise ship or plane; turned and gazed up and down the length of the beach.

Nothing. Even the bonfire had died. He stood on tiptoe and tried to peer past the high dune, to where the beach house stood within the grove of palmettos. Night swallowed everything,

He turned back to the waves licking at his bare feet. Something stung his face, blown sand or maybe a gnat. He waved to disperse it, then froze.

In the water, plumes of light coiled and unfolded, dazzling him. Deepest violet, a fiery emerald that stabbed his eyes; cobalt and a pure blaze of scarlet. He shook his head, edging backward; caught himself and looked around.

He was alone. He turned back, and the lights were still there, just below the surface, furling and unfurling to some secret rhythm.

Like a machine, he thought; some kind of underwater wind farm. A wave farm?

But no, that was crazy. He rubbed his cheeks, trying to sober up. He'd seen something like this in Ocean City late one night—it was something alive, Leonard had explained, plankton or jellyfish, one of those things that glowed. They'd gotten high and raced into the Atlantic to watch pale green streamers trail them as they body-surfed.

Now he took a deep breath and waded in, kicking at the waves, then halted to see if he'd churned up a luminous cloud.

Darkness lapped almost to his knees: there was no telltale glow where he'd stirred the water. But a few yards away, the lights continued to turn in upon themselves beneath the surface: scores of fist-size nebulae, as soundless and steady as his own pulse.

He stared until his head ached, trying to get a fix on them. The lights weren't diffuse, like phosphorescence. And they didn't float like jellyfish. They seemed to be rooted in place, near enough for him to touch.

Yet his eyes couldn't focus: the harder he tried, the more the lights seemed to shift, like an optical illusion or some dizzying computer game.

He stood there for five minutes, maybe longer. Nothing changed. He started to back away, slowly, finally turned and stumbled across the sand, stopping every few steps to glance over his shoulder. The lights were still there, though now he saw them only as a soft yellowish glow.

He ran the rest of the way to the house. There were no lights on, no music or laughter.

But he could smell cigarette smoke, and traced it to the deck, where Leonard stood beside the rail.

"Leonard!" Robbie drew alongside him, then glanced around for the boys.

"They slept inside," said Leonard. "Too cold."

"Listen, you have to see something. On the beach—these lights. Not on the beach, in the water." He grabbed Leonard's arm. "Like—just come on."

Leonard shook him off angrily. "You're drunk."

"I'm not drunk! Or, okay, maybe I am, a little. But I'm not kidding. Look—"

He pointed past the sea of palmettos, past the dunes, toward the dark line of waves. The yellow glow was now spangled with silver. It spread across the water, narrowing as it faded toward the horizon, like a wavering path.

Leonard stared, then turned to Robbie in disbelief. "You idiot. It's the fucking moon."

Robbie looked up. And yes, there was the quarter moon, a blaze of gold between gaps in the cloud.

"That's not it." He knew he sounded not just drunk but desperate. "It was *in* the water—"

"Bioluminescence." Leonard sighed and tossed his cigarette, then headed for the door. "Go to bed, Robbie."

Robbie started to yell after him, but caught himself and leaned against the rail. His head throbbed. Phantom blots of light swam across his vision. He felt dizzy, and on the verge of tears.

He closed his eyes; forced himself to breathe slowly, to channel the pulsing in his head into the memory of spectral whirlpools, a miniature galaxy blossoming beneath the water. After a minute he looked out again, but saw nothing save the blades of palmetto leaves etched against the moonlit sky.

HE WOKE SEVERAL HOURS later on the couch, feeling as though an ax were embedded in his forehead. Gray light washed across the floor. It was cold; he reached fruitlessly for a blanket, groaned, and sat up.

Emery was in the open kitchen, washing something in the sink. He glanced at Robbie, then hefted a coffeepot. "Ready for this?"

Robbie nodded, and Emery handed him a steaming mug. "What time is it?'

"Eight, a little after. The boys are with Leonard—they went out about an hour ago. It looks like rain, which kind of throws a monkey wrench into everything. Maybe it'll hold off long enough to get that thing off the ground."

Robbie sipped his coffee. "Seventeen seconds. He could just throw it into the air."

"Yeah, I thought of that, too. So what happened to you last night?"

"Nothing. Too much Tecate."

"Leonard said you were raving drunk."

"Leonard sets the bar pretty low. I was—relaxed."

"Well, time to unrelax. I told him I'd get you up and we'd be at the beach by eight."

"I don't even know what I'm doing. Am I a cameraman?"

"Uh-uh. That's me. You don't know how to work it, plus it's my camera. The boys are in charge of the windbreak and, I dunno, props. They hand things to Leonard."

"Things? What things?" Robbie scowled. "It's a fucking model airplane. It doesn't have a remote, does it? Because that would have been a *good* idea."

Emery picked up his camera bag. "Come on. You can carry the tripod,

how's that? Maybe the boys will hand you things, and you can hand them
to Leonard."

"I'll be there in a minute. Tell Leonard he can start without me."

After Emery left he finished his coffee and went into his room. He
rummaged through his clothes until he found a bottle of ibuprofen,
downed six, then pulled on a hooded sweatshirt and sat on the edge of his
bed, staring at the wall.

He'd obviously had some kind of blackout, the first since he'd been
fired from the parks commission. Somewhere between his seventh beer
and this morning's hangover was the blurred image of Crayola-colored pinwheels turning beneath dark water, his stumbling flight from the beach,
and Leonard's disgusted voice: *You idiot. It's the fucking moon.*

Robbie grimaced. He *had* seen something, he knew that.

But he could no longer recall it clearly, and what he could remember
made no sense. It was like a movie he'd watched half awake, or an accident
he'd glimpsed from the corner of his eye from a moving car. Maybe it had
been the moonlight, or some kind of fluorescent seaweed.

Or maybe he'd just been totally wasted.

Robbie sighed. He put on his sneakers, grabbed Emery's tripod, and
headed out.

A scattering of cold rain met him as he hit the beach. It was windy.
The sea glinted gray and silver, like crumpled tinfoil. Clumps of seaweed
covered the sand, and small round disks that resembled pieces of clouded
glass: jellyfish, hundreds of them. Robbie prodded one with his foot, then
continued down the shore.

The dune was on the north side of the island, where it rose steeply a
good fifteen feet above the sand. Now, a few hours before low tide, the
water was about thirty feet away. It was exactly the kind of place you might
choose to launch a human-powered craft, if you knew little about aerody-
namics. Robbie didn't know much, but he was fairly certain you needed to
be higher to get any kind of lift.

Still, that would be for a full-size craft. For a scale model you could
hold in your two cupped hands, maybe it would be high enough. He saw
Emery pacing along the water's edge, vid cam slung around his neck. The
only sign of the others was a trail of footsteps leading to the dune. Robbie
clambered up, using the tripod to keep from slipping on sand the color and
texture of damp cornmeal. He was panting when he reached the top.

"Hey, Dad. Where were you?"

Robbie smiled weakly as Zach peered out from the windbreak. "I have a sinus infection."

Zach motioned him inside. "Come on, I can't leave this open."

Robbie set down the tripod, then crouched to enter the makeshift tent. Inside, bedsheet walls billowed in the wind, straining at an elaborate scaffold of broom handles, driftwood, the remains of wooden deck chairs. Tyler and Zach sat cross-legged on a blanket and stared at their cell phones.

"You can get a strong signal here," said Tyler. "Nope, it's gone again."

Next to them, Leonard knelt beside a cardboard box. Instead of his customary white tunic, he wore one that was sky blue, embroidered with yellow birds. He glanced at Robbie, his gray eyes cold and dismissive. "There's only room for three people in here."

"That's okay—I'm going out," said Zach, and crawled through the gap in the sheets. Tyler followed him. Robbie jammed his hands into his pockets and forced a smile.

"So," he said. "Did you see all those jellyfish?"

Leonard nodded without looking at him. Very carefully he removed the *Bellerophon* and set it on a neatly folded towel. He reached into the box again and withdrew something else. A doll no bigger than his hand, dressed in a black frock coat and trousers, with a bowler hat so small that Robbie could have swallowed it.

"Voilà," said Leonard.

"Jesus, Leonard." Robbie hesitated, then asked, "Can I look at it?"

To his surprise, Leonard nodded. Robbie picked it up. The little figure was so light he wondered if there was anything inside the tiny suit.

But as he turned it gently, he could feel slender joints under its clothing, a miniature torso. Tiny hands protruded from the sleeves, and it wore minute, highly polished shoes that appeared to be made of black leather. Under the frock coat was a waistcoat, with a watch chain of gold thread that dangled from a nearly invisible pocket. From beneath the bowler hat peeked a fringe of red hair as fine as milkweed down. The cameo-size face that stared up at Robbie was Maggie Blevin's, painted in hairline strokes so that he could see every eyelash, every freckle on her rounded cheeks.

He looked at Leonard in amazement. "How did you do this?"

"It took a long time." He held out his hand, and Robbie returned the doll. "The hardest part was making sure the *Bellerophon* could carry her weight. And that she fit into the bicycle seat and could pedal it. You wouldn't think that would be difficult, but it was."

"It—it looks just like her." Robbie glanced at the doll again, then said, "I thought you wanted to make everything look like the original film. You know, with McCauley—I thought that was the point."

"The point is for it to fly."

"But —"

"You don't need to understand," said Leonard. "Maggie will."

He bent over the little aircraft, its multicolored wings and silken parasol as bright as a toy carousel, and tenderly began to fit the doll-size pilot into its seat.

Robbie shivered. He'd seen Leonard's handiwork before, mannequins so realistic that tourists constantly poked them to see if they were alive.

But those were life-size, and they weren't designed to resemble someone he *knew*. The sight of Leonard holding a tiny Maggie Blevin tenderly, as though she were a captive bird, made Robbie feel light-headed and slightly sick. He turned toward the tent opening. "I'll see if I can help Emery set up."

Leonard's gaze remained fixed on the tiny figure. "I'll be right there," he said at last.

At the foot of the dune, the boys were trying to talk Emery into letting them use the camera.

"No way." He waved as Robbie scrambled down. "See, I'm not even letting your dad do it."

"That's because Dad would suck," Zach said as Emery grabbed Robbie and steered him toward the water. "Come on, just for a minute."

"Trouble with the crew?" asked Robbie.

"Nah. They're just getting bored."

"Did you see that doll?"

"The Incredible Shrinking Maggie?" Emery stopped to stare at the dune. "The thing about Leonard is, I can never figure out if he's brilliant or potentially dangerous. The fact that he'll be able to retire with a full government pension suggests he's normal. The Maggie voodoo doll, though . . ."

He shook his head and began to pace again. Robbie walked beside him, kicking at wet sand and staring curiously at the sky. The air smelled odd, of ozone or hot metal. But it felt too chilly for a thunderstorm, and the dark ridge that hung above the palmettos and live oaks looked more like encroaching fog than cumulus clouds.

"Well, at least the wind's from the right direction," said Robbie.

Emery nodded. "Yeah. I was starting to think we'd have to throw it from the roof."

A few minutes later, Leonard's voice rang out above the wind. "Okay, everyone over here."

They gathered at the base of the dune and stared up at him, his tunic an azure rent in the ominous sky. Between Leonard's feet was a cardboard box. He glanced at it and went on.

"I'm going to wait till the wind seems right, and then I'll yell, '*Now!*' Emery, you'll just have to watch me and see where she goes, then do your best. Zach and Tyler—you guys fan out and be ready to catch her if she starts to fall. Catch her *gently*," he added.

"What about me?" called Robbie.

"You stay with Emery in case he needs backup."

"Backup?" Robbie frowned.

"You know," said Emery in a low voice. "In case I need help getting Leonard back to the rubber room."

The boys began to walk toward the water. Tyler had his cell phone out. He looked at Zach, who dug his phone from his pocket.

"Are they *texting* each other?" asked Emery in disbelief. "They're ten feet apart."

"Ready?" Leonard shouted.

"Ready," the boys yelled back.

Robbie turned to Emery. "What about you, Captain Marvo?"

Emery grinned and held up the camera. "I have never been readier."

Atop the dune, Leonard stooped to retrieve the *Bellerophon* from its box. As he straightened, its propellers began turning madly. Candy-striped rotators spun like pinwheels as he cradled it against his chest, his long white braids threatening to tangle with the parasol.

The wind gusted suddenly: Robbie's throat tightened as he watched the tiny black figure beneath the fuselage swing wildly back and forth, like an accelerated pendulum. Leonard slipped in the sand and fought to regain his balance.

"Uh-oh," said Emery.

The wind died, and Leonard righted himself. Even from the beach, Robbie could see how his face had gone white.

"Are you okay?" yelled Zach.

"I'm okay," Leonard yelled back.

He gave them a shaky smile, then stared intently at the horizon. After a minute his head tilted, as though listening to something. Abruptly he straightened and raised the *Bellerophon* in both hands. Behind him, palmettos thrashed as the wind gusted.

"Now!" he shouted.

Leonard opened his hands. As though it were a butterfly, the *Bellerophon* lifted into the air. Its feathery parasol billowed. Fan-shaped wings rose and fell; ailerons flapped and gears whirled like pinwheels. There was a sound like a train rushing through a tunnel, and Robbie stared openmouthed as the *Bellerophon* skimmed the air above his head, its pilot pedaling furiously as it headed toward the sea.

Robbie gasped. The boys raced after it, yelling. Emery followed, camera clamped to his face and Robbie at his heels.

"This is fucking incredible!" Emery shouted. "Look at that thing go!"

They drew up a few yards from the water. The *Bellerophon* whirred past, barely an arm's length above them. Robbie's eyes blurred as he stared after that brilliant whirl of color and motion, a child's dream of flight soaring just out of reach. Emery waded into the shallows with his camera. The boys followed, splashing and waving at the little plane. From the dune behind them echoed Leonard's voice.

"Godspeed."

Robbie gazed silently at the horizon as the *Bellerophon* continued on, its pilot silhouetted black against the sky, wings opened like sails. Its sound grew fainter, a soft whirring that might have been a flock of birds. Soon it would be gone. Robbie stepped to the water's edge and craned his neck to keep it in sight.

Without warning a green flare erupted from the waves and streamed toward the little aircraft. Like a meteor shooting *upward*, emerald blossomed into a blinding radiance that engulfed the *Bellerophon*. For an instant Robbie saw the flying machine, a golden wheel spinning within a comet's heart.

Then the blazing light was gone, and with it the *Bellerophon*.

Robbie gazed, stunned, at the empty air. After an endless moment he became aware of something—someone—near him. He turned to see

Emery stagger from the water, soaking wet, the camera held uselessly at his side.

"I dropped it," he gasped. "When that—whatever the fuck it was, when it came, I dropped the camera."

Robbie helped him onto the sand.

"I felt it." Emery shuddered, his hand tight around Robbie's arm. "Like a riptide. I thought I'd go under."

Robbie pulled away from him. "Zach?" he shouted, panicked. "Tyler, Zach, are you —"

Emery pointed at the water, and Robbie saw them, heron-stepping through the waves and whooping in triumph as they hurried back to shore.

"What happened?" Leonard ran up alongside Robbie and grabbed him. "Did you see that?"

Robbie nodded. Leonard turned to Emery, his eyes wild. "Did you get it? The *Bellerophon*? And that flare? Like the original film! The same thing, the exact same thing!"

Emery reached for Robbie's sweatshirt. "Give me that, I'll see if I can dry the camera."

Leonard stared blankly at Emery's soaked clothes, the water dripping from the vid cam.

"Oh no." He covered his face with his hands. "Oh no . . ."

"We got it!" Zach pushed between the grown-ups. "We got it, we got it!" Tyler ran up beside him, waving his cell phone. "Look!"

Everyone crowded together, the boys tilting their phones until the screens showed black.

"Okay," said Tyler. "Watch this."

Robbie shaded his eyes, squinting.

And there it was, a bright mote bobbing across a formless gray field, growing bigger and bigger until he could see it clearly—the whirl of wings and gears, the ballooning peacock-feather parasol and steadfast pilot on the velocipede; the swift, silent flare that lashed from the water then disappeared in an eyeblink.

"Now watch mine," said Zach, and the same scene played again from a different angle. "Eighteen seconds."

"Mine says twenty," said Tyler.

Robbie glanced uneasily at the water. "Maybe we should head back to the house," he said.

Leonard seized Zach's shoulder. "Can you get me that? Both of you? E-mail it or something?"

"Sure. But we'll need to go where we can get a signal."

"I'll drive you," said Emery. "Let me get into some dry clothes."

He turned and trudged up the beach, the boys laughing and running behind him.

Leonard walked the last few steps to the water's edge, spray staining the tip of one cowboy boot. He stared at the horizon, his expression puzzled yet oddly expectant.

Robbie hesitated, then joined him. The sea appeared calm, green-glass waves rolling in long swells beneath parchment-colored sky. Through a gap in the clouds he could make out a glint of blue, like a noonday star. He gazed at it in silence, and after a minute asked, "Did you know that was going to happen?"

Leonard shook his head. "No. How could I?"

"Then—what was it?" Robbie looked at him helplessly. "Do you have any idea?"

Leonard said nothing. Finally he turned to Robbie. Unexpectedly, he smiled.

"I have no clue. But you saw it, right?" Robbie nodded. "And you saw her fly. The *Bellerophon*."

Leonard took another step, heedless of the waves at his feet. "She flew." His voice was barely a whisper. "She really flew."

THAT NIGHT NOBODY SLEPT. Emery drove Zach, Tyler, and Leonard to a Dunkin' Donuts where the boys got a cell-phone signal and sent their movie footage to Leonard's laptop. Back at the house, he disappeared while the others sat on the deck and discussed, over and over again, what they had seen. The boys wanted to return to the beach, but Robbie refused to let them go. As a peace offering, he gave them each a beer. By the time Leonard emerged from his room with the laptop, it was after three A.M.

He set the computer on a table in the living room. "See what you think." When the others had assembled, he hit Play.

Blotched letters filled the screen: "The Maiden Flight of McCauley's *Bellerophon*." The familiar tipsy horizon appeared, sepia and amber, silvery flashes from the sea below. Robbie held his breath.

And there was the *Bellerophon* with its flickering wheels and wings propelled by a steadfast pilot, until the brilliant light struck from below and the clip abruptly ended, at exactly seventeen seconds. Nothing betrayed the figure as Maggie rather than McCauley; nothing seemed any different at all, no matter how many times Leonard played it back.

"So that's it," he said at last, and closed his laptop.

"Are you going to put it on YouTube?" asked Zach.

"No," he replied wearily. The boys exchanged a look, but for once remained silent.

"Well." Emery stood and stretched his arms, yawning. "Time to pack."

Two hours later they were on the road.

The hospice was a few miles outside town, a rambling old white house surrounded by neatly kept azaleas and rhododendrons. The boys were turned loose to wander the neighborhood. The others walked up to the veranda, Leonard carrying his laptop. He looked terrible, his gray eyes bloodshot and his face unshaven. Emery put an arm over his shoulder and Leonard nodded stiffly.

A nurse met them at the door, a trim blond woman in chinos and a yellow blouse.

"I told her you were coming," she said as she showed them into a sunlit room with wicker furniture and a low table covered with books and magazines. "She's the only one here now, though we expect someone tomorrow."

"How is she?" asked Leonard.

"She sleeps most of the time. And she's on morphine for the pain, so she's not very lucid. Her body's shutting down. But she's conscious."

"Has she had many visitors?" asked Emery.

"Not since she's been here. In the hospital a few neighbors dropped by. I gather there's no family. It's a shame." She shook her head sadly. "She's a lovely woman."

"Can I see her?" Leonard glanced at a closed door at the end of the bright room.

"Of course."

Robbie and Emery watched them go, then settled into the wicker chairs.

"God, this is depressing," said Emery.

"It's better than a hospital," said Robbie. "Anna was going to go into a hospice, but she died before she could."

Emery winced. "Sorry. Of course, I wasn't thinking."

"It's okay."

Robbie leaned back and shut his eyes. He saw Anna sitting on the grass with azaleas all around her, bees in the flowers and Zach laughing as he opened his hands to release a green moth that lit momentarily upon her head, then drifted into the sky.

"Robbie." He started awake. Emery sat beside him, shaking him gently. "Hey—I'm going in now. Go back to sleep if you want, I'll wake you when I come out."

Robbie looked around blearily. "Where's Leonard?"

"He went for a walk. He's pretty broken up. He wanted to be alone for a while."

"Sure, sure." Robbie rubbed his eyes. "I'll just wait."

When Emery was gone he stood and paced the room. After a few minutes he sighed and sank back into his chair, then idly flipped through the magazines and books on the table. *Tricycle, Newsweek,* the *Utne Reader;* some pamphlets on end-of-life issues; works by Viktor Frankl and Elisabeth Kübler-Ross.

And, underneath yesterday's newspaper, a familiar sky blue dust jacket emblazoned with the garish image of a naked man and woman, hands linked as they floated above a vast abyss, surrounded by a glowing purple sphere. Beneath them the title appeared in embossed green letters.

Wings for Humanity!
The Next Step is OURS!
by Margaret S. Blevin, PhD

Robbie picked it up. On the back was a photograph of the younger Maggie in a white, embroidered tunic, her hair a bright corona around her piquant face. She stood in the Hall of Flight beside a mock-up of the *Apollo* lunar module, the Wright Flyer high above her head. She was laughing, her hands raised in welcome. He opened it to a random page.

> *. . . that time has come: with the dawn of the Golden Millennium we will welcome their return, meeting them at last as equals to share in the glory that is the birthright of our species.*

He glanced at the frontispiece and title page, and then the dedication.

For Leonard, who never doubted

"Isn't that an amazing book?"

Robbie looked up to see the nurse smiling down at him.

"Uh, yeah," he said, and set it on the table.

"It's incredible she predicted so much stuff." The nurse shook her head. "Like the Hubble telescope, and that caveman they found in the glacier, the guy with the lens? And those turbines that can make energy in the jet stream? I never even heard of that, but my husband said they're real. Everything she says, it's all so hopeful. You know?"

Robbie stared at her, then quickly nodded. Behind her the door opened. Emery stepped out.

"She's kind of drifting," he said.

"Morning's her good time. She usually fades around now." The nurse glanced at her watch, then at Robbie. "You go ahead. Don't be surprised if she nods off."

He stood. "Sure. Thanks."

The room was small, its walls painted a soft lavender-gray. The bed faced a large window overlooking a garden. Goldfinches and tiny green wrens darted between a bird feeder and a small pool lined with flat white stones. For a moment Robbie thought the bed was empty. Then he saw that an emaciated figure had slipped down between the white sheets, dwarfed by pillows and a bolster.

"Maggie?"

The figure turned its head. Hairless, skin white as paper, mottled with bruises like spilled ink. Her lips and fingernails were violet, her face so pale and lined it was like gazing at a cracked egg. Only the eyes were recognizably Maggie's, huge, the deep slatey blue of an infant's. As she stared at him, she drew her wizened arms up, slowly, until her fingers grazed her shoulders. She reminded Robbie disturbingly of a praying mantis.

"I don't know if you remember me." He sat in a chair beside the bed. "I'm Robbie. I worked with Leonard. At the museum."

"He told me." Her voice was so soft he had to lean close to hear her. "I'm glad they got here. I expected them yesterday, when it was still snowing."

Robbie recalled Anna in her hospital bed, doped to the gills and talking to herself. "Sure," he said.

Maggie shot him a glance that might have held annoyance, then gazed past him into the garden. Her eyes widened as she struggled to lift her hand, fingers twitching. Robbie realized she was waving. He turned to stare out the window, but there was no one there. Maggie looked at him, then gestured at the door.

"You can go now," she said. "I have guests."

"Oh. Yeah, sorry."

He stood awkwardly, then leaned down to kiss the top of her head. Her skin was as smooth and cold as metal. "'Bye, Maggie."

At the door he looked back, and saw her gazing with a rapt expression at the window, head cocked slightly and her hands open, as though to catch the sunlight.

TWO DAYS AFTER THEY got home, Robbie received an e-mail from Leonard.

> *Dear Robbie,*
> *Maggie died this morning. The nurse said she became unconscious early*
> *yesterday, seemed to be in pain but at least it didn't last long. She had*
> *arranged to be cremated. No memorial service or anything like that. I*
> *will do something, probably not till the fall, and let you know.*
> *Yours,*
> *Leonard*

Robbie sighed. Already the week on Cowana seemed long ago and faintly dreamlike, like the memory of a childhood vacation. He wrote Leonard a note of condolence, then left for work.

Weeks passed. Zach and Tyler posted their clips of the *Bellerophon* online. Robbie met Emery for drinks ever week or two, and saw Leonard once, at Emery's Fourth of July barbecue. By the end of summer, Tyler's footage had been viewed 347,623 times, and Zach's 347,401. Both provided a link to the Captain Marvo site, where Emery had a free download of the entire text of *Wings for Humanity!* There were now over a thousand Google hits for Margaret Blevin, and Emery added a *Bellerophon* T-shirt to his merchandise: organic cotton with a silk-screened image of the baroque aircraft and its bowler-hatted pilot.

Early in September, Leonard called Robbie.

"Can you meet me at the museum tomorrow, around eight thirty? I'm having a memorial for Maggie, just you and me and Emery. After hours, I'll sign you in."

"Sure," said Robbie. "Can I bring something?"

"Just yourself. See you then."

He drove in with Emery. They walked across the twilit Mall, the museum a white cube that glowed against a sky swiftly darkening to indigo. Leonard waited for them by the side door. He wore an embroidered tunic, sky blue, his white hair loose upon his shoulders, and held a cardboard box with a small printed label.

"Come on," he said. The museum had been closed since five, but a guard opened the door for them. "We don't have a lot of time."

Hedges sat at the security desk, bald and even more imposing than when Robbie last saw him, decades ago. He signed them in, eyeing Robbie curiously then grinning when he read his signature.

"I remember you—Opie, right?"

Robbie winced at the nickname, then nodded. Hedges handed Leonard a slip of paper. "Be quick."

"Thanks. I will."

They walked to the staff elevator, the empty museum eerie and blue lit. High above them the silent aircraft seemed smaller than they had been in the past, battered and oddly toylike. Robbie noticed a crack in the *Gemini VII* space capsule, and strands of dust clinging to the Wright Flyer. When they reached the third floor, Leonard led them down the corridor, past the photo lab, past the staff cafeteria, past the library where the Nut Files used to be. Finally he stopped at a door near some open ductwork. He looked at the slip of paper Hedges had given him, punched a series of numbers into the lock, opened it then reached in to switch on the light. Inside was a narrow room with a metal ladder fixed to one wall.

"Where are we going?" asked Robbie.

"The roof," said Leonard. "If we get caught, Hedges and I are screwed. Actually, we're all screwed. So we have to make this fast."

He tucked the cardboard box against his chest, then began to climb the ladder. Emery and Robbie followed him, to a small metal platform and another door. Leonard punched in another code and pushed it open. They stepped out into the night.

It was like being atop an ocean liner. The museum's roof was flat, nearly a block long. Hot air blasted from huge exhaust vents, and Leonard motioned the others to move away, toward the far end of the building.

The air was cooler here, a breeze that smelled sweet and rainwashed, despite the cloudless sky. Beneath them stretched the Mall, a vast green game board, with the other museums and monuments huge game pieces, ivory and onyx and glass. The spire of the Washington Monument rose in the distance, and beyond that the glittering reaches of Roslyn and Crystal City.

"I've never been here," said Robbie, stepping beside Leonard.

Emery shook his head. "Me neither."

"I have," said Leonard, and smiled. "Just once, with Maggie."

Above the Capitol's dome hung the full moon, so bright against the starless sky that Robbie could read what was printed on Leonard's box.

MARGARET BLEVIN

"These are her ashes." Leonard set the box down and removed the top, revealing a ziplocked bag. He opened the bag, picked up the box again, and stood. "She wanted me to scatter them here. I wanted both of you to be with me."

He dipped his hand into the bag and withdrew a clenched fist; held the box out to Emery, who nodded silently and did the same; then turned to Robbie.

"You too," he said.

Robbie hesitated, then put his hand into the box. What was inside felt gritty, more like sand than ash. When he looked up, he saw that Leonard had stepped forward, head thrown back so that he gazed at the moon. He drew his arm back, flung the ashes into the sky, and stooped to grab more.

Emery glanced at Robbie, and the two of them opened their hands.

Robbie watched the ashes stream from between his fingers, like a flight of tiny moths. Then he turned and gathered more, the three of them tossing handful after handful into the sky.

When the box was finally empty, Robbie straightened, breathing hard, and ran a hand across his eyes. He didn't know if it was some trick of the moonlight or the freshening wind, but everywhere around them, every-where he looked, the air was filled with wings.

The
Devil on
the Staircase

by

Joe

Hill

I was
born in
Sulle Scale
the child of a
common bricklayer.

                                              The
                                          village
                                    of my birth
                                  nested in the
                                highest sharpest
                                ridges, high above
                              Positano, and in the
                            cold spring the clouds
                          crawled along the streets
                        like a procession of ghosts.
                      It was eight hundred and twenty
                    steps from Sulle Scale to the world
                  below. I know. I walked them again and
                again with my father, following his tread,
              from our home in the sky, and then back again.
            After his death I walked them often enough alone.

Up

    and   each

       down   with   step

            carrying   until   it

                 freight   seemed as

                                              if the bones

                                    in my knees were

                            being ground up into

                       sharp white splinters.

The
cliffs
were mazed
with crooked
staircases, made
from brick in some
places, granite in others.
Marble here, limestone there,
clay tiles, or beams of lumber.
When there were stairs to build my
father built them. When the steps were
washed out by spring rains it fell to him
to repair them. For years he had a donkey to
carry his stone. After it fell dead, he had me.

                                                     I

                                            hated

                                           him of

                                        course.

                                   He had his

                                  cats and he

                              sang to them

                         and poured them

                    saucers of milk and

              told them foolish stories

          and stroked them in his lap

      and when one time I kicked one—

   I do not remember why—he kicked me to

the floor and said not to touch his babies.

So I
carried
his rocks
when I should
have been carrying
schoolbooks, but I cannot
pretend I hated him for that.
I had no use for school, hated to
study, hated to read, felt acutely the
stifling heat of the single room schoolhouse,
the only good thing in it my cousin, Lithodora, who
read to the little children, sitting on a stool with her
back erect, chin lifted high, and her white throat showing.

                                           I
often
imagined
her throat
was as cool as
the marble altar
in our church and I
wanted to rest my brow
upon it as I had the altar.
How she read in her low steady
voice, the very voice you dream of
calling to you when you're sick, saying
you will be healthy again and know only the
sweet fever of her body. I could've loved books
if I had her to read them to me, beside me in my bed.

I
knew
every
step of
the stairs
between Sulle
Scale and Positano,
long flights that dropped
through canyons and descended

into tunnels bored in the limestone,
past orchards and the ruins of derelict
paper mills, past waterfalls and green pools.
I walked those stairs when I slept, in my dreams.

                                        The
                                      trail
                                  my father
                              and I walked
                            most often led
                        past a painted red
                      gate, barring the way
                    to a crooked staircase.
              I thought those steps led to
            a private villa and paid the gate
          no mind until the day I paused on the
        way down with a load of marble and leaned
      on it to rest and it swung open to my touch.

My
father,
he lagged
thirty or so
stairs behind me.
I stepped through the
gate onto the landing to
see where these stairs led.
I saw no villa or vineyard below,
only the staircase falling away from
me down among the sheerest of sheer cliffs.

                                  "Father,"
                            I called out
                        as he came near,
                    the slap of his feet
                echoing off the rocks and
            his breath whistling out of him.
        "Have you ever taken these stairs?"

When
he saw

me standing
inside the gate
he paled and had my
shoulder in an instant
was hauling me back onto
the main staircase. He said,
"How did you open the red gate?"

                                        "It was
                                    open when
                                  I got here,"
                                  I said. "Don't
                                they lead all the
                              way down to the sea?"

"No."
"But it
looks as if
they go all the
way to the bottom."

                                        "They go
                                    farther than
                                  that," my father
                                said and he crossed
                                himself. Then he said
                              again, "The gate is always
                            locked." And he stared at me,
                          the whites of his eyes showing. I
                        had never seen him look at me so, had
                      never thought I would see him afraid of me.

Lithodora
laughed when
I told her and
said my father was
old and superstitious.
She told me that there was
a tale that the stairs beyond
the painted gate led down to hell.
I had walked the mountain a thousand

times more than Lithodora and wanted to
know how she could know such a story when
I myself had never heard any mention of it.

                                    She said
                                the old folks
                            never spoke of it,
                        but had put the story
                    down in a history of the
                region, which I would know
            if I had ever read any of the
        teacher's assignments. I told her
    I could never concentrate on books when
she was in the same room with me. She laughed.
But when I tried to touch her throat she flinched.

My
fingers
brushed her
breast instead
and she was angry
and she told me that
I needed to wash my hands.

                                    After
                                my father
                            died—he was
                        walking down the
                    stairs with a load
                of tiles when a stray
            cat shot out in front of
        him and rather than step on
    it, he stepped into space and
fell fifty feet to be impaled upon
    a tree—I found a more lucrative use
for my donkey legs and yardarm shoulders.
    I entered the employ of Don Carlotta who kept
a terraced vineyard in the steeps of Sulle Scale.

I hauled
his wine down

the eight hundred
odd steps to Positano,
where it was sold to a rich
Saracen, a prince it was told,
dark and slender and more fluent
in my language than myself, a clever
young man who knew how to read things:
musical notes, the stars, a map, a sextant.

                                        Once I
                                    stumbled
                                  on a flight
                                of brick steps
                              as I was making my
                            way down with the Don's
                          wine and a strap slipped and
                        the crate on my back struck the
                    ‚   cliff wall and a bottle was smashed.
                      I brought it to the Saracen on the quay.
                    He said either I drank it or I should have,
                  for that bottle was worth all I made in a month.
                He told me I could consider myself paid and paid well.
              He laughed and his white teeth flashed in his black face.
I was
sober when
he laughed at
me but soon enough
had a head full of wine.
Not Don Carlotta's smooth and
peppery red mountain wine but the
cheapest Chianti in the Taverna, which
I drank with a passel of unemployed friends.

                                        Lithodora
                                    found me after
                                  it was dark and she
                                stood over me, her dark
                              hair framing her cool, white
                          beautiful, disgusted, loving face.
                    She said she had the silver I was owed.

                    She had told her friend Ahmed that he had
                insulted an honest man, that my family traded
            in hard labor, not lies and he was lucky I had not —
"— did
you call
him friend?"
I said. "A monkey
of the desert who knows
nothing of Christ the lord?"

                                        The way that
                                    she looked at me
                                then made me ashamed.
                        The way she put the money in
                    front of me made me more ashamed.
                    "I see you have more use for this than
                you have for me," she said before she went.

I almost
got up to go
after her. Almost.
One of my friends asked,
"Have you heard the Saracen
gave your cousin a slave bracelet,
a loop of silver bells, to wear around
her ankle? I suppose in the Arab lands, such
gifts are made to every new whore in the harem."

                                        I came
                                    to my feet
                                so quickly my
                            chair fell over.
                    I grabbed his throat
                in both hands and said,
                    "You lie. Her father would
                never allow her to accept such
            a gift from a godless blackamoor."

But
another
friend said

the Arab trader
was godless no more.
Lithodora had taught Ahmed
to read Latin, using the Bible
as his grammar, and he claimed now
to have entered into the light of Christ,
and he gave the bracelet to her with the full
knowledge of her parents, as a way to show thanks
for introducing him to the grace of our Father who art.

                                              When
                                           my first
                                        friend had
                                     recovered his
                                    breath, he told
                                 me Lithodora climbed
                                 the stairs every night
                                 to meet with him secretly
                              in empty shepherds' huts or in
                                 the caves, or among the ruins of
                                 the paper mills, by the roar of the
                                    waterfall, as it leapt like liquid silver
                                 in the moonlight, and in such places she was
                              his pupil and he a firm and most demanding tutor.
He
always
went ahead
and then she
would ascend the
stairs in the dark
wearing the bracelet.
When he heard the bells he
would light a candle to show her
where he waited to begin the lesson.

                                                 I
                                               was
                                         so drunk.
I set

out for
Lithodora's
house, with no
idea what I meant
to do when I got there.
I came up behind the cottage
where she lived with her parents
thinking I would throw a few stones
to wake her and bring her to her window.
But as I stole toward the back of the house
I heard a silvery tinkling somewhere above me.

                              She was
                          already on
                       the stairs and
                    climbing into the
                  stars with her white
                dress swinging from her
              hips and the bracelet around
            her ankle so bright in the gloom.
My
heart
thudded,
a cask flung
down a staircase:
doom doom doom doom.
I knew the hills better
than anyone and I ran another
way, making a steep climb up crude
steps of mud to get ahead of her, then
rejoining the main path up to Sulle Scale.
I still had the silver coin the Saracen prince
had given her, when she went to him and dishonored
me by begging him to pay me the wage I was properly owed.

                                      I put
                                  his silver
                               in a tin cup
                          I had and slowed

to a walk and went
along shaking his Judas
coin in my old battered mug.
Such a pretty ringing it made in
the echoing canyons, on the stairs,
in the night, high above Positano and the
crash and sigh of the sea, as the tide consummated
the desire of water to pound the earth into submission.

At
last,
pausing
to catch my
breath, I saw
a candleflame leap
up off in the darkness.
It was in a handsome ruin,
a place of high granite walls
matted with wildflowers and ivy.
A vast entryway looked into a room
with a grass floor and a roof of stars,
as if the place had been built, not to give
shelter from the natural world, but to protect a
virgin corner of wildness from the violation of man.

Then
again it
seemed a pagan
place, the natural
setting for an orgy hosted
by fauns with their goaty hooves,
their flutes and their furred cocks.
So the archway into that private courtyard
of weeds and summer green seemed the entrance
to a hall awaiting revelers for a private bacchanal.

He
waited
on spread
blanket, with

a bottle of the
Don's wine and some
books and he smiled at
the tinkling sound of my
approach but stopped when I
came into the light, a block of
rough stone already in my free hand.

                                        I
                                    killed
                              him there.

I did
not kill
him out of
family honor
or jealousy, did
not hit him with the
stone because he had laid
claim to Lithodora's cool white
body, which she would never offer me.

                                        I
                                      hit
                              him with
                        the block of
                  stone because I
        hated his black face.

After
I stopped
hitting him,
I sat with him.
I think I took his
wrist to see if he had
a pulse, but after I knew
he was dead, I went on holding
his hand listening to the hum of the
crickets in the grass, as if he were a
small child, *my* child, who had only drifted
off after fighting sleep for a very long time.

                                          What
                                       brought
                                     me out of
                                 my stupor was
                                the sweet music
                             of bells coming up
                          the stairs toward us.

I leapt
up and ran
but Dora was
already there,
coming through the
doorway, and I nearly
struck her on my way by.
She reached out for me with
one of her delicate white hands
and said my name but I did not stop.
I took the stairs three at a time, running
without thought, but I was not fast enough and
I heard her when she shouted *his* name, once and again.

                                             I
                                         don't
                                    know where
                                 I was running.
                             Sulle Scale, maybe,
                          though I knew they would
                       look for me there first once
                    Lithodora went down the steps and
                 told them what I had done to the Arab.
              I did not slow down until I was gulping for
           air and my chest was filled with fire and then
        I leaned against a gate at the side of the path —
you know
what gate —

                                        and it
                                   swung open
                              at first touch.

                              I went through the
                          gate and started down
                       the steep staircase beyond.
                     I thought no one will look for
            me here and I can hide a while and —
No.

                                              I
                                        thought,
                                   these stairs
                             will lead to the
                          road and I will head
                       north to Napoli and buy
                a ticket for a ship to the U.S.
            and take a new name, start a new —
No.
Enough.
The truth:

                                              I
                                      believed
                                   the stairs
                             led down into
                          hell and hell was
                     where I wanted to go.
The
steps
at first
were of old
white stone, but
as I continued along
they grew sooty and dark.
Other staircases merged with
them here and there, descending
from other points on the mountain.
I couldn't see how that was possible.
I thought I had walked all the flights of

stairs in the hills, except for the steps I
was on and I couldn't think for the life of me
where those other staircases might be coming from.

                                              The
                                           forest
                                       around me
                                    had been purged
                                 by fire at some time
                              in the not so far-off past,
                           and I made my descent through
                        stands of scorched, shattered pines,
                     the hillside all blackened and charred.
                  Only there had been no fire on that part of
               the hill, not for as long as I could remember.
            The breeze carried on it an unmistakable warmth.
         I began to feel unpleasantly overheated in my clothes.
I
followed
the staircase
round a switchback
and saw below me a boy
sitting on a stone landing.

                                              He
                                           had a
                                       collection
                                    of curious wares
                                 spread on a blanket.
                              There was a wind-up tin
                           bird in a cage, a basket of
                        white apples, a dented gold lighter.
                     There was a jar and in the jar was light.
                  This light would increase in brightness until
               the landing was lit as if by the rising sun, and
            then it would collapse into darkness, shrinking to a
         single point like some impossibly brilliant lightning bug.
He
smiled

to see me.
He had golden
hair and the most
beautiful smile I have
ever seen on a child's face
and I was afraid of him—even
before he called out to me by name.
I pretended I didn't hear him, pretended
he wasn't there, that I didn't see him, walked
right past him. He laughed to see me hurrying by.

> The
> farther
> I went the
> steeper it got.
> There seemed to be
> a light below, as if
> somewhere beyond a ledge,
> through the trees, there was
> a great city, on the scale of Roma,
> a bowl of lights like a bed of embers.
> I could smell food cooking on the breeze.

if
it was
food — that
hungry-making
perfume of meat
charring over flame.

> Voices
> ahead of me:
> a man speaking
> wearily, perhaps
> to himself, a long
> and joyless discourse;
> someone else laughing, bad
> laughter, unhinged and angry.
> A third man was asking questions.

"Is

a plum
sweeter after
it has been pushed
in the mouth of a virgin
to silence her as she is taken?
And who will claim the baby child
sleeping in the cradle made from the
rotten carcass of the lamb that laid with
the lion only to be eviscerated?" And so on.

                                          At
                                         the
                                        next
                                     turn in
                                   the steps
                                  they finally
                              came into sight.
                          They lined the stairs:
                       half a dozen men nailed on
                     to crosses of blackened pine.
                    I couldn't go on and for a time
                    I couldn't go back; it was the cats.
                  One of the men had a wound in his side,
                a red seeping wound that made a puddle on
              the stairs, and kittens lapped at it as if it
            were cream and he was talking to them in his tired
          voice, telling all the good kitties to drink their fill.
I
did
not go
close enough
to see his face.

                                          At
                                        last
                                   I returned
                                 the way I had

```
                              come on shaky legs.
                           The boy awaited me with
                        his collection of oddities.
"Why
not sit
and rest your
sore feet, Quirinus
Calvino?" he asked me.
And I sat down across from
him, not because I wanted to but
because that was where my legs gave out.
```

Neither of us spoke at first. He smiled across the blanket spread with his goods, and I pretended an interest in the stone wall that overhung the landing there. That light in the jar built and built until our shadows lunged against the rock like deformed giants, before the brightness winked out and plunged us back into our shared darkness. He offered me a skin of water but I knew better than to take anything from that child. Or thought I knew better. The light in the jar began to grow again, a single floating point of perfect whiteness, swelling like a balloon. I tried to look at it, but felt a pinch of pain in the back of my eyeballs and glanced away.

"What is that? It burns my eyes," I asked.

"A little spark stolen from the sun. You can do all sorts of wonderful things with it. You could make a furnace with it, a giant furnace, powerful enough to warm a whole city, and light a thousand Edison lights. Look how bright it gets. You have to be careful though. If you were to smash this jar and let the spark escape, that same city would disappear in a clap of brightness. You can have it if you want."

"No, I don't want it," I said.

"No. Of course not. That isn't your sort of thing. No matter. Someone will be along later for this. But take something. Anything you want," he said.

"Are you Lucifer?" I asked in a rough voice.

"Lucifer is an awful old goat who has a pitchfork and hooves and makes people suffer. I hate suffering. I only want to help people. I give gifts. That's why I'm here. Everyone who walks these stairs before their time gets a gift to welcome them. You look thirsty. Would you like an apple?" Holding up the basket of white apples as he spoke.

I was thirsty—my throat felt not just sore, but singed, as if I had inhaled smoke recently, and I began to reach for the offered fruit, almost reflexively, but then drew my hand back for I knew the lessons of at least one book. He grinned at me.

"Are those—" I asked.

"They're from a very old and honorable tree," he said. "You will never taste a sweeter fruit. And when you eat of it, you will be filled with ideas. Yes, even one such as you, Quirinus Calvino, who barely learned to read."

"I don't want it," I said, when what I really wanted to tell him was not to call me by name. I could not bear that he knew my name.

He said, "Everyone will want it. They will eat and eat and be filled with understanding. Why, learning how to speak another language will be as simple as, oh, learning to build a bomb. Just one bite of the apple away. What about the lighter? You can light anything with this lighter. A cigarette. A pipe. A campfire. Imaginations. Revolutions. Books. Rivers. The sky. Another man's soul. Even the human soul has a temperature at which it becomes flammable. The lighter has an enchantment on it, is tapped into the deepest wells of oil on the planet, and will set fire to things for as long as the oil lasts, which I am sure will be forever."

"You have nothing I want," I said.

"I have something for everyone," he said.

I rose to my feet, ready to leave, although I had nowhere to go. I couldn't walk back down the stairs. The thought made me dizzy. Neither could I go back up. Lithodora would have returned to the village by now. They would be searching the stairs for me with torches. I was surprised I hadn't heard them already.

The tin bird turned its head to look at me as I swayed on my heels, and blinked, the metal shutters of its eyes snapping closed, then popping open again. It let out a rusty cheep. So did I, startled by its sudden movement. I had thought it a toy, inanimate. It watched me steadily and I stared back. I had, as a child, always had an interest in ingenious mechanical objects, clockwork people who ran out of their hiding places at the stroke of noon, the woodcutter to chop wood, the maiden to dance a round. The boy followed my gaze, and smiled, then opened the cage and reached in for it. The bird leaped lightly onto his finger.

"It sings the most beautiful song," he said. "It finds a master, a shoulder it likes to perch on, and it sings for this person all the rest of its days. The trick to making it sing for you is to tell a lie. The bigger the better. Feed it a lie, and it will sing you the most marvelous little tune. People love to hear its song. They love it so much, they don't even care they're being lied to. He's yours if you want him."

"I don't want anything from you," I said, but when I said it, the bird began to whistle: the sweetest, softest melody, as good a sound as the laughter of a pretty girl, or your mother calling you to dinner. The song sounded a bit like something played on a music box, and I imagined a studded cylinder turning inside it, banging the teeth of a silver comb. I shivered to hear it. In this place, on these stairs, I had never imagined I could hear something so right.

He laughed and waved his hand at me. The bird's wings snapped from the side of its body, like knives leaping from sheaths, and it glided up and lit on my shoulder.

"You see," said the boy on the stairs. "It likes you."

"I can't pay," I said, my voice rough and strange.

"You've already paid," said the boy.

Then he turned his head and looked down the stairs and seemed to listen. I heard a wind rising. It made a low, soughing moan as it came up through the channel of the staircase, a deep and lonely and restless cry. The boy looked back at me. "Now go. I hear my father coming. The awful old goat."

I backed away and my heels struck the stair behind me. I was in such a hurry to get away I fell sprawling across the granite steps. The bird on my shoulder took off, rising in widening circles through the air, but when I found my feet it glided down to where it had rested before on my

shoulder
and I began
to run back up
the way I had come.

                                        I
                                  climbed
                             in haste for
                            a time but soon
                       was tired again and
                       had to slow to a walk.
                    I began to think about what
                  I would say when I reached the
              main staircase and was discovered.

"I will confess everything and accept
my punishment, whatever that is," I said.
The tin bird sang a gay and humorous ditty.
It
fell
silent
though as
I reached the
gate, quieted by
a different song not
far off: a girl's sobs.
I listened, confused, and
crept uncertainly back to where
I had murdered Lithodora's beloved.
I heard no sound except for Dora's cries.
No men shouting, no feet running on the steps.
I had been gone half the night, it seemed to me but
when I reached the ruins where I had left the Saracen
and looked upon Dora it was as if only minutes had passed.

I
came
toward
her and
whispered
to her, afraid
almost to be heard.
The second time I spoke
her name she turned her head
and looked at me with red-rimmed
hating eyes and screamed to get away.
I wanted to comfort her, to tell her I was
sorry, but when I came close she sprang to her
feet and ran at me, striking me and flaying at my
face with her fingernails while she cursed my name.
I meant
to put my
hands on her

shoulders to hold
her still but when I
reached for her they found
her smooth white neck instead.

                              Her
                           father
                          and his
                      fellows and
                   my unemployed
                friends discovered
               me weeping over her.
            Running my fingers through
          the silk of her long black hair.
        Her father fell to his knees and took
       her in his arms and for a while the hills
     rang with her name repeated over and over again.

Another
man, who held
a rifle, asked me
what had happened and
I told him — I told him —
the Arab, that monkey from the
desert, had lured her here and when
he couldn't force her innocence from her
he throttled her in the grass and I found them
and we fought and I killed him with a block of stone.

                              And
                           as I
                         told it
                    the tin bird
                began to whistle
              and sing, the most
            mournful and sweetest
           melody I had ever heard
          and the men listened until
     the sad song was sung complete.

I
held
Lithodora
in my arms as
we walked back down.
And as we went on our way
the bird began to sing again as
I told them the Saracen had planned
to take the sweetest and most beautiful
girls and auction their white flesh in Araby —
a more profitable line of trade than selling wine.
The bird was by now whistling a marching song and the
faces of the men who walked with me were rigid and dark.

Ahmed's
men burned
along with the
Arab's ship, and
sank in the harbor.
His goods, stored in a
warehouse by the quay, were
seized and his money box fell
to me as a reward for my heroism.

No
one
ever
would've
imagined when
I was a boy that
one day I would be
the wealthiest trader
on the whole Amalfi coast,
or that I would come to own the
prized vineyards of Don Carlotta, I
who once worked like a mule for his coin.

No
one

would've
guessed that
one day I would
be the beloved mayor
of Sulle Scalle, or a man
of such renown that I would be
invited to a personal audience with
his holiness the pope himself, who thanked
me for my many well-noted acts of generosity.

The
springs
inside the
pretty tin bird
wore down, in time,
and it ceased to sing,
but by then it did not matter
if anyone believed my lies or not
such was my wealth and power and fame.

However.
Several years
before the tin bird
fell silent, I woke one
morning in my manor to find
it had constructed a nest of wire
on my windowsill, and filled it with
fragile eggs made of bright silver foil.
I regarded these eggs with unease but when I
reached to touch them, their mechanical mother
nipped at me with her needle-sharp beak and I did
not after that time make any attempt to disturb them.

Months
later the
nest was filled
with foil tatters.
The young of this new
species, creatures of a new
age, had fluttered on their way.

I
cannot
tell you
how many birds
of tin and wire and
electric current there
are in the world now — but I
have, this very month, heard speak
our newest prime minister, Mr. Mussolini.
When he sings of the greatness of the Italian
people and our kinship with our German neighbors,
I am quite sure I can hear a tin bird singing with him.
Its tune plays especially well amplified over modern radio.
I don't
live in the
hills anymore.
It has been years
since I saw Sulle Scale.
I discovered, as I descended
at last into my senior years, that
I could no longer attempt the staircases.
I told people it was my poor sore old knees.

But in truth I
developed a
fear of
heights.

ABOUT THE CONTRIBUTORS

Dublin-born **Roddy Doyle** has written novels, play, and screenplays. His novel *Paddy Clarke Ha Ha Ha* won the Booker Prize in 1993. His Barrytown trilogy has been filmed as *The Commitments, The Snapper,* and *The Van.*

Joyce Carol Oates has published more than fifty novels, as well as numerous short story collections and volumes of poetry and nonfiction. Her novel *Them* won the National Book Award.

Joanne Harris is the author of *The Evil Seed* and *Chocolat,* which was a number one best-seller on the *London Sunday Times* and was shortlisted for the 1999 Whitbread Novel of the Year. *Runemarks,* published in 2007, was her first book for children and young adults.

Michael Marshall Smith is a British novelist, screenwriter, and short story writer. He has won the British Fantasy, the August Derleth, and the Philip K. Dick awards. His book *The Intruders* was picked up by the BBC for a major new drama series.

Joe R. Lansdale is the author of scores of novels and short stories, including the popular Hap and Leonard mystery series. He is a multiple winner of the Bram Stoker Award. He lives in Nacogdoches, Texas, with his wife and family.

Walter Mosley is the author of more than twenty books in many categories, but is perhaps best known for the highly regarded and popular Easy Rawlins hard-boiled detective novels. Born in Los Angeles, he now lives in New York City.

Richard Adams is the author of *Shardik, The Girl in the Swing*, and many other novels, but is perhaps best known for *Watership Down*, which was a national best-seller, and was awarded the Carnegie Medal and the Guardian Award for Children's Fiction.

Jodi Picoult is a number one best-selling author, with more than 14 million books in print worldwide. She won the New England Bookseller Award for fiction in 2003, and currently lives in Hanover, New Hampshire.

Michael Swanwick began publishing in the early 1980s, and is currently based in Philadelphia. He is the winner of the Hugo, World Fantasy, Theodore Sturgeon Memorial, and Nebula awards.

Peter Straub's novel *Ghost Story* is generally considered a high point of the modern horror novel. He has won the Bram Stoker, World Fantasy, and International Horror Guild awards. Born in Milwaukee, Wisconsin, he now lives in New York City.

Lawrence Block is the highly acclaimed author of two series set in New York, featuring Private Eye Matthew Scudder and burglar Bernie Rhodenbarr. In 1993 Block was tapped as a Grand Master by the Mystery Writers of America.

Jeffrey Ford is known for his iconoclastic and literary dark fantasy novels. He is the winner of numerous awards for both his short stories and longer works. He lives in southern New Jersey with his wife and family.

Chuck Palahniuk is the author of *Fight Club* and numerous other novels, including the recent novel *Pygmy*. He is the recipient of many awards, among them the Pacific Northwest Bookseller Association Award. He lives in Washington State.

Diana Wynne Jones has written many fantasy novels for adults and children, among them the Chrestomanci series, which won the 1977 Guardian Award for children's books. Her *Howl's Moving Castle* was made into a notable film by Japanese director Havai Miazaki. She lives in Great Britain.

Pittsburgh native **Stewart O'Nan** is the author of numerous novels, such as *Songs for the Missing* and *The Good Wife*. His first short story collection, *In the Walled City,* was awarded the Drue Heinz Literature Prize in 1993.

Multiple award-winning science fiction and fantasy writer **Gene Wolf** is perhaps best known for *The Book of the New Sun,* which comprises four volumes. He lives in Illinois.

Carolyn Parkhurst is the best-selling author of *The Dogs of Babel* (which was also a *New York Times* notable book in 2003) and *Lost and Found.* She lives in Washington, D.C.

Kat Howard currently lives in Minneapolis. She earned a law degree, then acquired a Ph.D. in English literature, both from the University of Minnesota. She is a 2008 graduate of the Clarion Writers' Workshop. "A Life in Fictions" is her first published story.

Jonathan Carroll, generally considered a magic realist, is the author of the novel *The Land of the Laughs* and many others. He has won the Bram Stoker, World Fantasy, and British Fantasy awards.

International number one best-selling author **Jeffery Deaver**'s books are sold in 150 countries and have been translated into 25 languages. He is the winner of numerous awards. His most recent books are *The Bodies Left Behind* and *More Twisted: Collected Stories, Volume II.*

Tim Powers, another magic realist, has won the World Fantasy Award two times, for his novels *Last Call* and *Declare.* Born in Buffalo, New York, he grew up in California, where he still lives.

Kurt Andersen is a novelist and host of the public radio program *Studio 360.* A cofounder of *Spy* magazine and former editor in chief of *New York* magazine, he has also written for *Vanity Fair, Time,* the *New York Times,* and the *New Yorker.*

Michael Moorcock has published science fiction and fantasy novels, as well as more overtly literary works. As editor of *New Worlds* magazine, he helped foster the new wave movement in science fiction, which helped bring it into the literary mainstream.

Elizabeth Hand grew up in New York and currently lives in Maine. She is the winner of the World Fantasy, Shirley Jackson, and International Horror Guild awards. Among her novels are *Illyria* and *Generation Loss*.

New England native **Joe Hill**'s first novel, *Heart-Shaped Box*, was a bestseller. He has won many awards. His first short-story collection, *20th Century Ghosts*, was published in 2005, and his most recent novel is *Horns*.